THE GREAT CAPTAINS

BY HENRY TREECE

Novels

The Great Captains

The Dark Island

Verse

Towards a Personal Armageddon

Thirty-Eight Poems

Invitation and Warning

The Black Seasons

The Haunted Garden

Collected Poems

The Exiles

Criticism

How I See Apocalypse

Dylan Thomas

Herbert Read

A Selection of Algernon Charles Swinburne

Drama

The Dark Island

Tristram and the Watchers

The Tragedy of Tristram

The End of a World

HENRY TREECE

THE GREAT CAPTAINS

RANDOM HOUSE • New York

1956

 Published in New York by Random House, Inc., and simultaneously in Toronto, Canada, by Random House of Canada, Limited.
Library of Congress Catalog Card Number: 55-8146
Manufactured in the United States of America by
H. *Wolff, New York*

CONTENTS

Places in the Story, vi

Preface, ix

"The Great Captains," xi

PART ONE
THE JOURNEY TO THE WEST
1

PART TWO
UTHER PENDRAGON
45

PART THREE
THE GREAT BATTLES
99

PART FOUR
THE VENGEANCE
219

PART FIVE
TOWARDS BADON
243

PART SIX
CAMLANN
291

Sources, 301

PLACES IN THE STORY

Abus—*The River Humber*
Agned—*Edinburgh*
Anderida Silva—*The Weald Forest*
Aquae Sulis—*Bath*
Avallon—*The Celtic Heaven, Valhalla, The Isle of Apples*
Bassas—*Tumulus in Sussex*
Bodotria—*The Firth of Forth*
Byzantium—*Istanbul*
Caer Leon—*Caerleon-upon-Usk*
Caerwent—*Caerwent*
Caledonia—*Area south of the Firth of Forth*
Calleva Atrebatum—*Silchester*
Camulodunum (Camulod, Camelot, Camlann)—*Colchester*
Cantii—*Kentish tribes*
Cissaceaster—*Chichester*
Demetia—*Southwest Wales*
Deva—*Chester*
Dubglas—*Boundary between Kent and Sussex*
Dumnonia—*Devon, Cornwall*
Durotriges—*Tribe of Wessex*
Eburacum—*York*
Glein—*River Glynde, East Sussex*
Glevum—*Gloucester*
Gwynnedd—*Wales*
Gwent—*Approximately Shropshire*
Hadrian's Wall—*The Roman wall from Wallsend to Carlisle*
Lindum—*Lincoln*
Lis Pengwern—*Shrewsbury*
Londinium—*London*
Mancunium—*Manchester*
Mons Badonicus—*Fortified hill near Swindon*
Powys—*Midland area of Wales*
Sabrina—*The River Severn*
Scythia—*Area about the Black Sea*
Siluria—*South Wales*
Sorbiodunum—*Old Sarum*
Strathclyde—*Area south of the Clyde River and including Cumberland*
Tamesa—*The River Thames*
Tribuit—*Chichester*
Vectis—*The Isle of Wight*
Venta Belgarum—*Winchester*
Verulam—*Saint Albans*
Vricon (Viroconium)—*Wroxeter in Shropshire*

BRITAIN IN THE TIME OF ARTHUR

Preface

THIS IS THE STORY OF "KING" ARTHUR, AS I THINK IT MIGHT HAVE happened. It is not easy now to throw off all the accretions of legend and, later, poetry and to see the situation with an objective historical eye. They were men, yet to see them only as men, stripped of their doom-driven greatness, is to represent them on too trivial a scale. To draw them as massive heroes only would be to re-create them as inhuman cyphers.

But whatever one does, they loom and fade, slide sideways, shift out of focus, the pathetic and malevolent ghosts of a period quite unlike any other in the history of Britain and for which we have no adequate terms of reference.

Yet it is a tale which sooner or later most storytellers wish to set down in their own way, for the struggles and characters portrayed are archetypal, and there is no getting away from them!

I do not presume to have found out who Arthur was; all I know is that Malory and Tennyson were wrong! Men very much closer to his time called him *ursus horribilis,* which should give a clear enough clue. Looking at the problem decently from a number of directions, I sympathise with Medrawt, who has had a poor defence in the Court of History. And this Court, may it be said, took its case from a biassed Knight writing in 1469, nearly a thousand years after the event.

The only safe assumption in a case like this is that we are all wrong—but it makes a good story.

Henry Treece

"THE GREAT CAPTAINS"

The great Captains, do they sleep
Careless as other men, with dangling arm?
Or do they roll from side to side,
Wide-eyed and sweating through the night,
Shuddering at every bird-cry, starting up
With hammering heart as distant doorlatch clicks,
Or nightwind carries nearer far-off feet?
Does dawn still find them living through the past,
Where never-ending film to the numb brain
Shows tumbled bodies, killed by directive,
Smashed faces grinning in the drizzling dawn,
And victory only lull before the same
Rehearsal yet again, and yet again?
The great Captains, do they ever weep
Before tedium drags them down to sleep?

P A R T   O N E

THE JOURNEY TO THE WEST

At the old world's edge, the fuchsia was in flower
And bugloss and poppy stood among the corn.
Isca Legionis, Verulamium, even Londinium,
Slept out the length of some long afternoon.
From Corstopitum down to Chichester
Foxglove and eglantine
Grew up towards the sunlight
From between the crumbling stones.

But when the moon came out along the Roman roads,
Along three thousand miles of weed-grown tracks,
Roads straight as arrows from York to Colchester
And back from Exeter to York again,
In the still air the marching feet still echoed,
And above the lonely peewit's cry
The proud centurion's voice set trembling
The dangling pine cones in the wood.

No, they are gone. It is all afternoon.
The distant thunder speaks in the hills
But goes unheard.
The blood-red sun will sink, to light another world.
Here in the country villas paint flakes from the columns,
And the ghosts, the tired gay ones,
Sit by the sunlit vineyard wall, yawning,
And speculating on predestination.

Now it is all late summer's afternoon,
Where the cow nuzzles her bursting udders,
Lowing to be milked,
And the lazy bees mumble as they stagger
Among the pitifully moss-grown urns.

I

TWO MEN STOOD IN THE SUNLIGHT ON THE CLIFF-TOP, LOOKING DOWN towards the sea. The disturbed gulls circled low over their heads, squawking with anger at their intrusion, but the men ignored the birds. They had other problems to think of; the wings that echoed in their minds were the pinions of death.

The old man was gazing over the glittering water with the fixed, immobile set of the head that is often seen in the blind, or the nearly blind. He was tall and almost emaciated. His long grey gown of coarse woollen stuff hung loosely about him, sometimes whipped in the wayward breezes that flicked across the open headland. It looked as though it had been made for a much bigger man. His close-cropped, grizzled hair gave him the look of a hermit, a recluse from the luxuries of common man. Yet upon his feet he wore high sandals of such leather and of such exquisite craftsmanship as might only have been purchased by one of substantial means. Nor was the sword, which swung in a heavy bronze scabbard from the thong about his waist, the weapon of an austere and penniless holy man. It was of the old Roman pattern, but much longer, and its hilt and pommel were not of the customary style. The hilt was of chiselled Irish gold, teased into spirals of plaited basket-work; the great round pommel was of silver, set with a large red stone that gleamed richly as he moved in the morning sun.

As the light struck in a new shaft from behind a high cloud, this old man pressed his hand closer to his eyes, straining to see. "Can you still see them, Medrodus?" he said. "Have they reached the ship yet?"

The young man smiled to himself. His own sight was as sharp as that of a bird of prey.

"They are pulling hard against the tide, Ambrosius," he said. "But the current is strong. It will be long before they are aboard. Must we wait?"

His keen eyes strayed to the rich sword with something like envy. Then he lightly shrugged his shoulders and began to whistle softly. The old man made a small gesture of annoyance, as though irritated at his dependence. He did not seem to like that carefree whistling, but the young man affected not to notice this.

"We must stay," said Ambrosius. "But, by the gods, I almost wish I was with them now, for it seems my time here is done. Britain is beyond my cure."

The young man stopped whistling suddenly, his heavy lids half veiling the scorn in his dark eyes. Of medium height and build, his swarthy skin and oiled black hair, which hung in small curls to the nape of his neck, gave him an exotic, almost an Eastern appearance. On his proudly held head he wore a light hood of leather, onto which many small iron plates had been rivetted for protection against a surprise sword cut. As a guard for his ears, two inverted triangles of chain mail dangled from the hood, clinking as he moved and lending his expression something of the Babylonian warrior.

"You are still the Count of Britain, Master," he said. "While you are with us Rome is not dead in Britain."

His voice was well modulated and ingratiating and on the surface he spoke with sincerity. The old man nodded gravely, accepting the title without embarrassment, as a king does. Yet the young man's thick red lips had curled as he spoke. The thin fringe of dark beard about his chin picked out the irony that lay so lightly concealed in his heart.

The old man turned away from him, his head lowered and his hand over his brow.

"The Count of Britain," he said sadly. "It is a threadbare robe now, that title. It no longer keeps out the Saxon cold. I wonder how much longer I shall wear it."

"You will live many years, Master," said the young man, looking towards the sword again like a girl before a trinket-maker's booth.

He was dressed in a short blue tunic of heavy linen, embellished by threads of woven silver; but now its hem was torn and its embroidery tarnished. A worn and greasy hide jerkin reached to his waist, laced round his broad chest by thongs of twisted leather. His strong legs were bare but for his thin woollen nether-stocks, made after the fashion of a legionary's winter breeches. Upon his feet he wore the caligulae, the marching-boots of a Roman soldier, but of such a lightness and softness of leather, such a delicacy of nail-work, that only a young dilettante of the officer caste would have dared to wear them.

"Yes, you will live for many years, dear Master," he said again, smiling down at his feet.

The grey old man turned his blank face once more towards the northern sea. Far below him huge limestone rocks, eroded by wind and water, towered in their sombre shapes. About them the white seabirds wheeled and cried mournfully, splashing the grey stone with their droppings.

Ambrosius said, "I sometimes feel that it will not be long before I go to meet my emperor. Then some other man will be as I am now, a king without a country, without even an army. A king without hope. It may be you, Medrodus, who knows? It may be you."

The young man turned away from him and walked a little closer to the edge of the cliffs. He saw the longboat bobbing clumsily in the water, pulled by twenty men unused to the oars, their round helmets gleaming dull in the sunlight, soldiers, the last of the Romans.

By now they were within a hundred paces of the ship that waited for them, a tall corbal-built vessel that stood too high out of the water for easy handling. Its sewn-hide sails were already unfurling as the boat approached, as though its captain was anxious to get away without delay.

Medrodus called back carelessly, over his shoulder, "The last of your army will soon be safe on their way to Gaul—or else to Hades!"

The Count of Britain stumbled towards him. Medrodus watched him coming, helplessly, screwing up his eyes in the hope of being allowed some transitory glimpse at least of his departing friends. If one stood aside, thought Medrodus, what is there to warn him of the cliff's edge? What could prevent him from falling onto the rocks below? He is an old man and would die easily.

For a brief instant, his hands clenched as though he might take the quickest way and push Ambrosius forward. Yet something got in his way; it was not conscience, or loyalty, but rather some vague unworded apprehension. It would not be like killing an ordinary man. Ambrosius was the chosen of Rome, and the vengeance of all the Imperial gods would drag down whoever laid a finger on him. Yet, if the old man might only make the mistake himself, who could be blamed?

Ambrosius lurched forward, the rising wind now whipping his coarse woollen robe against his thin body as he approached the cliff-edge. He could see nothing but a dull expanse of leaden grey, blurred painfully at times by passing flashes of brilliance as the sun struck spitefully at his eyes across the rolling North Sea.

With a gasp, Medrodus saw the sword, the great sword, actually swinging over the edge of the drop. If that went, all authority would die. The sword must not fall, too; it was his only proof of leadership when Ambrosius was gone. Even as the old man stumbled on, Medrodus put out his arm and held him closely.

"Master, Master," he cried, "you are too near the edge. You must not risk your life, Master."

The old man began to shudder. Medrodus could feel the bones of that old body shaking under the robe, and smiled again.

"Sit down, Ambrosius," he said. "You were near death then."

The old man's eyes filled with sudden tears. "You are a faithful friend, Medrodus," he said. "The only one who would have done that for me."

Then without warning he broke away and stood again above the rocks, his face distorted with a sudden anger. He shook his fist petulantly in the direction of the sea.

"Go, you traitors," he shouted. "Leave me here, you dogs! I will find better men than you, by the gods! Go, and take your payment with you, carrion!"

As he spoke he thrust a thin and weatherbeaten hand into the shallow goatskin pouch at his side and brought out a handful of small glistening coins, things hardly bigger than hailstones. He made a slight pretence of weighing them in his palm for an instant, then he smiled ruefully and with a sudden gesture of disgust flung the Roman minims out over the cliff-edge. The small particles of metal glittered like summer rain as they fell in a broad shower among the birds that circled the rocks below. Then, as though ashamed of his action, he said, "Yet they do right, I fear, to seek peace and a thatched roof of their own, in Rome or Gaul, yes, even in Saxony. There is nothing left for them here. Not even an oath to bind them any longer."

Medrodus smiled and said softly, "At this moment your good warband is nearer Saxony than it knows, perhaps!"

Far off, beyond the view of the watcher in the crow's nest of the boat below, a long grey shape swung patiently with the tide; a heathen longboat, its sails furled, its oars at rest; a grim sea-wolf, waiting for the plunder that it knew must come sooner or later. Medrodus could see it clearly now as the mist moved away. He felt no sympathy with the men who had marched half the length of Britain with him, who had been his comrades but a few hours before. He smiled callously and wished that the view might be uninterrupted, so that he could watch the boarding when it came.

Ambrosius made the Roman farewell sign and turned away from the cliff. Medrodus, who knew that it would be useless to ask him to stay after that farewell, followed him petulantly, kicking at the turf in irritation. Why couldn't the old man have let him stay long enough to see the Saxons draw up alongside these craven dogs!

Old Ambrosius stopped after a few paces and half turned his head, impatiently.

"I am coming, Master," said Medrodus smoothly, curling back his girl's red lips at the tall straight figure of the deserted leader, like a dog that would bite but dares not. Not, at least, until it is quite sure of its master's weakness.

II

AT LENGTH THE TWO SILENT MEN CAME TO THE MARSHLAND THAT lay some miles away from the coast. Here, despite the sun's warmth, which beat down on their shoulders as they went, the countryside was brooding and melancholy. Mile after mile of uneven tussocky grass lay before them, half shrouded in a thin mist, the moisture which the sun's heat had drawn up from the damp ground as the day wore on. It was an open loveless land, and quite deceptively cruel. It might have seemed an easy matter to set one's course across it towards the thickly wooded slopes of the hills that fringed the horizon, yet no man with eyes in his head would attempt such a movement. No man, that is, with sense enough to observe the whitened bones of sheep and cattle that strewed the place, the rotting tree-stumps and the half-submerged farmcart that heeled forlornly over, grown round with weeds and the creeping emerald-green lichens.

Medrodus stopped and scratched his chin. The marsh ooze was already up to his ankles.

"Let me take the sword, Count of Britain," he said. "It would be less for you to carry."

Ambrosius stopped suddenly and shook his head, reaching down to clasp the weapon more securely. "No, my son," he said, as gently as he could to offset this tell-tale movement. "It must stay by my side until the destined moment, the ritual day. Then you, or some other, shall carry it as long as there is faith left in you;

but not till then. We must obey the law, made by a greater one than ourselves, that the Count of Britain shall have held no other weapon before this. He must come as a virgin comes to the couch of her lord."

The young man shrugged as though the whole affair were valueless. He turned to the more urgent matter.

"Which way shall we take, Master? If we go further we shall sink into the slime."

As Ambrosius wondered, trying to remember what the military maps had said about this area, Medrodus' quick eye caught a movement from behind a high clump of alder-bushes, and almost immediately afterwards a man appeared, a cowherd, driving before him three miserable-looking creatures whose bones came near to breaking through their dung-caked hides. The man was deep in thought, or perhaps so weak that he could not raise his head without a great effort. He moved with the listless dragging steps of a fugitive from a long and arduous battle, his hands dangling at his sides, his chin almost on his breast. From time to time, as the cattle stopped to graze at some small clump of herbage less poisonous than the rest, the man still staggered on, bumping into the beasts and then standing still, staring on the ground, until they moved on again.

Medrodus cupped his mouth with his hands and called, "Greetings, friend! Is there a path through the marsh?"

His voice seemed to echo unnaturally in the still air. The cowherd looked up in terror, then he turned and shambled away, his rags flapping about him, the way he had come. The three beasts stopped, looking up disinterestedly, and then began to graze where they stood. Medrodus flew into a sudden anger and cursed the man for a fool. He looked about him for stones or flints with which he might maim the cattle as a punishment to the idiot.

Ambrosius sensed his anger and said, "You must be patient. These country folk are afraid of all strangers. They would not wish to meet an enemy in a place like this."

The young man grumbled, saying that if these were the country folk it was his destiny to protect, it seemed a waste of time and life. But Ambrosius spoke to him with patience and with gravity, telling him that Rome recognised no inequalities of status.

"That man is a citizen, as much as you or I," he said. "At least, he would be so, if there were anyone in Rome now to recognise him."

Medrodus snorted a little too loudly this time and the old man's face took on a severe expression.

"This sword will only be carried by the humble, my friend. Have no doubts about that," he said quietly.

Medrodus sensed that the old man was waiting for a reply, and he held back his anger and was silent. Ambrosius heard that silence and understood it. He knew that he was in the power of this hot-blooded young man. He was too blind to make his way alone across this treacherous country now. He smiled a little and said, "Medrodus, your father gave you to me for training. I had faith then that I could mould you in my own fashion, to become a Roman."

Medrodus flushed. "I am a Roman, Ambrosius; as much as any man in Britain. My people were citizens. My great-grandfather came from Rome herself—when she was greater than she is today."

The old man smiled drily and said, "The mixture has been warmed up with a dash or two of Scythian, I suspect. But we can let that pass. There are few of us left now who can lay claim to pure Roman blood. That is the price we pay for throwing open the doors of the Empire."

Medrodus laughed in his secret heart at the old man's pride. This old leader looked on himself as the last of the Romans left in Britain; one invested with the power that Julius had taken to himself, or that had been given to stuttering Claudius by the drunken Palace Guard, the legionaries who had found a puppet for themselves, they thought. Yet it was Claudius who at last had conquered Britain. . . .

Ambrosius was clucking, as he did when he was angry with his blindness. He was rubbing his horny knuckles into his eyes, milky with cataracts. "If I had my sight," he said, "we should not be in this torment. Yet there is something here which rings a chord in my memory." He stood facing the west and stretched out his left hand. "I recall that there is a broad river in that direction, the Abus. That way would lead us south, if ever we could cross that river again. I think my comitatus took the last ferry boat when we came across three nights ago. Yet what lies south but the brute and ravaged Civil Zone? There is no life there, no trade, no civilisation. The villas are laid waste, the farms are deserted, the towns are peopled only by Saxons and those that love the Saxons. No, there is nothing in the south but treachery and blood. Nothing but our enemies."

Medrodus nodded. "What is there in the north that is better?" he asked. "What has the old Military Zone to offer? What answer did we get, when we wrote asking them to join with us? They sent back a crow's skull and a broken knife! Yet there, once, the greatest of the Legions set up their standards in Eburacum."

Ambrosius nodded gravely and said, "There was more to that message than you knew, Medrodus. By bone and iron, we, the comitatus and myself, knew that the men of Eburacum could spare no man for any venture and that the enemy camped under their very walls. They could not get out to us, nor we in to them. There are five ship's companies of sea-wolves there, under the walls of Eburacum."

Medrodus frowned. "Why was the message hidden from me?" he said. "Why should all others know the meaning of bone and iron, and leave me in darkness?"

The old man patted him on the shoulder. "You are still young, Medrodus. Most of the others were nearly twice your age."

"Yes, and now they have sailed away and left you, despite their age and experience. What use is their knowledge to them now, Ambrosius?" he said.

Ambrosius turned on him then with such an expression of anger that Medrodus almost struck him down and snatched away the sword, feeling that he could not stand much more of this treatment. Yet he controlled himself, for there was something repugnant about striking the Count of Britain, one appointed so many years ago to take the place of the Roman Emperor in this faraway province. Wherever Ambrosius went, men knew him and respected him, even the chieftains and *reguli*. His position was inviolate. Without being a king, without possessing any territories of his own, he was powerful above all kinglets, was entitled to call on the men and coffers of them all, in the name of Rome.

It was even whispered in many places that this Ambrosius had sent for Germanus, Bishop of Auxerre, many years before, and had commanded him to investigate the misconduct of the British Church. Such was his power that even the men of God must obey his orders. . . . But such rumours spread in the steps of all great captains, especially in Britain now, when darkness had descended over the island again and no man knew truly what was in another's mind.

As Medrodus looked into the staring grey eyes of the Count, a chill crept into his heart. These were the eyes that had outstared Hengist in the middle of a drunken feast, and had sent the sea-rover muttering out into the darkness, his boasts forgotten. These eyes had caused the confused Vortigern to offer a hundred men, secretly, to harass the Saxon by night—even though, at that time, he was negotiating with them by day. Looking into those eyes, Medrodus understood something of the old man's power. If they affected one now, when they were helpless and almost blind, how much more must they have put men to fear when the sight shone from them like the glaring rays of the sun!

Medrodus looked away in embarrassment. If he had to kill the old man, it must be when he was not looking, he decided. His mind slid away from the idea of killing Ambrosius, however, unless it became absolutely necessary. It would be almost like killing a god. It would be a crime that always followed him and lay with him in bed at night. Every man he met would ask, "Where is Ambrosius? Where did he die? Where is he buried? Why did you not take better care of him; you were his chosen follower, weren't you? You were his official son, his disciple, his heir, weren't you?"

It would be too dangreous to kill Ambrosius, thought Medrodus, unless it became necessary to join with the Saxons later. Then it would be some sort of credential, to have killed the last of the Romans. Medrodus smiled at this new thought. He turned and saw that the old man's eyes were still on him, but this time he did not drop his head. Instead, he faced the leader and nodded, and smiled back at him, almost into his face.

Then Medrodus moved away, singing a camp song that he knew the old man disliked. It was a rough ballad which told how the King of Babylon came home one night to find his favourite wife making love to the Captain of the Guard. The chorus described the angry king's revenge on them both. It was the sort of bawdy ditty which was common among the soldiers of Rome, and which had spread from the Legions among the population, with the help of the camp-followers and entertainers who gained their subsistence from the cohorts.

Medrodus paused. "Why don't you join in the chorus, Master?" he said tauntingly. "It would help your steps along."

Ambrosius snorted but did not reply. Medrodus smiled at the old man's narrow-mindedness.

"Caesar would have joined in," said the young man. "Yes, even Claudius, and no man could have accused him of being a libertine."

Ambrosius said, "Who are you to say what the great ones would have done? Does the mouse enjoy the confidences of the eagle?"

"No," muttered Medrodus, "but this mouse does not worry about that. He is at least alive, and even the greatest of the eagles is now only a bundle of rotting feathers!"

III

AFTER THEY HAD MADE THEIR WAY FOR THE BEST PART OF AN HOUR alongside the outer rim of the coarse marshland, Ambrosius stopped like a hound that scents the air and held up his hand in a signal to the young man who now lagged behind him.

"It comes to my memory," he said, "that somewhere here should lie a small road that the Legion put down many years ago, to join the inland fortress with the coast. Can you see anything, Medrodus?"

A quarter of a mile away a high line of sedges seemed to run almost straight across the treacherous bogland. They went towards that tell-tale line, the tall dry reeds that stalked over the flat land like some skeleton army. Yet before they reached them, Ambrosius drew the other to his side and spoke to him gravely.

"This is the road we must take," he said. "We are perhaps fortunate to find it. And yet again, it may be the beginning of all our troubles. One way or another I do not expect to see much more of life, either the troubles or the glories. My sword arm is crippled with rheumatics in winter and my eyes are troubled at all times and seasons."

Medrodus said what he had said before, though he believed it no more than he did when he first said it. "Master, you will live to see many years yet, good years for Britain."

Ambrosius shook his head impatiently. "Do not treat me like a fool, Medrodus," he said. "We know each other too well to deal in such trumpery coinage. I know well enough how my heart leapt when I said good-bye to the men who had followed me for a dozen years, over a score of British battlefields. It jumped as though it would break through the skin of my breast, and my old blood thumped in my ears until I thought my head would burst. That is a sign, Medrodus, a sign which I cannot neglect now. Once I could ride, day and night for a week, and feel no such beating of the heart, no such struggling of the blood to be free. But now, if a lark rises suddenly from under my feet, my blood rushes so ardently into my throat, I can hardly breathe for the thickness of it. How can I last long, being so outworn?"

Medrodus was silent for a while, but at last he spoke with gravity and with some deference, for the old man's words had moved him in a strange way.

"You have chosen me," he said, "from among all the young men whom you knew in the Civil Zone. I am to follow you, nominated by yourself, as the new Count of Britain, when you elect to give up your office, Master. I have followed you faithfully all this time, trying to prepare myself for the honour that Rome will do me through your mouth. I have tried to discipline my mind and body, in readiness for such an honour. Now, would it not be appropriate for you to speak the words here, as we stand, and put the great sword in my keeping? Now, when your heart beats fiercely and when you fear that you may not walk the earth much longer?"

Ambrosius did not answer immediately, but passed his hand across his brow in a gesture of tiredness and uncertainty, as though he were trying to think out a problem that always evaded him. At last he replied, "My son, there are times when I doubt the rightness of my own judgement. Perhaps he who shall be the new Count should be chosen by others and not by myself. There is no law which says I must make the choice, Medrodus."

The young man answered with some heat, "Do you doubt my suitability, then, Master?"

The old man replied gently, "I do not know. I cannot always see the face that goes with your words. Voice and heart are often at variance, and it is the voice that lies. The heart is pictured faithfully in the face. . . . There have been times in these last perilous weeks, as we have been flying northwards, when I have sensed in you something which I had not known before—something indefinable, but most like a fault in a column that will bring the whole portico crashing down when the wind blows too suddenly, or too long from one direction. I once thought you might grow to be as firm as the rocks on the great plain, as straight as the pillars of the temple at Camulodunum. Yet sometimes I wonder now . . ."

Medrodus bit his lip in annoyance at the old man's frankness. "Ambrosius," he said, "you do not speak gentle words. Allow me the same privilege then, for we speak as one Roman to another."

The Count of Britain inclined his head. Medrodus ignored this gesture of permission and went on almost without a break. "Ambrosius, this is the wrong time to have doubts about your choice. Consider, we are alone, in a deserted part of the Province. On every side of us there may be enemies, either our own people or the Saxon folk. If you doubt me, what am I to do? Am I to go on guarding you, as I have always tried to do, or am I to take you at your word and leave you, so as not to waste any more years of my life, following a promise that will never be realised? Which am I to do, think you? Or, Ambrosius, am I to . . ."

The old man stopped him before he could finish what he was about to say. "Do not speak those words," he said. "I know what is in your mind now. Yet do not think that you would go scatheless from killing me, my young friend. In my time, I have been called on to put an end to many strong and evil men, in the name of Rome. I know that I am older now, and nearly blind; yet you are younger and less powerful than the others I have sent to their fathers. Now that you have forced me to speak in this way, I shall tell you that should you raise your hand against me in anger or revenge, or to snatch from me like a thief that which I must give you freely or not at all, I should use what life was left me to take you with me, to whatever place awaits us. Your young hand and your sharp eyes might achieve the sudden blow. But I would clutch your hand, your wrist, the hem of your tunic, and I would hold you however you struggled or struck again. You would never again be free of me, I promise you, Medrodus."

The young man looked up in horror at the face of Ambrosius. He saw no softness, no pity, only the indomitable Roman spirit, the gravity and the inflexible will that had driven countless thousands of such men to march the length and the breadth of the known world, over icy peaks and across crevasses, over burning sands, even through steaming jungles—the Roman Legions. And as he looked, Medrodus knew that this half-blind old man was one of these Romans, and that he himself was not.

He said, "Forgive me, Master. My anger rose when you seemed to doubt me. A man would do as much if you doubted his love for his mother, and Rome is my mother."

Ambrosius said, "You must learn to bear the doubt of men impassively. That too is part of your training. A man who squeals at the pinpricks of another's doubts is surely no fit man to give new life to Britain." The old man's voice softened a little. "You may be the future Count of Britain, but you cannot be invested here, in this deserted place. The declaration must take place before men, among those men of Britain who will pledge themselves to follow you to death."

"And where may they be, Master?" asked Medrodus, half sneering once again.

Ambrosius waved his hand across the stinking waste of slime and reeds, and the cry of the curlews lent a strange prophetic quality to his words. "They will be in the west, my son," he said. "Always in the west. There, beyond marsh and woodland and mountain, live strong men, untouched by the decay of cities. They will remember the old days again when we go amongst them. They will vow to follow you, if they trust you. It is among such folk that you must take this sword from my hands, and the blessing from my lips."

Then they struck the little narrow road, still visible, but half sunk in weed-covered brackish water. On either side of the stone path, the sedges rose so high that a man could not see beyond them.

Medrodus said, "This would be a bad road to be ambushed on, Master."

But Ambrosius only smiled and groped with his foot to find the firm way. "Yet we must take it," he said. "It leads towards the west, and perhaps the gods require that we should tread this road as a testing-feat. If we come safely along it, then perhaps they will smile on us once again and lead us on to the place where we shall gather an army to bring back the Great Peace to this wounded land."

He said no more, but walked on down the sinking road. Medrodus followed him, half afraid, his eyes constantly staring before and behind; his ears quick to every sound that was carried on the rising breeze, from the cry of the circling birds to the soft hissing of the marshland that seemed to fill the air on every side of them, whispering of death.

IV

LATE IN THE AFTERNOON, WHEN THE SUN STOOD IN THEIR EYES, LOW on the horizon, the two men came to the end of the swamp, and passed from the ominous shelter of the high reeds to find that their narrow path was crossed, almost at right angles, by a broad military road, running from south to north. And even as they came out into the open again, they stopped in sudden alarm, for to their left stood a thick clump of gnarled and tangled oaks, which hid the road from their sight, and from behind which they heard the sound of hooves and the rumbling wheels of a wagon.

Medrodus dragged the old man back into the shadow of the sedges, where they crouched for a while. Men did not hasten to greet each other in Britain now, but shrank away until they were sure of friendship. They were not anxious to meet on the open roads—much less in sunken lanes or in forest glades—and the home-going peasant, hearing footsteps on the road at night, would crouch in a ditch like a hunted animal until the air was still again and the feet had passed on. So the British people hid from their fellows, each wrapped about with his fears, his hatreds, his despairs; and so Medrodus and the Count were hidden, squatting on their haunches, listening for the clink of arms, parting the sedges slightly in order to observe what manner of men now travelled the open road towards them in full daylight.

At last Medrodus gave a whistle and said, "It is a covered trade-wagon with two oxen. There is a rider with a javelin behind it, keeping watch back down the road. Shall we wait until they have passed?"

Ambrosius said, "Why should we hide like dogs, away from our own folk? It is perhaps a provision wagon going to the militia in Eburacum. If so, perhaps the driver will be a generous man when he knows who I am. Perhaps he may even give us a loaf of bread and a slice of goat's cheese. My jaws are tired with chewing the dried meat we brought with us. Even a piece of cheese seems like an emperor's feast to me now."

Medrodus rose as the wagon approached, and holding the old man's hand, stepped out before the oxen, putting on a smile and holding up his right hand in the Roman greeting.

The wagon was a heavily built vehicle, its square hide covering capable of sheltering a dozen men. The fat and unshaven driver, who wore a dirty horsehide about his body and a broad iron knife in his belt, raised his whip as though he would strike at Medrodus, then shouted back down the road in a rough form of camp-Latin that jarred on the ears of the two wanderers. The outrider cantered up from behind the wagon and rode straight for Medrodus. He was an elderly man, wearing a battered and rusty corselet of the old Roman type, with a conical leathern helmet to go with it. His legs were swathed in dirty linen breeches. Even his javelin-shaft had been broken, and then respliced so that it sat crookedly in his grasp.

Medrodus called out, "Halt, friend! We are hungry travellers who mean you no harm. We are Romans like yourselves. Our only request is for food, if you will spare us a crust or two."

The horseman reined in his thin pony, and lowered the point of his lance, as though relieved not to have to do any fighting. His face was a frightened one, as though he had little taste for his function as a guard. Yet in his eyes and in the set of his crooked mouth there were craft and cruelty too.

He said, "Be off with you. We are no Romans. We are our own men now. We have little enough for ourselves to be giving bread away to any beggars who care to stop us on the roads."

Medrodus suddenly took hold of the pony's bridle and, as the man raised his lance-butt to strike at him, grasped him by the ankle and pitched him out of the saddle onto the road. The man lay still where he fell, and Medrodus bent and picked up the javelin which had fallen from his hand in the shock of the tumble.

Then the driver climbed down from his seat and shambled forward with a bag, which he thrust towards Ambrosius. "Have mercy, lord," he said. "We are but poor men who go to visit friends in Pictland. We mean no harm either. My brother there on the road is a harmless man, but he is afraid to give our food away, for many are starving in Britain today, and no one knows where the next bite will come from. The fields are laid waste by the sea-wolves, and the children have not as much as a husk of corn to still their hunger. Take this, lord, but do not kill my brother."

Medrodus did not answer. He smiled down at the shuddering wretch and then deliberately kicked him in the mouth, watching the effects of his sudden blow. The guard tried to smile up at him, as though asking for mercy, but Medrodus kicked him again, about the ears. Then, turning away, he ground the lance-butt into the man's groin.

"When next you meet the Count of Britain on the roads, remember this," he said. The driver dropped his bag of food and shrank back from Ambrosius, his fat cheeks shaking with fear. Medrodus turned quickly and took him by the neck of his rough tunic.

"Why are you so afraid to meet the Count, friend?" he asked grimly. "What is it you have done?"

The driver began to gabble in a confusion of Celtic and camp-doggerel, sinking to his knees and holding up his hands in terror. Medrodus glanced back at the face of Ambrosius. It held the expression of a general who sits in judgement at a court-martial. There was no pity, no mercy there, not even curiosity. It seemed that he sensed the young man's inquiring glance.

"Do as you think fit, Medrodus," he said, no longer a beggar on the British roads, but now a lawgiver once more, the Roman Emperor by proxy who, at whatever cost of mercy, must keep his people together in times of disruption.

Medrodus nodded and thrust the javelin-point so hard into the man's ribs that blood came through the greasy horsehide. The wretch shrieked out, "Have pity, lord! It is not us! It is the man in the wagon. We are his dogs to obey him. My brother and I were his slaves. He promised us freedom if we did as he bade us."

Medrodus pushed the gasping creature away from him, beside his brother, who still lay, his hands between his legs, in the road. Then the young man leapt into the darkness of the wagon and for a moment there was silence.

Yet that silence did not last long, for suddenly there was a muffled shout from within the wagon and then a scream of pain. Medrodus appeared, dragging with him a middle-aged man, dressed in a well-cut but rumpled linen tunic and a long woollen travelling cloak. Medrodus had the man's arm twisted behind him, so that he fell from the wagon onto the road, bent double with pain. Medrodus jumped down after him and punched him hard in the small of the back with the spearshaft. The man crawled away for a pace or two, then fell again at the feet of Ambrosius, holding up his hands for mercy.

Medrodus stood above him, the lance poised. "This dog is not carrying food," he said. "There is enough gold packed in the corn-sacks at the back of the wagon to buy an army of cavalry, and equip them all with parade armour."

The man who grovelled at the feet of the Count spoke urgently, though in the voice of an educated man. "Count," he said, "I do wrong, I know. Yet it is my own gold, plate and vases, not coin. I am no tax-gatherer, running away with the revenue. I am an honest man, a landowner who put all his profit into gold plate against a day like this. I am merely taking it to some place of safety, where the Saxon will not find it. I swear to you, lord."

Ambrosius looked down on him with his incurious half-blind eyes. "You are a liar," he said without malice. "You know the law by the sound of your voice, or at least you should. Each of your vases must be stamped and may be used as money for taxes should the Province need it. You are a tax thief and your crime carries the penalty of death. You know that, don't you?"

The man turned again to Medrodus, thinking that he might expect more mercy perhaps from the younger man. But the eyes of Medrodus were terrible and the man lowered his head again, putting his hands over the nape of his neck, as though he expected the blow to fall there.

Ambrosius sensed the danger that hung over the crouching wretch and held up his hand to stay Medrodus. Then he spoke down to the man, almost gently, but with the cold venom of the evangelist in his voice. This was the voice that many old men still remembered in distant parts of Britain; and many great ones had died with it in their ears. Vortigern had known those tones, though the voice which had spoken them had been younger and more flexible; Germanus, Bishop of Auxerre, knew them, and had thought twice about refusing the invitation to come back to Britain for a second time. Now this half-crazed magnate heard the dread voice and remembered all he had ever known about Ambrosius Aurelianus; and what he recalled stilled all hope in his thudding heart. Among the country folk the Count had the reputation of scrupulous fairness, no less and no more. He dealt justice impartially to friend and foe alike, and was incorruptible.

"You are a rat and a louse and an eater of dung," Ambrosius was saying gently. "You are such a creature as opens the door to the invader by your renegade work. Such men as you have poisoned the heart's blood of Britain, just as surely as though you had thrown hensbane into the wells of Londinium."

The old man paused, for his heart was aching in his chest and making speech hard. There was nothing theatrical about his words; he believed them with the intense credulity which patriotism brings to a man. To Ambrosius, in that instant, the wretch who groaned before him in the dusty road was the symbol of all self-seeking landowners who had weakened the Province and had dragged it down to disgrace.

"If I did my duty," went on the old man at last, "I should have you crucified at the next tree that would bear your greasy weight. If I did less than my duty, I should let my man here poke out your eyes with his thumbs. . . ."

Medrodus sensed the slight in the words, "my man," and writhed with the indignity. But he made no show of having heard, and his mouth still smiled. Yet it was something else to remember, one day, if he felt his heart softening too much towards the Count of Britain. . . .

Ambrosius went on speaking. "Yet I am old now and shrink at the smell of blood. Too much British blood has been spilled already by the Saxon. It would ill befall me to cause more of it to flow—yes, even the rank blood of such as you."

The landowner cringed and stammered, the spittle dribbling from his terror-slackened lips onto the fine linen of his tunic. He was trying already to give thanks for his deliverance when Medrodus rammed the spear-butt into his back once more, to silence him while Ambrosius spoke on. The man on the road began to cough savagely and fell onto his face, his hands clasped to his broken ribs.

"I shall not condemn you to such slow torments," said Ambrosius, his slow memories taking him back to the pillared halls of his youth where he had once dispensed justice to men who lived daily by Roman statute. "I shall send you on along the road without your gold, without your stolen wealth. You shall go as a free man again, but with my curse upon you for a rogue. I have finished."

Ambrosius stood silent then, expecting some word from the man whom he had in effect pardoned. But there was only silence, silence punctuated by the broken dry coughing of a man whose every breath flung up a gout of blood onto the roadway before his glazing eyes.

Medrodus said, "That dog will not bark again. He is dead."

Ambrosius came out of his trance of past glory, shaking his head from side to side. "I had not thought my curse was still so strong," he said softly. "The conscience of a man is past understanding. Perhaps I made a mistake. Perhaps he was an honest man, after all."

"Perhaps," said Medrodus, glad in a way that the driver and his brother had made their way off down the road while the talk had been going on. Then he rolled the spattered body among the reeds and turned the oxen into the marsh, prodding them in the belly and forcing them to overturn the richly laden wagon into the deep, sucking slime. Almost as an afterthought, he disembowelled them, but with his eyes turned away from their starting blood-rimmed beseeching, for at heart Medrodus had certain of the delicate instincts of the poet and did not like too much bloodshed, especially of animals. He rejoined Ambrosius on the lonely road, with a small sack in one hand and two golden dishes in the other.

"This food will last us three days, with care," he said. "There are bread, meat, onions and cheese. A good goat's cheese, Master."

"Is that all you carry, my friend?" asked the old man.

Medrodus said, "No, I have two dishes, but they are very heavy, almost all one could carry with comfort. It is a pity that we must leave that treasure behind."

The old man said, "What is the manner of the dishes, Medrodus?"

The young man answered, "They are well chiselled. Look, this one has a man and a woman on it. They are dancing—away from each other, the fools! Every muscle! Look at the folds in her dress! See what they show! Oh, it was a man who knew women who made this!"

He was holding the plate before the blank eyes of the old man, almost taunting him with his blindness by the description. Then, as though recollecting himself, he said, "Pardon my words, Master, I had forgotten."

Ambrosius, a man who had never felt the need for a woman, made a grimace of distaste and said coldly, "Give me the thing."

The young man drew back momentarily, avarice ugly in his dark eyes. But the old man's hand reached out, insisting, shaking with impatience. Medrodus could stand it no longer. He put the dishes into the thin commanding hand. Ambrosius held them for a while, contemplatively, his fingers searching the surfaces which Medrodus had described. Then, as though his conscience smote him, he stopped and said drily, "Where lies the swamp?"

"To your left, Master," said Medrodus, still astounded that he should feel such a child before this feeble old man.

Ambrosius turned with the stiff speed of the blind, and swinging his arm wide, flung the two golden dishes away from him. Medrodus watched them skimming like two golden birds in the last rays of the sun, away over the dry sedges, above which the clumsy peewits circled, daft with their own keening and crying. His sharp ears heard the splash these precious things made as they fell into the slime, among the roots of a decaying oak, to be forgotten now for two thousand years.

He dared to say at last, "That was waste, Master."

Ambrosius said, "We should not have killed that man. We had to make a payment to the gods. You do not understand everything, Medrodus."

Medrodus flared up for an instant. "Men think you are a Christian, Master," he said. "Yet you offer sacrifices, like the old ones."

Ambrosius answered, "When a land is in its death-throes, what matter the form of the religion, provided there is a religion at all? And is not the Mosaic law, 'An eye for an eye'?"

Medrodus could not argue with such a man. He said, "All the same, those dishes were of value. They would have bought men."

The old man said, "The men who shall serve us must do so without payment. Yet, my son, should you find that you can get no one to follow you without money, you will always know where it lies hidden. You, of all folk, will never forget that half a day's march from Eburacum there lies a wagon sunk in the slime that could buy back the freedom of Britain. Aye, and all the many islands that cluster round her for shelter from the storm."

Medrodus grasped the rough javelin firmly. He could speak no more with this old dotard. "Come," he said, "if we do not start towards the west again, darkness will overtake us on this road."

Ambrosius nodded. "We must hold the road northwards awhile before we turn to the west. The forests beyond this road are dangerous too. We must set our course across the moorlands which lie nearer Eburacum."

V

NORTHWARDS NOW LAY MILE UPON MILE OF UNDULATING GREY ROAD, upturned every few hundred yards where fungus and dandelion had set their vegetable strength against that of stake and pile and stone; upturned and left to moulder by men who had no interest in restoring what they would never own, or by other men who had never known such roads before and looked on them as being the work of the gods, not of hands like their own. The marauding Saxon saw these roads as something like the seasons, or the budding of the chestnut, or the springing of the corn. The roads had been nobody's business for the past two hundred years and more.

Twenty miles away, within the swaying walls of Eburacum, a few score men, British soldiers who still aped Roman manners and training, looked over the ramparts and sighed towards that straight ribbon of road; but they did not think of it as a thing which they might mend. They looked on it as the way to freedom, either to north or to south, if only they could pass invisible between the scattered huts and awnings that lay below the walls, the stinking homes of the besieging foreigner from Saxony. The half-hearted garrison dared not make such a sally, though. By now they were too weak or too spiritless to run such a gauntlet, whereas their tow-haired enemies rested, waiting with sharpened swords or long-bladed axes across their knees, only too ready to join a sporting Roman in a moonlight chase across the moorland, or along the crumbling white road that led both north and south.

The sea-rovers grinned and sang their rough songs which poured scorn on Roman courage. It had been almost a week since the last Roman had signed himself hurriedly and had begun that frantic rush over the rubble and across the Saxon midden-heaps towards the great road. And he had been a little fat one, nearly dead with fatigue and heart failure even before the first axe fell upon his weeping head. The invaders resigned themselves to a summer of rough cider and games with the knuckle-bones—poor drink and poor gambling, but dice must serve where men have no chess-boards, and cider take the place of mead among men who must conserve the last ear of corn for their winter bread-making. And the Saxons were laying in stores now, for they had no intention of leaving this year, or next either, if only this garrison would make up its mind to surrender, or to starve and have done with it. They must do one or the other before long; then everything would be pleasant and comfortable, with no enemies at one's back, barring a road to the sea should one need it in a hurry. From the Saxon point of view, there was only one drawback—there were no women of a marriageable age in the fortress. But they consoled themselves that next spring a ship or two might make the crossing again and bring back enough hardy Woden-born lasses to start a plantation in earnest.

Medrodus and Ambrosius stood on this road to Eburacum and sensed all this. It had not needed much imagination to do so, after the evidence they had stumbled upon by the roadside. Seeing a huddled form in the fast deepening twilight, the young man had shouted out a warning to it, suspecting a British ambush from the skirmishing troops of the citadel; but there had been no answer, and Medrodus had cast his javelin so expertly as to strike the man through the shoulders. The fellow had not moved, and when Medrodus had crept forward cautiously to find out the reason for this, he had discovered that this was a militia-man, a legionary of sorts, who must have been dead for some days. The Saxons had cut his throat—as they always did unless they were surprised before they could perform the ritual act—with their little knives. They had left behind the rusting Roman breastplates and loricae as not being worth pillage. The round Imperial helmet lay a few feet away, half full of rainwater. Medrodus went back to the old man and said, "He wears the ribbons of a decurion. An old man—fifty if he is a day."

Ambrosius made a small gesture of tolerant resignation and said nothing. A wood lay facing them on the western side of the great road. The final rays of the sun glinted behind it, throwing up each bough in black silhouette. Above the hunched and melancholy trees, rooks swirled in the orange air, like scraps of burnt paper caught in a wayward breeze. Below the wood, at shoulder-height, a great white owl glided silently, seeking mouse or vole, ignoring the two wanderers who had now left this dangerous road to strike further inland.

Beyond the wood lay the open moorland, punctuated here and there by rough spinneys, self-set, self-nourished, Nature's unceasing attempt to repair the ordered chaos of four hundred years of Rome. From time to time the travellers skirted shallow valleys and hollows, some of them noisy with the voice of waters, but most of them as dark and silent as the tomb.

Above one such hollow the men halted. The acrid scent of wood smoke wafted up to them in the growing moonlight. Mingled with it was another smell, that of burning flesh.

Ambrosius sniffed the night air. "They have burned their cattle down there," he said. "All waste! All waste! This land is a dark wasteland now, where men destroy and never build again."

Medrodus grasped his arm firmly, indicating that he should be silent, for such country could provide cover for a score of assassins, and an arrow might fly as accurately towards a sound as a sight.

"Master," he said, "let us go on, skirting this place. We can set our course beyond that far wood and come round at last to the high land of the west. So may we skirt danger."

Ambrosius sniffed the heavy air again and said, in his dry old man's whisper, "Danger is everywhere in Britain now, my son. The man who runs from it, like our little landowner in his wagon, is likely to find it waiting for him at the next crossroads. We shall go forward, Medrodus, remembering who we are, reminding ourselves of Rome."

Later they halted again at the edge of a high escarpment, the long, silver-black panorama of a menacing countryside lying down below them, to all intents still and deserted. Yet even in the few minutes that they watched, wondering which way they should take, bright orange-red points of light sprang up here and there across the long valley; sprang up and persisted for varying lengths of time, then died down again and fell to blackness. The night air carried a faint, musklike suspicion of smoke, that increased in density as the breeze blew up into their nostrils, and faded away like a morning dream when the wind turned from them once again.

"Down there men are setting fire to farms," said Medrodus. "They are laying waste to the country with a vengeance."

Ambrosius said bitterly, "Yes, with a vengeance. That is what we were told would happen once it was known that my own poor Legion had finally been disbanded. They did it in Gaul, too, the *Bacaudae,* the discontented peasants, and now they are doing it up and down Britain. It is as though they love no man, not even their masters who once put rye bread into their bellies and good neat's leather on their feet."

Medrodus said, "The British peasant loves the Saxon invader a little more than he does his own master, if the truth be known. The Saxon never beat him or took his dish of gruel away from him for short work! Somehow or other, it seems that the British have lost their honour, their pride, their unity."

Ambrosius stood for a little while in the moonlight. "Do you think that they ever knew such things? Only the nobles, the officers, the eminent of one sort or another, have ever known what it was to have honour and pride and unity—and not all of them, either!"

Medrodus said, "You are turning cynical, Master."

Ambrosius spoke as though to himself. "Perhaps that is a privilege of age. But I have observed this small province of a great empire falling to gradual ruin. I have seen loyalty wither and fade, and have watched selfishness flourish until its branches have touched the sky. We of Rome once brought a great ideal to this island; we shared our material advantages with a lesser people, hoping we might wean them away from their savage practices. We gave them the ideal of Empire, of citizenship; we gave them stability and uniformity. We gave comfort and education. . . ."

"And took away the life of the people," observed the young

man quietly. "I have heard that the physician, curing a wound, may accidentally bleed his patient to death."

Ambrosius smiled at him sadly. "Yes," he said, "perhaps it is something like that, but worse. For the doctor can only kill the body, yet Rome, by its well-meaning error, has destroyed the very heart, the soul, the spirit of these poor British folk."

Medrodus had never heard the old man speak such words. He stared at him in amazement. "What can we do for them, then, that Rome herself failed to do, Master?" he said.

"If I had the power, I would give them back their heart," said the old man. "I would give them back their faith in Rome, but not the Rome we know, the Rome that was once clean and just, proud and yet humble. That is what I would have done, perhaps. That is what my successor must pledge himself to do, to rebuild Rome on British soil. This sword shall only be given to the man who can pledge himself to that dream as fervently as I do myself. No woman must stand in his life, no other pleasure, no other vision. He must live a dedicated man, almost a sacrifice. Yes, that is what he must be, a sacrifice, the king who dies for his people."

Medrodus eyed the great sword and wondered, wondered whether its golden lure was profit enough for such an act of dedication, wondered almost whether he had not been a fool to follow so far a dream which should demand what amounted to the destruction of the self. And he looked at Ambrosius with new eyes now, seeing him as a religious maniac almost, less the old fearless battle-leader than a man obsessed, one who had crushed out of himself any ideal or pleasure that conflicted with this narrow, rooted passion for an ordered world, the world of some fantastically perfect Rome. . . . Yet a maniac who in his moments of clarity could see that perfection bred the seed of death in its own womb; a maniac who acknowledged the failure of Rome, yet would in his own fashion relive that failure again and again, and would train others to uphold and to nourish the growth of that seed of decay. Now we are reaping the harvest, thought the young man. He took the old leader's thin arm and together they began to walk down the slope into the valley.

After many hours they gained the other edge without having met any man. It was as though the world fell dead before their feet and only came alive again when they had passed. They moved through a small wood and then struck an old road, now thickly overgrown with springy turf and heather. It was an ancient provision track leading to some suburb, but now long forgotten. Ambrosius tried to recall where it might have led, but now from hunger and fatigue his mind was swimming beyond him somewhere and would not come back when he called it. They rested for a while in a pine copse where the needles lay thick on the ground and there was some shelter from the chill night wind, and when they had eaten a little of their bread and goat's cheese, they walked on again.

When they had gone for the best part of an hour, Medrodus suddenly became aware of a new sensation, though less a true sensation than the outside aura of one, the fringe of another consciousness. The air seemed different, the casual sounds of the night more strange. It was as though he trod the rim of a different world.

Beneath his feet he felt the ground falling gradually, and as the moon came out again from behind a cloud, flooding a broad and shallow valley with its equal silver light, the young man saw clearly and for the first time what really lay before them. It was a deserted city, a dead and long-forgotten place of crumbling stone. Here and there lay toppled columns, chipped by the barbarous axe-blade, eroded by the voracious tooth of wind and of rain, casting grotesque shadows across the bare wide space of what once had been a forum. This square grey place seemed to heave and roll like a frozen sea in the moonlight, its broad flagstones cast up fantastically by the unaccountable slow power of weed and of toadstool.

And beyond this dead place of meeting rose the buildings of the town; some of them colonnaded and porticoed after the Grecian manner; some of them built in a plainer Roman style, for use rather than for beauty. But all of them decayed now beyond repair, crumbling in the colourless light, an old, unburied civic corpse.

Somewhere beyond the forum, Medrodus saw a cupola sway gently, tiredly, without interest, in the moon's rays, then slowly heel over and slide sideways with a whisper that grew into a rattling crash as the heavy pediment swept across the loose tiles of the building below it.

Ambrosius made a grimace in the wan light. "In some ways this is Rome herself," he said. "This place which first rose in pride and grew to fatness in prosperity is now only the chattering-place of defeated spirits."

As he spoke, a long and melancholy howl sounded down an echoing alley-way to their left.

". . . and outcast dogs, like us," he ended.

The old leader pulled his threadbare toga more tightly about his thin shoulders. Medrodus saw the shudder that passed across the muscles of his face and neck.

"Are you afraid of this dead city, Ambrosius?" he asked.

"This is a part of my own past," answered the old man. "A part of my life that lies rotting here in the moonlight. I am not afraid of it, any more than I am afraid of my own body's death and decay. But I do not like it. That is all."

Medrodus looked about him. This was not his life, his Rome, his body. He was suddenly conscious of his arms and legs and the hard set of his stomach muscles. No, not his body! Never in his lifetime had men lived in cities like this. One only saw them in the north or the far west. Nowhere else. In other parts the sensible citizens had torn them down, to use their stones for pigsties and roads and for making bridges. No ghosts live among the stones that wall off a field, or a privy, he thought lightly.

"I will go and find a place where we can sleep tonight," he said aloud. "There'll surely be one municipal office with a sound roof left on it."

Ambrosius caught his arm. "No," he said. "Indoors the ghosts would yearn about us all the night; we should not sleep." Then, as though he had exposed a weakness which he would have kept hidden, he added quickly, "It would not be safe. This place totters and falls from hour to hour almost. We might be crushed if we sought shelter among these crazy stones. Let us raise up a few loose flagstones, for I can feel them beneath my feet. They would keep off the wind and we could build a fire to warm us through the night. That would be a better plan."

Medrodus had not truly relished the idea of groping unarmed among the sinister ruins. He shrugged his shoulders and said, "As you will, Master. I shall obey you in this, as in all else."

Leaving Ambrosius seated upon a stone, he went back to the edge of the forum, to gather furze and brushwood for the fire. Then they made their wind-break and drank brackish water from the goatskin flask that the young man carried at his belt, and chewed at the gritty bread and the strips of pickled meat from the stores which they had taken from the renegade's wagon. And at length old Ambrosius settled himself down in the moist earth that lay where the paving-stone had been. Medrodus watched his eyelids fluttering and smiled thoughtfully to see that the old man's fingers were clasped about the gold hilt of his sword, even as sleep crept over him.

No man should bind himself so closely to a symbol, the young man thought. He made to turn round and warm his hands before the crackling twigs of the fire, but as he did so his blood seemed to freeze and his heart leapt into his throat with a great bound.

A man was sitting watching him from the shadows thrown by the upturned flagstones on the other side of the fire, a small man with long hands like the claws of a bird and eyes that burned in the fire-glow like surging opals. His black hair hung down over his features, so that for a while in the fluttering light it seemed that he was faceless. Yet his head was bent forward, watchfully, as though he had been there a long time, waiting for Medrodus to look up and see him.

VI

THE YOUNG MAN'S FIRST REACTION WAS TO JUMP UP AND MOVE TO safety behind one of the heavy stones. Then he regained control of his shuddering muscles, remembering his own reputation among the Legion of Ambrosius as a wrestler and knifeman. Besides, the creature that faced him across the fire was small and old. The arms showed through his rags as thin as sticks, not the arms of a dangerous man. Medrodus gave a light laugh and rose to his feet in the firelight. His face, now darkly bearded with the stubble of three days, was set in a cruel smile. He moved, lithe as an animal, round the fire and stood before the bundle of rags that now sat rocking and crooning in the fire-glow.

"You are not welcome, my friend," he said viciously. Then with a sudden violence he reached down and grasped the wrists of the stranger, meaning to fling him across the stones, away from the fire.

Yet the strong hands of Medrodus gripped nothing, and the thin dry wrists were outside his own taut fingers. Medrodus grabbed at the man again, and once more grasped only the air. And now the stranger flung the thick hair back from his face and was looking up at him, his eyes hooded, his toothless mouth open, black as a pit and grinning.

Medrodus was, despite his cruelty, a brave man who did not accept defeat readily. Yet he was also a man of imagination, sensitive as a leopard or a snake in spring. He stared down in wonder at the ragged watcher by the fire, and as he did so the man began to rise to his feet, unaided it seemed by any movement of the arms or legs, moving without effort, like a leaf caught in some slow upward turning of the winds.

For a moment the eyes of Medrodus seemed to deceive him,

for the man rose and rose among the flickering shadows about the dying fire until he grew to a strange and supernatural height. Now he was taller than a javelin, and looked down, laughing silently, at the shrinking Roman, the long rags flapping about him with the scent of the tomb, his stark white ribs showing through the rents of his garment like the charnel stairs to hell.

Then he held out his arms towards Medrodus. "Take my wrists now, little one," he said. "Hold me fast a prisoner now." There was menace, even death, in that invitation, the young man knew. He shuddered in the foetid breath that swirled about his face as the thing spoke, and his ears were suddenly bewildered with the cry of birds. Of carrion kites and crows. He shook his head and tried to back away. Yet as he moved, that dark shape seemed to bend over him, preventing his escape, smothering all his courage. He tried to cry out for Ambrosius, like a child for his father, but no sound came from his mouth and the ghastly blank face still smiled down into his. Medrodus made a great effort and half turned in his terror towards Ambrosius; but he could see that the old man was asleep, in a safe world of his own, crouched in the shelter of the flagstones, still clasping the great sword as a child might hold a favourite toy in slumber.

Then Medrodus felt himself falling, and rolled aside just in time to avoid tumbling into the hot ashes. He lay on his back, breathing heavily, on the warm stones, unable to speak. And when at last he dared to look up again in the long silence, he saw that the stranger was sitting once more beyond the fire, crooning and rocking gently among the shadows, the hair of his gaunt head hanging before his face, like some black waterfall of the night. And Medrodus said in fear, "Who are you, Master? Why are you here?"

For a while there was a great stillness again. Only the night wind swept across the open crumbling place, and the sparks blew up from the white ashes with a faint, purring crackle. The young man listened to his own voice asking the questions, and it seemed that the words would echo forever in his bewildered ears, like a pebble falling down an eternal well, striking one side and then the other, and never reaching the black waters at the bottom.

Then at length, as though coming on the thin wind from some distant wasteland, Medrodus heard a voice, the keening voice of the Ice Land, the voice of nothingness. "Look at my breast," it said. "Look at my breast, Medrodus, and tell me what you see."

Medrodus, his great eyes trancelike now, did as he was bidden and saw the great gold lunula that gleamed below the creature's rags; the moon sign of the ancient priests, the druid symbol of holiness. Medrodus saw this and was afraid, for the tree-priests had been gone from the land for many centuries, wiped out at first by the Roman gods, destroyed at last by Christ Himself.

Medrodus bowed his head as a slave might do, for this thing was his master. He was nothing but a dog before such power, and he knew this in every beat of his frightened heart.

"You are of the old religion, Master," he said humbly.

The man nodded, and held out his hands, one on either side of himself, at arm's length. Then Medrodus saw a small snake rise from one of them, an adder; and from the other, a stoat. And these creatures stood still in the palms of this man's hands for a while, their small unwinking eyes fixed on Medrodus. He stared back at them in awful fascination. He saw the adder leap suddenly from one hand to the other, and in the palm of that one hand he watched the snake coil about the creature of fur, and saw both disappear in an ever-lessening spiral of bright light, until that hand, too, was empty. He rubbed his eyes in wonder, and then looked back to see the creatures now struggling in the druid's other hand. But suddenly the man clapped his palms together and the creatures were gone.

"Now do you know who I am?" he asked softly, smiling behind the hair that hid his face.

Medrodus answered in fear, "Yes, I know now. You are Merddin, the lost one, the maker of dreams."

Then Medrodus put his shaking hands to his ears, for the forum was suddenly filled with the obscene laughter of hyenas, and it seemed that long grey wolf-shapes swept here and there across the open space between the ruins.

"Have you come to take me?" whispered the Roman at last.

The other said, "How can I take you? You are a Christian and beyond my heathen power, are you not?"

The young man lowered his head, afraid to meet the wide lights that burned out towards him from the tumbling hair.

The druid's mocking voice said, "Is your God stronger than mine, Medrodus?"

Medrodus spoke in shame. "I am powerless, Master," he said. "I am in your hands. What am I to do?"

Then the hyena laughter came again into the deserted place and the grey shapes ran so close about the fire that Medrodus could smell the sweat of their hides and hear the scraping of their nails upon the stones.

And as from an immense distance beyond the farthest stars, the voice of Merddin floated down across the void, saying, "Whoso shall bear the sword of Ambrosius, to him great power. His the Yea and Nay, the life and the death; the setting up of stone, the throwing down of the cross. He shall remake Britain, be the axle-tree. His the mouth that shall speak the prayer for all."

Medrodus understood the words as though he had spoken them himself. "What shall be his reward when he throws down the cross and sets up the druid stones in the earth again? How shall the Count of Britain profit if he brings the old gods back and casts away the Christ?"

Even as he gasped with fear at his own boldness, the empty place seemed to heave about him, as though the earth would open and fling him down into a great pit. Astounded, he looked at the rocking figure and saw that Merddin was pointing downwards through the stones, as though commanding the Roman to follow his gaze.

And Medrodus looked down, and it was as though the great flakes of granite melted before his eyes, or became glass, green and oozing, so that he could see through them and beyond them, down and down, into the rich black soil below the place where he lay.

And there he saw a vast treasure house, of gold and silver, and of rare stones and ornaments, drinking cups and salvers, dishes and jewelled urns. Scattered thickly here and there, they lay in heaps, one upon another, waist-deep, it seemed, all bright and lustrous among the twining roots of the earth plants, new as the day they had come from the furnace and the polishing-wheel. An immense treasure that no man could assess, for it seemed to stretch beyond that lonely forum and away along the farthest avenue of that strange city of the night.

"Will that be his?" asked Medrodus. "With such a treasure a man might sail and take Byzantium, might be a Caesar by the Middle Sea again. Such wealth could buy back Rome and set the Eagles moving on the earth once more."

Then the voice came from beyond the stars again, saying, "Such trinket-stuff could buy back the old glory of the world before Bethlehem. That is the bargain!"

Medrodus knew a great fear when he heard these words. "But what if the Count-to-be should set the Christ before such treasure on earth. What would be his reward, then, Merddin?"

Once more the great thunders rumbled about the deserted city, and the stones divided once more as though they were curtains of silk, torn back by a vicious hand. Medrodus looked down and then covered up his eyes from what he saw. For there, in the place where gold cups had lain and diamonds had glittered, were men, a vast legion of the dead, all tumbled in the ghastly patterns of decay, with the worm at their eyes and the sly rat at their breasts, and the armour rusted on their arms and the dry white bone showing through the rotting hair.

"Such a legion could have conquered Asia," said Medrodus. "Should so many die because a leader chose the cross?"

But this time there was no answer, only a shuddering of the stones, and the thin night wind sweeping back over the lonely place. Medrodus looked for an answer to where Merddin had been sitting. But there was only the lichened shadow on the pavement where he had been and a dry toad dragging his wrinkled belly away from the last glow of the fire to a place where the darkness had already reached as it stretched its hand across the ruined forum.

Medrodus got to his feet, his brain on fire with confusion and horror. He bent above Ambrosius, then shook him with a sudden resolution. "We must go from here, Master," he said. "The old gods have come back. Here a man might be tempted away from Christ."

As he spoke he seemed to hear the sound of hyenas again, but distant now, as though they were beyond the tottering buildings that lay across the square. His teeth chattered with fear. "Hurry, Ambrosius," he said. "We must go from here."

The old man rose and followed him, half asleep, still clutching the sword and mumbling as he walked. And when the night was at last waning and the first grey hint of dawn moved like a shudder across the eastern sky behind them, the two staggered into a little gully where the wind was less chill. And there they lay down as best they could, huddled together for warmth, and at last fell asleep.

In the dawn light, the old man's face was serene in sleep; but the lips of Medrodus moved constantly and his throat worked, as though he were talking, pleading, arguing with one who would not let him go. The look on his face was that of a man who struggles against an opponent, but already senses defeat.

"Merddin, oh, Merddin," he whispered as he slept. "Must I forsake the Christ?"

A grey bird of morning swept over the little gully and looked down with its bright eye on the two sleepers. One had the peace of a tree about him; but from the other came a wave of suffering and pain. The bird wheeled into the high air and flew back towards the wood

VII

AT LAST MEDRODUS WOKE AND LOOKED ABOUT HIM. THE PLACE WAS quite different from what he had imagined it might be when they had stumbled into it.

The narrow declivity which sheltered them was steep on either side and heavily moss-grown, as though it had once been damp, before the hot summer sun had come to the land. At their feet ran the thinnest trickle of water, which wound in and out among the pebbles and rounded stones, strong enough to give nourishment only to water-weeds, which grew along the path of the runlet, a deeper shade of green than those that grew elsewhere.

Medrodus, like a man drunk, turned his head slowly to see where the water came from. A miniature aqueduct ran across the tiny valley to his left, supported on elegant stone columns meticulously fluted and decorated at base and capital with carved vine leaves. Despite the gnawing tooth of wind and weather, these pillars still held something of their old classical dignity, some element of grace and poise carried from a nobler world to this dark island and surviving in spite of bloodshed and ruin.

The water dripped down the wall below the shallow stone runnel of the aqueduct from the mouth of a leaden satyr, who leered, his features twisted and worn smooth by the centuries. Once this small valley must have been an irrigation ditch, fed by the surplus water from the aqueduct, which no doubt went to a bathhouse or piscatorium in the villa of some landed magnate in the early days of the Province.

Medrodus felt a strange and inexplicable emotion of yearning as he gazed at the pockmarked lead and the lichened stone. This was Rome, a glory he could never claim, a world of vanished glory.

He looked away to Ambrosius. The old man lay sleeping like a child, his pale lips smiling, his wizened hands about the hilt of the sword. Ambrosius belonged to Rome. He was part of this ruined glory, a true Roman.

For a moment, Medrodus remembered his own painful past; the flaking walls of Colchester, in whose slums he had been born, in whose back streets and stinking alley-ways he had played as a child. The son of a minor tax-official, hardly able to earn enough to feed himself, much less his seven unkempt brats . . . Medrodus recalled his father's worried face with loathing. A face too often distorted with sudden spasms of frustrated anger when the poor little man felt that he was working himself to death while his slatternly wife and rebellious family lived on the fat of the land. Cabbage soup and black barley bread! Meat once a week, if one were clever enough to be at the marketplace when some farmer came in with a diseased sheep or a heifer that had died in calf.

In the little green gully, Medrodus recalled his childhood, and could have wept. He let his eyes move to where the Count of Britain lay smiling, and spat with contempt, as he remembered this same Ambrosius riding through the slum where he lived one spring morning, with his men behind him, smiling at their leader's caprices in visiting such a dung-heap, and holding their noble noses in disgust. Medrodus saw again the picture of the great warrior as he was then, leaning down from his warhorse, that same sword at his side, leaning down and smiling, as a moral to his followers, and saying, "Mark my words, gentlemen, but this little savage who rolls in the gutters of Colchester shall one day stand for election in my place."

Perhaps he had only meant it as a joke, or to bring his proud followers to their senses, but one of them, a descendant of Romans for ten generations, had ridden up and had said with contempt, "But Ambrosius, this is a barbarian."

And the Count of Britain had put on that gravity which had become an automatic act with him and had said, "His hair and eyes are dark enough, Cato. He must be as good a Roman as any here—if only he had parents to prove it!"

Medrodus remembered his shame, even then, a small boy bespattered with filth, and shoeless, as the warband clustered round him on their fine horses and teased him, calling him Emperor. . . . He had wished to slit the bellies of their horses with the sharp stick he carried for his game of soldiers, and then spike them as they rolled on the cobblestones of his alley-way.

Ambrosius had lifted him up onto the saddle while the tears were still in his eyes, and had made the lad lead them to his father's house. Medrodus recalled that his mother had wept when the great man had taken him away, but his sad-faced father had clutched the broad bright gold pieces thankfully and had even kissed the bridle of the Count's horse, not daring to approach the great lord himself.

Medrodus had not been sorry to leave his family, though he had cried in the night for a short while when he thought of his lame sister, Claudia, for she was the only one he played with, being the weakest and least able to punch back when he lost his temper. Yet he had loved her in his way, and when he was feeling magnanimous—which was always after he had hurt her and was afraid she might tell his father when he came home late at night—he would make up stories for her amusement, stories in which she was a queen, and he always the more powerful king. And always they would kill their enemies, putting them to death a score of ways that occurred to a small boy's mind as he remembered the wrongs done him by the other occupants of the slums in which they lived.

So Medrodus became the ward of old Ambrosius, and so he came to be lying in the ditch beneath the grinning satyr that morning, still waiting for the Count to die. . . .

Suddenly the young man leapt up and ran to where the leaden mouth dripped its water down the wall. By reaching up he could just touch the creature's carved beard. His fingers grasped it and he pulled down with all his weight. The long leaden neck seemed to shudder for a moment; then slowly and irrevocably it bent and twisted, and the leaden pipe buckled and broke. Medrodus sat down among the damp mosses with the ruined thing in his hands, while the water trickled down over his head and shoulders, taking a new course now that the satyr was destroyed.

Ambrosius was sitting up and looking towards him, shading his eyes with his hand.

"What are you doing, Medrodus?" he asked. "Are you breaking something?"

Medrodus passed his hand across his damp forehead. Then he smiled and said, "I was testing my strength against Rome, Master!"

Ambrosius clucked and turned away from him, "You are foolish with hunger, my son," he said. "Such words are almost blasphemy now."

Medrodus rose from where he sat and strode up and over the sheltering bank. He did not dare speak back to the old man, for he felt a strange new rebellion growing in his heart and was afraid that he might speak more than he should.

Before him the countryside stretched in a gently rolling mosaic of greens, pocked here and there by quarries from which great builders had once hewn their stone, or covered in thick patches by the dark woodlands of the Midlands. Away on the horizon the blue hills lay in the new sun of morning, and from where he stood Medrodus could see nothing that jarred on his tensed nerves.

Once he looked back into the gully to see old Ambrosius wiping the sword blade on the skirt of his threadbare robe with patient rhythmic movements, lost in his dreamlike senility.

Medrodus turned away from him and went down the hill. A lark rose from under his very feet and mounted into the clear air with a startled whir of its small wings. He laughed at its fear and wished he were a hawk to race it into the skies and then poise above it before rushing down to the kill.

Among the gorsebushes at the hill's foot a group of rabbits crouched, sniffing about their sandy warrens. They had stopped nibbling at the lark's shrill warning, but Medrodus was treading so lightly in his morning pride that as yet their keen ears did not pick him up. He stopped and took up a large flint, then waited awhile until the animals had lost some of their suspicion and were eating again. Where they clustered together most thickly, he threw his stone, straight and strong. The rabbits scattered in the sudden terror of the flint, leaving one of their number behind, a doe heavy with young, who still kicked her hind legs and jerked her head from side to side, the glazing eyes wide open.

Medrodus went down and stood above her, watching the movements with a disinterested calm now, as though the sacrifice of this silly creature had appeased his anger. He felt the impulse to bend down and finish her suffering, but he controlled it, asking himself why he should meddle with the creature's pattern of life and death.

The flint which had killed her lay a yard away, its jagged edge bloody and decorated with a tuft of soft white fur. In a sudden movement which he could not explain, Medrodus picked it up and then daubed the blood across his forehead and the backs of his hands. It was as though a voice had told him to do this, a voice which came from behind a cascade of dark hair. Medrodus looked up in sudden fear. The sun on the eastern horizon seemed to wink at him like a gold lunula. He flung the bloody flint away from him in terror.

The rabbit was dead now, its limbs already stiffening. Medrodus rolled it beneath a gorsebush with his foot and began to go back up the hill. Yet now he had lost some of his confidence. He did not dare let Ambrosius sense that darkening streak across his forehead. He wiped it away with the sleeve of his tunic. His skin felt sticky after it had gone, as though it had left an inescapable stigma behind it. The flies began to buzz about him as he got nearer the gully once more, and in his mounting fear, Medrodus heard them speaking with the voice of Merddin. He ran down to where the water still trickled from the broken leaden pipe.

"Unclean, unclean!" he muttered as he rubbed the water over his face and the backs of his hands. Ambrosius, still cleaning the sword, did not hear him.

P A R T   T W O

UTHER PENDRAGON

Like ghosts in companies the dancers run
Under the lowering sky among the stones,
Anonymous, the men with antlers swirling,
Their faces stiff with grinning back at death.

The men of leaves and straw form whorls about
The clay-daubed girls who fall and shriek,
Shuddering as the jerking figures strike,
Feeling the Corn King trembling on their thighs.

And last, the men with sticks, the lily-white,
Their green cloaks whirling in the night's last breath.
Click-clack! Click-clack! *Their faces grave,*
Reliving glory and rehearsing death!

VIII

THEY HAD BEEN WALKING FOR TEN DAYS, NOW, TOWARDS THE WEST, meeting few men, avoiding such meetings when they could. Ambrosius slept well, like a young child, smiling in his dreams. Yet by day it was apparent that his strength was failing. He tired easily and often forgot why they were making the long journey across unfriendly country. Then Medrodus would try to tell him what their purpose was, speaking to him slowly and gently and holding his hand to emphasise certain points.

"We go to the western territories," he would say, as though to a backward child. "We go to raise men who will drive out the Saxon from Britain and let us live again as we did under Rome."

And Ambrosius would nod and smile and repeat his words. Yet sometimes, suddenly and without warning, the old man would sit up with a jerk, dragging his hand away, to ask why Medrodus should treat him like a fool. Then he would get to his feet and go off walking again, as though he were young and virile once more. Yet he would tire before long and then Medrodus would smile and wrap him up, away from the night wind, under a hedge or in a convenient ditch.

Medrodus himself had changed since that night in the ruined city. Now he felt his mind divided in a way he had not known before. Previously his only concern had been whether or not Ambrosius would honour his word and create him Count of Britain, once they had come to their journey's end among the tribes of the west. But now the situation was more complicated. Now the argument was carried a grim stage further. Suppose Ambrosius *did* make him Count, then what was he to do—press back the invader in the name of the Holy Cross, and gain death; or set up the old heathendom that Britain had known and followed before the Romans came, and gain vast wealth on earth, and everlasting torment when at the end he had to die? Such was his dilemma that at times, as he turned from side to side in the damp night watches, hearing the owls hooting about him and the field mice scuttering past him in the dark, he groaned aloud and wished to God that the problem had never been offered him to solve. Sometimes, when he was driven almost to despair, he thought of getting up from the ditch and running away, somewhere, he knew not where, to live as a hunter or a fisherman, beside some quiet stream. . . . Yet as dawn broke and healing sleep came to his eyes again, he forgot these things, and when the sun rose was ready once again to march with Ambrosius with the sun at his back.

Their journey was uneventful now. Once indeed they came to a stinking wooden village, where only old men and women sat propped against the palisade, chewing roots or pieces of tree-bark, the famine and despair grinning from their withered faces. All the young ones had left, they said; now there was only death for them. The two travellers passed on, breathing hard to keep the plague from their nostrils.

Once they met a crazed old woman picking sticks in a sunken lane, dropping as many as she gathered. She cackled at them and said, "Uther Pendragon lies at Lis Pengwern! Find him, Ambrosius! Find Uther Pendragon." Ambrosius, who was astounded at the old hag's knowledge of his identity, gave her a handful of small coins, which she dropped straightway, and could not find again.

Yet her words had so impressed the Count that he said, "That is an omen, Medrodus. We must go first to Uther Guletic, in Lis Pengwern. He is a good man, I have heard say, and will know where we should go next if we are to raise the tribes."

Medrodus said, "For God's sake, Ambrosius, let us go wherever you please, as long as we get there while I still have my reason!

This journey has put twenty years on my life. I am anxious to end it soon, whatever may happen."

Ambrosius smiled and said, "You need to cultivate more patience yet, my friend. Remember the great Legions. They walked up and down upon the earth for hundreds of years to gain their glory."

Medrodus said bitterly, "And where are they now! Heaps of refuse underneath the soil, while the Saxon and the Jute, who have never even made a road in their history, laugh at our fortresses and throw their carrion into our wells!"

Ambrosius did not answer, but set his thin lips and clutched the sword tightly to him.

Late that evening they came upon the first of the great hills of the west. As they approached it, Medrodus stopped with a gasp and pointed up to its summit. In the last rays of the setting sun, a horseman stood, his hair and cloak blown back from him by the night breeze, the blood-red light from behind him picking out the helmet on his head and the long lance in his hand. He seemed to be watching for them, like a bird of prey, Medrodus thought. Then, as suddenly as he had appeared, he went behind the hill.

When the two travellers reached the summit, he was nowhere to be seen. They descended the hill and entered a wood.

Breaking through the wood at last, they came to a long and rocky slope which led down to a river valley, beyond which the great hills of the west rose gradually, to reach their heights some miles away on the horizon, a dim purple grey in the mists of the morning.

Below them, where the rock-strewn surface of the land gave place to the more lush water meadows, a man was ploughing.

Medrodus stared at the clumsy wooden implement and then at the beasts that drew it. They were bulls, black and heavy in the chest, their long savage horns probing out before them as they moved snorting along the furrow.

"By Jupiter," he said, "but a man who ploughs with bulls must be worth joking with!"

Ambrosius was weary now almost to the point of falling. The weeks of rough country and of little food were more than his old body could tolerate. He said, "Joke with a man who uses cows, my friend, but walk clear of one who can make a bull walk straight."

Medrodus smiled at him and then put his hands to his mouth and called out, "Ho, there! The gods draw near. Fall to your knees, ploughman, lest you offend them!"

Ambrosius clucked with displeasure, but Medrodus was too full of his own jesting self-importance to notice that.

The ploughman halted and turned his head up towards them. Then he spat on the ground and shook the heavy thong reins. The black bulls began to move on again. Medrodus saw this and drew in his breath with annoyance. He began to run towards the man, the rage thumping in his temples.

"Stop, you clown!" he called. "Stop when the Count of Britain comes towards you."

The ploughman stopped once more and stood still to wait for Medrodus. He was tall and barrel-chested; so heavily developed were the muscles of his shoulders that he looked at first sight almost hunchbacked. His broad face glistened in the sunlight with sweat, which he wiped away from time to time with the back of a large and calloused hand. His sandy hair was chopped off at the nape of the neck, in the old barbarian style, but hung in two small plaits, one from each temple, almost hiding the heavy gold rings which dangled from his ears.

In spite of the man's rough horsehide jerkin and crudely banded woollen trousers, Medrodus sensed that among his own folk he must be a man of some substance. The embossed bronze gorget, the coral-studded arm-rings, and the ivory haft of the knife that hung from the leathern lace across his breast all contributed to this impression.

"Ploughmen are rich in the west," sneered Medrodus.

The man's face showed no emotion, no recognition. It was as impassive as a roughhewn block of sandstone—and roughhewn it was indeed, for below the unblinking pale blue eyes, the cheekbones were raised by thick horizontal ridges, the result of some ritual surgery, into which blue dyes had been rubbed, giving the broad face an inexpressibly savage look. Medrodus felt a slight shudder pass down his neck as he looked back into this face.

By now Ambrosius had stumbled up to them. He gave the old greeting sign and said, "Hail, friend. We come in peace. Have you a welcome for us?"

The man did not move, and for a moment even allowed the runnels of sweat to stream down his red face unchecked. Medrodus noted the cruelty of expression which the broad mouth held, turned down at the corners in a fixed smile. His hot temper would allow him to keep silent no longer.

"When a Roman asks, even the dogs must bark an answer!" he said, his voice bold, his legs shaking with the strain of this strange interview.

The man's mouth curled ever so slightly. Then he shrugged his heavy shoulders and turned again to the plough stilts. He shook the reins slightly, as though to warn the waiting creatures that they must begin their work again.

Medrodus was beside him in a stride, his own hand upon the reins, the muscles of his sallow face working with frustrated anger. Yet before he could put into words the hurt pride that was in his heart, the ploughman had turned with surprising swiftness, had taken him roughly by the hair on the crown of his head, and with one easy movement had flung him sprawling among the furrows.

Bewildered by the man's animal speed and strength, Medrodus lay where he fell, his eyes wide with sudden fear, snarling but speechless.

Ambrosius stumbled forward, squinting hard so as to see, his hands stretched out helplessly.

"Peace be with you, friend," he said. "Know that we are harmless folk, come from afar to speak with Uther Pendragon."

The ploughman turned and gazed at the old man. Then he spoke, but as one unaccustomed to frequent conversation. His voice sounded almost foreign to their ears. It was not the voice of a man who habitually spoke Latin, or even any Roman dialect of Celtic that they knew.

"Uther Guletic! Uther Guletic!" he said, shaking his great red head. "When he speaks the birds fall from the sky and timid men make a mess in their breeches! Ah, Uther Guletic!"

He nodded a time or two, wiped the sweat from under his chin, then turned from them as though they had ceased to exist.

The bulls strained at their harness and began to pull. Medrodus raised himself slowly and stood staring after him.

"If I had a bow," he snarled. "Oh, that would bring you down to my level, my friend!"

Ambrosius said, "These folk are sensitive. They are not to be hectored. We Romans had long years learning how to deal with them."

Medrodus turned on him, nettled. "I am a Roman, too," he said angrily.

The old man's lips drew back in a straight line but he did not speak. Just then the ploughman halted at the end of his furrow, and turning back to them, called, "Uther Guletic! Uther Guletic! Over there, and take a pair of clean breeches!" He began to laugh, and waved his hand broadly towards a low hill beyond the river. He then turned back to his plough and bent over the share, his shoulders heaving with laughter.

Medrodus swore in anger, but Ambrosius checked him. "A man who would rule a people must first learn to rule his own tongue," he said coldly.

Medrodus came back at him hotly. "We shall see, Ambrosius," he said. "There are many ways of doing these things."

"But only one right way," said the Count of Britain, "and that you will learn, if these western men let you live long enough to learn anything."

The young man's lips curled back in anger. "I shall live, never fear, Master, while there is the muscle in my arm to drive a knife."

Ambrosius smiled, as though he were thinking of other things. "I have known many men who said something like that," he said, "yet the worm has crawled in the mouths of them all by now."

Medrodus struck himself hard on the thigh, unable to contain his rage.

"Do not distress yourself," he said. "I am marked for other things than the worm."

At the river bank they found a raft pulled up among the stones. They crossed the narrow stream on it, Medrodus pushing with the long pole, and muttering a curse with every movement. Some of the curses were spoken against the western men, some against the Saxon, and some against an enemy unnamed. As the young man muttered, he looked towards the blind Ambrosius, who sat with his back towards him, fondling the great sword on his thin knees.

IX

SO AT LAST THEY WALKED INTO UTHER'S DUN. THE PLACE THEY HAD come so far to find lay sprawled in confusion beneath the lowering grey stone crags of a high hill. Wooden and wattle huts were strewn, haphazard, on all sides of a large, roughly square area of earth, beaten hard and flat by many feet for many generations. Beyond that square lay the ruins of what had once been a Roman villa, four-square and red-tiled, its courtyard containing fruit trees and a stone fountain. Yet the building which overtopped all, although it was set away from the others, almost at the foot of the steep rocky slopes of the hill, was a temple, domed and columned in a barbaric imitation of the classical style, but made of wood, an immense parody of a civilisation which had now passed into man's most distant dreams.

The grotesque hunched shape seemed to brood above the settlement, its columns blackened by fire, its irregular dome decorated by long pikes, at the summit of each of which grinned a parchment-coloured head, some of them still wearing their frayed and tattered trappings of braid and eagles' feathers.

Within the temple, fires burned at altars raised to many gods, throwing out a black and greasy smoke that hid whatever it swept across and hung about the ragged tents and wattle huts before it dispersed in the direction of the river.

Medrodus shuddered and held his nose as the waves of billowing smoke swung in his direction.

"The Kings of the West live in style," he said drily.

"At least they live," said Ambrosius, "which is more than we can say for many jewelled emperors we have known."

Everywhere about them there was movement, the patternless violent to-and-fro of any primitive encampment. Women dragged long sledges laden with brushwood, or passed wooden buckets from hand to hand from the stream up to the huts; children rolled in the dust between the wattle huts, or stood on the manure heaps shouting and pushing their companions headlong down; drovers brought in their herds of sheep, to the accompaniment of barking dogs; cattle strayed here and there about the houses. Over the carcass of a fallen bull, a group of half-naked men worked, some of them astride the beast, laughing as they hacked, their chests spattered with warm blood. In the beaten-earth square, two parties of young men attacked each other with cudgels, the fight swaying backwards and forwards as one side and then the other gained the mastery. Beyond the Roman villa, a company of horsemen swept in a wide circle, picking with their long lances at some object which rolled on the ground.

Medrodus said, "God, how the place stinks!"

The old man's face took on a cynical smile. "Almost as bad as the alley-ways of Colchester, I seem to recall." Medrodus felt a fierce shiver pass down the hairs on the nape of his neck to the muscles of his back, the muscles that would drive a knife into a man. But he controlled himself and said, "Master, you do wrong to taunt me. I am what you have made me. If that is a bad thing, then your training and not my heart may be at fault."

The old man stopped and said, "I am fallible, like any other man, Medrodus, that is all."

And Medrodus read a strange menace in that simple speech,

though he could not put his finger on the cause of the menace at that time.

There was hardly time for more words, for the horsemen had sighted them and had swung round towards them, galloping furiously. Soon the two men were surrounded by this swarm of half-naked Celts, their long hair streaming behind them, their painted bodies bent low over their horses' necks as they swept about their visitors. Medrodus made a firm stand, determined not to let them force him to show fear. He smiled above their heads, towards the black smoke of the temple, trying to impress them with his Roman gravity. Old Ambrosius, his eyes made still more blind by the thick dust that swirled about them now, put out a hand to find Medrodus and whispered, "What is it? Are they attacking us, Medrodus? Who are they, think you?"

Medrodus put out his arm to steady the old man, who was in danger of falling down in the giddy confusion. Yet it was not kindness alone that prompted this movement. He intended these savages to see it as a protective gesture to a weak old man, expecting that they would respect that weakness and draw away.

Yet he misjudged these men, to whom an old man was not an object for pity but for sport. One great horseman, his corn-coloured hair caught back on his shoulders by great whorls of copper, drove in so close that he jostled Ambrosius sideways, against the pony of another man, a small dark man whose face was criss-crossed with many ritual scars. The Count of Britain stumbled and fell to his knees. Medrodus acted by instinct and stood above him, one leg on either side of the old man's kneeling body. He reached down for the great sword, which Ambrosius still clasped as a mother might hold a child. Seeing his intention, the man with the corn-coloured hair gave a rough shout and, levelling his lance, drew back to make a charge at Medrodus, who now felt the sweat of fear trickling the length of his back.

It was at this moment that a great shout sounded behind them, from the river, at which the horsemen halted, and sat waiting, still as carven statues. Medrodus looked behind him to see the man who had been ploughing with bulls. He strode with authority now, his broad head thrown back.

"Hold your lance, Bedwyr!" he called. "The old one means no harm. It is only the young one who offends."

Ambrosius struggled to his feet and looked towards the ploughman.

"I owe you thanks," he said. "Your followers are a little overboisterous in their play."

The ploughman ignored the old man's words. He spoke to the horsemen.

"Get back to your work," he said. "You, Bedwyr, take these to the Guletic. And keep your lance out of them until he has seen them."

The horsemen saluted him before they galloped back to their lance-play. The corn-haired savage who had intended to kill Medrodus now laughed just as readily and swung his own horse round towards the decaying villa. "Artos commands," he said, when Medrodus would have hung back. "Men obey him."

The ploughman, Artos, had walked away to a wattle hut at the edge of the compound, disinterestedly. He did not once turn round to see if his orders had been obeyed. Medrodus envied his assurance, hating its success at the same time.

The horseman snarled over his shoulder, "Make better speed or I will ride behind you. Then you shall learn a way to make men hurry."

They followed him through the wide gateway of the villa and across the derelict courtyard, to where Uther Pendragon sat in state, among his chieftains, laughing under an awning by the further wall.

Like Cunedda and Vortigern of earlier times, this Uther was a northern Celt, who had seen more profit in moving westward and appropriating territories outside the sway of the Legions. Of all the *foederati*, however, he had best learned how to mind his own affairs. There was no record that Uther Pendragon had ever become involved in the many skirmishes that had flared up and faded away along the Borders, in those last ruinous years of Roman domination. When minor wars started, Uther found occasion to visit relatives in Strathclyde, or to go on a long hunting expedition in farthest Gwynnedd. So he was still strong, not having wasted his men in futile battles and his money in entertaining visiting Roman delegates.

The laughter under the tattered awning ceased as the two travellers made their way towards the group. Uther Pendragon stood up on his throne steps as Ambrosius drew near and raised his hand in a careless gesture, as though gibing at the Roman greeting sign. He was a tall and robust man, despite his seventy years. His hair was still plentiful and red, and hung down below his roughly beaten gold head-ring, in two plaits onto his broad shoulders. His drooping moustaches mingled with the fierce fork of his beard below a hooked and hawklike nose. His most remarkable features were his pale grey eyes, that seemed like holes in his head, so faded was their colour—and an old sword-cut that puckered up the left side of his face from temple to nostril, so that he always seemed to be grinning in a savagely humorous way.

His voice was as courteous as he could make it, though sibilant from that same sword wound, which had knocked out his teeth on one side of his jaw.

"Welcome, Ambrosius," he said. "We wondered how long it would be before you came."

At these words, there was a subdued rustle of laughter among the chieftains. Medrodus wondered what the reactions of Ambrosius would be to such a jibe. Yet the Count of Britain seemed hardly to hear what Uther Pendragon had said. He stood in the courtyard, his arms folded, a strangely confident little smile wrinkling the corners of his mouth. This was Ambrosius Aurelianus, the Roman, now, and no longer the weary and faintly comic old dotard he had seemed at many points along the journey.

"Uther Guletic," he said quietly, "what is there left for me to do, for Rome to do? If you will not come to us when we send for you, then we must come to you, as the father must go to his grown up son, however wayward the boy may be."

The laughter under the awning turned to a faint gasp of astonishment, and men looked up now to see what Uther Guletic would do as answer to such impertinence. And for a while there was silence while the thick black smoke from the temple altars swept across the enclosed courtyard.

Then Uther Pendragon descended the three steps on which his carved throne-chair was set, and he went to Ambrosius Aurelianus, a smile upon his grim face, his red head slightly bowed. And he held out his hands to the old man, who stood still, staring above him all the while. And Uther Pendragon kneeled in the dust before the Count of Britain and said, quietly, yet so that all should hear, "Master, if such as you had sat on the golden chair in Rome, the world would not be a jungle now." Lightly he touched the hem of the old man's tattered robe with his lips. Then, with a movement so feverishly quick that for an instant Medrodus almost suspected treachery, Uther Pendragon swung round to his henchmen under the wall and said defiantly, "This is a man. Look at him and remember that I have said so, should the devils of mischief enter your heads tonight, or any other night."

Many there present had never heard of Ambrosius, but had feared Uther Pendragon from their cradles. They gazed with wonder on the thin old man who stood before them still clasping the great sword, his blind eyes looking beyond them into a past, or a future, towards which they could not reach. Medrodus saw the little twitch of the Count's lips, the signal for some cynical comment. Then he saw the mouth straighten itself again, and knew that Ambrosius would leave unsaid that which had come to his mind. Ambrosius said, "Thank you, friend. May this moment heal the wound the silent years have made."

Uther looked a little uncomfortable for a moment and then he turned and called out for a slave-girl to fetch water so that the feet of Ambrosius should be washed, a ritual sign of hospitality. Medrodus suddenly recalled an incident of his childhood, when his mother had been asked to attend a ceremonial dinner at the municipal offices in Colchester. She had assumed that her invitation was due to the fact that her husband was a person of some standing, at least in the tax department. She borrowed a dress from a neighbour and spent hours trying to make her face and hands look as though she were a lady of leisure. Yet in the end, she still looked much the same as she had for years. The wrinkles were too deep, the callouses too hard, for a mere day to remove them. And that evening, she found that she was not to sit at the great table of the visiting Vicarius, but had to stand, with other wives of petty officials and clerks, along the wall, as a servant. Her special task was to hold the golden bowl of rosewater, with which the feet of the Vicarius were washed. Medrodus recalled her tears when she returned to their wretched home that night. Now he watched the slave-girl washing the feet of Ambrosius. He clenched his lips tight.

"Soon they shall wash my feet," he said to himself, "those laughing savages under the awning, Uther Guletic himself. Yes, and the one who ploughed with the bulls. Especially he. I will throw the water into his face afterwards."

Medrodus looked again at Uther Pendragon. He noted the full red cloak, held at the shoulder by a massive garnet brooch, its setting of dark bronze; the sky-blue tunic, pinched in about the waist by a belt of a hand's span in breadth, bossed at intervals with red coral, from which hung a silver-hilted hunting knife in a scabbard of heavy Spanish leather.

His envious gaze travelled down the man's body, to the bright red and yellow breeches, strapped round thigh and calf with thongs of plaited hide. He observed the thinness of those legs, the limbs of a man who had walked little for exercise, but who had lived a long lifetime in the saddle. Medrodus made a mental note that if ever he had to face the Guletic in anger, it should be on foot and not mounted.

He came from his daydream to hear Ambrosius say, "This is my ward, Medrodus, who has served me well since his boyhood." Nothing more than that; no announcement of the election. Medrodus looked up in irritation, but then was forced to walk forward to take the hands of Uther, who waited to greet him. The Guletic's grip was so strong that for an instant Medrodus knew himself to be powerless. The young man made another note, not to meet the Guletic unarmed!

"Young man, you are welcome for the sake of Ambrosius," said Uther Pendragon. Then he went back to his chair and seemed to forget him.

Now the Count of Britain was sitting among the war lords, who regarded him with respect, listening to his halting Celtic as he explained that Britain could only be free again if the people of the west joined forces and swept the Saxon invader from the coasts.

Uther listened attentively, stroking his beard and grinning because of his sword-cut. Only once did he interrupt, when he said, "The western folk are many. It would need a strong man to hold them together. You and I are too old for that task now, Ambrosius." The heart of Medrodus leapt into his throat, for he expected that the old man would make his announcement now. But Ambrosius was silent, as though in his blindness he forgot that Medrodus still stood there. And the moment was lost, for Uther went straight on, saying, "Moreover, friend, we can never bring back Rome again, even if we wished to do so, for Rome has gone from the world's face; she is as torn and bleeding as we are. By force, perhaps, we might drive out the Saxon, but it would be to create a rule of our own, and not of Rome."

Ambrosius bowed his head. "I am not a fool, Uther," he said. "I know there is a price to be paid. Men fight for different dreams, and yours is not mine. Yet the end could be the same, peace and comfort for a well-ordered land. Britain is still rich, if one only knows where to look for the riches. Her people still have strength, if one only knows how to call it forth. Together, you and I, Uther, might lead this land back to ordered peace and prosperity. No, not as warriors, I know; but as counsellors. A British Council, over which we presided, you and I, having chosen a *dux bellorum,* a battle leader, to do our fighting, would be the answer."

The chieftains began to talk to each other now, shaking their feathered heads and beating their hands, one upon the other, to stress their words. Pendragon listened to them for a space and then said to the old man, "We are not certain. We are tribesmen and not legions. We have never followed anyone but our blood leaders, no, not from the beginning. We are a roaming people, who fight here and there as the whim takes us and as the loot draws us! And when we are not fighting, we have our cattle to tend, and our fields to plough, and our babes to get and rear. It is not easy for us to follow an idea like the one you speak of, for we have never known an ordered comfort, friend."

Medrodus had edged to the foot of the throne steps, and would have raised his own voice at that moment, had not a slave-woman offered him a horn-cup of wine. As he set it to his lips, he noticed that Uther and Ambrosius were also being offered wine, but from golden cups. It seemed to him now that everything possible was being done to humiliate him. Yet he would show them that he could control himself as a Roman should. He put the cup to his lips and drank a little. The wine was thin and sour, made from local grapes, he thought. His grimace went unchecked.

Then Uther Pendragon leaned forward in his chair and knocked the cup from his hand. The wine spilled at the feet of Medrodus, splashing over the pavement onto his sandals. He turned in anger to meet the cold light eyes of the Guletic. Uther was smiling differently now and the gap in his teeth was openly displayed.

"I would not have my guests suffer from my hospitality," he said. "Our wine is not to your taste. We shall not inflict it again."

Some of the tribesmen were on their feet, looking down at him, their eyes flaming like those of animals. Somehow they assumed that this stranger had insulted Uther, their overlord. Medrodus made himself smile.

"Guletic," he said, "I have travelled far and am weary. My manners may improve when I have rested."

Uther still bared his teeth, a nerve at the side of his neck throbbing with suppressed anger.

"There is a bed for you," he said; "may it be more to your liking than our wine was."

Ambrosius half rose, as though he realised at last that the young man was going to leave him among these strange folk. But Medrodus could not wait now. He saluted Uther Pendragon and followed the slave-girl who waited to take him to the room set aside for wandering guests.

As Medrodus sat on the thong pallet, dangling his legs and biting his knuckles with frustration, the door-curtain opened and a young fair-haired man came in. Medrodus saw his wavering blue eyes and the sharp, mean nose. He sat in silence, trying to summon up as much dignity as his anger had left him.

The young man said, "I was there when he spilled the wine over you. He is a violent man. You must always beware of his anger."

Medrodus did not speak. He feared that this might be some trap. The other sensed this and went on hurriedly. "I am not of this folk. You may trust me. I am from Dumnonia, Ambassador to Constantine. I only say, take care. Uther Guletic is to be watched. Yet his son, Artos the Bear, is even more fearful."

Medrodus said, as urbanely as he could, "I look forward to meeting a son who contains within himself more graces even than the father."

The Ambassador looked at him strangely. "But you have met him," he said. "I saw him through the archway, stopping Bedwyr from running his lance through you."

Medrodus said, "So that is Artos! Artos the Bear! He is well named, indeed. Tell me, my friend, is it his usual habit to plough the fields with bulls in the yoke? That seems a strange custom, even for such an unusual people as this!"

The other came forward, but listened before he spoke lest there should be someone in the corridor that led to this room.

"Friend," he said, "you have met a man who is under a curse of the gods. Artos is cursed. He is forced to plough with bulls as a penance. His father, Uther Pendragon, put that punishment upon him. It is one of their old punishments. Most often the bulls are intractable and gore the ploughman. Yet this Artos subdued them, and can now plough as straight a furrow with bulls as another man can with oxen."

Medrodus looked back at him in bewilderment. "His father caused him to risk death?" he asked. "But why should that be? A father does not do that to his son if he loves him."

The other said, "Make no mistake, Uther loves Artos, but the priests made him pass the sentence, for it is the old law. Artos had offended the oldest of laws. Had he been the son of a mere warrior, they would have cut his throat over the altar stones and said no more about it. But Artos is of the precious blood, the oldest blood, of kings."

Medrodus said simply, "What has he done to merit such punishment?" But the fair-haired man drew back. "I may not tell you," he said. "The word must not be said, lest the old gods hear it and bring me to the same thing in my dreams."

Medrodus said, "Get out of my room, for God's sake! I have come from a different land, I see, although I have only crossed a few hundred miles of waste dungheap. Go, and keep your gossip for the other old women you know. They will relish it about the smoking fire, no doubt. But I am tired."

He flung himself onto the bed, his face to the rough stone wall, and closed his eyes.

"You will not live long here, my friend," said the other, turning from him. "Your temper is too quick—yet even so, it cannot match the fury of Uther Pendragon. A man must stay awake all night to catch Uther with his breeches down!"

Medrodus sat up again. "We shall see who is master," he said, unable to control himself. The young man laughed quietly and went to the door.

"At the feast," he said, "we shall doubtless see many things. There you will learn more perhaps than you wish to know."

He turned then, and without saying another word, went through the door-curtain. Medrodus bit his knuckles until the blood came in thin trickles. Then he beat his bleeding hand against the grey stone wall, unable to contain his anger any longer.

X

THE RESINOUS SMOKE HUNG AT HEAD-HEIGHT IN THE HALL, BLOWN back from the chimney hole in the tiles by a contrary wind. Here and there the torches flared up and died again, coaxed by slaves. In the night, on the hills above the ruined villa, wolves howled to each other in the moonlight.

A harper plucked at his strings in a dark corner and sang a yearning ballad of his own country, for he was a slave, captured in war. Uther's folk had put out his eyes so that he might sing the sweeter. Now he saw only the things he dreamed about, and his dreams were so much sweeter than the reality had ever been. He sang of his country as though it had been a place of golden apple trees and everlasting sunlight; though in fact it had been a thousand acres of stoney outcrop, on which the rain fell all the summer and the seas beat all the winter.

Medrodus lolled back, tipsy with mead, for the Guletic had kept his word, and the woman who tended Medrodus would not bring him wine.

Ambrosius, seated at the head of the table with the Guletic, drummed on the oak boards with his thin fingers, drinking little and eating only bread. He was old, anyway, and needed little food; besides, in two weeks, travelling across Britain, he had had so little to eat that his stomach had shrunk and he was not hungry now.

Uther Guletic did not notice that. He was jesting with a broken-nosed warrior on his right, and drinking horn for horn with any man who dared challenge him.

Medrodus was bored. Ambrosius had not spoken to him the whole evening. The young man was too hurt to make any overtures. So they were silent. Outside, another wolf pack had scented the first and were loping over the harsh scree to find meat.

A juggler stood in the firelight, throwing up a dozen coloured balls. The men at the tables hooted at him. He shrugged his shoulders and then juggled with a dozen sharp knives. They made little circles in the torchlight as they seemed to pass in a whirl about his white hands. Yet the men thought little of his skill.

Medrodus thought that there was one who could show them something to applaud, if only he might be there at that moment. He recalled the grinning skulls beneath the forum. These savages would marvel at that! Then Medrodus recalled that Merddin was the priest of such men as these, and he was silent, even within his mind, again.

A girl came into the firelight and danced in a wide, swaying circle. At first she smiled, the fixed smile of the professional dancer, for she had been reared in the theatres of Byzantium; she had come to Britain, hearing that the savages there did not know the value of good gold. In the dark corner, the harpist still longed for his land of golden apple trees. As the dancer passed round the hall, men leaned over their tables and tore her clothes from her. She danced on, naked. Her face still held the fixed smile of the theatres.

Then one young man, anxious to impress his fellows, flung the remains of his wine over her as she passed him. She turned and gave him a smile, for she was a brave creature. Now every man flung his wine over her body, so that she swung glittering through the firelight. Men began to regret their wine, to find her smile poor recompense. At last an elderly chieftain from Gwent put out his razor-keen hunting-knife as she passed in the fury of her dance.

She stopped suddenly, a long thin streak of red round her flank. The tables rocked with laughter. This was entertainment. The girl took the laughter as a challenge and continued her dance. Now as she passed each table, her body was cut; yet her courage made her dance. Medrodus leaned forward now, his boredom forgotten. His eyes were wide open and his lips apart. He took his knife from its sheath and thought what an example he would give! Yes, one to make men respect him. He leaned over the table, even though her eyes begged his tolerance in the torchlight.

Then, just as his arm went out to make the stroke, Uther Guletic spoke, and his voice sounded, as though he spoke in the ear of Medrodus, to him alone.

"I have always led warriors, not cowards! You swine have rooted up a delicate flower that is worth more than any one of you."

There was silence in the hall now, and the dancer stopped swirling. She looked at Uther Pendragon with gratitude in her dark eyes. He ignored her and spoke on. "Look you, my little friends, since the talk is of knives, and this dancer has not even clothes to protect her body—since the challenge is that and no other, which of you warriors will jump into the firelight, bare of your shirt, and take a knife to this little girl?"

In the silence the wolves could be heard, giving battle among the grey stones. The harper had fallen asleep, his fingers crooked about the strings. Now summer and gold apples would never come. Only winter and the harsh salt surf on the rocks were there.

Medrodus was leaning over the table, his knife out, when Uther announced his challenge. All men looked towards him and he shuddered that such a test should be given him that night.

Now men began to laugh about the hall, and one of them threw the girl a long slim skinning-knife, which she caught, with a smile. Medrodus tried to speak, to assert his dignity, as was befitting a man who expected soon to be called to command over these tribesmen. But they did not know his ambitions. They saw only a rather foolish-looking young man, half drunk with mead, leaning on a table.

"The warriors ask for you, young sir," said Uther Guletic, smiling over his wine-horn. As for Ambrosius, he was now withdrawn into his blind world of pearl-grey, and did not know what was afoot.

Medrodus looked from side to side, the thought coming to his mind that never in history could a man have been so cheated by fate of his rightful dues. For who would follow into battle a man who had fought with a naked girl at a feast?

Now the men at the tables in the firelight began to beat the oaken boards with their knives and chant, "Let him fight! Let him fight! Let him fight!" Until the words sounded like some horrible sentence of doom to the weary Roman.

Medrodus was almost at the point of begging Ambrosius to help him when a voice behind him whispered, "Well, friend? Perhaps you understand my warning now?" The fair-haired young man leaned against Medrodus, as he passed, to whisper these words.

Now there was such a noise in the hall that all men laughed in the expectation of blood. At this point, Medrodus, sensing that he was alone and must make his way without help from any source, human or divine, leaped over the table, his knife in his hand.

Suddenly there was silence again in the ruined corridor. The noises of the night came down through the chimney-hole once more. The dancer, who had laughed before, hardly understanding what was going on, expecting at any moment that the whole thing would turn out to be a jest, now shrank back towards a table. She was pushed forward to meet the advancing Medrodus, whose knife was held before him, stiffly, as he usually attacked.

Yet, when he was within a yard of her, and when some of the young men about the tables were rising to kill him should he succeed in killing her, Medrodus halted. He, too, understood the terror that stared from the girl's wide eyes. It was in his own heart at that moment. So he stopped and bowed to her, and held out his knife to her, hilt foremost, and then what few coins he had, in the other hand.

"Lady, you have slain me," he said, smiling uncertainly. The girl looked at him for a moment and then, with the quickness of the alleys in which she was reared, saw his meaning. She stepped towards him, and as she took the money from his hand, stabbed at him with her long knife. She had intended the thrust to be as much a pantomime as his performance was, but the knife was long.

Medrodus gave a short gasp, and then smiled on, his hand clasped over his stomach. The men nearest to him saw the thin trickle of blood that came between his fingers as he smiled.

Then the girl turned and was gone into the shadows, to another part of the villa. And the warriors sat down again, calling aloud for wine.

Medrodus went to his seat, alone and forgotten by the men who had watched him so carefully but a minute before. Now he knew that although he had chosen the right answer in this last affair, he could never lead these folk into battle with the Saxon.

XI

THEN OLD AMBROSIUS ROSE, LIKE A MAN COMING FROM A DEEP trance, shaking his head and holding the sword in his hand as though he had not known it was there before. The noise about the tables was at its height, and here and there men began to quarrel, pushing at each other drunkenly. Uther Pendragon looked at Ambrosius curiously, even insolently, as though amused that the Count of Britain should, by his rising, call for silence on such an occasion.

Medrodus felt the tears coming to his eyes. This was not the moment, he thought. He beat on the hard board before him in self-pity and despair.

Ambrosius was speaking now, though none listened. Medrodus caught a phrase or two, precisely formed in a Roman tongue that few in that hall could have understood, even had they heard them. "He who shall carry this sword . . . the glory of Rome in a new world . . . ordered commonwealth . . . unto the death."

Suddenly a spasm of annoyance passed over the face of the Guletic, Uther Pendragon. He, too, rose, and beating on the table with his drinking-horn, called for silence.

"When the Count of Britain speaks," he said sardonically, "even the men of the west must cease their gossip."

It was at this point, when all men looked towards the tired old man, and when the slaves had thrown logs upon the fire in the centre of the room, that the curtains which covered the main door were flung open. A party of men stood in the doorway, as drunk as those within, from the way in which they swayed on their feet.

Artos the Bear was their leader, and Bedwyr of the corn-coloured hair stood at his left hand. The small dark man whose face was crossed by ritual scars stood at his right hand. The drinkers at the tables saw that their visitors carried staves, but no other weapons. There were many others in the courtyard, judging from the sounds of feet and of voices.

Artos spoke thickly. "Hail, Uther, Father and Guletic," he said, bowing his head. "We come to visit you."

Uther Pendragon stared back at his son, in anger. "This is a place where only men of honour may sit. Artos, my son, you were not invited to sit at this feast, nor was your warband. Go back to the huts and drink your fill there. You shall not disturb this gathering."

Out in the courtyard, men began to laugh, and many about the tables regretted that they had obeyed the rules of hospitality and had come without a sword. Others, who had hidden knives about their clothes, began to fccl for them in the firelight.

"We come as friends, unarmed, as you see," said Artos, holding up his long cudgel. "Give us wine, Uther, and let us go our ways again."

Uther's eyes flashed at this impertinence. His great pride was hurt that many men laughed at the young man. He was about to speak harshly to his son, when the whole situation changed and went beyond any man's recall.

Ambrosius still stood, gazing upwards into the smoke, the great sword held up before him, a symbol with which he was illustrating his speech. The eyes of Artos the Bear turned to the sword. In his drunken state, he saw it as the excuse for a jest. Before any man could stop him, he had run forward and taken the great weapon from the old man's hand. And in a loud mocking voice he said, "I accept your present, O guest of my father!" Then, turning to the wondering feasters, he said, "Even as a young warrior accepts the sword given him by his lady, I accept this from the depths of the lake of dreams. I who came here unarmed shall walk out with a sword at last."

There was a great gasp about the hall, for Artos had been forbidden to carry a sword while the punishment was on him.

Uther began to rise again, but his friend pulled him down, with a whisper. "Do not anger him, Guletic. He may do someone an injury now he is armed." Ambrosius was holding out his hands piteously now, unable to see what had happened to the sword he cherished. Uther now took him by the arms and forced him back into the chair. Medrodus felt the blood suddenly pound in his head. He had followed the Count all his youth, to hold this sword at the end, and now a drunken ploughman had burst into the hall and taken it as easily as that!

Without stopping to consider the results of his action, Medrodus vaulted the table and went towards Artos the Bear, who swayed in the firelight, still waving the great sword and laughing drunkenly.

"That is my rightful weapon," said Medrodus, his voice thick with anger. "No hand but mine shall hold it when the Count lays down his authority. Give it to me, Artos the Bear."

The man turned and stared at Medrodus, still laughing good-humouredly. "He who would hold a sword must be prepared to take a sword," he said. "And will you take this from me, then?"

So great was the rage that surged up in the breast of Medrodus that he forgot the other's superior strength, forgot his reputation, his crowded followers who swung their cudgels in the courtyard, waiting for a chance to use them.

"By the gods, I will," shouted Medrodus now, and made a movement towards the laughing chieftain. There was something about that act which seemed to warm the heart of the drunkard towards him. Medrodus, alone in a strange hall, surrounded by men of a different race, had dared to challenge one who had already flung him to the ground as a child might fling an unwanted doll. Artos the Bear looked down at him with a smile and said, "You do not lack courage, stranger."

Then, with a movement of such sudden violence that no man expected it, Artos the Bear swept the great sword round, so that its bright blade described a silver arc in the firelight, and struck at a massive, knotted log that stood beside the ashes and was used as a chopping-block for the pieces of meat that were roasted in the fire. The bright blade sheared down into the twisted oak, driven by the strength of the drunkard's muscled arm. And there it stayed, the golden hilt quivering when Artos let it go.

Medrodus stared at him, aghast. "Now, stranger," said Artos the Bear, "I would not spill your blood tonight, for you speak bravely. But if you want your sword, take it. And if you cannot, let that man who can draw it from the oak-bole have it for his own."

The mood about the tables had changed. Now men began to smile again, and those who had pulled out knives secretly began to put them back, just as secretly. Even Uther Pendragon settled back in his chair and held out his drinking-horn to the slave-girl who tended him.

Medrodus paused and looked towards the Count. Ambrosius seemed now to understand the drift of affairs. He was shaking his head as though he were powerless. His thin hands were spread before him on the table. He was saying, again and again, "So be it. So be it." As though unable to impress his will on others any longer.

Medrodus spat towards him in contempt, and with a great heave of the shoulders grasped the shivering hilt. In his heart he knew, then, that he must drag out the blade or forever lose his ambition. As he pulled in the silence, he heard the sinews of his arms cracking, and felt the sweat running down his body. And when the blood beat so urgently in his head that he thought he might faint, he knew that he would never pull out that sword from the oak-bole. At last he staggered back, and the men at the tables stared at him as though he were already dead, for his face had gone white and his limbs were trembling with the shock of his great exertion.

Now Artos stepped forward, and pausing before the long hilt, called out, "Look you, Bedwyr, fling a bucket of water over this thing to swell the wood. I am in a mood to make my task more difficult tonight."

Bedwyr of the corn-coloured hair ran forward and did as he was bid. All the men about the tables laughed and nudged each other, for they thought that Artos was too drunk to know what he was about. At last the son of Uther moved towards the log and set himself firmly before it. Then he, too, bunched his heavy shoulders and took hold of the golden hilt, that looked so little in his hands. All men waited now, hearing their own hearts beating and the muscles of Artos groaning with the exertion of his effort. So great indeed was his trial that the hide belt about his waist suddenly burst, and some men thought for a moment that he had torn out his own bowels in his dragging.

Then suddenly he turned towards his father, laughing, his face and neck dripping with sweat, his eyes almost starting from his head, bloodshot and wild. In his right hand he whirled the great sword, free of all encumbrances.

"Hail, Uther Guletic," he shouted. "Whose sword is it now, my father?"

The followers in the courtyard now began to crush into the hall, shouting for their young leader. The men at the tables began to shout, too, "It is your sword, Artos!"

Uther Pendragon paid no heed to Ambrosius, who sat with his hands over his face, weeping. "My son," he said, "it can be no other man's but yours. You have won it in your own way. Yet you carry it without my blessing, for your trial is not yet ended."

Then all the men in the hall called out, standing, their hands raised, "Hail, Artos the Bear, Count of Britain!" And those awful words seemed to echo on up the rocky hillside, into the forests beyond, to the lair of the bear and the dens of the wolves and the setts of the badgers, on and on, across Britain in the ghostly moonlight.

Medrodus fell to his knees in the firelight, weeping. "May you know eternal agony, Ambrosius," he said, praying savagely to whatever god would listen to him. "May you know the agonies I have known, old dotard! May Rome perish from the face of the earth forever! That is my wish!"

Now the warband in the hall and in the courtyard began to chant, "Lead us, Artos! Lead us in battle! Let your dogs tear the throats of all who stand against you! Lead us, Artos!"

And even Uther Pendragon shifted uneasily in his chair, for he knew that this was a dangerous time, and that the drunken tribesmen needed only the faintest suggestion from Artos and then they would tear down his own authority, perhaps even lay him across the smoking altars of the temple and slit his throat in the moonlight.

He stood. "Hail, Artos," he shouted with the rest. "May you come to victory and then to grace, for the gods seem to will it so."

Artos turned and surveyed his father with a wry look. "Uther Guletic has spoken," he said. "Now shall no man deny me!"

Then, with a movement so gentle that few men saw it, he bent towards the still kneeling Medrodus and laid a hand on his back.

"Have courage, friend," he said. "You tried hard and I doubt if any other man here could have done so much. We shall come to know each other."

Artos strode from the feast hall with his followers. Many men about the tables rose, too, and went with him. And at last Uther Pendragon led old Ambrosius away. Two old men who at last knew their defeat.

Medrodus still kneeled in the dying firelight. He felt another hand upon his shoulder. It was the fair-haired young man who had visited him in his room. He was smiling down at him. "Wait but a little longer, friend," he said. "I, Aurelius Caninus, have promised you my friendship, and that may come to mean much. You and I are two men who have yet their kingdom to get, but our time will come, if only we trust each other."

These were the kindest words any man had spoken to Medrodus for many months. He rose and looked hard into the other's eyes.

"Aurelius Caninus," he said, "I believe that this is either my end or my beginning; the bitterness of my heart will not let me know which. But I accept your friendship gladly."

Aurelius took his hands and said, "I, too, am tied to a dotard who hampers me. Yet that is a little obstacle which a woman's bodkin can overcome. It shall not keep me from my kingdom when the time comes."

Then he went from the hall, and Medrodus was left alone. Although he knew that the time of Ambrosius was finished, that the old man could no longer call himself the Count of Britain, yet he still burned with anger that this senile creature had by his weakness deceived him in all his hopes.

Medrodus made his way outside, his heart full of hate for all men, except perhaps for Aurelius Caninus, the ambassador whose name meant "The Dog."

XII

AMBROSIUS GROPED HIS WAY TO THE BATHHOUSE, SEEKING AN OLD man's solace in the warm comfort of water. The underfloor heating system, laid down in the time of Agricola, had long since ceased to function and rats had made their homes in the shelter of the flues. But a slave-girl had heated enough water on the wood fires in the kitchens to fill the shallow scooped-out stone bath almost to the brim.

They had spilled rather a lot of water on the stone floor, and Ambrosius was irritated that he was forced to splash through it, his long robe dragging in the wet. It clung damply about his ankles as he moved. He swore a defeated old man's oath, without force or conviction. His tottering mind tried to picture what would have happened to such slaves in the time, say, of Caligula, or even of Claudius. But that was so long ago, it was like a dream that no one believed could ever have happened.

He reached forward and trimmed the smoking wicks of two small fat-lamps that stood on the ledge in the wall, beside the bath, throwing barely enough light to reach halfway across the long and barnlike room. Had not both lamps been on one side of the bath, the night might have ended differently, but where they were, they cast no shadows.

Ambrosius slowly dragged off his clothes and then eased his aching old body down into the bath. The water was a little too warm for him. As he lay back, his heart began to thump painfully. The fumes of pine came up from the water, a heady scent that made the old man's eyes stream with water.

The mind of Ambrosius went back to the feast now, and he almost wept to remember how the sword had been taken from him. He began to hate Medrodus a little for not protecting him as he should have done. Perhaps he had done wrong at the beginning in taking that young man into his service. Yet at the time he had thought to impress his followers with the ideals of equality. Medrodus was not worthy to be Count, thought Ambrosius. He would not elect him, after all, unless he improved a great deal.

Then Ambrosius recalled that the new Count was already chosen, had chosen himself, in fact. This was not what Rome decreed, surely, for a man to elect himself? Why, it was like the bad old days of Cunedda and Vortigern again, when a barbarian could stand up and, by saying that he was the king, make himself so. Ambrosius determined to see Uther Pendragon in the morning. They must take the sword away from that man and let Ambrosius be Count of Britain again. Yes, that is what they must do, thought the old man.

He began to feel very sleepy and found that he was smiling to himself. Then suddenly he was brought back to his senses by a fluttering in the far window. His heart began to beat with excitement, until he realised that the noise was made by a frightened starling that had beaten itself against the stone window frame in an error of flight. Ambrosius smiled sadly, conscious of his limiting weakness, his blindness, seeing himself as helpless as that bird for a moment, fluttering in fright against the stone-work of a harsh world.

He lay back again and peered at the water that swirled below his chin. He could see as far as that, could even see the pine cones bobbing up and down near his waist, and the whitish scum that floated on the surface of the hard water.

In the morning, he thought, I will go to Uther Pendragon and he will make them give me the sword again. Then I shall go away, to the south, perhaps, and find men who will respect me, will want Rome back again. That is what I must do, for the gods will protect one who has served Rome so long. . . .

Then he was conscious of the fluttering bird again, somewhere near the window. The stupid creature, he thought. It will kill itself! The two lamps on the ledge by his head burned on steadily, a thin line of black smoke rising straight up from their rush wicks.

Ambrosius heard himself sigh deeply, though he had not meant to. Then he heard the blood rush up into his ears, whistling fiercely as it pulsed, as though it would burst through the eardrums. Surprised at this, he looked down at the water near his chin and saw that it was of a deep red. This was something he did not know. The water had not been that colour before.

With a vaguely felt alarm, the old man tried to rise from the bath, but the long knife in his left side kept him there. He tried to drag it out, bewildered and afraid, but found that he could not grasp it firmly now. He sank back, lower and lower, until the red water covered him entirely.

Then the fluttering of the bird became a man's footsteps, treading softly through the puddles of water that lay on the bathhouse floor, towards the door, towards the dark and secret night.

XIII

THE DEATH OF AMBROSIUS WAS GREETED WITHOUT OVERMUCH CONCERN. Since he was found grasping the hilt of the knife that killed him, many men assumed that he had driven it into his own side, after the custom of the old Roman officers after a defeat. Medrodus testified that Ambrosius had sworn to commit suicide should the choice of a new Count go against his own wishes.

Uther Pendragon looked at him hard when he said this, but Medrodus returned the look with a confident smile.

The body of Ambrosius was placed in a hollow on the hillside and a cairn of stones put over it. The wolves scratched at the stones for a night or two and then everyone forgot about the old man.

At first Medrodus had ideas of leaving Uther's Dun and of making his way southeast, to offer his services to the Jutes of Kent, who seemed an enlightened people. But Aurelius Caninus spoke with him secretly and told him that it would be wiser to stay in the west, however inconvenient for the time being, since great changes were likely before long.

"You see," he said, "I myself am here to induce Uther and his son to join with the other western kings so that we may ride to the Roman east and gain what we may. Already the kings are massing, Cuneglassus, Votiporix and my own master, Constantine. They bring to their standards the warriors of the Midlands, Gwynnedd and the lands of Dumnonia. It would be a mighty host, and it will need a leader, a *dux bellorum*, my friend."

Medrodus said, "But Artos, who is by force the new Count, will surely be elected? What chance is there for any other man?"

Aurelius bared his teeth in a sharp smile. "Perhaps I could find a way to give you the leadership," he said, looking down at the ground.

Medrodus said, "What payment do you require, my friend?"

Aurelius answered, "Your help in putting the old man, Constantine, out of the way. He has named me as his successor, since he is without children. Yet he lingers on so long, I am impatient."

Medrodus pretended to consider this proposition. His face expressed more doubt than he really held. Aurelius was quick to take offence, and he said, "You will have no scruples, surely, my friend? We might arrange for Constantine to take a bath, for example!"

Medrodus did not smile at this remark. He looked above the other's head and said, "Very well, Aurelius Caninus. I will do what I can." They did not shake hands on the bargain.

A little further from where they stood, a young woman sat outside a wattle hut, her long yellow hair hanging in great heavy plaits to her waist. She suckled a small baby at her breast. Medrodus observed her rich, honey-coloured skin and the fullness of her breasts. He made a comment about them to Aurelius, who turned back to him with a grave face.

"No one must touch her," he said. "She is the woman of Artos, and cursed as he is. That is their son, Anir. Her punishment is to keep the altar fires burning in the temple for the rest of her life. Anir will be taken from her as soon as he can leave her and she will not see him again. She is condemned to serve the temple now, until she herself is stretched over the stones."

Medrodus said with a dry smile, "It seems a great waste. She would bring pleasure to many a man."

Aurelius said, "Her name is Gwenhwyfar, the golden one. Artos found her in a village in Powys and got her with child."

Medrodus said, "That is no crime. Most men do it from time to time."

The other man smiled and said, "Yes, that is so. Uther Pendragon once found her mother just as attractive. She has his nose, if you will look."

As Medrodus turned in horror to look at the woman, a great hound ran from the wattle hut towards the two men, its hackles up and its fangs displayed.

The girl called, "Troynt! Troynt! Come back, you fool!" The hound heard her and stopped. Then it turned and loped back to her and lay down at her feet, obediently.

"That was the hound of Artos," said Aurelius. "Yet now it will not leave the woman and has forgotten its old master entirely. Men say that the hound would kill anyone who touched Gwenhwyfar or the child."

"Even Artos?" asked Medrodus.

"I think so," said the other. "But Artos is forbidden by law to look at her, in any case. He has not been within a hundred paces of her since the child was born, they say!"

The two men walked on to where horsemen were riding at

lance practice. Aurelius said, "Join with them. One day you will be their leader, I promise you."

Medrodus said, "I thank you, King of Dumnonia."

Aurelius walked back to the villa alone.

XIV

SEVEN NIGHTS AFTER THE WANDERERS HAD COME TO LIS PENGWERN, fires were lit along the hilltops surrounding the settlement. They blazed fiercely in the night wind, causing cries of wonder from the children of the tribe. Medrodus asked why these fires had been lit.

Cei, a warrior in the band of Artos, answered, "They are to guide the feet of the antler-men." Then he turned away, grim-faced, and pretended to busy himself taking a stone from his horse's hoof. Medrodus cursed him silently for a barbarian, but all the same kept his eyes on the hilltops, wondering what was about to happen.

At length a great load of brushwood was dragged in on sledges and erected as a mound at the centre of the hard earth compound where the horsemen did their training. Men stayed round the heap, expectant and pointing excitedly. Medrodus noted that the women and children had been sent to the huts, as though they must not see what was to take place. The men sat on their haunches, their hands dangling loosely before them, waiting like hounds sniffing the air, their eyes wide and bright in the light of the torches. And at last, the king's litter was carried slowly out from his house to the place, some fifty yards from the heap of brushwood, where a painted wooden chair had been set for him. Old Uther sat down stiffly in the chair, Artos standing behind him, and after a moment or two, during which he muttered to himself and rolled his eyes, he raised a horn to his lips and blew three long blasts. A young man ran forward, carrying a torch in each hand. Five yards from the mound he stopped, and whirling the resinous branches, flung them with a shout onto the heap. The dry brushwood burst into flame, lighting up all who sat in the compound.

A low and shuddering sigh went up from the men who squatted, waiting. Medrodus, who stood a little behind Artos, felt the hairs at the nape of his neck prickling. He clenched his fingers about the hide belt he wore, to disguise his trembling. He had heard of these ancient fire festivals since childhood, but had never met anyone who had seen them. Men spoke of them in whispers, as though they were fearful things, to be ashamed of. They were like some obscene dream that had haunted the minds of the Celts since the earliest times; since the great stones themselves had been pushed into place, above Sorbiodunum. The Romans had very definitely forbidden such things in the Civil Zone. One governor had actually issued an edict, condemning any man who lit a bonfire at the spring or midsummer festival times to the loss of his right hand.

Medrodus shivered as he waited with the fierce firelight half blinding him. Artos stared up towards the hilltop. Old Uther's chin was sunk in his hands. He looked like one in a state of trance. The men who squatted began to beat with their palms on the hard earth in a strange surging rhythm that rumbled dully among the huts around them. They were already working themselves up into a condition of excitement. Many of them were half drunk with corn-wine.

At last, when the rhythmic thudding on the earth had become almost unbearable, the fires on the hilltops began to go out, and from a distance came an answering sound, down the slopes. At first it seemed like the humming of an immense swarm of bees, low and vibrant, throaty and male. Then, as this sound came nearer, it was joined by another, a high-pitched squealing sound, based on three separated notes, those of a primitive flute. And almost obscured by the more vigorous overtones already throbbing on the air, came the rattle of drumsticks on tightened parchment. Now the night was filled with sound, of all registers and beats. The noise seemed to come forward at a frightening pace. Uther was breathing through his nose, rapidly now, and the lips of Artos himself had fallen open as he strained to see what was happening beyond the fire. Then, when the waiting men could hardly bear this suspense any longer, there was a sudden scurry from the darkness at the bottom of the hill, and into the fire-glow ran the music-men. They were all dressed in black, hooded and bound round with thongs of leather, from which dangled shells and pieces of flint that clinked as they moved. These men stood together in two long ranks, away from the tribesmen, leaving a broad space in the area nearest the fire itself. The big men with the bull-roarers leapt into the air with frenzy from time to time as their white bone instruments hummed at the ends of their cords. The others holding the flute in one hand and the drumstick in the other, jigged up and down on one spot, like strange insects, their long drums gripped tightly between their thighs. And when the music-makers were in position and it seemed that the noise they made had reached its highest pitch, there came a wild shriek from the deep shadows and a score of creatures materialised with a vicious flurry of dust—the horn-men.

The warriors crouching on the ground sucked in their breath between their teeth. "Aieee!" they said, their eyes now fearful in the fire-glow. "The deathly dancers!" Almost identical with each other in appearance, these dancers moved with wicked twitching steps, something between a limp and an epileptic spasm, the long antlers that were strapped to their heads clacking with each movement, the sinews of legs and arms and neck tensed and relaxed with each formal motion, their faces, heavily ochred with clay, set like grim masks.

Medrodus saw the bars of red clay that streaked their faces and bodies horizontally, and groaned. They represented a past which apparently still simmered just below the surface of life in Britain, the past which Rome had thought to eradicate, but which had come back in the west as strongly as ever.

Now the antler-dancers circled the fire, the weasels' tails tied below their knees flurrying in the night air, the pigs' bladders, which hung from their necks on a hide thong, bobbing up and down against their clay-daubed chests, the horsehide kilts that hung almost to the ground casting grotesque shadows across the compound. The drums rattled on, the high flutes screamed, the bull-roars filled the air with a throbbing nightmare of reiteration. And now the leader of the line of horn-men leapt into the air and began the chant, to be joined immediately by his followers, a low nasal whine, punctuated with harsh and guttural barks, like those of badgers.

At this point Artos turned to Medrodus and stared at him keenly. Medrodus looked back at him as steadily as he could. Then, in such low tones that Medrodus was hardly sure that they had been uttered, Artos seemed to say, "I would crush them as a foot does the beetle. They are evil." Medrodus was about to answer him when there was a great cry from the assembled tribesmen, "Oh look, the lily-white ones!" And from behind the music-men, twenty prancing figures appeared, their faces and bodies white with clay, their heads bedecked with leaves, their green kilts and cloaks floating out behind them. And as they came, they sang a wailing melody of three notes that seemed to undulate above them. They had the bodies of men, but their voices were those of women, high and shrill. Artos turned once more, and smiling grimly said, "That surely is an act of dedication!" Medrodus stared at them with fascination. Then the music-men played again, and the two groups of dancers moved in contrary motion, about the fire, until at last the leader of the gaunt antler-men held up his arms in some cryptic signal. Now the two bands turned to face each other and the music-men played louder and faster, as though they were coming to the summit of some ghastly orgasm.

Then each dancer took out two white sticks, the peeled wands of willow, and clicking them together in the air, rushed at his opponent, the horn-men against the green ones. For a moment they performed certain prescribed motions with their wands, and then came together in the act of fighting, using their willow staves as weapons. The tribesmen craned forward to see what was happening.

And when the surging tangling bodies were almost exhausted in this fantastic struggle, Uther blew once more upon the horn at his side. The conflict stopped, each green-clad dancer falling to the ground before his horn-bedecked partner. Now the music stopped also, and in the strange silence about the fire, each antler-man pulled out a broad flint knife, and making as though to stab himself to the heart, slashed open the pig's bladder that hung from his neck, bending over his partner and letting the red liquid spurt over him.

The tribesmen shouted now, "It is well done! The corn will grow!" Uther turned in his chair and smiled back at Artos. "This will be a good year," he said, "for not one of the green men died on the sticks. It is not often thus."

Medrodus watched the panting dancers as they knelt together on the earth, filthy with dust and the blood that covered them. He felt disappointed in a curious way. This was nothing more than mere mummery, he thought; he had expected death.

But even while this thought was in his mind, there came a high scream from beyond the fire and a young bull burst through the flames, scattering the embers right and left, bellowing with fear and pain. Men wearing the antlers drove him through the flames, into the middle of the compound where all men might see him. His eyes were wide and red-rimmed, long strings of slaver hung from his mouth and dewlaps. The beast stood still for a moment, breathing noisily, and then the leader of the horn-men circled him twice, and at the third movement round him, leapt onto the bull's back. Other men crowded round him, some at his horns, some dragging at his tail. And as the bull-roarers and flutes started up again, two men at his rear slashed the beast behind the hams so that he fell onto his haunches, bellowing with sudden pain. And even as he did so, the leader of the antler-men reached forward, and jerking back the bull's head, passed his own knife deeply across his throat. The bull's bellowing became a low gurgling and he spewed blood over all who stood before him. Then he was down, and immediately the horn-men clustered over his body, like ants over a dead dog. They tore at his flesh, spattering themselves with blood, and then, thrusting their hands inside him, dragged out the steaming organs, tearing at them with their teeth and screaming out ancient words which had long lost their meaning for any man present. Their leader staggered from the mutilated heap towards Uther, dragging a length of offal behind him. His movements were those of a drunken man and his eyes were rolled back, so that the watchers round Uther could see only their whites.

A pace or two from the king, he stopped and began a sing-song whining chant in which he offered the bull as surety of good harvest and success in war. Uther smiled back at him, silent and nodding. This had happened to him many times before. He knew these words as well as he knew the few Christian prayers he had been taught by his Roman masters. The antler-leader came forward and, first, wiped the steaming entrails down the king's chair, then across his forehead and down his cheeks. Uther still smiled, holding his face steady so that the man might fulfil his office.

But when he had finished, the man straightened himself, and looking past the king's chair said for all to hear, "Artos the Bear should share Uther's good fortune."

The tribesmen laughed at this, for it seemed to them that the horn-man was now having his own sort of fun, after carrying out his rites. Artos said in a low voice, "Your task is finished, horn-man. Go to the hall where food awaits you."

But the grotesque creature was carried away by his office. He sprang forward and thrust the stinking mess into the face of Artos, splashing him with blood, laughing and shrieking as he did so.

Artos took a step backwards and now said angrily, "Go, if you wish to kill the bull another year. Go, I say!"

The tribesmen sucked in their breath. No one had ever dared to speak like that to a horn-man.

The drums and flutes struck up again, madly, and the antlered leader's eyes flared wide with excitement. He came at Artos again, brandishing the entrails, his own face now slavering like that of the bull he had slaughtered.

As he wiped the mess down the face of Artos once more, the prince slid sideways with an angry roar. The antler-man stumbled a little, and then all men saw Artos raise his right hand and bring it down heavily on the man's neck. The horn-man fell forward, his arms outspread, his antlers falling from him when the straps broke.

The music stopped and men began to mutter, afraid. Artos bent and drew his knife from the man's neck. He wiped it on the hide kilt before he put it back in his sheath. Then stepping into the dying firelight so that all the tribesmen should see what he did, he snapped the antlers over his knee and flung them onto the steaming carcass of the bull. And raising his voice, he called out over the place, "The power of the horn-men is great, my friends. But the arm of a prince is greater." Uther did not speak, but his lips were moving in silent agitation, as though he spoke prayers that would ward off disaster to them all. The fire was built again and the dancers placed the body of their leader and the remains of the bull on it. They did not express an opinion one way or the other. They were not unused to seeing men die, for their only trade was the spilling of blood. Its fuller meaning lay beyond their understanding. And now they were hungry and thirsty: that was all they knew.

XV

LATER THAT NIGHT, WHEN ARTOS HAD LEFT THE FEASTING IN THE hall, and sat by a small fire against a hide windbreak with his friends, Bedwyr said, "Only a man who feels the gods in his heart would dare slay the horn-man." Artos warmed his hands over the fire and smiled. "Who knows?" he answered. "It seems to me that any man who dares might gain greatness." He looked at Medrodus as he spoke, but the dark-haired one looked away, recalling how the sword had been taken from him by a trick.

Then Cei said, "I know nothing of greatness, Bear. But I do

know that a brave king with five hundred horsemen could take Britain now and hold it for his own." He looked straight into the eyes of Artos as he spoke.

"Do you hanker after a kingdom, friend?" asked Medrodus slyly.

Cei did not turn to face him as he replied, "I am only a dog, the dog of Artos. All I desire is a bone."

Medrodus clenched his fists angrily. "And that is all you are likely to get," he said.

Cei said to Bedwyr, ignoring the speaker, "If I travelled among a strange people, I would keep my mouth shut lest someone push a knife into it."

Bedwyr was about to make a similar reply when Artos whipped round suddenly, his two hands full of white ashes from the fire. He flung them over the warriors without warning and then laughed as they coughed and tried to brush the fragments from their hair.

"You are like two old women," he said, "forever gossiping about 'if' and 'might.' For my part, I'll shake the hands of any stranger who dares come into my steading and tell me I am a fool!"

He held out his hands towards Medrodus, who took them hesitantly, remembering the reception he had got from Artos when they had first come upon him, ploughing beside the river.

Cei said, "You are as fickle as the winds, Bear. If the young Roman is wise, he will sleep with a dagger in his hand after that show of friendship!"

Artos grasped him by the ankle and dragged him towards the fire. "Kiss the hot embers, little Cei," he said. "That will cleanse your tongue of all evil."

Cei struggled hard but could not break from the prince's grip. And at last when Artos had him by the shoulders and was forcing his head down so low over the flames that his hair was singeing, he gasped, "You are a better man than I, Bear. I will beg the dark one's pardon."

Artos flung him sideways, so that he rolled at the feet of Medrodus. Even as he was scrambling to his feet, an old man and a boy came into the glow cast by their fire. The man leaned on a long stick and nodded his grey head continually, as though he were palsy-stricken. His only garment was a blanket of coarse and tattered grey linen, which was wound about his waist and then thrown over his upper body, much after the manner of the Roman toga. The boy, who was abject and thin, his greasy black hair hanging unkempt to his shoulders, wore a long jacket of ragged sheepskin, held into the waist by a length of hempen cord.

The two halted before the warriors, holding up their right hands in salute. "Greetings, friends," said Artos, smiling, "which graves have you crawled from?"

The old man replied without humour. "We have travelled from Ireland, Master. We are making our way to the north, to Pictland."

Bedwyr said, "They will cut your throats there and feed you to the pigs. The Picts are savages."

The old man looked him in the eye and said, "We are Picts, Master, but so far we have fed no one to our pigs."

Cei said, "That is because you have never had any pigs, you old fool!"

The young boy, who had been standing miserably so far, laughed at this remark. The old man turned on him sharply, striking him across the legs with his staff. The boy did not cry out, did not even rub the place where the stick had fallen. Instead, he lowered his head and stood as in repentance, his hands at his sides. Artos said grimly, "You treat the boy sternly, old man. Who is he?"

The old man answered, "He is my daughter's child and was born in Ireland. Her village has been smitten with plague. The men have died and the women can hardly keep life in their bodies until the corn grows."

"So you fetch the boy back to look after him?" Artos asked.

The old man shrugged his withered shoulders. "He has talents," he said. "They will make him into a singer, a bard. When they have blinded him, he will sing the sweeter. I shall be his eyes then and we shall have food and lodging among the villages."

Bedwyr looked at the still repentant form of the boy and then said, "Old man, you are so close to death that a hungry crow would come back unsatisfied from picking at you. When you are dead, which may be before another winter has passed, what will happen to this boy, if you blind him?"

The old man's lips drew back in a bitter smile. "What does it matter," he said, "if I live the summer through? After that he must fend for himself, as I have always done."

Medrodus said with contempt, "They did not blind you, Pict."

The old man said, "That is because I have no talent as a bard, Master. One must pay the gods for their gifts."

Medrodus remembered Merddin and wondered.

Artos broke through his memories. "Let us hear what this boy can do," he said. "We have gifts to give, as well as the gods."

The old man rapped his stick across the boy's shins again and spoke to him sharply. The lad flung back his hair, and feeling inside his sheepskin coat, pulled out a small bone flute. Then, capering in a simple round-dance, he played a crude melody that kept time to his movements. At the end of each round he halted, and in a clear high voice chanted a song:

"Burnished the helmets, their banners waving;
The women wept to see them go;
The warriors rode forth into the forest,
Their sword-edges hungry for the taste of flesh.
At the day's end the owls cried and the wolves howled;
The women waited fearfully by fires.
They wept for the helmets and the pretty flags,
But they did not see these things again.
In the dawn, only the horses came back,
Came through the woods, bearing bloody saddles."

When the boy reached the end of his song, he fell on his knees before Artos, his head bowed, his knuckles touching the earth.

Artos said, "Who taught him to sing that song, old man?"

The man replied, "It is an ancient song of our people. I taught him the song as we walked through Britain."

"Then you are the one who should be blinded, are you not?" asked Artos.

The old man shrugged his shoulders, "As you will, Master," he said. "At least then I might stay here and feed well until my raven croaks for me."

Artos said, "You who wander the roads are always so near to death that it means little to you. Take the boy to the feast hall and tell them there that Artos commands they feed you well and give you warm clothes to keep these mountain winds away from your bodies."

The boy still kneeled, "Thank you, Emperor," he said. "Then must we go on to Pictland?"

Artos surveyed him narrowly and a strange smile clipped his mouth shut. At last he said, "The old man will go to Pictland, or to wherever he may wish. But you shall stay here, my friend. Your eyes are too pretty for blinding."

The old man said, "You take my living from me, Prince."

Artos drew a bracelet from his wrist, a heavy thing of gold set with corals. He flung it at the old man's feet.

"That is a good bargain, you robber," he said. "Remember, I could pass my sword through you just as easily, then where would your living be?"

The old man merely smiled, and when he had hidden the bracelet away, took the boy towards the hall, leaning heavily on his shoulder as they went.

Medrodus remembered Ambrosius again and shuddered.

XVI

ARTOS WALKED WITH MEDRODUS TO THE PLACE WHERE HE SLEPT. AT the door he stopped and said directly, "Your eyes are keen, Roman. What do you see? What do you think of me?"

Medrodus smiled and said, "How may I answer that? I see all that comes before my eyes, and my opinions on what I see are worthless."

Artos took him suddenly by the wrist. "Look you," he said, "you come from another world, your thoughts will be good ones to hear. In this place I hear only what men think I might wish to hear. They are bound down and blinded by loyalties which you do not know. Will you not tell me with honesty what I am?"

Medrodus sensed that Artos was unsure of himself, that his quick barbarian's mind had suddenly grown to doubt what he saw about him. Yet Medrodus saw no reason why he should put his vision, his philosophy, to this usurper's use. He half turned into his room and said lightly, "I see you as a prince, a strong man who takes what he wants without waiting to be given it."

Artos said, "You are thinking of the sword. Yet consider, if I had not taken it, another would have done so. It is sure that they would not have let you take it, to rule them as you wished. When you came here with the old man, you walked into a hornet's nest, my friend. I only took what you could not have kept."

Medrodus turned back to him. "Perhaps," he said. "I had not considered it in such a light. Then let me expand my opinion of you and say that you are a quick-thinking man, a philosopher, a swift arbitrator. Will that do?" He smiled into the face of Artos, who stared back at him, almost bewildered. "Your words bring me no comfort," said the Bear. "They seem to float away from a warm meaning. I do not understand them, or you, or myself."

Medrodus inclined his head and said, "May you sleep well and wake with a clear mind."

Artos nodded and walked slowly away from the villa. When he had gone, Medrodus said, "I'll tell you what you are, Artos! You are a feather caught in a north wind, a shred of cloth flung into a fire, a fish swimming towards the hook. You are the toy of the gods, my friend!"

He smiled grimly then as he swung himself onto the bed. Yet even Medrodus had doubts, for in Artos he sensed something else, some fineness, some resolution, some ambition, which he had not thought to meet among the savages of Lis Pengwern. Even so, these doubts did not prevent Medrodus from falling almost immediately into a deep sleep.

In a wattle hut at the furthest edge of the settlement, Artos lay beside the woman Gwenhwyfar. A small rushlight floated in a clay saucer on the earthen floor, throwing its light up into their faces. It was the same face, rudely handsome in the man, strongly beautiful in the woman. They lay close together and their hair was of one colour, as though it belonged to one person only.

The woman said, "You should not come to me here, husband. It might bring death to you."

Artos whispered, "Cei and Bedwyr are hidden outside. They would quieten any man who pried where his business did not lie."

She smiled, "And good Troynt lies before the door. He would not let Uther himself pass. Yet this is not the life our hearts would lead, my love."

Artos held her close to him and said, "One day, my love, we shall change the world. Then, when I am king, you shall be queen."

He spoke so simply that she had to smile, although the tears were gathering in her eyes. She could not reply.

At last Artos said, "Well, wife, what do you say to that? You are too silent for such great news."

Then, knowing that she would hurt him, but feeling that she must speak, she said, "I do not think the gods will let us be happy together, with our great sin hanging over us like a summer's cloud."

Artos was still for a while and then he answered, "There is this consolation, that once a man has assured himself of damnation, he can thereafter commit any sin he wishes without fear. Tonight I killed the horn-leader."

Gwenhwyfar drew in her breath quickly. "A woman told me of it," she said, "but I did not believe her. All the folk lie so much about what you do and what you say, it is hard to keep a picture of you in my mind when you are not here with me."

Artos pressed her to him until she almost cried out. "This is the only reality," he said. "Think of these arms, this body. That is what I am, my love."

Then she began to weep because she was suddenly and strangely very happy with him beside her. At last she said, "Soon you will go away, they say. They say you will ride with the black-haired Roman."

Artos answered, "That is true, my queen. I shall go to prepare your kingdom for you, and when it is gained, I shall send for you to sit with me on a throne of gold."

Gwenhwyfar began to weep again. "Perhaps you will forget me," she said.

"May my heart shrivel within my breast if I do," said Artos.

Before dawn he rose quietly, leaving her asleep, the tears still on her cheeks, and went to the door. The baby slept in a basket. Artos touched him lightly on the forehead in salute and then passed between the huts. Bedwyr and Cei rose stiffly from their bush where they had lain and followed him, grumbling, back to the settlement.

Later that day Medrodus met Artos and said, "The old man has gone and has taken the little singing-boy. They are nowhere to be found."

Artos rubbed his eyes and yawned. "Then I have lost my gold bracelet," he said. "I only bought the boy because of his song. I learned it when I was much smaller than he is."

Medrodus smiled inwardly at this softness of heart. "Now the boy will be blinded so that he may sing it all his life," he said. "It is a curious custom."

Artos yawned again, noisily, as though the matter no longer interested him. "If the truth were known," he said, "they are a pair of rogues and thieves. No doubt the old man has sold the boy in every steading in the south, to soft-headed lords who have sympathy for a pair of dark eyes."

"True," said Medrodus, watching him narrowly. "You do well to put it from your mind."

Artos excused himself, saying that he must go to the fields beyond the river. When he was out of sight of Medrodus, he called two men to him and ordered them to scour the countryside towards the north, and if they found the old man and the boy, to kill the one and bring the other back with them.

Medrodus heard of this later from Aurelius, who had been standing behind a hut while Artos gave his orders.

The horsemen returned at sunset without the boy, and Medrodus smiled to see how cruelly Artos struck them across the face with the back of his hard hand. Yet at the same time, his heart misgave him that this man could be so cruel and yet so kind. He had not known such a man before.

XVII

UTHER PENDRAGON LAY, TROUBLED, IN HIS BED. A FEW DAYS AFTER the death of Ambrosius, the Guletic had been riding through a wood to the north of Lis Pengwern when a little green snake had fallen from the bough of a tree and had bitten him in the thigh before he could brush it off. He had laughed at the wound then and had ridden on to a house where a young widow awaited him.

Now his thigh was so swollen that he could not walk. The throbbing from the infected place was so fierce, it seemed as though his stomach was on fire. He had tried many remedies, including the sacrifice of three young slave-girls. Now he lay rolling about in his agony, his belly and upper legs encased with the mashed remains of a score of little green snakes, that had already caused the death of one warrior in their collecting.

Uther Pendragon had sent for his son, Artos. The young man was long in coming, for he was training a new corps of horsemen, a second comitatus, to follow his first and tried warband. He came into the room at last, covered with mud and staggering with fatigue. He knelt before his father and did not speak until the old man had first addressed him.

Uther Pendragon propped himself up with difficulty and said, "Artos, I fear the death-pain is on me. I must have committed some great sin to cause the gods to punish me like this. Perhaps I was wrong to let you take that sword. I fear now that it was the will of the gods to give it to Medrodus."

Artos by now had become deeply attached to the sword, which was so much finer a weapon than the crude iron affairs that tribesmen usually carried. He had even christened it Caliburn. It had become like another limb to him, he loved it so. He was determined not to give back the sword, even though his father demanded it.

Uther said, "I must confess that I was glad when you took the title of Count of Britain upon you. But now I fear that it belongs by rights to Medrodus. I cannot demand that you give up what you have acquired by your strength, but I beg of you now to share the honour with the man who was the chosen of Ambrosius. Take him as your brother, let him lead a troop of horse. I beg you to do this, or I fear that the gods will not let me live."

Artos promised to do as his father had begged, relieved that he had not been commanded to give back the sword.

That night, by a great fire set in the midst of the compound, Artos took Medrodus as his brother in view of all the warriors. Their wrists were gashed and bound together so that the blood mingled and the mouths of their wounds kissed each other so long that they seemed to grow together and were painful to break apart. Then Artos gave his brother a new name, Medrawt, which was the Celtic form of his Roman name.

Artos told them all that his father had commanded this, and so they were perforce satisfied. They were not pleased when they heard that Medrawt was to lead a troop of horse, but they were forced to accept the situation.

Later, when Medrawt was riding back to his room in the villa, Aurelius came out to meet him. "You have mounted the first step, you see, my friend," he said.

Medrawt regarded him with a proud smile. "But not with any man's help," he said, and passed on through the courtyard. Aurelius stared after him. "Take care, my friend," he said softly. "There is still far to go, and a wise man treads gently over a nest of adders."

In the morning the news went round the settlement that Uther Pendragon was much improved and that the swelling had gone from his thighs, though as yet he could not make water without pain.

"The gods are still keeping an eye on him," said Bedwyr; and Artos laughed and punched his friend hard in the chest, to show that he appreciated the joke.

During these weeks Medrodus worked hard to fit himself for his new status. Being little practised as a horseman, he was forced to submit to much raillery until he became competent. This he did with as good a grace as he could find, allowing even the youngest of his troop to address him by name, in the Celtic tribal fashion, and to mock at him when he made a mistake in his horsemanship. Soon the new troop had become attached to him, in a rough and ready way. He had let his hair grow and wore garments cut in the style of those of his followers. On one occasion, after they had drunk more mead than they could carry, he had even stripped down, as they did, and had painted his face and upper body with bluc war-paint. Some of his comitatus were so impressed by this that they gave him rings and armlets of their own to wear, so that he should truly become of them and not of Rome.

Artos watched this change with amusement. But Bedwyr and Cei, the small dark man with the ritual scars across his face, were not greatly pleased.

"If he should submit to scarring, I would believe that he was of us," said Cei. Bedwyr agreed with that, and the next day Artos put the point to Medrawt.

The young man knew that this was a testing-point which he could not escape. Though he hated pain, he bowed his head to the words of Artos, who went straightway to Uther and told him.

The old man was strangely pleased. "I shall be carried on my litter to do the cutting myself," he said. "It is appropriate for me to do it. Tell them to make the temple ready."

He lay back in his bed then, pondering over the ritual and seeing in his mind's eye where he should make the incisions for the scars to form. When he had resolved what he would do, he lay back again and slept soundly, like a child, with a peaceful smile on his grim face.

Aurelius Caninus came to Medrawt as he sat waiting for the horns to blow, his naked body wrapped about with a long woollen cavalry-cloak.

"You are a fool, Medrodus," he said. "How do you know what they will do when they have you on the stones? That old devil Uther is a madman when once he holds the sacrifice knife. He will take away your manhood, and then what does it matter if they give you a whole legion of cavalry to lead? That will not bring your manhood back."

Medrawt had been afraid of this before, but had not dared to speak the words. He turned on Aurelius in wrath, but the other was not offended this time. The matter was too serious a one to permit easy offence.

"Then, for your own sake," said Aurelius, "make yourself drunk with mead before you go to the temple. So you may not feel the knife so keenly." Then he left Medrawt, who suddenly found his body to be very precious to him.

Yet, even though he followed the advice of Aurelius, he still felt the edge of the knife as it visited various parts of his body. Many times he would have screamed had they not tied a hempen rope round his jaws and behind his head; many times would have started from the stone, had not Cei and Bedwyr held him fast, smiling down at him and nodding from time to time.

When at last old Uther sat back in his litter, breathing heavily, Medrawt was still on the fringes of consciousness. The two loosed his arms and took the gag from his mouth. Medrawt tried to smile and placed his hands between his thighs. Then he stood up and made obeisance to Uther Pendragon, almost thankfully, for the old man's fatigue had come at the right time, it seemed. Bedwyr caught Medrawt as he tottered and fell, and while he lay unconscious, a slave-woman rubbed the blue dye into his wounds so that when they healed he would carry the tribal marks forever.

Yet it was many weeks before they did heal, for Uther had used a knife made dirty by the sacrifice of many creatures of field and woodland. And during those pain-wracked weeks, when the world seemed to be a place of agony and sickness, Medrawt often regretted that he had come so far to the west, regretted that the Count of Britain had picked him from the gutters of Colchester.

But among his followers, had he known it, Medrawt was now a leader to be followed to the death, for all of them knew the pain he had suffered to be as they were, being of his own age and young enough to recall it still, with a shudder.

PART THREE

THE GREAT BATTLES

At the pinewood's edge
The badger's kittens roll in the fern,
Trying their teeth in the sun,
Recklessly snapping at sticks.
Then anguish of hoof
Beats on their ears,
And startled they watch from the wood
Cloaked horsemen skirting the hill.
In the moonlight, daring the open,
They follow their curious noses
And whimpering drag to their covert
The embroidered glove of an earl.

XVIII

IT WAS LATE SUMMER BEFORE THE WAR PARTY SET OUT FROM Uther's Dun, on their way to Caerwent, to hold conference with the Kings of the West. All told, they now numbered four hundred horsemen, and since they had sworn over the hot fires and the steaming blood ever to help each other, whatever might befall, they called themselves the Cymry, that is, the Comrades. Artos led the main force of two hundred and fifty, while Medrawt was in command of the second force of one hundred and fifty, mainly the youngest and least-tried of the cavalcade. The great savage, Bedwyr, still rode beside Artos and would not be parted from him. The small dark tribesman, Cei, was seconded to the troop of Medrawt, to act as his lieutenant. In spite of his saturnine features, Cei was something of a humourist, and though Medrawt suspected him of being a spy for Artos, he felt confidence in him as a war-comrade and was glad to have him. Aurelius Caninus insisted on travelling back in a gilded litter, to show his exalted rank. He went beside Medrawt, for there was much he still wished to arrange with him, when there occurred any opportunity for private conversation.

So the Cymry trooped out of the settlement and over the hill, leaving behind women and children to the care of the other warriors who were pledged to Uther. This would not be a campaign like others, perhaps, when the families followed the warriors in wagons, for the Cymry had far to go and might be away for a long while.

The Cymry took only the most immediate of supplies, since they expected to obtain everything they needed at the court of the Western Kings. What little they took was dragged behind pack-horses, on rough sledges made from poles and trailed along the ground.

The first night out, as the two troops built their fires and erected small tents where they could, a dark horseman galloped past the encampment of Medrawt, his face smothered by a thick cloak and his head down. He did not answer any greetings but went on into the darkness, back the way they had come.

Medrawt, sitting with Cei, said, "Why should we send a messenger back to Uther's Dun so early?"

Cei was cutting a piece of meat. He stopped with his knife halfway to his lips and said, "What messenger? I saw no one pass." Then he grinned at the fire and put the meat into his mouth and could not talk afterwards for chewing.

At dawn, Medrawt woke to hear a horse's hooves and looked out of his tent flap. It was the same man, but this time he did not have his face covered, for it was so early that he must have expected all the Cymry to be still sleeping. Medrawt drew his head inside the tent, for he recognised Artos the Bear. When the horse had passed, Medrawt looked out again. A man in the next tent was also awake and watching the Bear riding back to his company. It was Aurelius Caninus. He smiled and whispered, "It is a strong love that pulls a man back like that. He has not spent a night away from her since the boy was born."

Medrawt said softly, "But were they not separated, under pain of death?"

The other shrugged his shoulders and said, "They do not fear death, those two, for they would go together and meet elsewhere when it was over. I am surprised you did not know about it. Everyone else did, except Uther and the old men."

They withdrew to their tents then and tried to sleep again.

Cei was very kind to Medrawt during the journey, in a brusque soldier's fashion. He administered any discipline that was needed among the young men, and even kept watch over Medrawt in the night. Once Medrawt was awakened to find that Cei was pulling a blanket over him, since a heavy mist had come up in the night as they travelled along the valley of the Sabrina. Medrawt had thanked him, but the man had only grunted and then made his way back to his own pallet of straw. Then when they were four days out, one of Medrawt's wounds burst open again and he was thrown into a raging fever. It was impossible to stop the army and make it wait until the leader was well again. Medrawt had to ride on, but Cei rode at his side always, supporting him in the saddle and holding the water-skin to his parched lips. When they made camp at night, Cei had water heated and bathed Medrawt's wound, tenderly, like a woman, but never saying a word. Medrawt fell into half-consciousness one day, when the sun was stronger than it need have been, and cursed Cei and tried to strike him. Cei smiled calmly and submitted to the weak blows, and did not mention it again, though Medrawt carried a vague memory of the occasion and wished he could have expressed his remorse.

Then all was well again, and the party began to draw near to Caerwent. At night as they camped, they were always aware that they were being watched from the high ground above them; and if they ever ventured into the woods on the western side of the river, they always heard footsteps retreating before them. Medrawt spoke of this to Aurelius, who smiled and said, "All must be well. If it were otherwise, you would be dead by now. They would shoot you with poisoned arrows at night. It is only the Kings of the West who are keeping a watch on you, to see that you arrive safely."

At first Medrawt doubted his words, until one night when a drunken trooper of his own company flung a javelin at a sound he heard among the bushes and then went to investigate the success of his cast. They heard him scream in the darkness, and then his horse came back into the firelight, its saddle fouled with blood. They found the trooper among the bushes when they dared to go to seek him. His head was a mess of arrows and his javelin hand had been severed at the wrist. After that, Medrawt gave orders that the night guard was to ignore any sounds of whatever sort that were heard during the duty-tour. This worked well, for no other men were lost on the way, from wounds—though three were killed in private fights, and one from the bite of an adder when he bent over a water-hole to drink, not seeing that the viper was already there.

So two weeks after they had trooped from Uther's Dun, the two companies of Cymry approached ancient Caerwent.

It was a gaunt grey citadel of ruined Roman stone, its massive parapets standing proudly on the gentle hillside. As the Cymry drew nearer, they saw that warriors paraded along the walls, keeping watch over the surrounding countryside. It would be a difficult place to defend, thought Medrawt, unless one had very many men. Yet it would take many men to capture it. Such a town could spill much blood, he thought. He wondered whether they would ride out of it as easily as they entered it.

Then Bedwyr galloped up to him and begged him to join Artos, for they must meet the Kings of the West together, as was fitting for two captains. They rode through the gates, the war-horns howling in their ears and the dogs of Caerwent running beneath their horses' legs.

XIX

CUNNEGLASSUS, KING OF THE MIDDLE LANDS, LEANED ON THE GILDED arm of his great chair, his pendulous lips bright with wine, his carved emerald to his short-sighted eye. Medrawt noted with envy the moulded arm-rings and the heavy bracelets that adorned this libertine's wrists, the pearl he wore in the fleshly lobe of his right ear—worth a hundred horses, Medrawt computed. Cunneglassus was about to speak, and all other talk fell away to fearful silence.

"But, young man," he wheezed, swaying a little with drunkenness already, though the night was yet but halfway through. "But, young man, we have talked of this scheme of yours for three days now, and still I cannot agree with the reasons you put forward."

He paused to take a breath and Artos, who had been drumming with impatience on the table-top before him, opened his mouth to speak. Yet before he could pronounce a syllable, the fat king had regained his breath, and shaking the thick and oiled curls of his dark head, continued. "You see, my boy, we are old in strategy; we have been warriors for thirty years, each one of us, and we know the difficulties. Is that not so, Votiporix?"

Beside him, in a chair of equal magnificence, a lithe old man sat watching him with the sharp eyes of a hawk; Votiporix, King of the Demetae, dark-faced and contemptuous, of a line so ancient that no man knew when it began. Votiporix, whose skin was so swarthy and whose eyes were so dark that he might well have been nurtured under the hot suns of Africa; who belonged to an earlier age in the history of the islands, the age of the tribal guletics such as Uther Pendragon, when men wore conical leathern helmets decorated with the feathers of eagles, and clothed their lower limbs in breeches of red and yellow squared tartan, bound to the knee with criss-crossed thongs of embossed hide. This Votiporix stared back at Cunneglassus, his cruel lips haunted by a smile of disdain. He nodded his head, slowly, and but once.

"Speak, Lord of the Middle Lands," he said, playing with a silver-hafted knife.

Cunneglassus made a small bow in return. "Yes," he said, "we know the difficulties. First, you see, these Saxons are old hands at warfare; they are not untried youngsters, you know. They can cut a horse from under a man, before he knows which rein he is pulling on. Can they not, Votiporix?"

The King of the Demetae yawned openly. "You tell me so," he said. "I have never met them. My estates call for all my attention."

Cunneglassus, vexed, drank from his wine cup. He did not return to that point, but said, "And after all, Artos, son of Uther Guletic, though we all know of your fame, and your strength, and, of course, of your love-making"— He paused for a laughter that did not come, for all men in the hall were secretly afraid of the red-haired chieftain. "Though we have heard of these things, we have yet to hear that you can manage a great force of cavalry, such as this campaign would need."

Artos the Bear rose now to his feet and stared the fat king in the eye so that even he lowered the emerald through which he saw the world, and turned away for an instant.

Artos was angry, indeed, but yet these men were powerful and must not be offended. He spoke as calmly as he was able. "King of the Middle Lands," he said, "I have led a warband since I was as high as this table we sit about. I have with me such captains as would help me in my command. As for the Saxons being good warriors, I do not gainsay it—yet which man among us would dare stand now and tell me that they are our masters in war?"

There were murmurs of approval from many parts of the hall, even from the followers of the Western Kings, who already chafed with the idleness thrust upon them by the long delay they had endured.

Votiporix said quietly, "All this may be so, Artos, son of Uther, but how many men do you bring? Think of the number we should have to give you. Would they follow you? Who would pay the cost of keeping them for long stretches in the field? These are practical matters which must not be jumped at."

Cunneglassus turned to him and smiled. Medrawt saw the fat lips and the hanging jowls and wished to strike the man across the face.

Now it seemed that the patience of Artos had almost run its course. He sat to reply, as though he no longer regarded these kings as being his superior. "You ask how many men I bring. I tell you, I bring enough to take a city, such is their courage. You ask whether your men would follow me. Then let me speak to them in the square tomorrow, and I warrant you they will trample upon each other to swear the oath to me. You ask who would pay for their long marches to meet the enemy. I tell you that the return journey will pay for the outward ride. When you see what treasure we shall come back with, then you will know how the battles shall be paid for. That is my answer."

Bedwyr began to hum a little war-song that the Cymry had put together on their ride south. It was a jaunty thing and was taken up here and there in the hall, for by now many men there were who had heard enough of talk and wished to be at something, the wine of Caerwent was so good. One man listened to another, the men of the Western Kings, and soon the ditty was being passed on, growing in its volume, first as background to the speakers, then as the master sound of the gathering. Artos smiled but otherwise ignored the song.

"Give the Cymry bones for bread,
Let them sleep on stones for bed;
Cut their hearts out, spike their eyes,
They'll be up at next sunrise;
Though of their heads you lighten them,
You will never frighten them;
True Cymry fight without their heads—
Beware, you fat-gut lie-abeds!"

As the song gathered impetus, the bundle of sheepskin in the third gilded chair stirred and became a man; a very old man, almost too old to sit upright. Aurelius Caninus, a sickly smile on his weasel's face, leaned over and helped the King of Dumnonia to rise. Constantine, senile madman, eldest of the Western Kings, was sitting up and taking notice at last, at a time when all men but Aurelius had even forgotten his presence. Constantine, his wrinkled yellow skull like that of a bird, his palsied fingers too shaking to hold a cup to his blue mouth, his thin shoulders too rotten with creeping eczema to bear the weight of a silken shift upon them. The King of Dumnonia was about to speak.

All men were silent, even the singers dropped their voices, for this old man ruled over vast territories and was wealthy beyond man's dreams. Besides, he was mad, and among primitive peoples that is always a good reason for listening to what such oracles have to say.

Old Constantine peered about him with red-rimmed eyes for a moment. He was taken with a spasm of coughing, brought on by a sudden waft of wood smoke in his direction. When Aurelius had patted him on the back and his head had stopped shaking a little, he formed his mouth to speak. Now even the drunken Bedwyr was silent.

Constantine said, "Where is my little dog, Aurelius?"

Aurelius looked round the room, as though denying any association with such a fool, but Bedwyr shouted, "Yes, where's his dog? Give the king his dog." Though Bedwyr was not a lover of dogs, and had never heard of this one before.

Constantine looked in the direction of Bedwyr. "Let that man stand," he said, his voice taking on a new strength. Cei who sat next Bedwyr whispered, "Good-bye, friend, he will have your eyes put out! He's as mad as a spring badger! Ho! Ho!"

Bedwyr stood, his knees trembling a little, not that he feared any man alive, but this thing was hardly a man, and was scarcely alive, by ordinary reckoning.

Constantine regarded him for a moment and then beckoned Aurelius to listen. "Mark that man, Aurelius," he said. "It is a good man, a warrior and a true Christian man. I would do him some service. Let him come to me in the morning, and I will give him gold and a horse. Yea, he shall have a wife, too, three wives. Mark that, Aurelius, I am getting forgetful. But mark it, my friend."

Artos began to laugh then, for he knew how Bedwyr hated women. Bedwyr was about to beg the king to remit most of his bounty, but a Dumnonian who sat near him turned and said, "Have no fears, friend, he will forget what he has said. If you did go tomorrow, he would most likely have you tied over an anthill till dusk!"

"Thank God for that," said Bedwyr, wiping the sweat from his forehead.

Then the song started again, and although Cunneglassus and Votiporix were obviously annoyed, Constantine tried to beat time to it with his febrile hand.

"Slower, slower, boys," he squeaked, all thought of his little dog forgotten. "I will sing with you boys, wait for me."

The Cymry entered into the spirit of the jest and sang slowly, shouting out the words so that the old madman might understand them. But his brain was of no more use to him than a handful of sheep dung, and the words he succeeded in forming were meaningless, even to the mad rooks who cawed above his tumbledown shack of a palace in Dumnonia, so far away.

Then, when the jest seemed played out, the old man sat up in his chair and looked at Artos with strangely sharp eyes.

The Dumnonian near Bedwyr whispered, "This is his dangerous mood, for now he understands and speaks sense. Take care now, friend. This can be death, or glory! We have suffered both under him."

The old man stretched out his hand and pointed with a long, emaciated finger towards Artos the Bear. Men saw that his hand did not shake any more.

"Son of Uther, son of my oldest friend," he said, "I greet you. I have dreamed of you these long days gone by. Artos, son of Uther, greetings, for you shall be *dux bellorum*, the Captain of Battles!"

Votiporix and Cunneglassus started with this new shock. They turned and tried to remonstrate with their mad companion, but his thin shriek of a voice rose above theirs and was heard by all men.

"I have spoken, I have spoken! A man who leads such as these song-makers, the Cymry, deserves to be Captain of Battles! Nothing less is fit for him!"

Artos rose in his place, trying to make peace among the shouting kings, but again Constantine cried out, "I tell all men who can hear me, that if Artos be not declared Captain of the Battles, then I will call him to me now and give him my own crown and he shall be greater than any of you!"

A great hush fell upon the hall. The old man had risen, and stood like a crazy prophet, still pointing towards Artos, though now his hand had begun to shake again.

Aurelius, his face white with consternation, tried to ease the old king back into his seat. Medrawt smiled grimly to see the concern in the face of Aurelius the Dog, who was afraid of losing the crown he so much envied now.

"Do you declare him Captain? Do you Votiporix? Do you Cunneglassus, then? Speak now, or it will be too late!"

Constantine began to fumble by the side of his chair. An old Greek helmet stood there, its sides dented with the years, its plume hackles broken and motheaten. It was his only symbol of kingship. Votiporix saw the movement of the old man's hand, and said in great haste, "Very well, Constantine, I give my vote; he shall be *dux*. Though we shall live to regret this foolishness, my friend."

After that there was nothing the outvoted Cunneglassus could do but agree, and the great shouts that greeted this election sounded far out over the city of Caerwent, and along the hillside above it, to the distant hovels where common men crouched in fear, alike from the wolves and from their overlords.

So Artos became Captain of the Battles, the General of all the British cavalry. An honour bought by a song, and such a foolish song, but sung by men who believed what they sang, foolish or not, and who would have cleared the Saxon out of Britain that very night, had they been sober enough to sit on a horse long enough to find a Saxon.

Constantine had fallen back into his chair when the vote was taken, and now lay like a dead man. Aurelius wrapped his sheepskin about his throat with fingers that would have relished the task of crushing it instead. Medrawt watched him carefully, and when Caninus carried the old king from the hall, followed him as unobtrusively as he could, into the courtyard, towards the old king's thatched billets.

Artos stood upon the table and all men drank to him and then flung the rest of the wine over him, in some primitive memory of libation, anointing the warrior-god, but with wine, which is blood, and not with Christian oil.

"Artos! Artos! Artos!" they shouted, stupid with the glory that was to be.

XX

THE DAY SET ASIDE FOR HUNTING TURNED OUT TO BE A WET ONE AND few of the lords were anxious to ride out. Yet news had come in that two wolves, a male and a female, had made their home within the thick wood that lay beyond the second ridge and that these beasts were ravaging the farmsteads outside Caerwent, dragging down the precious ewes wantonly and even attacking the shepherds. One wild-eyed man told the lords that he had been followed as he came down from his flock two nights before. He carried only a staff, which he broke in his nervousness, striking out at a stone which looked like a wolf in the moonlight.

When his pursuers saw that he was unarmed, and smelled the fear which he left behind him in the wind, they closed in on him, slavering and urging each other to pull him down, he said. In his terror, he ran blindly across a field with which he was not familiar, and tumbled headlong into a ditch that brought water down from the hills to his village.

This ditch gave him a drenching but saved his life, for the wolves seemed to suspect some sort of trap and would not come down there after him. Instead they prowled round until dawn, trying to reach down at him, snarling and letting their slaver drip over his face as he lay staring up at them. When the first light came, they left him, and he crawled back to his village, half crazed from his ordeal.

When Artos heard this tale, he said, "These are two wolves a man would be glad to meet. They seem to have spirit and courage."

And so the hunting party set off through the driving rain, their cloaks wrapped tight about them, looking more like embalmed corpses than men. Cunneglassus and Constantine stayed within doors: the first because he was far too fat to ride easily, the second because his senses had left him again and he was now convinced that he must stay and guard some queen or other while her husband sailed for Troy. Aurelius Caninus stayed with the old madman, stroking his hand and periodically dosing him with potions that contained enough foxglove to kill a normal man.

Artos rode with the gaunt, dark-faced Votiporix, at the head of the column. Medrodus rode with Bedwyr and Cei at a short distance behind them. They carried only light boar-spears and swords. The wolfhounds were left behind, since the thick mud on the hillsides would put them at a disadvantage against two such wily quarries and the hound-keeper had no wish for his animals to be disembowelled on such a slight occasion.

At the top of the first rise Cei's horse cast a shoe. He gazed down ruefully for a moment and then smiled as he turned back for home. Bedwyr taunted him, saying that he would lend him his horse. But Cei shook his head and said, "This is the hand of my God, friend. If I went on into the wood after this, the dog-wolf would eat my heart!" He rode away down the hill, laughing.

When he had gone, Bedwyr said, "He is a crafty one, that Cei. He has killed more wolves than most men, some of them on foot, with a little knife, yet he still respects them."

Medrodus replied, "Does he not fear them?"

Bedwyr took some time to reply. "Cei is afraid of nothing," he said. "How many wolves have you slain, my friend?"

Medrodus flushed with annoyance. "I have never before lived in such a countryside where one might find them. I have lived in places where men have cleared away such savage beasts."

Bedwyr replied, "It is well for a man to be prepared, wherever he has lived. Do not speak lightly of the wolves until you have carried home ten pelts, and even then, speak softly, for the eleventh beast might drag you down."

Medrodus snorted and said no more. All the same, he felt secretly to see that his sword was loose in the scabbard, so that it would fly out easily if there came a sudden attack.

When they reached their hunting ground, Artos sent Bedwyr with the other riders to encircle the wood and to drive the wolves before them, while he waited, accompanied by Votiporix and Medrodus, to strike them when they broke cover. These three sat drenched and shivering with cold beneath the dripping boughs, even their legs wet from the tall bracken which reached up to their horses' bellies.

Votiporix said at length, "Let us go into the wood. There, at least, we may be dry, even though we may lose our quarry."

Artos bowed his head and, turning, pressed his horse forward among the knee-high brushwood and under the trees.

Within the wood, greenness pressed on the riders. Even the light which vibrated uncertainly between the leaves had about it a tinge of damp green. The horses slipped on the green lichen that crept over the stones on the forest floor. Their riders drew back from the dank green moss that clothed the tree trunks on every side of them. Above the riders, on the roof of the forest, the rain beat down to create a continuous heavy whispering, oppressive and foreboding. Layer on layer of dark and rotting leaves thickened the air with their stench as the horses plunged through them.

Medrodus blew down his nostrils in disgust. "The scent of tombs," he said.

Votiporix glared at him darkly. "Speak no contempt of woods, Roman," he said. "The Gods of the West live in the groves."

Artos looked back impatiently at them, his boar-spear levelled beside his horse's neck.

"We are seeking wolves, my friends, not gods or tombs," he said.

"You may find them together," muttered Votiporix.

"Then I shall wish I had stayed by the fireside," Artos said and laughed, bending low to avoid a swinging bough and spurring his horse forward into a small glade, where the bracken gave place to lush grass. In his anger Votiporix did not see the bough until it was almost too late. It caught him across the breast, causing him to swing his horse sideways. Medrodus did not wait to see what happened to the chieftain, but pressed his horse forward, after Artos.

It was at this moment that the thick furze and bracken at the far side of the glade parted violently and Medrodus glimpsed the sudden and vicious scurrying motion of a shaggy grey body which launched itself towards Artos, who gave a high shout of excitement and rode to meet the she-wolf. Such was the fury of the beast's attack as she leapt at the horse's throat that the boar-spear ran through her body, its point protruding for two feet beyond her.

The terrified horse screamed at the slavering mask which tore at its own twisting body. Artos gave a grunt of satisfaction and let the spearpoint fall, with its heavy weight, towards the ground. He half turned to shout to the others, when the bushes at his unprotected side parted violently and the great dog-wolf leapt onto him, snapping at his head, bearing him from the high saddle as easily as though he were a child. The screaming horse wheeled, mad with terror, dragging Artos here and there, his foot caught in the stirrup, while the great wolf worried at him, trying to break through the thick hide of his shoulder-plates.

Then Medrodus passed on like a rushing wind, his jaws tightly set. His long sword swept down and the dog-wolf's headless body fell across Artos, spouting warm blood over him. Half turning, Medrodus slashed again, cutting through the stirrup leather that had almost killed Artos. The crazed horse, now free, galloped madly among the trees, neighing at the smell of blood.

Medrodus was on his knees above the Bear, laughing and pointing. Artos sat up, to find that the dead wolf's teeth had clenched so immovably into the thick hide of his armour that the severed head still hung, like some savage decoration, on his left breast.

"By the gods," he said, "I will wear this until it falls of its own accord! It was a brave wolf."

But Votiporix ran up and slashed the wolf head away with his hunting-knife. "You fool," he shouted, "so you would draw all the wolves in Britain upon us!"

Artos stared at him coldly, then turned from him with contemptuous deliberation, and taking the hands of Medrodus in his own, said, "Medrawt, my dear brother, may the dogs of hell gnaw at my belly for a thousand years if I forget this day's work." Then he clasped Medrodus to him warmly, placing his scarred face close to the other's pale cheek.

Medrodus said, "I did it only because Bedwyr taunted me."

Artos smiled broadly. "Who cares why the cow is milked, as long as we eat the cheese?" he said.

Votiporix had already left them and was riding from the wood in fury when he met Bedwyr and the rest of the party. He nodded back towards the glade. "Do not go in there," he said, his lips curled back in a sneer, "you would disturb the lovers."

Bedwyr came near to killing him for those words.

XXI

DURING THE FOLLOWING DAYS, THE CYMRY, OR THE LEGION OF THE Bear, as men came to refer to it, made urgent preparations for the campaign against the Saxons of the southeast, for it was of the utmost importance that the new army should be on the move before the winter snows might impede them, or lock them in the west until spring, when the invaders might have accumulated fresh multitudes of supporters.

All told, the Legion now numbered upwards of eight hundred cavalrymen, besides armourers, grooms, cooks and huntsmen, whose function was to enable the horsemen to livc off the lands they passed through.

Artos and Medrawt led the first and second companies of Cymry, Bedwyr the two hundred Dumnonians who had chosen to follow the new *dux bellorum*, and Cei, since he was of the same Silurian race, the men of the Demetae, who had ignored the censures of Votiporix and had vowed not to return to their country until they could boast of having proved themselves against the Saxon.

As far as was possible, the Legion was equipped in the old Roman style, in plumed helmet and kilt, but with a stout leather jerkin to replace the cuirass, for lightness' sake in riding. Moreover, these cavalrymen carried the long slashing sword, and not the foot soldier's short stabbing weapon. Each man was armed with a lance and none carried shields.

For casc of recognition in battle, the four troops carried their own banners, which were not the signs of the tribes to which they belonged. It was natural that Artos should keep to his long pennant on which was embroidered a slavering bear; but the other companies bore simple squares of coloured cloth, without insignia —black for Medrawt, red for Bedwyr and blue for Cei.

Artos created another innovation in having constructed a new type of provision wagon; its wheels were spoked and not solid, and the front axle was pivoted so that the wagon might be manoeuvreable in winding roads. The body-work was light, and constructed of two main spars, over which was lashed a flooring of tightly woven wattle. There was no superstructure to add to the weight of the vehicle, whose only object was to carry food and water barrels, and not to shelter its occupants. Only ten of these wagons were to be taken, and they were to be drawn by such horses as would be fit to employ as war horses, when such replacements became necessary.

It was essential, the Bear had decided, that the Legion should move with great speed and a minimum of outside entanglements, and so he commanded that no camp-followers should be allowed to accompany the army. This decree irritated such of the Dumnonians and Demetae who had become used to the relatively soft life of Caerwent. But it did not worry the older Cymry, who knew that living off the land implied other things than bread and water.

By the time autumn had established itself in the west, all was in readiness for the campaign. The settled route was to take the Cymry to Aquae Sulis, and then via Calleva Atrebatum direct to Londinium. Once the Sabrina had been ferried, the road would be almost due east and would avoid most of the too thickly forested areas. Once in Londinium, they would make their final plans of attack, in the light of whatever new information they might receive in the ancient capital.

Medrawt heard all these plans, and smiling, agreed to everything Artos had decreed. He felt in his heart that his time was about to come. The senile king, Constantine, had not survived his weakening outburst at the election of Artos. He had been found dead in his bed the morning after, the froth still on his lips, from what seemed to be a particularly violent heart attack. Aurelius had shown such grief as was appropriate to a young man who had served the king so long, and had seen to it that the old man had a good send-off. Constantine's little dog, together with the three slaves who had been in the house at the time of the king's death, accompanied their master to whatever place shelters the spirits of insane kings.

Aurelius was elected King of Dumnonia on the day of Constantine's funeral. No one gainsaid him, for Constantine had no sons, and many men had heard the old king in his ravings address Aurelius as "Emperor," and even make him wear the old Grecian helmet. Votiporix and Cunneglassus almost welcomed Aurelius as a fellow-monarch in the Confederation, for they knew he was a weak man, and expected to influence him to their own advantage.

Artos did not care who was King of Dumnonia, as long as he was *dux bellorum;* and Medrawt saw this new accession as a move to the good in his own progress towards becoming the Count of Britain. So, in all respects, the sad demise of Constantine caused little consternation.

Yet, in its way, it gave rise to an incident which was to echo down through history, though changed by the centuries through which it passed. For it happened that one day, shortly before the

Legion rode out of Caerwent on the great adventure, that the Kings of the West, together with the leaders of the four companies, were on a hill overlooking the citadel.

It was a miserable day and the rain, blown on the rising wind, was whipped against the stern faces of the riders. They pulled their long cloaks about them, and turning away from the autumn storm, decided to make their way to shelter in the city.

As they descended the hill, they came to a place in the ramparts where the stones had fallen one upon another, so that there was space for only one rider to pass through at a time. Artos pressed forward and would have passed into the city, but Votiporix placed his hand upon the Bear's shoulder and restrained him.

"Patience, Bear," he said. "A king goes before a captain."

Cunneglassus then spurred forward, smiling, but serious in his heart, and rode knee to knee with the King of the Demetae.

"There is another king here, too, friend Artos," he said, thinking to ride through with Votiporix.

The fierce rain streaming down his rugged face, Artos sat and smiled at them strangely. He watched Aurelius spurring on to gain the gap before Bedwyr, and Cei anxious not to be the last.

Then Artos gave a great shout and said, "Between God and myself, but this is more like a maidens' corn-dance than a meeting of great captains! Each one anxious to be first, afraid to be last! Has God truly put men's hearts into bodies that act so like those of swine snuffling for husks on a dung-heap?"

The kings turned on him, angrily. But the Bear only laughed at them. Then he reached down at his side and unhooked the great round bronze buckler that swung from his pommel-horn. He took it firmly by its embossed edge and flung it away from him, so that it lay, its round boss uppermost, in the heather. The horsemen looked at him, wondering.

He beckoned to them then. "Come," he said gently, as though to backward children. "Sit on your chargers round this shield."

The men obeyed him, for his voice was already one of command. And when they were disposed about the great buckler, he turned to them and said, "Now, at this table, who holds the place of honour?"

They looked down at the shield and then up at the *dux bellorum*. "Why," said Votiporix, "there is no place of honour. All places are the same, round a shield."

Artos smiled at him and said, "Exactly so, King of the Demetae." Then, with a swift movement, he leaned low out of the saddle, took up his buckler, and without another word, rode through the gap, letting whoever would follow him in the order they might.

XXII

WHEN THE RIDERS WERE SEVEN DAYS OUT FROM CAERWENT THEY reached a high and ancient earthworks, at the summit of which had been constructed a rough fortification of unhewn stones, built much after the fashion of the Roman mile castles, along Hadrian's great wall. It was such a fortress as might give shelter to a hundred defenders, though there was little enough for such a castle to protect in the poverty-stricken countryside about it; nor would any enemy force, working its way along the river valley below the hill, be taken by surprise should a sudden sally be made from the rude fortress, since it would be possible from a long distance to observe the movements of any men who descended the bare hillside.

Artos put forward this opinion to his chief captains who rode beside him. Medrodus, the keen-sighted, reined in his horse and pointed.

"Look," he said, "there are men on the walls watching us. They are not there to guard the valley. They are in a state of siege, poor devils. Either the Saxon is near at hand, or they are expecting him to come."

Artos stared and then said, "They are our people, though we cannot stay to protect them. That they must do for themselves. We have our own way to make and our battles to fight. Yet at least you and I could ride up to greet them, to put new heart into them, perhaps."

Bedwyr said, "They would value two sacks of meal and a jar of wine more highly."

Artos smiled and nodded. "You are a practical man, Bedwyr," he said.

So he and Medrodus rode up the hill, followed by a man leading a pack-horse laden with meal and wine. The Cymry waited, taking this opportunity to eat and drink a little themselves.

As they approached the fortress, Medrodus said, "They are excited. They are clustering above the gate. They seem more like living corpses than men, they are so starved."

High over the topmost bastions, small heads looked down. Someone shouted in a high-pitched voice, and arms like thin sticks were waved.

Artos said, "This is a tomb, not a fortress. Why should our people suffer so? I swear to God that I will take ten Saxon heads for everyone that looks on me now."

Medrodus smiled down at his saddle-horn but did not speak.

Then Artos cupped his hands about his lips and shouted, "We are your friends. We come to bring you food. Open the gates."

From the further side of the gaunt fortress, a flock of birds rose, squawking, ravens or rooks, fluttering like pieces of burnt paper.

Artos was still holding his hands about his mouth, and looking upwards, when the air above him was filled with a vicious whirring. His horse gave a grunt and a deep sigh, and then rolled over, flinging Artos from him. Eight feathered arrow-flights showed in the welling blood of the creature's belly. Medrodus gave a sudden cry and clapped his hand to his head. Then he looked at the blood on his hand and felt his ear again. Smiling wickedly, he said, "You bastards! May you rot before you can even eat each other!" Then, bending low, he took Artos up onto the saddle and spurred down the hill again, the winged flights humming behind him, splintering harmlessly on the rocks where his horse had been but a second before. The man with the baggage horse was not so fortunate, nor was his horse.

Artos looked back grimly. "You are welcome to the feast, you carrion," he said. "It will but remind you of your great hunger."

Bedwyr brought him another horse and they rode on.

"It will be another story when we get to Londinium," said the Bear. "These folk are crazed and do not know which way to turn, or whom to attack."

Medrodus, who regretted the hole made in his ear, said, "If we did justly, we would roast them in their stone oven. They cannot have too many arrows left."

Cei smacked him playfully on the behind and said, "Oh, how bloodthirsty you are, playfellow! I don't know if we are safe with such an ogre."

The men near at hand laughed at this, but in their hearts most of them sided with Medrawt.

That evening the story took another turn. Five miles from the fortress, in a hilly place along the valley, the foremost riders smelled smoke, and creeping to the top of a hillock, sighted a dozen small fires, lit on the rolling downs.

Artos saw them and said, "This is the enemy that keeps our gentle British brothers locked in their stone tower."

A party of archers crept up like anxious hounds, already putting arrows to their bows. Their leader, a grizzled man of Gwent, surveyed the fires and the dark figures moving about them. The place was littered with skin windbreaks and awnings. Tethered goats and cattle grazed beyond the fires. "They keep no watch, Bear," he said. "If I took twenty men down there, we could skewer them where they stood. They would never see where the shafts came from."

Artos smiled grimly and said, "That would be a pity. There would be no satisfaction in that for either side. Better to let them know, at least for a minute or two, what did kill them! No, some of us will ride down on them with sword and lance. My new horse needs a little battleplay to bring his courage to a fine edge."

The archers went down, disappointed, and Artos quietly chose fifty of the best-tried horsemen of the Cymry, men notorious for their love of battle. Medrodus went with them, but Cei and Bedwyr stayed behind, grumbling, to command the waiting force.

The attackers led their horses quietly into the valley and among the thick green foliage that bordered the little river. When they reached the open country and saw the Saxon fires flickering before them, they mounted with hardly a jingle and, their faces grimly set, began their gallop, dividing into two companies, so as to embrace as many of the unsuspecting enemy as they could.

The Saxons, sprawling here and there about their fires, laughing or gnawing at the strips of dried meat which they carried with them, were suddenly aware of the vicious thud of hooves about them. A young boy, who stood amid a circle of warriors, singing an ancient song of their flat reed-fringed homeland, stopped in the middle of a phrase, his eyes wide with terror, and pointed towards the rank of dark horsemen who bore down on them, red cloaks flying, the firelight already glinting on their gold bracelets and neck-rings, and on the silver-bright points of spear or edge of slashing sword.

The Celts swept out of the western darkness, like the warriors of the old gods, the killers from the nether world.

A high Saxon voice screamed, "The Lordly Ones are upon us! Fly, fly, for we cannot stand against them!"

Then the slaughter started, in the firelight, on the lonely moorland. And soon, as sword rose and fell, or lance thrust again and again, the fires went out, smothered by the bodies that fell upon them, careless in the agony of death.

The Celts howled and laughed in their ecstasy; the Saxons, now grimly silent, fell without a word, most of them hardly raising their hands to ward off the fearful blows. Medrodus, however, noticed one young man who ran here and there, his short scramasaxe red with blood, in and out among the horses, slashing at their bellies. He swung his charger round, and coming on the Saxon from behind, took him between the shoulders with his lance. The man half turned and slashed at the ash-shaft of the spear, vicious even in the shadows of death. Medrodus shook the man clear of his lance point and then turned to find another enemy.

Artos had quickly drawn clear of his followers, revelling in the balanced keenness of the sword he had won from Ambrosius. Men fell before his onslaught like corn before the reaper's scythe. At length he saw before him a band of Saxons clustered on the far side of a fire. In their centre was a grey-bearded old man, who stood baying like a cornered hound, his leather helmet awry on his fierce head. Three women kneeled by him, one of them clinging to him and weeping. Half-naked, ragged children crouched by him, staring up at him, or wide-eyed towards the fearful horsemen.

For a second Artos was reminded of his own father, of the families he had known at Lis Pengwern. He saw that this old chieftain had brought his folk with him across the grey seas, to find a better home for them in gentle Britain, and his heart misgave him at the man's simplicity and guilelessness in walking so unprepared into the jaws of death.

Then, shutting his ears to the whimpering of children and the high crying of the women, he set his horse at the clustering family and, splashing through the fire, was upon them, shouting and hacking with his sword, Caliburn.

The old Saxon faced him bravely, his eyes red with anger, his clumsy axe swung back to decapitate the horse. But Artos leaned from the saddle and struck the chieftain across the head, while yet the heavy axe was moving towards him. The man crumpled and fell upon those of his family who kneeled about him. The axe flew through the air into the darkness. Artos wheeled his terrified horse about, and rode to young Medrodus, hoping that he had not harmed the children in that wild flurry of hooves.

As the Celts rode back to the waiting Cymry, Artos said, "These were better men than those who snarled at us from the hill-fort."

Medrodus shrugged his shoulders and said, "Perhaps. Yet they were our enemies, just as those who shot at us were our countrymen. In war, one must not give way to gentle feelings."

Artos said, "My mind is troubled. I hope that our problems are solved when we reach Londinium."

Medrodus said, "There you will learn what it is to be the Count of Britain. There you will discover the glory of the trust which is given you with your title."

Artos answered, "Yes, it will be different in Londinium. There our greatness will begin."

XXIII

LONDINIUM SWEATED, SWEATED AND ROTTED IN THE HEAT OF A DAY that had surprised autumn by its sudden advent. But Londinium had sweated and rotted for two hundred years now, and was little changed after it all. This was perhaps the principal virtue of the city, that being ugly from its birth, it had no fear of the ravages that time would make on a comelier face.

The ramparts stood or fell as they pleased, for no one cared. If they stood, they provided a home for the probing roots of nettle and of willow-herb. If they fell, they provided masonry for another hovel to spring up, haphazard as weeds themselves—like most of the other dwellings, now that Roman order was so long forgotten.

The river was still as busy as ever and far dirtier than before. Yet somehow its bustling life had an indestructible reality about it. It was a stinking river, which spoke with a raucous voice, viciously, but which was still a great waterway, Rome or not.

Londinium was an open city now, friend to none, foe to none, a dwelling-place for any man who knew how to fend for himself. In its winding cobbled streets a dozen languages could be heard at any hour; in its taverns, greasy coins from over half the known world were legal tender, had there been any law to recognise them; in its temples, the same chipped marble god answered to the names of Mithras and Woden; in its high and clustering slums, red head lay beside black, yellow skin by white; and it was a fortunate child whose dreams did not contain a violent death, of man or woman, before it was seven years old.

Artos, the *dux bellorum*, had never seen Londinium before, except in his own dreams. Then it had been a place of cultured order, its regular white buildings matched only by the clean dignity of its noble citizens, the children of Rome. During the long ride from Aquae Sulis, Artos had indeed expected that time and the savages of Saxony might have marred this dream a little, yet he was sure in his mind that it would still be recognisable, that it could eventually be re-created when the invader was destroyed.

But Artos was not prepared for the city he was to find that steaming autumn day. There were no trumpets, no flags, no flowers cast down by grateful citizens before the horses' feet.

As the Legion approached the crumbling Western Gate, the leaders saw the beginnings of the confusion that was so soon to follow their entry. Groups of men, no bigger than black dots, appeared in parties, stood still for a while, then moved rapidly within the ruined wall, to show themselves again in a little space on top of the stones themselves, staring, pointing perhaps, then disappearing once more. The many booths, gay with coloured awnings, that stood outside the city bounds, were suddenly dismantled, their gaudy sunblinds folded up and carried away.

Medrawt, riding beside Artos, said, "Do not hope for too much, brother. Londinium is not the place for a man to give his heart to nowadays."

Artos stared fixedly before him. "You are a cynic, brother," he said. "I believe that Rome could rise again here."

Medrawt turned his face away to hide his smile. "We shall see, Bear," he said. "It depends on what you mean by Rome. Some men mean different things by the same word."

Artos sensed the mockery in his voice. His rough face became flushed with displeasure. He set spurs to his white horse, holding up his right hand to indicate that the leading troop should break into a canter now, so as to enter the ancient citadel in grand style.

At first it seemed that their quest had led them to a deserted city, a place perhaps of the dead, for no one was to be seen. Yet as they began to file through the broken gates, the weed-grown walls were suddenly alive with men. Stones flew through the air, and then a flight of arrows whistled down on the laughing men and their proud horses.

Artos reined in his charger, a broad cut across his cheek, from which the blood welled angrily. He had the look of a frustrated animal about him now. Medrawt shouted to him urgently, "Ride on, Bear! Do not halt. You are asking for death to stay here."

Even as he spoke, the white horse was struck between the eyes by a sling-shot and reared violently. Artos was flung to the ground and then the charger, slipping on the cobblestones, fell beside him, legs threshing in its death agony. Acting on a sudden impulse, yet at the same time wondering at his own stupidity, Medrawt rode in and, leaning low from the saddle, took Artos by the broad belt about his waist. So, clapping spurs to his horse's side, he dragged the Count of Britain away from the murderous hooves. Bedwyr now rode up, leading the Count's second horse, a dapple-grey, and less nervous than the other had been.

"The hand of God is kind to you, Master," he said, helping Artos to mount. The Bear turned and grasped the hand of Medrawt. "Yet this one is more immediate," he said, his grim face twisted into a smile. Then, almost as though he wished no one else to hear, "That was an act I had not expected, Medrawt. Things have happened between us, things of fate for which no single man can be responsible. But may God give me the power to reward you when the time comes. Ride always by my side, brother, and let no man come between us."

Bedwyr said quietly to Cei, "It would make more sense to say 'no woman,' I think, friend!"

Cei shrugged his shoulders and said, "Which of us would not have done the same for him? It was only that Medrawt was the nearest."

Medrawt was still wondering why he had saved the Bear. It was as though a power greater than his own envy and disappointment had made him lean down from his horse to save the life of the Count of Britain.

Then the stones and the flights of arrows began again from the walls and from the upper windows of the houses, and the many horsemen were flung into a deadly confusion in the narrow streets. So tightly packed were they that one horse being struck carried two others down with him, or one man falling knocked his companion from the saddle. And once down, it was hardly possible to escape injury from the many plunging hooves. Some who were still near the city gates would have turned back and ridden outside the place for safety, but Artos gave the signal to charge, though there was no visible enemy before them. And so the Legion entered Londinium, rejected by those whom they had come to protect.

At last, as they rode towards a place where four roads met, Artos held up his hand for the cavalry to slow down. A group of men stood waiting for them, barring their way with upraised arms. Medrawt's quick eye saw that they were not soldiers, but civilians of various sorts—councillors, perhaps, merchants and such like. Nor were they all of one race. The pale hair of Saxon moved beside the darker head of Celt. One man even wore the rough black pelt of a bear above his tunic, as they did in the dim forests of the northern lands still.

"Halt, you who enter this city unbidden!" called a tall, grey-haired old man who wore the long robe of a municipal officer.

Bedwyr grumbled, "Put a lance into him, Artos!"

But Artos signalled for the leading company to halt, and he rode forward to within ten paces of the deputation, Medrawt closely behind him, his sword loose in the scabbard in case of a sudden act of treachery.

Artos spoke impassively, without malice, for he already regarded himself as the saviour of Londinium, almost its ruler. Perhaps his voice carried the slightest hint of proprietorship, which the old man may have sensed.

"We come as friends," said Artos, "to protect you, men of Britain. Yet we have received a poor welcome today."

The old councillor answered, "We did not invite you. We can protect ourselves, horseman. We are not men of Britain; we are men of Londinium. We have been left to fend for ourselves so long that we have learned to fight with other things than swords and lances."

Medrawt said bitterly, "Yes, with pieces of stone from attic windows!"

The old man ignored him and said to Artos, "Leave us, and go wherever you are wanted, for you are not wanted here." The men who clustered behind him laughed at this and nodded their heads in approval.

Bedwyr said, "They have courage, whatever else they lack, these old men of Londinium."

Then the impatient Cymry were silent as Artos spoke again, and his words were contemptuous ones, as though addressed to a menial and not to a civic official.

"Old man, by your looks you have but little time to go before death locks up your mouth. Do as little damage with your tongue as you can before you go into the shadows. We, the Cymry, are here on a greater errand than you seem aware of."

And the old man answered him in like manner, while his companions laughed again and the Cymry fidgetted angrily in their saddles.

"My death is no man's concern but my own, horseman. Nor do I care by what name you call yourselves, or even what you think your purpose to be—though, if I spoke my mind freely, I should say that you came here as many other men have come in history, to fill your bellies and your purses."

Now Artos could restrain himself no longer. In his great anger he shouted, "We come to free Britain from the Saxon, dotard, and to set up Rome again."

Then the men in the group began to laugh and to nudge each other, as though Artos had made a great joke; and those who jeered loudest were the fair-haired ones.

"Who are you, horseman, to take on such a task?" called out one of them, whose flaxen plaits hung almost to his waist.

Artos looked above their sneering heads, his eyes wide with fury. "I am the Count of Britain," he said.

His words were greeted by a roar of laughter that was echoed from the high walls of the houses above them. Men, women and even little children leaned out from the windows, laughing and jeering. Then from one housetop someone flung a handful of garbage down upon Artos. As though this were a signal, hands reached out now from every window, each with its missile of filth.

The old councillor openly laughed now. "That is our answer to you, horseman. There is no Count of Britain. Who was the Count, a blind old madman called Ambrosius, died many years ago in Rome. That was the end of such nonsense!"

Medrawt said viciously, "You are a liar!"

Then he was drenched by a bucketful of slops from above. His hot temper could be restrained no longer. Suddenly his horse was rearing above the old man and his sword was slashing down wherever his blind rage would let him see a head to strike.

The Cymry gasped behind him. Artos spurred to him, saying, "Have patience, brother. We must not kill those whom we came to save!"

But now the pavement was strewn with bodies, and those of the councillors who could had escaped into open doorways. Medrawt was weeping with anger, his hands shaking uncontrollably.

Then from above them, from all sides of them, came catcalls and missiles. Bedwyr rode up. "Our men are getting wounded, Bear," he said. "What are we to do?"

One of the leading Cymry shouted out, "Let us sack the houses and burn down this nest of vipers, Artos!"

The Bear said, as calmly as he could, "See that the man who spoke then is rewarded with a hundred lashes for his advice tonight, Bedwyr."

In the grim silence that now settled on the Legion, Artos called out, "Turn your horses about, Cymry, and ride from this place."

Then he turned his face up towards the windows in the square and yelled, "We shall never set foot on this dung-heap again, though you come crawling on bleeding knees to beg our help."

His words were greeted by ironical cheers and wild laughter. Children imitated the Bear's uncouth accents. Medrawt felt suddenly ashamed to be riding with him.

So began the ride back. The Legion took the way it came, out of Londinium, in silence. And all the way they were pelted and besmirched with ordure and droppings. As they passed through the gates at last, Bedwyr reported that the ride had cost them a score of men.

"That will not weigh heavily on my mind, friend," said Artos. "They would have died later. What troubles me is that Londinium does not love the Count of Britain."

Medrawt, who had not spoken before, said, "The man who wishes to be loved does not accept such a title. It is only for the hardiest in mind."

Artos did not answer him, but rode on gripping the pommel of his high saddle.

XXIV

GLEIN WAS THE FIRST OF THE BATTLES OF ARTOS, AND THE LEAVES OF autumn were falling from the trees. The turf of the Sussex Weald still grew thick and lush; flowers still nodded in sheltered places beneath the trees. The maturity of the year was echoed in the mellower sounds of the birds' voices. It seemed a season of wood smoke and amber lights. Not one of blood.

Beyond the brow of a hill overlooking the River Glein, the Legion of the Bear was waiting. Below them, somewhere in the deep woodlands that bordered the sluggish river, lay their enemy, men of the Jutish Cantwara. A scout had ridden in the night before to say that these men, some of them old settlers in Britain, were on their way westward through the forests to join the Saxon kinglet, Aelle, and his son Cissa. The man had come near to riding full pelt into a company of them, at dusk, and brought back a long axe-slash in his saddle to prove his words. But it had been impossible for him to estimate the number of the enemy. So, as they waited, there were many among the Cymry who licked their dry lips and felt frequently to see if their swords were still there.

One old veteran said to the shivering lad at his side, "Once it begins, the sweat will stop drowning the palms of your hands. You will forget this waiting. Look, my own hands are shaking now."

He held out his calloused palms. The boy could discern no movement, but he nodded his head. His teeth were chattering too hard for him to risk speech.

The old man said, "On this hill was once built a great fortress, in the days before even Julius came here. Old Britons lie beneath our horses' feet, men who knew the secret of the great stones. They will be sending their good wishes with us tonight."

Dusk came down suddenly like a dark cloak. From the woodlands, below the waiting Cymry, came the night-time calls of owl and badger, as though nocturnal life had now inherited the earth. Some men felt that they should not be there at such a time, intruding on a world that did not belong to them.

Artos sat silent and still, the great sword Caliburn across his knees, his heavy cloak pulled high up about his face. He stared down into the darkness, like a warrior carved from stone. Bedwyr who sat nearest him at that time saw that his lips were moving, gently and yet with the marked rhythm that might have signified a prayer, though Bedwyr had not seen his master pray before, except with wild shrieks and groans before the smoking altars of Lis Pengwern. But this was a different thing.

Medrawt sat a little way behind Artos, withdrawn into his own thoughts. He noticed with concern that the nerves of his right leg and thigh were twitching uncontrollably. It was a little unnerving to be in the vanguard, that long line of horsemen which draped itself like some grim black ribbon across the brow of the sombre hill.

Medrawt sensed the solid phalanx of cavalry behind him, the

many hundreds of the Legion. They would be sweating like himself and, at the same time, licking their dry lips, lips on which the dust of the day's long ride would still be caked. Medrawt thought, Many of them will not ride far from this mound of death. They will not see the sun set tomorrow. They will not even break their fasts. Many will never do this again, ever.

And as he thought these things, Medrawt suddenly wanted to make water. Then he knew that he was afraid, mortally afraid. It would be impossible to relieve himself, he knew, without drawing the attention of the others to his fear. He sat still, biting his fingernails and squeezing his legs tight about the great pommel of his saddle.

All his past experience had been different from this. Before, when he rode with Ambrosius, it had been the quick ambush, the sudden rush on an unsuspecting village. . . . Then it had been a matter of horses' hooves, and swords sweeping out of the sunlight, and men falling back as one charged, and one's blood racing with the sheer joy of it all, and never a thought spared to death, or even to wounds. One had no time to think of being hurt, and only discovered the scratches on one's legs afterwards, back at camp. But this waiting, above the darkening forest, was different.

Medrawt suddenly thought to himself, In God's name, why am I here? Artos will gain from this battle, not I. Why did I follow him? I should have been happier had I returned to Camulodunum when old Ambrosius betrayed me. What do I care about a new Rome!"

Bedwyr suddenly turned his horse about and came towards him through the dusk. "I wager they will flee from us like fire," he said. "Our great number will make them think that Jehovah has come out of the clouds against them. You and I will never see a blow struck, my friend!"

Medrawt wondered whether his teeth had chattered so loudly as to cause the warrior to console him thus. He ran his tongue round his parched lips and said, "Why are you afraid, Bedwyr?"

The warrior grinned in the dusk and said, "I have never gone into a battle in my life when the shirt hasn't stuck to my back.

But that goes as soon as I have killed a man. I prefer the sword, or failing that, the axe. You know you have done it, then; but with the lance you get no confidence. You can be killing them all night without knowing it, if they fall off decently, that is, without twisting sideways and causing a lot of trouble."

Medrawt hardly heard what the man was saying. He was suddenly aware that his breeches were wet and chill about his thighs. He beat upon the saddle before him with his left hand and bit his lip until he tasted the salt of blood. He could smell only death in the twilight.

"For the love of Christ leave me, Bedwyr," he said, and turned his horse away from the man.

The slope fell down into a little hollow and there, bunched together, a group of riders muttered in the chill evening breezes. They were Demetae and the eagles' feathers of their helmets fluttered above their dark bent heads. One of their number suddenly began to gesture wildly with his hands and arms, flinging himself about in the saddle, his voice rising to a shout. One of his fellows leaned over and clapped his hand over the man's mouth and silenced him. But only for a while. The man began again. "We are doomed," he said. "Let us leave. We are Demetae and not the dogs of Artos!"

Bedwyr came near Medrawt again. "I wish to God the horn would blow soon," he whispered. "Such waiting breeds fear. It is spreading along the hill. Some of the Dumnonians have already deserted."

Medrawt lowered his head, wishing he were with them. Then when the man's voice was raised again, Artos swung round in his saddle and made a sign to Bedwyr, who rode forward into the little hollow and did not stop until he came to the group of Demetae. It was now too dark for Medrawt to see exactly what happened, but Bedwyr seemed to lean towards the yelling tribesman. The voice rose suddenly to a high shriek and did not sound again, though all men about him waited for its fall.

Bedwyr rode back past Medrawt. The little knot of men in the hollow were silent. They had dismounted and were laying their burden down on the turf. A shock of terror ran the length of Medrawt's spine. He knew that the same thing would happen to him, to anyone. He began to pray that he did not shriek like that.

A curlew winging down out of the night sky over the ridge made as to alight on the turf he knew so well. At the last moment his sharp bird's eye sensed men and horses and bright weapons. He rose again, with a frightened fluttering of pinions and a gaunt scream. His cry sounded like the premonition of doom in men's ears. They began to rock in their saddles, sliding their hands along the javelin shafts for something to do, trying to remember rhymes they had learned when children. . . . The sensitive horses were tossing their heads, jingling their iron and bronze ornaments, pawing the turf with their sharp battle-shoes.

Medrawt was suddenly aware that his knuckles were gleaming like white bones on the reins. He tried to unclench his hands but found that they would not obey him. Then as he looked down the steep hillside, the thought came to him that, if he clapped spurs to his horse and galloped forward without warning, he might get down to the thick forests before anyone could stop him. Then wryly he thought that the Jutish Cantwara might not welcome him. He knew enough of them to support this view; rough, sturdy-minded men, they were, good farmers, but too handy with the whip and the branding-iron. And again, suppose his horse stumbled as he put it at the concentric lines of earthen ramparts that lay round the hill—or suppose one of the Cymry already had an arrow fitted to the string. . . .

Then, as his thoughts whirled this way and that, and his pulse thudded in the side of his head like a mad thing, a tiny light flickered below them, in the river valley; then another and another, all as small as the lights of glowworms.

And Artos was standing up in his stirrups, his great head thrown back, his throat moving, as though he were offering thanks to the God of War, or asking for a blessing before the bloody shambles began.

Bedwyr said, "They are lighting their fires below, the fools!

They are making their camp between the woods and the river, on the flat river meadows. They must be crazy!"

Medrawt said, "Then we shall trap them, friend."

Bedwyr looked at him strangely. "That is in the hand of the gods; we cannot say. But see that you strike at anything that moves on two feet! And see that you do not fall from your horse!"

Then, almost by his ear, Medrawt shuddered at the sound of the war-horn. Its high-pitched howling rose like the scream of a soul in the torment of eternal damnation. It went on and on until Medrawt was at the point of crying out for it to stop. He began to tremble in every limb now and could hardly breathe with the great surging of blood in his throat. He tore at the bronze ring about his neck. For a moment his eyes clouded and he was blind.

Then, as though he did not know himself any longer, he turned to Artos and smiled at him, drawing back his lips as far as he could. His hands had gone dry. His legs were firm again.

He was the master of his voice. "By God, Bear," he heard himself say, "they shall know what it is to outface Rome now!"

Artos did not even turn to answer him. But Medrawt heard him say, "Yes, yes, brother! They shall know! Yes, they shall know!"

Then he raised his right hand in a high and commanding gesture. The Cymry felt godhead move in their veins at that moment. Then the whole line of horse began to move forward relentlessly down the dark hill.

XXV

MEDRAWT SAT BENEATH A GAUNT HAWTHORN TREE, HOLDING A crust of bread and a pannikin of water in his hands, though he did not regard them. The morning sun beat onto his back, for the warm spell still held, and the clouds rose to great turreted heights in a blue sky. From time to time his eyes strayed to the bodies that lay here and there about him, on the fringes of the wood. He did not look at them for long, however. By now he knew well enough what a Jute was like, and one was much the same as another. They had fought well, these farmers and herdsmen, but the might of the Cymry had been too much for them.

One who lay nearest to Medrawt stared up at the morning sky, pleasantly, as though trying to weigh up what sort of day it was going to be. He seemed to have died thinking of the late barley crop, or of a new milch cow he had bought in the market last week, wondering whether he'd been cheated after all. Yet that was impossible; he must have been thinking of very different things. Medrawt noticed the broken nails of his hand, a hard-working hand that had hacked down trees from this very forest to make a place for his farm, his farm and his family, all tow-headed folk like himself, no doubt, unless he had done what so many Jutes seemed to do nowadays, and had found himself a British girl, one who was easy, who found foreigners more attractive than her own countrymen. This Jute wore a broad copper arm-ring, a crude affair that he must have beaten out himself, perhaps on a wet day when work in the fields was out of the question. Medrawt thought at first that he might take the ring, as a souvenir. Some heathenish thing, he thought. He bent over the man and looked closer at the ring. Scratched on it roughly, as though with the point of a dagger, for instance, was a cross and a fish. Medrawt knew this to be a primitive Christian sign. It did not seem right for this wild man of the woods, this invader, to wear a Christian symbol on his arm. Perhaps he had stolen it. Perhaps he had lived so long in Britain that he had forgotten Woden. Medrawt decided not to take the ring, for it might carry with it the vengeance of the Christian God. He thought for a moment about this, and then sat down again.

Cei was sitting next to him, already burnishing his helmet, which was very dented and not at all as beautiful as it had been when they first set out on their journey to the southeast. Cei looked up and said, "Eat your breakfast, Medrawt. One gets used to this sort of thing in time. It no longer interferes with the appetite. The main thing is to see that you eat, for it keeps the spirits up. A hungry horseman is no horseman at all."

Medrawt smiled at him, tolerantly now. "I eat little, friend," he said. "It is a habit I have been accustomed to since I was a child. If you had paid attention to my habits, you would have seen that I seldom eat before midday, wherever I am. But to still your mind, I will eat and drink now, to show you that my tablemates do not upset me."

He began to eat the dry crust, to prove his words. Last night, before the battle, when they were all waiting on the dark hill, Medrawt had been afraid. But once the charge had begun, his fear had left him. He now knew it to have been the fear of an unknown situation and not of the enemy. He thought back to the sudden vicious flurries between woodland and river, and recalled men coming at him with axes or crude iron swords, and himself riding at them, taking the war to them, thrusting until his arm tired and his lance splintered. Then slashing downwards, again and again, until there was no one else to kill. For no quarter was given, or asked, in that first dark battle against the invader.

"They were brave men," said Cei. "We were too many for them, that was all."

Medrawt replied, "These Cantwara have the name for being a brave folk. No one can deny them that title. But they are fools. They let us hustle them into the open, between forest and water, and there they were powerless. They should have enticed us to the woods, and there they might have held us."

Cei was polishing his helmet still, hissing like a groom over a horse, as he scrubbed at its battered surface.

"They were not prepared. Look at them, not a shirt of mail between them, and such swords and bucklers as no man ever saw since the time of Caesar! Blunt bars of iron for the one, and round boards covered with oxhide for the other. A man must be confident in his weapons or he is no soldier. I tell you, if only we could get hold of a company of these men and train them to sit a horse and hold a lance, we should be doing a very wise thing."

Medrawt said, "They have never heard of Roman ways, most of them. Would you employ such savages, then?"

Cei grinned up at him and replied, "We could teach them about Roman ways—at least, those of us who know about them—once we had won the final victory. That is the important thing, to make ourselves masters in Britain. All else will follow."

Medrawt nodded, for the man spoke sense.

"All else will follow." Medrawt saw himself for a moment leading a great company of Jutish cavalrymen, wresting back from Artos and the Western Kings his own rightful inheritance. He toyed with the thought for a while—himself as the Count of Britain, but brought to that eminence by the enemies of Britain! There was an irony about that speculation which attracted him. A *dux bellorum* whose friends were the enemy, and whose enemies were his own people!

He recalled the man with the copper arm-ring. An enemy, but a Christian. What a supreme irony it would be if the cross were brought back to Britain by those who were called "heathen." Medrawt saw himself as the Paladin of Christ, setting up the cross where it had so long been forgotten or despised when remembered.

What if both he and Christ were brought to power by the Jutes?

Then, as though a bowl of water had been flung into his face, he shuddered. A dead man lay under a bush, a Jutish warrior, the arrows thick in his chest. His hair hung over his face, hiding his features. He was an ordinary man of barn and byre, yet there was something in his crouched attitude, in the hair that fell like a waterfall over his gaunt visage that reminded Medrawt of another one, a man he had met in a ruined city. Medrawt thought of Merddin, and of the threats and promises of that fearful night. Set up the cross, and death will be your portion. Bring back the old gods, and great treasure will be your reward.

Medrawt's whole life had been one of craft, of survival in whatever circumstance presented itself. He had risen from the swarming life of the city gutters by his animal quickness, his rat-like compromise. He did not lack courage, the courage of the snake that will strike when it must, and preferably at the unsuspecting foot. He did not lack beauty, the sleek and febrile beauty of the leopard. Medrawt was a man who hated and despised poverty, who admired and envied power. To gain power and to avoid poverty, these were man's only aims, he thought. And whichever god lent his aid to such an aim was the god to follow. A man must do the best for himself, he thought, looking back at Cei.

The warrior was surveying his own grizzled reflection in the side of his helmet, well satisfied with the polish he had put upon it by his rubbing. A simple brute beast! thought Medrawt. A man of the tribes, who wanted only to serve a leader unto death, to eat and drink and collect what booty there was about, to roll in the village straw with any woman who was not positively repulsive, and to pass on the next morning without a thought of her, or of any of the many others he had taken as the will moved him, just as he would take a crust of bread or a horn-cup of mead.

Cei turned and met his gaze. "Sit down and rest," he said. "Why, you are as nervous as a cat. You'll never live through this campaign unless you learn to rest when the occasion allows it. The man who lives longest in a battle is the one who rests most between bouts!"

Medrawt replied, "How wise you are, friend Cei! I do not know what I should do without you." He sat down beside Cei, who looked hard at him, trying to decide whether or not Medrawt was making a fool of him. Although he followed Medrawt loyally, he did not like him overmuch. He went with him because Artos had commanded it, and for no other reason.

"One day I shall slit your throat, Medrawt," he said pleasantly, trying on his helmet.

Medrawt replied, "What will be, will be, friend. But I advise you to do it when I am fast asleep, for otherwise I should forget my Spartan training under Ambrosius, and might reach up and take you with me."

Cei said, "That is always a possibility when one kills a man."

So they spoke with each other, teasing in the way of men who half mean everything they say, and yet are good-tempered about life. And as they weighed each other up, under the rustling boughs, a rider suddenly broke through the undergrowth from the opposite side of the encampment and galloped shouting to the tent of Artos. Men scattered on every side of him, and then joined to follow him, to find out what news he brought that had moved him to such haste.

Cei rose. "Come," he said. "We shall be wanted."

In the tent of Artos they heard the news. The battle of Glein which they had just fought was a mere beginning, and the Jutes they had met were little more than an advance party, whose intention it had been to test the strength of the Cymry.

The messenger gasped, "They are in full force, on the Dubglas, to the north of Anderida Silva. It will be a day's hard riding, and bloody business at the end of it, if I mistake not."

"Who leads them, messenger?" asked the Bear. "One of their Jutish kinglets?"

The man smiled ruefully. "They are not the men you have just met, Artos," he said. "These are men to make a man think twice before attacking. They are not of one sort, but are a vast company of Jutes and South Saxons, berserkers, by all accounts. They are led by the old devil, Aelle. His son Cissa rides with him. Together they are a fearsome pair."

Bedwyr snorted loudly and arrogantly, blowing his long moustaches out like a badger. "Tush, tush, tush!" he said. "A hollow turnip looks like a skull to a little lad!"

The messenger turned on him furiously and opened his leather jerkin. "But this skull can bite, Brock!" he said. All men about him saw the red weal that circled his body.

"That is the mark of a whiplash," said Medrawt, thinking that the man was about to boast of a battle encounter.

The messenger nodded to him with sarcasm. "Yes, oh Great One," he said. "That much Cissa did to me as I rode past his troop, with my head covered at dawn. I was as close to them as I dared be, hoping to drive a knife into their leader. I covered my head so that I might be mistaken for one of them in the dawn light. Cissa keeps a hard discipline among his men, and when I got too close he turned and gave me this. That is Cissa, my friend, a fearsome man, I tell you."

Medrawt said, "Keep with me, messenger. If I get the chance I will have this Cissa strung up and you shall inscribe his body with your own lash."

XXVI

THE SAXONS AND THEIR ALLIES OF THE CANTWARA WERE ENCAMPED on the northern bank of the Kentwater, between two ancient Roman roads that ran southwards to the broad river. The scouting parties of the Cymry returned to say that their position was a good one, for there they could not be touched by the cavalry, since they had the forward protection of the river. Moreover, they had two good roads, one at either end of their elongated encampment, by which supplies might come to them and by which, should it be necessary, they might make their retreat to the north. Artos asked how many men they had and was told twice the number of the Legion.

He bent over the table, on which were spread maps and charts of the country. "The greater will be our honour, then," he said.

That night the Legion bivouacked on the edge of the great forest, not exposing themselves, and looked across the river at the campfires of their enemy. When the wind was in the right direction, it was possible to hear them talking, even to pick up the words of the drinking songs with which they passed the night.

Medrawt, who shared a tent with Artos now, said, "There is a confession I want to make, Artos."

The Bear looked up at him slowly, as though he had been expecting this and was not surprised. "What is it?" he said.

Medrawt answered, "I do not think that the gods denied me a sort of courage at my birth, but until the battle starts I am always afraid. Waiting makes a coward of me."

Artos sighed, as though this was not the confession he expected, or even wanted. "That is not surprising," he said tiredly. "We are all painted with the same brush, brother."

"Yes," said Medrawt earnestly, "but if I might go into action without delay, I might stave off my fear. Look, Artos, let me go quietly into the water, unknown to any of the men, and swim to the other side. I might find out something about them. I might get a sight of their leaders, and if I took a knife with me . . ."

Artos regarded him gravely. "I shall not let you out of my sight, brother," he said. "You are under my command to stay within this tent until morning."

He turned back to his maps, tracing the line of the river with his thick, lance-hardened finger.

"Do you not trust me, Artos?" asked Medrawt angrily.

The other did not reply for a while, but at last said, "I do not want to risk a single warrior before our storm breaks upon them."

Medrawt went to his pallet-bed, and lay in the darkness for a long time, wondering whether Artos really suspected his intentions. As dawn came, he lay watching the Bear, whose head was flung back and half off the rough pillow, his mouth wide open, his arms outstretched, like a sacrifice on the great stones of Sorbiodunum. Medrawt's mind was dark for a while with the thought that it would be so easy to kill Artos as he lay asleep, and then to ride his horse across the river and make his peace with Aelle and Cissa.

Then Artos woke and saw Medrawt watching him. He smiled and said, "The great captains sleep well before a battle, brother. Do you not throw off the cares of tomorrow until they come?"

Medrawt said, "I have slept all I need, Artos. I lay awake for a while to watch over you."

Artos pulled on his thick hide breeches. "That was a waste of time," he said, "though I value that love you bear me. But Bedwyr lies before the tent door. He would not have let anyone come in."

Medrawt shuddered a little at that.

Then a slave came in with food and drink, and the two men broke their fast and shortly began to decorate themselves for the battle.

No trumpets were blown to signal the attack. The Cymry had been awakened early by trusted men who went from troop to troop, shaking the riders and warning them to eat quickly and prepare themselves, for the hour of battle was at hand. Then, at a low whistle, the horsemen moved forward among the trees, mounted on reaching the edge of the forest, and galloped the last hundred yards down the slope to the swift river. Artos scarcely expected this first attempt to succeed, and so, in the vanguard of the attack, he was hardly disappointed.

Scarcely had the Cymry reached the river banks when hail upon hail of arrows fell amongst them. The enemy had been well aware of their presence, all night, it seemed, and had long awaited this attempt. Now men fell from their high saddles to left and to right. Wounded chargers reared and screamed in agony, bringing down those who pressed closely from behind. For a while the green meadows that led down to the river were a nightmare of confusion, and what had been green was soon red.

Now there was no point in attempting to keep their presence a secret, and Artos caused the retreat to be sounded.

Back in the forest, Artos made a survey of the damage that had been done in those few minutes. The levies of the Western Kings had suffered most, by chance. Among the Cymry, horses had paid a heavier penalty than men, it appeared. In all, a hundred and forty men had been lost in that short ride across the meadows.

Now Artos decided to wait until dusk and then to make the attempt again. Men tried to sleep through the afternoon, so as to be alert against this new and formidable enemy. But only a few could shake away the memory of that bloody morning and gain the relief of slumber.

As night fell, the Cymry led their horses over the green slope, and mounted only the moment before they entered the water. Once again, the Saxons were waiting, and had arranged pine flares along their side of the river bank, so that the neigh of the first horse caused a long row of lights to spring into being. This time the hail of arrows was not so deadly, for the shadow was often mistaken for the man. All the same, a landing was impossible, and the Cymry withdrew, having lost twenty men or so, and a number of valuable horses, some of which had to be poleaxed on landing, since they were irreparably lamed by arrows or stakes.

So ended the first day of Dubglas. After their easy victory at Glein, many of the Cymry felt their hearts sink within them. It was characteristic of their Celtic blood that they should be so much the prey of their emotions. Some of them went into the woods of Anderida Silva that night and did not return. Medrawt was not among them.

The second day was less eventful. Artos, knowing the feelings of the Legion, determined not to strain their loyalty too hard and so allowed them as much rest as was possible.

That evening, before the pine torches could be lit on the Saxon side, a hundred archers of the Legion crawled down to the bank and sent flight after flight of arrows into the reeds on the opposite shore. Then, under this protective barrage, two hundred picked men of all the companies swam over, their bodies naked, after vowing to kill a man each. They carried only short knives and cudgels, tipped with iron, such weapons as would be easy to carry and might be effective at close quarters, especially among an enemy taken by surprise.

All men waited anxiously to see the result of this foray. At length the Cymry saw them come back, dripping with water and laughing. This attack had been successful, they said, except for the thirty men they had left behind. The Saxons, confident after their victory the previous night, had left only a small guard among the reeds, and the barrage of arrows had effectively silenced them. The two hundred had run up the Saxon bank, like silent wolves, right into the camp, where the enemy lay about unprepared and drinking, sure of their position.

One of the Cymry assassins, a thin man from Vricon, short of an eye from a street brawl in Deva, said, "It was like robbing children. They lay helpless, most of them, some drunk, some making love. I took six of them before my cudgel broke, then I maimed four others before we came back. And every man of the Cymry did as well, Artos."

The Bear said, "You were always a liar, Cromac. I shall credit you with half that number."

The man smiled and nodded. "The Bear's eyes see through doors of iron," he said. "But I tell you it is the truth that a dozen of us got within a yard or two of Aelle, and should have brought back his head, but for that son of his! I tell you, Artos, Cissa is a great warrior with the axe. He uses it in long sweeps and a man cannot get near enough to damage him. He saved his father, I tell you."

"You must take a lance next time, Cromac," said Artos, affecting to be unimpressed; though when the man had gone, Artos said to Bedwyr, "We must vow to slay these two, Aelle and Cissa, or I can see that we shall never call southern Britain our own."

They made a vow, and Cei joined them. Medrawt made a special vow. "If I do not kill this creature Cissa," he said, "may he kill me."

Artos glared at him, for such a vow was a useless one. The good warrior's duty was to get the better of the bargain, not an equal one.

Now the good news spread through the camp of the Cymry like a forest fire, and many were the men who would gladly have rushed to the river to finish off what their scouts had begun. But Artos was wary and said that the Saxons were not notorious for forgiving an injury. To attack now would be to run into a nest of furious hornets. Instead, he doubled the night watch and even withdrew the campment a little further into the forest. That night all men had to sleep clothed and with their swords unsheathed by their sides. Many men grumbled, but they soon saw that their leader was wise.

And so, shortly before dawn, the warning horn blew urgently, and all men leapt from their beds, sword in hand. But the alarm was out of all proportion to its cause. The attacking party was a small group of berserkers who had jumped naked into the river to avenge their relatives and friends. The archers stationed at the edge of the forest picked them off as they ran up over the green meadows. Only one of them evaded the arrows and reached the fringe of the wood, where the officers were standing, the Bear in their midst. When the young Saxon rushed at him, his short dagger upraised, Bedwyr knocked him down with the haft of his great axe and then fell upon him and half throttled him until the berserk fury had gone out of him. Artos tried to question him, but the young Saxon would not talk, and when they loosed his hands, tore out his flaxen hair in great handfuls.

The Bear was curiously impressed by the youth's courage and had him dressed decently and sent down to the river bank, with the promise of a safe passage across. But the youth did not seem to understand what was being offered him. When they turned him loose, he ran, fast as a hare, zigzagging down the meadows, expecting to be shot at as he went. He stopped at the river's brink and looked back, to see the Cymry standing at the edge of the forest, laughing at him. Then he understood that they had not tried to kill him, and the humiliation was so great that he flung himself into the deepest part of the river, and without making a single stroke to save himself, was carried away from sight by the swift current.

Artos almost wept at this. He turned away and said to Cei, "That man was too good to be a Saxon. I would have given him a place among the Legion."

Cei said, "They are mostly like that, Bear. Just children. If you hurt their bodies they only laugh, until they die. But if you hurt their pride, they will suffer the torments of damnation, and will prefer to die rather than live to be laughed at."

"They are not like us," said Bedwyr cynically. "We prefer to live, whatever the circumstances, don't we, Medrawt?"

Medrawt did not answer him, but turned away.

On the third day, men woke to find the encampment of the

Legion much quieter than usual. The company of Medrawt had gone, like ghosts in the night.

Artos, in great anger, almost struck Bedwyr for sleeping when he should have been on watch. Bedwyr had no excuse, but said that he had been exhausted by two nights' watching and must have dozed off just at the moment when Medrawt had left the tent. Now men began to speak of withdrawing from the battle entirely and of finding other Saxons, elsewhere, who might be easier game. But the Bear's fury was such that no man persisted in the idea, and so during the morning the remains of the Legion began to prepare for a great attack.

Soon after midday, a strong party of Saxons crossed the river on broad rafts, which they must have dragged down to the banks on their side during the night. They were sighted soon after they had started, but though the arrows of the Cymry inflicted severe casualties on them, a large number landed and forced their way into the outskirts of the forest.

Now man met man among the low hawthorn and brambles, and the Cymry, caught away from their horses, had to learn to fight on foot again. For a time the battle was an even one, and then Artos arranged an encircling movement, cutting them off from the river. When they saw this, many of them seemed to give up heart, and dropping their axes, tried to run the gauntlet to the water's side. Only a few got through, for the Cymry struck rhythmically and with malice now.

That night Artos allowed each man who had fought that day a double ration of meat and two flagons of wine. Only the archers at the river's edge were forbidden to drink wine, though they were promised as much as they might drink the next day.

No one dared question the Bear that night, for he behaved like a madman, a quiet madman who stares before him, saying nothing, but biting his lips and sometimes clenching and unclenching his hands, as though under great stress for which there is no language.

The fourth day broke stormy and dark. It seemed that the fine sunny weather had gone from them now, to make way for winter.

Artos gathered the men together in a glade and spoke to them, gravely, saying that now they were fewer in numbers than before, but yet must get across the Dubglas that day, or die in shame. Men muttered harsh things against Medrawt then, and many there were who would have run at him with a knife had he been in that clearing under the trees.

Artos told them his plan. Generally, they were to let the horses fend for themselves as they crossed, and on landing were to mount any horse that was nearest. The men themselves were to make use of the rafts which the enemy had abandoned, but to use them in a different way. Twelve men were to stand on each raft, their long shields locked so as to provide a protecting wall in front. Behind these forward shields would kneel as many men as could find shelter. After each raft, stripped of their armour, as many men as could were to trail behind, holding each other's shoulders, and using the cover of the shields and rafts. In this way, each raft might give protection and carriage to upwards of sixty men, Artos said, and there were seven rafts. They were to have the usual covering fire from archers stationed on the river banks in the reeds. When this first striking force was across and at its work, the bulk of the Legion was to make its way over in the usual manner, without delay. They would cross without danger, he said, with a wry smile. The Cymry laughed at this, for they knew that this was a river of death, and that it would never be without danger until the last Saxon was destroyed.

Then they ran aboard, under cover of the shields. One of the rafts had some difficulty in getting out of the reeds. It followed some distance after the others. The men on the forward rafts called back at it, saying that it was built of cowardly wood and would sink if a water hen attacked it.

When the raft line was halfway over the river, the Saxon bowmen found the range of the ungainly craft. The air was filled with the sound of a myriad angry wasps, and then the enemy arrows rattled down unceasingly upon the bronze shields. Yet they did small damage, for they were tightly interlocked, in the usual manner of a shield-wall. Nevertheless, some of the forward shield-bearers were wounded about the feet or legs, and one or two men killed from those missiles which were aimed high into the air to come down beyond the shield-wall.

When the Saxons tired of trying to kill the raftmen, they turned their arrows onto the swimming horses. That day the Cymry lost many gallant beasts, who floated dying down the river, shot full with shafts.

Artos stood upright, so that all men should hear him. He cupped his hands about his mouth and yelled, "Mount immediately on landing. Charge up the slope. Your new war cry shall be, "Cymry and Holy Cross! May we meet in heaven, my friends."

Many men marvelled at this cry, for never before had Artos fought on the side of the cross. Then the rafts plunged into the reeds and the shield-wall broke up. Men leaped over each other to be first in the onslaught. For a minute or two, they struggled like enemies among the sedges, then they were mounted on the horses that had floundered after them, and were ready to charge.

As they formed into line, a great gasp went up, for suddenly, behind them, appeared an immense rainbow, shimmering in the misty air beyond the river. "An omen, an omen," some called. "We shall have victory." But one man said morosely, "Nay, lads! It's telling us we've left heaven on the other side!"

This man was the first to take an arrow in the neck as he rode up the green slope. A friend of his was by him at the time and said to him, "You were right, warrior." But the man smiled, even as he fell from his horse, and gasped, "What does it matter, I have found my place."

Those who had time to look behind found that the remaining Cymry were making the crossing unopposed, for now the Saxons held the little green hill above the river, where their camp was, and did not waste men down on the reedy shores.

Artos, Bedwyr and Cei fought knee to knee, high above the rout. Men came at them with spears and swords, but they held fast and mowed great swathes about them, laughing now with the grimness of it. Once a flaxen savage leapt past Cei and took the bridle of Artos. He swung up almost onto the horse's back, so that Artos could not shorten his sword sufficiently to run him through. The man was drunk and started to sing a song in the Bear's face as he tried to get his balance to stab the leader. Bedwyr knocked him sideways with a bronze mace and then trampled on him as he rolled on the grass. Artos said, "Thank you, friend, but I would have heard the first verse of that song."

Ahead of them, the three saw a knot of Saxons under a banner of sorts. They did not know the sign that was stitched in white on the blue ground, but they sensed that Aelle and Cissa were somewhere near it. Then Cei said, "Look, there they are, Bear!" and spurred forward, trying to be the first to reach them. Artos looked at Aelle in admiration, for he was a big man and knew how to wield an axe. He stood head and shoulders above all men there, and sang as he swung his terrible weapon, his red hair floating about his head, held only by a thin circlet of gold, for he disdained to wear a helmet. Artos wished he might have been close to that king, for he was a worthy opponent. Yet the son, Cissa, shorter, but equally strong, was a true man, too, he thought. His hair was plucked back into a rough bun, by a cord, and he worked with a curved sword, slashing up and down, up and down, and at each stroke, dealing vicious blows upon the attacking Cymry.

Once the King Aelle stopped in his axe-work and looked straight across the crowding men. He could see Artos and he shouted, "Come on, Bear! Let me take your hide with my little toy!" He began to laugh then, and began his grim work again, for his foes had pressed in while he was jesting.

Then suddenly Cei said in the ear of Artos, "It will not be easy, Bear. They are driving us down to the river step by step."

Artos said, "We shall fight then, for we can never cross it again."

And then a man of the Demetae came galloping towards them, shouting, "Withdraw, Artos! We are finished! A great troop of horse are coming from behind to reinforce them. We could not stand against them, for they ride like devils!" The man galloped on towards the river. Artos said, "Did you note that man's face, Cei? He shall hang tonight."

Bedwyr said, "If he speaks truth, we shall not be there to hang him."

And then they saw the Saxons on the hillock suddenly turn, and seem to melt away, crumbling like an old wall in a high wind. Aelle himself, left standing, looked up to see a warrior on a great white horse towering above him, lance at the level. He swung his axe, but the lance took him in the breast, and he was half lifted off his feet with the shock of the thrust. Medrawt smiled across at Artos and called, "Cymry! The Bear and the Cymry!"

Artos stared at the man, and at the many other horsemen who now swept onwards to greet their comrades of the first company.

"Medrawt did not desert us, Bedwyr!" he said. "By the gods, he came from behind them and scythed them away like dry grass!"

Bedwyr and Cei looked at each other, and rubbed their noses, wondering what to say. They had not expected ever to see that man again, certainly not as a friend.

Bedwyr said at last, "We did not need him. We should have conquered them in a little while."

Artos answered and said, "Better now than in a little while, friend. For in a little while, more of our comrades would have died too."

He rode to Medrawt and the two warriors clasped each other like brothers, but now brothers who loved each other dearly.

So ended the four days of Dubglas. Out of the Saxon host of two thousand, not more than five hundred survived, and they mostly old men or those too young for battle. Those who could, fled from the field. Artos would gladly have gone back across the river then, but Medrawt begged to be allowed to pursue the fugitives. Artos could not refuse him, after his work that day. So Medrawt rode on with half of his troop, and Artos saw to it that Aelle was buried as befitted his great courage. "I wish his son lay with him, though," said Cei.

XXVII

THE ESCAPING SAXONS KEPT TOGETHER AS WELL AS THEY MIGHT, taking the road westwards along the river bank. It was easier for men on foot than for cavalry and so for a while the fugitives made good ground. Here and there, the Cymry came upon exhausted runners, who gasped in the reeds, wide-eyed and waiting for death. Medrawt spared none of them, though his followers would have done so. When the sun was setting ahead of them, many of the riders hoped that they would be called off from this cruel chase, but Medrawt's face was grim. For the first time, he would force his will on friend and foe alike. Men began to hate him that day.

At length, the straggling fugitives reached the hill near where the river rose. Behind it lay deep woodlands. Some fear kept them from entering these woods. Instead, they took an old Roman road that ran towards the south, hoping perhaps to join their friends. When he saw this movement, Medrawt smiled grimly and shouted, "Ride now, Cymry, for the kill is at hand!" He set spurs to his horse, knowing that now they would make good speed on the metalled road.

The Cymry overtook the enemy on the outskirts of an ancient and decaying village, built by earlier Jutish settlers and now long abandoned. It lay in the shadow of a great tumulus that towered, humped and black in the fading light. It seemed a place of evil omen, a place of sad ghosts.

The Saxons now tried to form a pathetic shield-wall, snatching up anything that might serve as a shield, for they had cast away their round wooden bucklers in their flight. Now old boards, pieces of any sort of wood or stone, branches of trees must serve them. The Cymry rode among the tumbledown thatched huts, striking down with bad grace at old men and boys who had nothing better to fight back with than sticks or rusted iron chains.

One of the Cymry sneered, "The Battle of Bassas! I would have stayed at Caer Leon rather than share this glory!" He rode on, making a great show of striking at the enemy, but always using the flat of his sword so as to do no harm.

Yet at last it was over. The Saxons could stand no longer, and now they waited like patient beasts in a slaughter house, for the death which they knew must be inevitable.

Medrawt rode up to survey them as they clustered in the village compound. He smiled down at them darkly and then said, "Let ten among you step forward and offer themselves for punishment. The rest shall go free."

There was a movement everywhere at these words. The Saxons, old men and young, stepped forward, not one wishing to be beholden to another for his safety. Then the Cymry would have set them free, but Medrawt merely smiled and chose ten of the youngest and strongest-looking of the enemy. He made the others stand round them in a hollow square, so that they should always remember what happened to those who stood out against Rome.

Soon a great cry of horror swept up over the village. The ten blinded men staggered about, clutching their bleeding faces. Medrawt watched them intently. "Now make them walk across the square," he commanded. "And let those who walk straight be given the needles again."

He turned away then, and listened for the renewed cries that must greet this torment. The warrior who had been compelled to carry out the blinding wept to see the damage his hands had wrought. When those who walked straight were brought back to him, he only made a pretence of blinding them again. Yet his movements were so convincing that Medrawt was deceived, even he, whose own eyes were like those of a questing hawk.

And at length, those of the Saxons who could, walked over the dark hill, cursing Medrawt and the Cymry. Among them was Cissa, who had slashed off his long hair with a hunting-knife, even while he was running, and had torn his fine tunic so that it had looked like a beggar's garment. He had rubbed mud onto his face in the few minutes of respite before they were cornered in the village, and so no one had recognised him. He had stepped forward with the rest, being a brave man, but had had the good fortune not to be chosen when Medrawt selected his victims.

At the brow of the dark hill of the tumulus, Cissa looked down and smiled a wicked smile. "Woden bring you into my hands, O Medrawt the Black," he said, "and may I never reach Valhalla if I let you walk like a human man again!"

As he spoke, a black crow swept low over his head, and the dying sun lit up the man's shape as with fire. It was as though Woden had heard him, and those about him drew away, and made the finger-sign against all evil spirits, they were so afraid of him. Cissa seemed different from other men in that moment.

XXVIII

THE VICTORIOUS ARMY TOOK THE ROAD THAT LAY ALONG THE COAST, towards Venta Belgarum, on their way homewards. Artos ordered this, though many men had wanted to return to Londinium first, for there one might still find taverns and women and entertainment. But Artos set his face grimly and said with contempt, "No doubt they are lining the roads into Londinium now, expecting us, the coward dogs! They would not march with us before the battle and they shall not enjoy our spoils after the battle. I would see Londinium sacked and gutted before I would raise a finger to save her. She has made her bed and she must lie on it now."

Towards Medrawt, he was just as stern for a while. He had not approved of the massacre at the place of the tumulus. He said openly that he would have withdrawn and have left the survivors to make their way to their boats, if they had any. They were brave men and should be respected. Medrawt had reported that Saxons were not as other men; they were brave as a viper is brave, by nature, and that sort of bravery should be crushed under the heel, as a viper's is. Artos had turned away from him with an angry grunt, but had not replied. Later he told Bedwyr, "I have never forgotten an injury, or a service, friend. Medrawt acted like a devil to the Saxon, but yet he saved my life. A man must forget the little evil because of the greater good." And as the day wore on, he indicated that he wished Medrawt to ride with him at the head of the long columns again, and spoke and laughed with him as he had become used to doing by now. Medrawt smiled, in his enigmatic way, and took this change in the Bear's attitude as philosophically as he took most things now. The time would come, then he would have to bear no man's changes of moods, he consoled himself.

The numbers of the army had increased greatly since the battles, in spite of the losses sustained by the Cymry. True, they had taken no prisoners, as Artos had ordered, but as the army had made its way through Anderida Silva southwards, hundreds of foreigners, mainly Jutes, had come forward from among the trees and had given up their swords with the request that they be allowed to join the Cymry. One young Jutish princeling, Bethlac, had ridden especially to Medrawt and had offered himself and his hundred picked warriors. They were landless men, not like the older Jutes who had long been settled in the southeast. And that meant that they were anxious to prove themselves, to make a home for themselves, to do which they were free of any ties of race or family.

Medrawt had spoken long with Artos about this, and had said, "A month ago, I should have shot them full of arrows, as dogs and carrion. But I have seen how they can fight, these Jutes. I have seen how loyal they can be when once they have pledged their word. What does it matter to us how we regain Britain, with what fighting men, as long as our task is accomplished?"

Artos replied, "You were once the Roman and I the barbarian, yet now it seems that the tables are turning, my friend! Yet I agree with you, provided we watch these dogs. Let us take them, but offer them nothing yet, only death and torment if they so much as break their word by a syllable."

Medrawt had these words translated to the wide-eyed Jutes. They nodded their heads solemnly, and fell into line with the Cymry without another word. Bethlac attached himself to Medrawt and would not leave him. At the first stop, he went forward and kneeled before the Roman, taking his hands in his own. "I am your man," he said simply. "May the crows build their nests in my skull and the wolves of the forest crunch my foot-bones if I betray you."

Medrawt was touched by this primitive oath and saw to it that Bethlac was given a horse so that he could ride with him at the head of the column. Cei sniffed at this, and pretended he could not stand the smell of a Jute. He rode on the other side of Medrawt, and never looked towards Bethlac without nipping his nostrils together with thumb and forefinger. But the jest grew thin before long, and as Cei came to understand the young man's courage and to appreciate his princely bearing and horsemanship, he ceased to sneer at him, and even came at last to ride with him, knee to knee.

Beyond Venta Belgarum, the road west was crowded with fugitives, who had heard the news that a great army was approaching and had expected it to be a Saxon force, as usual. There were no young men left in the town now, and so on the road the Cymry saw only the old and diseased, or the women with their tired children, carrying bundles on their backs, or pushing what they could salvage from their deserted homes on crude carts. One old man dragged a rude sledge behind him along the dusty road. He was crippled with rheumatism and near-blind with cataract. As the horsemen clattered up, he did not run away into the rough heath and woodland that lined the road, as the others had done, but stumbled doggedly on, his head almost on his breast, his thin arms knotted with the effort of dragging a weight too heavy for him.

Bedwyr drew level with him and said, "Run fast, grandad, we

are terrible Saxons and will cut off your ears and feed them to our pet wolves."

The old man nodded and said, without raising his head, "Yes, I know you will, you brutes. I have heard all about it. But you cannot sing in your halls that I ran away from you. I have sworn to travel along this road, and travel I shall, though you hack my legs from beneath me. Think on that, Saxon." And he trudged on, sweating with exhaustion.

Bedwyr fell silent with shame at this. But Cei was always ready to jest without embarrassment and rode to the old man.

"What have you on your sledge that makes it so heavy, grandad?" he asked. "Is it gold and great goblets of silver?"

The old man sighed deeply and said, "Such gold as I would defend with my life, sea-wolf, if I were young enough to bring a sword to you."

Cei laughed and turned over the rough sacking covers with the point of his lance. On the sledge lay the bodies of an old woman, a girl and a brindled farm dog. They lay as though in their bed asleep. The old man was rescuing what was left of his family.

Cei fell back into the column, his face no longer smiling. Medrawt said, "The old man will kill himself before he has gone many miles farther, then they will all be together, Cei."

Cei said, "Pray God, I still have such courage when I am that old man's age."

But Bedwyr flicked him carelessly with his whip and said, "Have no fear, Cei long-nose, you will never live that long! Your raven is croaking already at Caerwent."

He did not know why he said this, but the words seemed to come unbidden. When he had said them he was troubled, for he had seen the little shadow pass across the face of his friend. When he rode close to him later and tried to tell him the words meant nothing, Cei turned away, his jaws clamped tight. "The gods spoke through your mouth, brother," he said. "I wish for nothing more."

Still further along the white road, the leaders saw a small party of men, four carrying a litter and two boxes on their shoulders.

The litter-bearers constantly looked back in fear, and as the cavalcade drew near, flung down their burden and took to the woods. The two carrying boxes stared about them, startled for a moment, and then followed their companions, still carrying their loads as though they might be too precious to fling away.

As Artos approached, he saw that the handles of the litter were of heavy silver-gilt and the hangings of cloth-of-gold edged with crimson silk tasselling. As he wondered who might be therein, the curtains parted and a woman looked out at him, smiling ruefully.

"I told the fools not to run away," she said, in a rich contralto voice which carried in it the accents of the Eastern Empire. "I could see that you were British. But the stupid asses were frightened out of their wits and would not stay."

She was a woman of almost thirty, Artos judged—his own age—and more beautiful than any other he had ever seen. More beautiful than Gwynhwyfar, even, he had to admit. As he thought of his dear wife, and of their son, Anir, he felt a great wave of yearning sweep into his heart.

The woman was rising from the ground and standing up now. Her limbs were as lovely as her face, her skin a light golden brown, as though it had known much warmer suns. Her black hair was coiffed with silver filigree and pearls. A great emerald shone at her throat, holding together the folds of her purple woollen gown.

She stood at his stirrup now and said, "Artorius Ursus, is it not?" The Roman name puzzled him for a time, but he understood and nodded wryly. "Men usually call me something else," he said. "But I am quite prepared to answer to that title, if you give it."

Her great brown eyes smiled up at him, a little impudently. "I, too, have heard some of the titles men give you," she said. "But I thought that it would be inappropriate to greet you with any of the current ones! I am Lystra, a citizen, but born in Byzantium. I have been staying with a friend, a municipal officer and a merchant of Londinium."

"You are off your track, madam," said Medrawt drily.

She turned and regarded him with interest. He looked well, sitting upright on his black horse, his Roman helmet on his saddle before him, the wind tossing the black ringlets of his long hair.

"Yes," she said simply, "I had the misfortune to employ rogues who did not know the way to the west. And now they have robbed me, I fear."

Cei rode up, closely followed by Bedwyr. Each man bore a box on the saddle. Artos said, "Your bearers did not get far with their loot, lady." He turned to the men and said, "Where are they?"

Bedwyr slapped his sword lightly. "Who knows to what heaven a baggage-carrier goes?" he said. Artos shrugged his shoulders and said, "We journey to the west, to Caerwent. You may travel with us for safety if you choose."

Lystra smiled graciously and with a slight wink said, "Do you often save women in distress, Artorius Ursus?"

The Bear smiled grimly. "It seems my function to distress them, rather than to protect them when they are distressed," he said.

"One must always make a start," said Lystra, getting back into the litter. She smiled at Medrawt as he called for four of the Jutes to come forward and take it up. He was much more handsome than the Bear, she thought. But would the fates bring him so noble a place in the land? Lystra was tired of fending for herself now and was seeking a more comfortable and lucrative life than the world had allowed her to that date. True, she had some riches, in that litter and those chests, but if the news spread that she had stolen them from the house of the merchant in the general panic that had followed the visit of Artos to Londinium on his way south, the municipal authorities would brand her on the breast, at least; perhaps crucify her. And in either case that would be the end of her hopes as a great lady.

The cavalcade pressed on towards Sorbiodunum. Lystra looked out from time to time, to smile at Artos, or, if he were not looking in her direction, at Medrawt. One or the other—did it matter which?

XXIX

THE CYMRY WERE TREATED WELL IN THE OLD CITY, THOUGH THE elders shook their heads with dismay when they saw the great number of the army, now over a thousand in strength, and wondered whether this act of hospitality might not bankrupt their treasure chests forever. The taxes must be increased forthwith, they decided; and in the same breath they wondered whether it might not be easier merely to commit suicide when the Cymry had passed on towards Caerwent. That was the old Roman military custom, for the commander to fall on his sword after a defeat, and what was this but a defeat, though a celebration of a victory, in a land which was now groaning in its beggary?

Yet they need not have feared. Artos gave orders that no man was to eat that night. A fast was declared, as an act of penance to whatever god it was that had given them such good fortune at the beginning of their great adventure. The men accepted the order impassively, as they had learned to do with Artos by now, though some of the Jutes were a little bewildered, for they had no victory to celebrate, they told their tribal leaders. What should they do? The leaders scratched their ears and said slyly, "You are Cymry now, and have gained a victory by proxy. But at the moment when the victory was gained, you were Jutes. Therefore, you must eat, for a defeated people does not know where the next meal is to come from, and they must always be prepared."

Some of the young Jutes foraged afar that night. They fell on lonely farms and took what they needed, but they killed no one. The next day many of them were severely whipped, even by those leaders who had told them to eat. They did not complain, for they knew that the leaders must do what they must do, and there was no saying more.

But Artos kept to his own decree. And after he had seen that his personal comitatus was well billeted, he rode out away from the ancient citadel, to the still more ancient circle of stones that brooded over the undulating plain, Stonehenge. The place of sacrifices to those who had followed the old religion.

He had never before been there, though always, since his earliest childhood, he had heard men speak of the stones as something which one should see before one died. In his mind, they were more than mere stones; they were the evidence of the old gods, their home, their memorial. He had thought they must be very high, like the pyramids of Egypt, as men had described them to him. Yet he was almost upon them, in the falling light, before he recognised their presence.

They crouched, rather than stood upright, on the plain, and Artos reined in his horse, feeling faintly disappointed. Yet as he rode down to them, he saw again the heavy magnificence of their setting. They had stood on that spot forever, and no man remembered them being any different from what they were as he gazed at them. For four hundred years the Romans had marched past them, staring at them as he did now; yet they had not fallen down before Roman gaze, Roman might, Roman gods. . . . They were as new and as old as they ever were, as they ever would be; the indestructible heart of Britain, he thought.

Artos tethered his stallion to a stout hawthorn that grew a little way from the stones, and went to them on foot, as was fitting, humbly. He passed through the centre ring and stood by the great stone of sacrifice. There he kneeled, as men did in the Christian churches, and tried to think of a prayer to say to the gods who had helped him in the Sussex Weald; but no prayer came to him, only a filthy marching song. He shook his head, impatiently, and tried to pray again, yet he knew that it would be impossible.

"Caesar was a gentleman
Of eminent renown;
He set his boys
Before the joys
Of his Imperial Crown."

The stupid ditty kept coming back, with all its drunken verses, and would not let the true feeling of gratitude break through. Yet this was not how he should feel before the great stones, the temple which his father, and all the old chieftains he had ever known, had respected with all their blood and bones and sinews. . . .

To Artos, it suddenly seemed that this conflict of his own was a reflection of a far greater conflict; perhaps the gods themselves were fighting here, and the lewdest winning. He wondered whether, if he had the courage to make the sign of the Christian cross, this conflict would vanish and he would be able to pray?

Above him the curlews cried, in their timeless cracked voices. They seemed like the souls of all lost men, the men who had ended their little lives on this very stone. Artos the Bear shuddered.

Then he heard his charger snort and begin to stamp his feet, a thing he did only when danger approached. But Artos turned to him and called out impatiently for him to be still. The stallion had seen what the great leader could not see in the darkness, a black cloaked form that had run swiftly behind one of the stones, not five yards from Artos the Bear.

Artos kneeled again, and pressed his bare head hard against the cruel stone, chafing the skin of his forehead so that the silly song would go away and leave him free to give thanks. He was deep in concentration at this thing, when someone stood beside him. He heard nothing, but suddenly his beast-keen nostrils caught a whiff of perfume, the thick and oily scent that women of the towns sometimes wore, the rich ones whose husbands had connections in the Middle Sea. Artos looked up with a start to see a pale face smiling down at him. He rose and clasped the woman, peering close into her hood. It was Lystra. She shuddered perceptibly as the man's strong hands pressed into her arms.

"They said you were mighty, Artorius," she whispered, "but I had no idea what that meant until now."

Artos held her as a boy might hold a rag doll, staring ahead and wondering what he might do with it, to break it, for suddenly he had remembered what this stone was for.

Something of the same had evidently come into the mind of the woman who shivered in his grasp, for Lystra said, "Artorius, I came down here to see the famous stones, not to lie on them as a sacrifice!"

Artos shuddered himself now as though his dream was coming true. He gave a strange groan and flung the woman onto the flat stone that lay before him. He was desperately powerful and she could do nothing to prevent him. As she lay there, the moon swinging up before her eyes, and this strange man above her, his face white and his breath sobbing in his chest, she began to laugh softly, out of terror, out of expectation of death, of mutilation. She did not know why she laughed, or what his moaning meant then.

And Artos the Bear, Count of Britain, *dux bellorum* of the Kings of the West, stared across her in his new madness, not knowing what he meant, feeling at one time for a knife, at another for the thong lacings of his garments. Like a man drugged or drunk, a man damned or on his way to heaven, Artos the Bear enjoyed her as she lay sobbing in fear under the great stones that had been there forever and would never fall.

A curlew croaked out his song of despair and a lone owl hooted with ecstasy at a mouse. The night wind sighed across the empty spaces of the plain. The moon grinned blandly, sadly, madly down at the life, death, birth and coupling of mankind, impartially, on palace and stinking slum, on ice and desert place, on lamb and leopard.

Then Artos rose from the stone, his limbs quivering. He passed his gaunt hand over his calloused brow, feeling the old scars anew. Now he was a man bewitched in the dead moonlight. At length the woman dressed in black moved and got down from the sacrificial stone. She did not look at him, but her shoulders quivered just as his did.

So they stood for a while, as the night birds cried and the great stallion made strange inarticulate requests in the darkness.

And at last Artos said hoarsely, "So be it. Woman, it was written that we should come together. I feel that it was written before my seed was sown."

Lystra was too overwhelmed to say anything. She felt chilled to the bone from that cold stone and had wondered from time to time why Artos had not come to her in her billets, where there was a bed of soft sheepskin.

Now he took her by the wrists and said, "Woman, whoever you have called yourself, you are now the Thing of Artos. Are you content?"

Lystra said, "Yes, Artos. I know what it must have been like in the old days now, on the stones."

He shook her until she could have cried out in pain. "Then it was a knife that entered, you fool!" he said savagely. "Take care, the old days might come back."

Lystra was subdued. She said, "The Saxons call this 'hand-fasting.' It is a form of marriage in law. Are you suggesting that to me?"

The Bear said, "I will kill the man who next uses your body, woman. Is that enough? What marriage in the church would require a man to make that vow?"

And Lystra said softly, "I am content, Artos."

Then he walked away from her to his stallion. He mounted the great beast, which snorted at the vicious wound of his spurs. The birds still shrieked about the place of death. The woman walked behind the horse, her head bowed, through the gates of Sorbiodunum.

In the morning Artos announced his hand-fast marriage to the Cymry, and no man spoke out of place, except one old warrior from above Lis Pengwern.

"When Gwenhwyfar gets to hear of this, there'll be trouble," he said.

The one standing next to him said, "They say he is making this one dye her hair gold, and is rechristening her Gwenhwyfar."

Those round about laughed, but it was true. Only Medrawt thought the marriage amiss, but he told his feelings to no other.

XXX

THE NEWS OF THE VICTORIES HAD ALREADY BEEN RECEIVED IN CAERwent. The Western Kings were delighted, they said, and had arranged feasts to celebrate the glad tidings. But after a brief description of the battles, Artos told them that he was tired from his journey, and would go on as soon as possible to Caer Leon upon the River Usk.

Cunneglassus wheezed, "Caer Leon! Good God, Artos, that place has been neglected for two hundred years. You'll die of cold, my friend!"

But Artos looked straight through him and said again, "I go to Caer Leon upon Usk, King. When you wish to dissuade me, find yourself another captain, and Britain another Count."

With that he turned and went from the room. Lystra was waiting for him in his tent and she said, "You are a hero, Artos. I am amazed that you let these little kinglets tell you what to do."

He rolled into the warm bed. "I don't," he said. "I am the Bear of Britain, whatever they are in their little principalities. The country is more than the county, my dear."

And then he forgot the whole affair, and remembered only the new Gwenhwyfar who lay with him, but a more magic one than the one he had known before, so many years before, the one who was too much like himself to give him that excitement he now found.

So it was that Artos the Bear set up his capital at Caer Leon upon Usk. And no one dared say "Nay" to him at that time.

This Caer Leon, the Fort of the Legions, sometimes called "Isca Legionis," had been set up after Caratacus had gone from Siluria to find friends among the more northerly tribes. The Second Legion had made their home there, and had stayed, gradually becoming less Roman and more British as the years had gone on, for three hundred years. It was a good town, set upon a little hill, with the greater hills of Gwynnedd rising behind it to the west. The River Usk flowed at its foot, and a bridge gave access to the greater River Sabrina. Caer Leon had a fortress on the summit of its hill, with barracks and a parade ground. It had wells from which the sweet water of the western mountains flowed. It had a civilian city without its military walls, of colonnaded shops and long-gardened villas. It had bathhouses and cemeteries, brick kilns and barns.

And, more than all these amenities, it had a theatre, an amphitheatre or circus, a bull-ring, or what one willed. This lay beyond the walls of the military citadel, or the civilian city, down the hill, towards the quiet Usk. Indeed, as Artos sat in his flat barge, coming from Caerwent, he saw that amphitheatre past the wharf and up a green hill, its walls still firm and erect, and he said to Bedwyr, who never left him, "My brother, I may be wrong in demanding this place from the Kings of the West, but I tell you that there is not a man of the Cymry, nay, or the Jutes, who will deny themselves this theatre!"

Lystra, who sat near Artos said, "My lord, I have been all my years in places of entertainment. I know what it is like to come to a new theatre, one which is not warmed by the friendship of a past appearance."

"What troubles you, my wife?" said Artos the Bear, now grown tender in the last weeks.

"Only this," said Lystra, "that if I were a gladiator, coming in a barge, as they must have done up this quiet river, I should be prepared for death, of course, that is understood. But I should not be prepared for death in this green countryside. There is something more awful in this looking over a field or two, and seeing the walls of the arena, than in straying past the fetid dens of lions as one went to death in Rome."

Bedwyr looked at her in scorn. He had not been to Rome. "But, lady," he said, using the formal term, since Lystra was now, in effect, a queen. "Lady, surely a man would rather die among green hills than among the stenches of the Roman bestiaries?"

Cei, who was a Silurian by extraction and more practical, said, "I think my lady is right. I would rather die in the dust of battle, with thirst in my throat, and a harsh mail vest chafing my side till it bled, than among a green and prosperous-seeming countryside. If I heard a cow lowing to be milked as my enemy came at me, I do declare, I would throw my sword away and ask him to wait awhile."

Artos gave Cei such a back-handed buffet as almost knocked him out of the barge into the Usk. Medrawt did not join in the joke. He looked hard at Lystra instead, for he could not see why this treasure of the Byzantine dance floors should ever stray so far from her proper habitat.

Yet the dream of Artos materialised, in a way. He took Caer Leon as his home, his citadel. And masons came and put the tiles back on the roofs of villas and barrack blocks. Other workmen came and cleared the soil and dung and rotted metal from the amphitheatre.

And at last Caer Leon upon Usk became a splendid place again, almost as it had been in the last years of its occupation. For instance, the roofs of certain buildings were found on scrubbing to be of lead and not mere wood or tiles. And later, a dome was discovered which glinted with solid gold, when it was cleaned.

Artos, who had never known such luxury, was enraptured. He dragged Lystra about with him from place to place, showing her this and that, pointing out, to the amusement of the masons, why that building should be restored, that neglected, until the girl did not know whether she had married a warrior or a maniac. Only Medrawt held his peace and waited, for he had received a most secret message from Aurelius, King of Dumnonia. The instruction was that Medrawt should dispose of the man who brought the message. Medrawt gave the job to Bethlac, the Jute, who took the creature to the guest house, gave him a long drink of heather-ale, and then eased a slim hunting-knife under his ribs, quietly, talking about the weather in the west all the time.

But Artos was happy, creating his new city. He said that it would be known as the Queen of the West in future times. Lystra observed that the important thing was what it should be known as now! Artos smiled and agreed that she was practical. Then he went to the soldiers' barracks and struck Bedwyr in the mouth for smiling at him. After that he told Cei that he should look after the horses of his company more efficiently—though the horses were three fields away and never seen by Artos. He told Cei to parade, with his whole company, at dawn, and stand at attention there until midday. He said, as an afterthought, that Medrawt would see that they did it.

Medrawt, told by Cei later, did not relish the prospect, and dismissed the company an hour after dawn. Yet before he could get back to his billet, a young warrior of the Cymry galloped up and saluted.

"Greetings, Medrawt," he said, raising his right hand in the orthodox Roman manner. "My commander requests your presence without delay."

Medrawt did not like the dark smile about the youth's lips. "You have not shaved today, my man," he said. "A Roman shaves every day, whatever the situation."

The youth had risen late and had been sent on this errand while the sleep was yet in his eyes. He was in the wrong. He lowered his head, not much, but enough for the sensitive Medrawt to see the movement. Medrawt smiled at the fellow. "Go back," he said, "and shave, and then bring the orders of the Bear to me, and not till then."

The horseman saluted him, much abashed, and rode back to his barracks, searching for a comrade who had a razor.

Medrawt woke Bethlac. "My friend," he said, "ride now to Caerwent. Tell Aurelius, my brother, to stand fast. Tell him to send a hundred horsemen to Caer Leon without any delay. My life may hang on it. Tell him, they can be termed a hunting party. But they must carry weapons for war. Now, go, without another word."

Bethlac galloped off through the gates, and Medrawt put on a bright garment, so as to reflect the spirit of the new day's sunshine.

At length he went to the villa where Artos lived. No man prevented his entrance. Artos lay in bed with Lystra beside him, drinking a cup of wine, his night-shift fallen from his shoulders to show the scars that wealed his chest. He greeted Medrawt cheerfully. "Why, brother," he said, "we had given you up! We expected you half an hour ago."

Medrawt looked at them both, undecidedly. He thought Lystra winked at him, but he could not be sure.

"What is your will, Bear?" he said, as meekly as he could manage.

Artos said, "Look, Medrawt, we must reorganise, brother. We must use these old buildings to the best advantage, you know. I see there are whole blocks given to one detachment, with an officer in charge of each body of men. His quarters are situated at the end of the corridor. Now, I know we are not leading foot soldiers, as they were when the buildings were designed, but I do think that our cavalry could be made to toe the line. If you were to get Cei to help you to choose sergeants of horse, who would sleep in those quarters to overlook their company of horse . . ."

The voice of Artos went on, and just outside the gates a hundred horsemen from Caerwent fidgetted in the morning cold. Medrawt shivered at last and smiled. "Artos, brother," he said, looking quizzically at the cut in his wrist, "do you realise that I have not breakfasted yet? And do you realise that it is a very cold morning? In fact the roof of the quartermaster's stores is white with frost."

Artos stared at him in amazement. He said, "But, Medrawt, you are shivering. Come into this bed, for I am ready to rise and inspect the new building. Come, I order you, it is warm here. Gwenhwyfar must get up, too, and see to her kitchen-maids, or whatever it is they are called."

He rose and shortly went from the room. They heard his stallion's hooves clattering away to a far part of the citadel. Medrawt lay beside Lystra, and smiled. "It is your husband's orders, lady," he said. "And who would cross him?"

Lystra said, "You talk too much, Medrawt."

Outside, the Caerwent cavalry blew upon their frozen fingers.

XXXI

THE MONTHS THAT FOLLOWED HAD SOMETHING OF THE SUBTLE QUALity of a nightmare for Medrawt. Always he felt that he was on the verge of something else, never the thing that appeared before his eyes, or sounded in his ears, the thing of the waking world, but some other emanation, something almost ineffable, beyond these tangible evidences of reality. For instance, although Artos seemed to love his new wife dearly, to have forgotten about his other woman, the first Gwenhwyfar, yet there was a sort of carelessness in his treatment of her that did not relate itself to his love. He would, for example, leave her with Medrawt for a day at a stretch, in circumstances which might be conducive to their love-making, were they so inclined. Medrawt did not understand it. He would not have left a woman such as this within reach of any man, friend or not. At last he spoke to Bethlac about it, since he was never sure of Cei's loyalty.

The Jute said, "I have observed it, Master. It seemed strange even to me, a savage, as you would say! Do you think that the Bear is trying to trick you into seducing the woman, so that he can be revenged on you both?"

Medrawt said, smiling, "I do not think that Artos is as simple as that. Besides, he values this woman too much to risk her. And he would not wish to be revenged on such a creature, who is, after all quite an acquisition to him. He would never find a more beautiful wife in the whole of Britain."

This troubled him for a while, until at last the idea came to him that Artos either loved him dearly and trusted him even with the woman who was more lovely than any other, or that in some primitive way, Artos was expiating some sin of love himself, tormenting himself as a necessary punishment.

Yet the Bear gave no outward sign that his love was a troubled one. He had had Lystra's hair dyed golden, and always addressed her as Gwenhwyfar when they were together. She only knew that this meant "the fair-haired one," and no one told her any more. Her only comment was that it meant more work for her, since the roots of her hair always showed dark when her long tresses had grown, and that meant she had to dye them again, until at last her hair was so light that no one, not even the wheezing old merchant of Londinium, who had of course known her intimately, would have recognised her. That is, but for a small mole which she had at the base of the spine, a tiny birthmark. This was what had first attracted her to him, the old man had said, when he saw her dancing in a tavern near Verulam.

Lystra felt secure at last, after all her wanderings, and was at first determined not to prejudice this new state by having any dealings with Medrawt. She smiled at him in a friendly fashion, and sometimes bathed with him near the bridge over the Usk, where the river swung round and there was a sheltered spot among the willows that came down to the slow water's edge. Sometimes she commanded him to dry her body after their swim, as though he were a slave-girl. But as he did this, she always stared away from him, and though she was teasing him, she would have resisted any acts of tenderness he had offered. Besides, whenever she went on these excursions, she always told Artos about them, and asked whether he would join them. Artos said, "I am no swimmer, Gwenhwyfar. Swimming is for fishes. I am a man. But go you and see that my brother Medrawt does not drown. There will be work for him to do in Britain before long, I feel."

XXXII

ARTOS SAT IN HIS GILDED CHAIR, DRESSED NOW IN A PURPLE VESTMENT that hung about him richly, like the robes of an emperor. At his sandalled feet lay a little greyhound, its neck encircled by a narrow golden collar. A young man smoothed the Count's hair, which he had now allowed to grow longer again, rubbing his scalp gently with heavy-scented unguents. A slave-girl knelt beneath the heavily embroidered wall hangings, drawing her fingers with slow rhythmic movements across the strings of a harp.

Artos stared at her thick-red gold hair, which hung glistening to her waist. He admired the slim beauty of the arms, the long sensitive fingers, the full and ivory whiteness of the naked breasts. The dark gold rings and armbands which he had given her seemed part of her colouring. The great emerald which gleamed between her breasts matched the colour of her eyes. The other slaves knew her as the Count's favourite, but mocked at her vanity once her back was turned. She was little more than an ignorant Irish savage, they said, who could hardly speak coherently. Artos, who was not concerned with elevated conversation in this instance, did not notice this deficiency, in the general richness of her equipment. But this day there seemed to be something different, something wrong.

Artos said, "What ails you, woman? Your face is pale; your fingers are heavy on the string this morning."

The slave-girl's hand stopped in mid-air. The little harp sank lower, onto her crossed legs. She faced the Count and smiled slowly. Her eyelids fell.

"I am a woman, Master," she said.

The youth who tended the Count's hair sniggered foolishly. Artos turned on him a sudden look which cut like a knife to his heart and silenced him.

Then Artos said, "What is amiss with you, woman? Are you sick from eating unripe apples? Speak out."

The slave-girl raised her green eyes until she stared back into those of Artos, directly and without fear. "I am with child, Master," she said.

Artos looked back at her for a moment. She shrank back from what she saw in his eyes.

"Whose child is it, woman?" he asked in a low voice.

After a while the woman said, "It is yours, Master. There has been no other."

The Bear of Britain struck one hand into the palm of the other, slowly, rhythmically, as though beating time to his marching thoughts. At last he said, "You are unfortunate, girl, either that or a fool. Are there no wise women in this place?"

Now the slave let fall the harp onto the mosaic of the floor and began to weep, covering her pale face with her heavily ringed hands.

Artos said, "Though the seed is sown, the harvest must not grow. There is only one child who shall come after me. There must be no other to contest his greatness."

The slave-girl rose and quickly crossed the room. She flung herself before him, clasping his feet, imploring wordlessly, her eyes filled with tears.

Artos turned from her with contempt. To the youth who combed his hair he said, "Take her. She is yours. See that the child does not live or you shall be tied together and flung into the Usk. Is it understood?"

The young man bowed his head before Artos. "It is understood, Master," he said, rejoicing secretly that this proud Irishwoman, who had once scorned him, should now be his, to use as he willed.

Artos turned from them both. "Take her away," he said. "You may keep her rings and wristlets but leave the emerald with me. That is the price you are paying me for her in this market."

He waved his hand in dismissal. The girl suddenly stood, and tearing the emerald from her breast, flung it into the Count's face. It struck him on the cheekbone, sharply, and fell into his lap. He did not flinch nor did his expression change. She would have torn off her rings and bracelets, but the young man, who saw his bargain dwindling, took her roughly by the arms and almost flung her from the presence-chamber.

When they had gone, Artos let the emerald fall onto the stone floor. He gazed at it for a while, fixedly, then ground his foot on it cruelly, as though trying to mar the beauty of its cutting. While he was doing this, the guard at the door entered, bringing with him a sullen-faced man whose black hair hung in elf-locks onto his thin shoulders. Dressed only in a greasy horsehide held into his waist by a thong, he swayed from foot to foot, looking away from Artos, who stared at him questioningly.

The guard said, "He dropped over the wall, Bear, and we took him immediately. He carries no weapons."

Artos said, "What do you want here, my friend?"

The man shuffled his feet and grimaced, but would not speak.

Artos said to the guard, "Go to the door and stay there. I shall call for you if I want you."

The guard replied, "Is that wise, Bear? This man might be dangerous."

Artos looked back at the guard so terribly that the man lowered his head, ashamed.

"I could break his back with one blow of my fist," said the Count. "And then yours with another. Go, as I have commanded."

The guard saluted and went out as Artos had said, and when he had gone, the man in the horsehide fell on his knees before Artos, who raised him up and slapped him on the back as though he were an old friend. "Well, Bledyn," he said, "how goes it, you old rogue? What message do you bring?"

The dark-haired one went to the door and looked out. Then he came back and, kneeling, said, "Things are not well at Lis Pengwern, Artos. The young men who were left have grown discontented and will not till the fields or herd the cattle. They say they have no leader now, that old Uther is not their chief but their fathers' chief. Most of them have left to join any lord who will give them a sword to carry and a horse to ride. Those who remain taunt Uther when he walks abroad. They have pulled down the temple and have overthrown the sacrifice stone. Lis Pengwern is open to the wolves."

Artos thought for a while, a strange dark smile twisting his lips. At last he spoke. "And what says Uther to this?" he asked.

The messenger did not meet his eyes as he answered, "He is afraid, Artos, and does not dare move out of his house now." He waited for the Bear to strike him for these words, but Artos merely nodded and smiled. The man went on, "It is Uther who sends me here to ask for help. He begs that you ride back to your village to uphold his kingship. That is your duty, he reminds you."

Artos rose now and paced up and down the room. The smile never left his face.

"I expected all this," he said. "Uther had grown too swollen with power, like a little cock on a midden-heap. But he does wrong to remind me of my duty. I do not forget that he sat in judgement on me for a sin that was his own in origin. I do not forget that what I have in this world, I gained by my own strength and not with his assistance."

The messenger said, "I do not dare go back and tell him that, Artos. He still has a few men about him who would take my tongue out for carrying such an answer."

Artos answered, "That would be a waste of a good spy, would it not, Bledyn? Well, we must give you another message to take, one that will let you keep that tongue wagging in your head for a few more years."

The messenger bowed, ironically. Artos gave him a push with his sandalled foot that sent the man sprawling his length across the floor.

Then lightly he said, "Take back this message—tell Uther my father that I shall see that he gets his dues. Tell him that."

The other said, "When shall I say that you are coming to Lis Pengwern? He will ask that."

Artos answered, "Who says that I shall come at all? You can tell him that I may not leave this place yet, or my own power will crumble. Then go on to say that I shall see he gets his due place in Lis Pengwern."

As he said this, he laughed and, pointing to the floor, said, "Take that emerald, my friend. That is your payment for this journey."

The man got up to go, but halfway to the door looked back into the eyes of Artos and saw the question that shone urgently through them.

"Yes, Artos," he said, "I saw her before I left. She is well."

"Is the boy well?" asked Artos, his voice unsure.

The messenger replied, "Yes, Master, the boy is well. He is a true little prince."

Artos hesitated for a moment and then said, "Damn you, you bargainer! What message did she send?"

He flung a gold chain at the messenger, who stooped and caught it with a smile, bowing his dark head in acknowledgement.

"She sends the message that you live day and night in her heart. She asks when you will come to her again," he said, his eyes no longer bold.

Artos punched the arm of his gilded chair until his great knuckles were bruised. Looking away from the waiting messenger, he said gently, "Tell her that one day there will be a place for her. There will be a place at my side. Now is not the time for that. I must be master of this Roman world before I can give her safety and riches and power."

He stopped for a moment, as though he might be fighting within his own mind, his inclination warring against the necessities of his situation.

At last he spoke again, his words bursting out almost against his will. "Oh God, tell her to come to me *when* she will, *where* she will. Tell her that my heart beats within hers, that while she lives, I live; that when her blood falls cold, so will mine."

The messenger touched his forehead with the back of his hand, as in obeisance to a great chieftain. Yet still he stayed, as though there was something which he wished to say.

Artos at last recovered himself and said, "Speak, man. What is it?"

The messenger licked his dry lips. "Do not kill me, Master," he said, "yet there is another thing which she will wish to know. We have heard in Lis Pengwern that there is another one, a beautiful one, who sits with you here."

Artos jumped to his feet and for a moment it seemed as though he might strike the man down. Then, as the messenger shrank before him, he smiled bitterly and said, "Tell my love that all things will be made right again, that nothing shall stand in her way. Tell her that all obstacles shall be removed."

The man nodded and saluted again, but when he was near the door, Artos strode towards him and pressed something into his hand. "Take great care of this," he said. "Give it safely into her keeping. Tell her that I send it to protect, not to destroy her."

The man looked down with wonder and fear at the little green glass phial in his hand. Then he nodded and put the thing into a doeskin pouch that was tied between his legs.

"Fare well, and come to me again, one day," said Artos. "But if you betray this trust, take a boat and sail beyond Ireland, or cut your throat without delay, or I shall leave no more of you in one piece than would feed a sparrow."

"I shall not betray you, Master," said the man. Then he was gone, and Artos went back to his chair.

When the young man came to him later to dress his hair, Artos rose suddenly and struck him in the face, knocking him against the wall.

The young man saw that the Bear had bitten his lips until the blood had run down into his short beard. He lay still on the floor, waiting for Artos to kill him.

But nothing happened. There was only silence. And when the young man dared to look up once again, he saw that the Bear sat hunched in his chair, his shoulders heaving with the dry sobs that smothered themselves in his throat. The young man crept away, marvelling at the womanly weakness of this upstart Count of Britain.

XXXIII

AS SUMMER TURNED TO AUTUMN, THE KINGS OF THE WEST GREW restive in Caerwent. Cunneglassus wished to return to his own country for the harvest, and Votiporix openly said that things had not turned out quite as he had hoped, and that he would be as well with his men in another place. Only Aurelius showed no sign of discontent yet, and lived a pleasant enough life in Caerwent, feasting and hunting in the woods above the city.

Then Artos called a council in his palace at Caer Leon, and announced to them all that he considered the first stage of the great war to be completed. The Jutes and the South Saxons were crushed, he told them. The sea-rovers who had settled along the eastern coasts could wait. They did little damage, and mostly occupied such marshy areas as no one else would want anyway. They could be cleared in a year's time, when Britain was a settled country again.

Cunneglassus said, "You are a soldier, Artos, not a councillor. We are of the opinion that you should ride again, to the east, and smoke out the heathen before the winter comes on the land."

Artos twisted a great gold ring in his fingers, and smiled. Bedwyr, beside him, smiled too. Medrawt, at his other side, looked down towards the table top.

Votiporix spoke then, his thin Welsh voice rising higher as he became more heated. "Do not forget, Artos, that we, the Western Kings, made you what you are. You are our *dux bellorum,* our Captain of Battles, not our master. Yet since you have been back from the south, you have acted like an emperor rather than a mere soldier."

Artos stared him in the eye and stopped twisting the ring. "My friend," he said, "I will grant most of what you say. But tell me, if you have a stallion of great worth, do you not groom him and feed him well, and keep him in a warm stall? If you have a hunting dog with fleet legs and a good nose, do you not pander to his tastes and give him meat when the other curs eat husks? So, would you not let me have my whims, who am more than a horse or a dog?"

Votiporix became suddenly angry. "You are diverting our minds from the real question," he said, his dark eyes flashing. "You have taken a wife without our permission, you have rebuilt a city without our approval, and now you will rest through the autumn when we think you should march again, to strike fear into the Saxons of our eastern coasts. That, in an ordinary soldier, would be rebellion, and we should flay him alive for it. Yet you expect to be praised and petted, not punished for your self-will."

Artos rose and looked across the long room. Now he did not address Votiporix alone, and his gaze wandered towards all men.

"Kings of the West," he said, "and your friends and councillors here present. The thing is simple, in spite of our foolish talk about horses and flaying. It is this: I will serve you faithfully as your Captain of Battles, for that I have sworn, and I do not break my word. Yet, do not forget my other status. I am Count of Britain, and not through your choosing but because of Ambrosius and my own strength. So, there is another part of me that does not belong to you, but is my own. When your wishes are those of the Count of Britain, then shall they be followed to the death. But when your commands seem foolish in the eyes of the Count, he will obey his own desires, even if that means offending you."

Cunneglassus leaned forward, his thick neck red with passion. "Do you mean to set yourself up as a king, Artos Pendragon?" he said, rapping the table impatiently with his heavily ringed knuckles to emphasise his words.

Artos said, "What does that word mean, Cunneglassus? We have no kings in Britain now. They died when Rome conquered the land. No, I am the Count of Britain, nothing more."

Now the kings looked at each other in consternation, for they saw that this upstart planned to depose them. Votiporix rose and said, "Artos, out of your own mouth you have condemned yourself.

You cannot serve us well with such rebellious thoughts in your mind. We shall send you back to your dung-heaps in Lis Peng-wern."

Then there was an uproar about the table. But Artos still smiled. "Gentlemen," he said, "be calm. We are not playing at castles and sieges now, we are talking about our plans for the future of this country. Follow my advice, and in five years, you will see an ordered commonwealth, in the riches of which we shall all share. Disobey my counsels now, and you will lose whatever little you have gained."

"How shall we, Artos?" asked Aurelius quietly. He had not spoken before, since he had already a plan of action in his own mind and was hardly listening to what these men were saying.

The Bear looked at him with distaste, for he had known him a long while and despised him. "Aurelius Caninus, in words which you will understand, I tell you that you will lose whatever you may have gained because you will not live to enjoy it. That is all."

Artos sat in his chair at the head of the table once more. Cunneglassus and Votiporix consulted with each other in whispers. Then Votiporix spoke up. "We have come here in peace, Bear, bringing with us only a handful of horsemen. It would be an easy thing for you to slay us treacherously, then. But have no fear, our armies would come back at you when the news reached them, and would destroy you in your turn within two days. Then what would the Count of Britain matter?"

Artos lolled in his chair, not bothering even to look at the chieftain. "Understand," he said quietly, "I do not threaten you. I merely place the arguments before you. It is you who talk of armies and treachery. Yet, since the word has been spoken, I will not ignore it. I will tell you that I have five thousand men here in Caer Leon, and the offer of another five thousand in other parts of Britain. Now tell me, my friends, can your own hosts match those I speak of?"

Votiporix rose hastily, his hand upon his sword-hilt. "I shall return to Caerwent, and then to my own country," he said. "You did ill to mass forces against us, your friends."

Cunneglassus wheezed slowly to his feet, leaning hard on the table to help him to rise. "Yes, Artos," he said, "Votiporix is right. It was an act of treachery and that will not be forgotten."

Aurelius Caninus moved up the room towards the Bear. Artos called out to the parting kings, "Take care my men do not ambush you as you ride through the gates, friends! Good day to you. Return to talk sense when your anger has died down."

Aurelius said to Artos, "You did right, Count of Britain. Know that I have three thousand picked warriors who will ride at your command when you should need them."

Medrawt looked up at him with a shock. Artos did not deign to look at him. "Go with your friends," he said. "They need your warriors, not I."

When all others had gone, Artos said to Medrawt, "That man is not to be trusted, brother. If he would betray his fellow-kings, he would betray me, too, think you not?"

Medrawt said, "I do not know, Artos. But I fear that you did unwisely this afternoon."

Artos slapped him on the shoulder and said, "Why, old Votiporix has never been known to sit a council out yet. He is always trying to pick quarrels. No one notices him, for he forgets it all on the next day. Have no fear, Medrawt, today's affair will only bind us closer to each other, for now they know that they must act with me or their schemes will come to nothing."

Medrawt shook his head darkly and went towards his billets. Bethlac waited for him there, and looked relieved when he came in.

"Master," he said, "Caninus has been here. He came secretly and departed with haste, but left you a message. He told me to say to you that you need only be patient, for you will assuredly drink from the cup soon. He said that I was to tell you he offered men to the Bear only to disarm his suspicions. Watch and wait, he said. And then he went through the door with his cloak about his face, like a murderer, or a ghost!"

Medrawt dismissed him and sat at his table, in the rushlight, thinking, when suddenly the curtains of his door swung back and Artos entered, his face now grave.

"Brother," he said, "I have been wondering about all this, and now my mind misgives me a little. Perhaps they are more crafty than I thought, after all. Perhaps I should take care of some sort, though it would trouble me to walk in fear of such carrion."

Medrawt poured wine for him into a cup of Samian ware. "What is in your mind, brother?" he said. "You are great and have many men to protect you."

Artos the Bear scratched his nose and smiled. "Not perhaps as great as they think," he said, "for my tale of the five thousand who would come at my call was a lie. I should be fortunate to scour up three hundred from the countryside. But that does not matter; together our two companies could hold them, and given the right terrain, defeat them. At least, we could maul them so badly that they would be the prey of any other enemy that came at them, and they would not risk that danger."

Medrawt smiled and nodded, "Yes, Artos," he said, "we must stay together, that is important."

The Count of Britain nodded and held out his cup for more wine. Medrawt poured it, a little smile flickering over his dark face as his back was turned towards the Bear of Britain.

Then Artos said, "You are my second in command, Medrawt, the Count-elect, when I should die."

"You must live for many years, brother," said Medrawt, recalling the same words he had once spoken to old Ambrosius.

Artos shrugged his shoulders and said, "So I shall, if the gods grant my prayers! But what I want to say now is this—that should I be away from my city when the Western Kings make their treacherous stroke, there must be someone to protect Gwenhwyfar. It must be you, brother, for you are my right hand now. You must stay with your company of Cymry and Jutes, wherever I am called, for it will be your place to keep my wife and my city safe in my absence."

Medrawt smiled sadly and said, "I wish nothing better than to fight by your side until my raven calls me away. But I obey your command, Artos the Count. So be it."

The Bear embraced him warmly and then went from the room. When an hour had passed, Medrawt sent for Bethlac and bade him ride to Caerwent secretly.

"Find Aurelius," he said, "and tell him that the cup comes towards me and that I shall soon drink."

Bethlac took a swift horse and went the long way round so as not to meet anyone. After he had gone from the city, another horseman followed him, just as secretly, right to the gates of Caerwent. Yet so quietly did he go, that he might have been a spirit, and Bethlac did not hear him.

On the following day other horsemen came into Caer Leon. They had ridden from the north and all carried grievous wounds. They demanded audience with the Bear and were straightway admitted to him.

"Artos," said their leader, whose hair and ornamental scars were like those of the Count himself, "you must ride hard if you are to rule more than half of Britain. Gomer, the King of the Picts, is moving south with a great army. He comes swiftly and must intend to conquer the north before the winter falls."

Artos gave the men food and drink and spoke with them in friendship, for they were of his own people of Strathclyde. He spoke their dialect, though badly now, since he had not used it for many years.

"How many men has he?" Artos asked. "A thousand?"

The leader of the northern men laughed sadly. "I think he leads the whole of Pictland, Bear," he said. "His two sons march with him, and each of them has a thousand in his warband. You must needs gallop fast and gallop strong, if you would save your kingdom."

Medrawt had heard this, and now Artos turned to him and said, "It is fate, my brother. You must stay behind and guard the city and the woman."

Medrawt said, "I am your other self, Artos. You may ride with courage in your heart."

Then Artos sent messengers to Caerwent, telling the kings of the new danger. They rode to Caer Leon when they had heard this news, and bade Artos godspeed.

"How many men will you give me, Votiporix?" asked Artos, sardonically. Votiporix shook his head and said, "It would be foolish to weaken our city by taking their soldiers from them, Artos."

He turned to Cunneglassus and asked the same question. Cunneglassus mumbled that Votiporix spoke for him, too. Then Artos looked at Aurelius with a strange smile. "I shall not ask you, Caninus," he said, "for I recall what you said but yesterday."

Aurelius Caninus looked away from him. "I ride south, Artos," he said, "to look to my own affairs. My people have revolted and I must first set my own house in order."

Artos turned from him. "The news of the revolt must have come today, Caninus, did it not?"

The other fidgetted and did not speak. Artos shrugged his shoulders and said, "Have no fear, my lords, the men I have will suffice this time."

They went from the room in triumph, though their faces had put on the look of gravity to meet with the situation.

Medrawt said to Artos, "You ride on a long journey, brother. Which way shall you take?"

Artos said, "North along the old road by Viroconium, to Deva, and thence by Mancunium to the Wall. After that, we ride in whatever direction the enemy lie."

Medrawt said, "When Britain is at peace again, we must rebuild the great Wall and keep a detachment of soldiers there, as they did in the olden times."

"That is a good plan, brother," said Artos. "But first let us find the peace that will let us have time to do it."

"Which way will you ride south again?" asked Medrawt.

Artos regarded him slowly. "I shall not tempt the gods by speaking such words," he said, "or they may not let me come away from the Picts."

Medrawt said with a warm smile, "Why, brother, you will live to be the king of this whole country, I know it."

Artos did not answer him, but turned away and got into the saddle.

He rode with Bedwyr and Cei towards the house of Lystra. "Cei," he said, "it grieves me that you will not be with me in this battle that is to be. But you must be my eyes and ears here. You followed Medrawt's man to Caerwent in the night and know that things may not be what they seem. I command you, if the time comes, you must strike him down and take command of the second company. You must hold Caer Leon until I return."

Cei bowed his head and said, "My knife is already sharpened. Fare well and bring back a victory, Bear."

Lystra was waiting for her husband, dressed in a white gown of samite. He kneeled before her and put his great sword into her hands.

"Give me this, lady," he said, "as though you were giving it to a warrior for the first time. Bless it in the name of whatever god you prayed to when you were a child, for I have a feeling that I shall need the support of as many deities as I can get in the next days."

And Lystra gave him his sword, speaking strange words, which he did not understand, over the blade of it.

"I hope it was a good luck charm," he said, taking her in his arms. "For if you spoke a spell of ruin over it, you will be responsible for my death and I shall sit at your bedside every night until you go to your funeral pyre!"

He meant this to be a grim joke, but she shuddered and said, "I would not betray you, husband, you know that."

Artos crushed her to him and said, "I know that, Gwenhwyfar. You and Medrawt are my truest friends. Trust Medrawt, my wife, for he is to be the Count here while I am away. Keep close to him."

Lystra did not speak about Medrawt. She let the loose folds of her samite gown fall apart so that Artos could see the beauty of her body.

"I am yours, Bear," she said. "Come back from the north whole again. I shall await you here."

The first rains of autumn began to fall as the long cavalcade rode out through the gates of Caer Leon. Artos did not once turn back, though both Lystra and Medrawt waved banners from the ramparts.

XXXIV

LYSTRA LEANED ON A BALUSTRADE AND WATCHED THE CAVALRY OF THE second company of Cymry wheeling and charging, halting and retreating. It was a wonderfully drilled mass of young tribesmen, now supplemented by those of the Jutes who were interested in riding, mainly the sons of petty chieftains who had been able to afford horses for their sons to ride. In the centre of the vast parade ground, Medrawt sat upright in the saddle, with Cei at his left side, his eyes never leaving his company. He saw every bit, every spur, every saddle-girth. He saw each man, from Roman helmet to heavy caligula, each sword-belt and neck-cloth; nothing missed his eye.

Nor did any point of Medrawt miss the eye of Lystra. She saw the proud carriage of his head, the red plume of his officer's golden helmet, that trailed halfway down his broad back in the graceful style of ancient Greece. She saw the strongly made arms and legs, the gilded buskins that reached to the knee, the purple cloak and the embossed amber-leather saddle. And what she saw pleased her.

At length the watchkeeper's silver trumpet blew and the centurions led off their parties of horsemen to the barrack mess. Medrawt still spoke with Cei, motioning gently with his right hand to stress the points he was making. At last Cei saluted his captain and cantered off across the square. Medrawt wheeled his black horse towards the palace of Artos, and then saw the woman. She smiled, as though she wished to speak with him, and Medrawt rode forward to where she stood.

Lystra inclined her head graciously when he saluted her, his sword held before his lips. "Your horsemen are like machines of death," she said. "What do they think about when they are not drilling?"

Medrawt scratched his head and screwed up his eyes. "Think about?" he said. "About the drill they will do tomorrow, I expect, Lady Gwenhwyfar. That is what soldiers are for, surely, to prepare themselves."

Lystra smiled ironically at his use of the Celtic title and then said, "Such singleness of purpose is splendid in theory, but would not you and I find such a life tedious?"

Medrawt said, "I do not think so, lady. Surely we both live for one thing only? That is true, is it not?"

Lystra answered, "Your eyes are sharp, Medrawt. I suppose that comes from watching your men so closely day after day."

The young officer replied, "What is it you would speak to me about, lady?"

Lystra said, "Why are you afraid of me? We have known each other long enough, have we not? We can be frank, each to other."

Medrawt dismounted and stood close by her so that no man passing might hear what he said. "Lady Lystra, let us not endanger our lives. Your husband the Bear is not a man to forgive lightly. You are right. We both have singleness of purpose; that much I have learned about you. You love the power your marriage brings you. Do not endanger it then by any act of foolishness with me."

Lystra smiled down at the ground and said, "Yes, you have sharp eyes, Medrawt, and sharp ears, and a sharp heart. You read me right. I have that same singleness of purpose which you, too, possess, the search for power. That is why I speak with you now. You tell me by your eyes that you are interested in what I say. So I will speak on."

Medrawt drew closer to her, under the colonnade. He was annoyed that she should draw him into this conversation now. Cei might return at any time from the barracks.

"I beg you, lady, be brief," he said. "I am weary from the parade and must write a report for Artos to read when he returns."

Lystra said, "Do not be a fool, Medrawt. You know as well as I that he never reads reports. Indeed, I sometimes think he has deceived us both into thinking he can read at all! But I will be brief, as you command me. Look, Medrawt, it runs strongly in my mind that Artos may meet with misfortune in the north, or elsewhere. If that were so, it might be a bad thing for you and me."

Medrawt said, "It is always likely that a soldier will meet with misfortune, yet I do not think that Artos is more prone to misfortune than any other man. What is in your mind, lady?"

The woman placed her hand on his arm and said, "Medrawt, you are a grown man and not a schoolboy. You know which way the wind blows. If Artos were to die, who would take his place?"

Medrawt held his chin in his hand, pretending to think for a while. "I am the Count-elect," he said, trying to sound as though the possibility were distasteful to him.

Lystra took away her hand. Her mouth smiled in a hard way that mirrored the nature of her thoughts. "The Count-elect," she said. "That means nothing. Caninus the Dog would take the title himself, have no fears of that. He has promised to support you in your election, but a man who could gain himself a crown as he has done, would gain himself a title too. Think on that."

Medrawt mused a little now, for that possibility had not occurred to him. He looked at Lystra with more respect now and said, "I did not think of that, lady."

Lystra said, "I know you did not. Your mind was too full of betraying Artos; you did not stop to think that others were about to betray both him and you."

Medrawt looked at her searchingly. Her face was set and sincere. She believed what she was saying, he could see that.

"What am I to do, lady?" he said simply.

Lystra shrugged her shoulders. "You are a soldier," she said. "You should know about tactics and strategy, not I. I can only advise you to prepare for what I tell you."

Medrawt said, "How should I prepare, lady? My company could not stand against the combined forces of the Western Kings, nor even against that of Artos, should the need arise."

Lystra answered, "No, indeed you are like a man caught between two millstones, liable to be crushed whichever way you move. You must not hope to become Count of Britain, I tell you. That much is clear to me. Your only hope of military success is to hold Caer Leon for Artos, until he can get to you, and then hope that one day, when he is dead, you may become the Count. That is poor consolation for one like you who itches for power, is it not?"

She waited so long for an answer that in the end, Medrawt nodded. "You read me aright, Lystra," he said. "What do you want?"

The woman said, "You and I, Medrawt, are not of princely blood. Each of us has known what it is to wrestle for scraps in the alley-ways. No, do not start, I know more of your history than you think. The tale of Medrawt is current in Londinium, have no fear; the gutter-brat snatched up to glory by the old man, Ambrosius. Know that I, too, was born among the offals of a great city that cares not whom it starves and destroys. I have danced in the halls of unrighteousness and lain with aged satyrs, not because I liked it, but because it was my only means of rising from what I was. I have known the repugnance of flesh against flesh, yet I have endured it. You, too, know that; I sense it in you. You are not a man who gives himself readily to a woman, however fair, because you carry within you the fastidiousness born of the gutters, the hatred of what you saw day by day and vowed to rise above. Is that not true, Medrawt?"

The young captain said, "You know too much for a woman, Lystra. Perhaps it would be better if I ran my sword through you now and rode south to the Saxons."

Lystra said, "That would be foolish, for together we might gain a power that Artos never dreams of. The Saxons will not help you to anything but death, so forget them. Nor will the Kings of the West, who look only to their own good fortune now and have already forgotten the Rome they wished to create again in suffering Britain. No, I tell you that it is not easy, but if you were prepared to struggle a little longer, the rewards might be great."

Medrawt said, "What should I do, Lystra? Speak freely, for I will not betray you."

The woman said, "Have no doubts about the situation, my friend. You cannot harm me; Artos would crucify you were I to speak one word against you to him. I am not afraid of your betraying me, Medrawt. No, I make this proposition; let us go away together, you with your company of horse, and I with the treasures of this city, which are already great. We could sell ourselves in Europe, even to Rome herself; or to any other government, perhaps farther east, who needed such an army, ready made. Why, Medrawt, within a year you could be a king."

Medrawt looked up suddenly, for he heard the beat of a horse's hooves at the other side of the square. It was Cei.

"I must go now, Lystra," he said. "We will speak further."

The woman smiled and shrugged her shoulders. "Let it be soon," she said, "or we are both likely to be crushed by the millstones, and there would end our dream of power, Medrawt."

The captain cantered across the square to meet his henchman. Cei looked up at him seriously and did not salute. Medrawt bit his lip with anger at this, but he knew better than to say anything to this man, who was one of the oldest friends Artos had.

"The Bear has been away a week now, Medrawt," said Cei, without any delay, "and I begin to hear strange talk among the men of the second company of horse. Some say that the Bear will never lead the Cymry again. They say that the Western Kings have named another in his place. Do you know anything of this?"

Medrawt said, "These are rumours, Cei, the sort of thing that soldiers are always saying, to pass the time away, nothing more."

For a while the two rode side by side, slowly. Then Cei said, "If you betrayed him, Medrawt, I should drive my knife into your side. You know that?"

Medrawt nodded and said, "Yes, Cei, I have always known that."

Then they parted. But now, as they were within sight of the barrack blocks, Cei saluted the captain, who smiled and saluted in return, the long red plume of his helmet nodding gallantly as he raised his hand in the old Roman gesture.

XXXV

THE CYMRY LIT THEIR FIRES AT LAST IN THE WOOD OF CALEDONIA. Although they were weary with their long ride north, they had caught something of their leader's new assurance and lit their campfires confidently, as though they dared the Painted Ones to rush from behind their sheltering trees and attack them.

Artos sat in his hide tent with Bedwyr and a young lieutenant named Drostan, a relative of Marcus of Dumnonia. He was a foolishly gay youngster, who invented dreams which he said he had dreamt, just to cause amusement. As they sat burnishing their weapons, Drostan told them of a monster he had killed in his dreams. It was a massive pig; and inside this pig he had found a dog; and inside the dog, a cat; and inside the cat, a mouse; and inside the mouse a wheat-ear. And when Drostan had taken out the wheat-ear, and had crushed it between his finger and his thumb, a sad, howling voice had come to him from afar, crying, "Oh, merciless warrior, you have killed my heart!" Drostan said that he looked up then, in his dream, and saw a giant, staggering about in the field outside, with his hand to his breast.

"It seems," said the young man, "that this giant, an Irish giant, I might say—no giant of the Cymry would be so careless—had hidden his heart in that manner so that he might live forever, proof against all sword thrusts. Alas, for the giants of Ireland—they are fools!"

Bedwyr had laughed, but Artos was preoccupied and staring before him in the rush-light. Bedwyr winked at the young man as though to urge him on to another flight of fancy.

Drostan told of a lovely golden-haired girl of Ireland, Yslod, he called her.

He said that his Uncle Marcus, in his dream, of course, asked him to sail across to Ireland and fetch this lovely creature back for him to marry.

"But alas, you know how it is," said Drostan, raising his auburn eyebrows nonchalantly, "she just couldn't resist me! Before we had got back in sight of the cliffs of Dumnonia, the job was done! I felt very bad about betraying old Uncle Marcus, but who could have disappointed a lady as beautiful, and as insistent, as she was?"

Artos looked up at him in the dim light, his lips pressed together and the muscles of his face working slightly. Drostan did not heed the warning and went on. "Of course, we had to confess when the time came. I told Marcus we had accidentally drunk a love potion on board, thinking it was the ordinary issue of ship's ale. But he did not believe that. There was nothing for it, I had to take ship to Gaul and lie quiet there until Marcus had grown so old that he did not greatly care any more."

Drostan looked round for praise. But Bedwyr coughed meaningfully behind his hand and busied himself with a stirrup-iron that suddenly needed polishing violently. Artos stared through the firelight at the young warrior.

"I have never dreamed about women in my life, Lieutenant," he said. "A soldier should not dream, or if he does, it should be of blood and the death of his enemies. Get outside now and take the northern watch. The cool air will ventilate your brain and clear it of such cobwebs before you come in to sleep."

Drostan shrugged his shoulders and strolled outside. He never knew how close that shrug brought him to death.

When he had gone, Artos said, "That young fool is fey. He must be sent back to his Uncle Marcus when we get back home again. He is of no use to me. That sort of talk is like a canker that eats into the solid core of soldiery."

Bedwyr smiled to himself. He knew well enough what had upset the Bear; it was the description of the young girl as being golden-haired, for it was the colour of Gwenhwyfar, for whom

Artos still yearned in his secret brooding heart. Yet he nodded to the leader and said that he would see that Drostan went back, the moment they reached Caerwent. But Artos had forgotten all about it the next day, and even laughed when Drostan got up to his foolishness later on, telling of a dream in which he had drunk the water from the Irish Sea so as to walk over dry-shod for a wager.

The Cymry moved their tents further into the wood, always keeping a sharp watch, but did not meet their enemy as yet. Some of them began to suspect that the rumour that had drawn them northwards was a trick to get them away from Caerwent for some reason or another. One man even mentioned the name of Medrawt, as being responsible. He did this carelessly, in the hearing of Artos, who had him hung by the thumbs from a lower bough of a pine tree, his toes barely touching the ground. And there he stayed from sundown to dawn. When the leader gave permission for his father to cut him down, the young man screamed with agony as his sinews tried to find their place in his wrists again. He was finished as a fighting man from that moment, for never again could he hold a sword. But Artos found him a job as an ostler, since he could grip a curry comb without the use of his thumbs. No man complained of this discipline, for they still loved and respected the Bear at this time.

On the third night, the sentries at the eastern side of the encampment blew their horns, and the Cymry sprang to their positions among the protective trees, for horsemanship was out of the question in such terrain.

It was a wet night and the rain dripped down from the boughs above, drearily and dishearteningly. No man relished the idea of fighting in such a disconsolate drizzle. The Cymry waited, their teeth chattering and their sword-arms shaking with the damp cold. It was too wet to let a man feel like a hero and no war chants were made to keep the blood flowing hotly that night.

After a long wait, the Cymry saw the glimmer of resinous rowan torches, and at last they glimpsed men moving towards them. Artos gave orders that they were to set arrows to string, but not to shoot until the intentions of the oncoming force were clear. But the torches came on and on, and at last a long column of men filed into the camp of the Cymry, dark-haired Picts, wrapped in their black cloaks and trying to keep as dry as they could.

Their leader, a bent old man who wore a circlet of hawk's feathers in his catskin cap, and had not a tooth left in his head, made his way up to Artos and held out both hands to him, empty of any weapons. Artos put up his own sword and took the old veteran into his tent. Bedwyr stood at the door, to guard against treachery, but all the Picts asked for was a great fire, and when that was made, they began to smile again and told the Cymry where the best hunting grounds were in the neighbourhood.

Artos tried to recall his dialect of Strathclyde again, to speak with the mumbling old chieftain. This was Gomer, of whom Artos had been warned in the message. Artos asked him where his sons and the army were. The old man took some time to understand the question and then waved his arm broadly and laughed, his toothless gums shining in the firelight.

"Why," he said, "my sons hold their marriage feasts still. Each has sworn to get a son before the other and they will not declare the feasting over until they know how it will be, one way or the other. They are like young stallions, Artos. Even as babies they sucked against each other, and when they grew older, ate against each other. Now they beget against each other! It is the way of twin sons."

Artos smiled at him sternly, for as yet he did not trust the old man, who was called "The Fox" by the folk of the north.

"Yes," said the Bear, "but where is the army?"

The old man waved his arm again. "Outside, Bear," he said. "The other half is hunting above Agned, getting in the winter meat for salting. You do wrong to call it an army, for we are a peaceful folk, hunters and fishers, and not harm-doers to any man, if we are left alone."

He smiled slyly when he said the last words. Artos was angry and said to him, "When did a man last call you a liar, Gomer?"

The old man's smile never left his face. He warmed his wizened hands nearer the blaze and said softly, "Perhaps yesterday, for all

I know, for I do not hear everything now that I am old. Yet I will tell you, Bear, that the last one to call me liar in my hearing lived no longer than to draw three more breaths."

Artos said, "What happened to him, old man?"

A knife was almost pricking his throat before he had finished his question. Artos looked down it and saw the unblinking eyes of the old man, the steady hand, wizened though it was, that held the knife. Artos shrugged his shoulders and said, "If you wish to keep your hands on the end of your arms, put that bird-spit away, Gomer the Fox. No man draws steel in this tent but by my wish."

The old man smiled back at him, with an equal self-possession. "What sort of fool are you, Artos Pendragon?" he said. "You asked what happened to a man who insulted me and I merely showed you. How else could I have proved my words?"

Artos leaned sideways as though to find a more comfortable position on his wooden chair, yet with the same movement he swung his left arm over and knocked the man's hand aside. The knife fell to the ground. Artos said, "I could tear your throat open with my hands, Gomer. You are very old and weak now, and I am still the Bear of Britain. What say you to that?"

Gomer picked up his knife and put it away, among the folds of his black robes. He grinned and turned away from Artos, as though he did not fear him.

"I should blow my whistle as I died," he said, "and before my body had dropped to the ground, my sons would pick out your eyes with the hot embers of the fire, and my armies would destroy your company and their horses so that no man would ever know that they had camped in the Wood of Caledonia. Even the ashes of their bodies my men would waft away with their cloaks. No one would know where Artos was buried then."

Artos nodded gently. "So your sons are with you, Gomer? In spite of your talk about weddings, they are here in the wood?"

The old man said, "Who knows, Artos? Perhaps they are, perhaps they are not. I forget when they held their wedding feast. I forget so much these days, now that I am old and, as you say, weak."

Artos said, "We came to tell you that now Britain is no longer your hunting ground, Gomer. What do you say?"

The old Pict said, "We have heard that Rome has come again and we wanted to see it, nothing more. We are not a warlike folk, Bear, as you know. All we ask is a stag to chase and a trout to fish, no more."

Artos said, "If you come south of the Wood of Caledonia, we shall slay you and feed your bodies to our hunting hounds. If you go north again and stay within your own country, we shall forget you."

Gomer said, "Tonight we came to see you, without too many weapons, for we have grown tired of watching your fires night after night, and we thought you would like to know that we meant you no harm. We come in peace, Artos."

Artos replied, "Go back north, Gomer, and we shall return to the place from whence we came. But if you ride south, we shall destroy you and your women and children. Our vengeance is great now that we have made up our minds to act at last."

Gomer rose to his feet and said, "We understand each other, Bear. Yet we have never been known in our history to meet our enemy and then return home without fighting. We must have a tale to tell. Shall we fight with staves, and then part friends?"

The notion appealed to the grim humour of Artos. He called Bedwyr and told him the old man's plan. So in the light of the great fire, men from both sides cut down sticks from the trees and formed themselves into two companies. Then, with Artos and Gomer sitting together in the firelight and watching them, they ran together and went through the motions of war. The parody continued until the warriors had exhausted themselves, then they sat together, the two peoples mingling, and ate and drank in the firelight, forgetting the rain that still drifted between the boughs of the great trees.

"Cat Coit Celidon," said the old man, ironically, raising his horn-cup to the Count of Britain. "So we shall both go home and say that we have gained the victory."

Artos laughed and said, "Where are your sons, Gomer?"

The old man answered, "In their beds with their wives, if they have any sense, Bear."

Then the men of both sides lay down where they were and slept in the silence of the great forest. And in the morning, the Picts had gone, though no man heard them go. Artos made an inspection of the encampment and found that they had taken a dozen pack-horses with them, but he did not begrudge them. He had not expected to get off so lightly against such a wary enemy.

When the Cymry had eaten again, they mounted and rode towards the south.

XXXVI

IN CAERWENT THE THREE KINGS SAT IN COUNCIL, ATTENDED ONLY BY deaf mutes, or slaves they had always known and trusted. Votiporix was beside himself with anxiety at the preparations they were to make. Cunneglassus, in his lazy way, was indifferent as to the means, and was only concerned with the result.

"It is so easy," he said, "that I wonder why we meet to discuss it. Artos will come to Caerwent to report his victory over the Picts, and we shall ambush him with a vastly superior number of men. He will be killed in the forum, and that will be the end of the affair. What is there more to discuss?"

Aurelius Caninus showed his yellow teeth in a smile. "Only one thing," he said. "Who will take his place?"

Votiporix leaned across the table in his haste. "Not Medrawt," he said. "That man is not to be trusted, any more than Artos was. We could use the horse of Medrawt, but not their master."

Aurelius said, "No, perhaps you are right, although he has always seemed a friendly man. Perhaps it should be one of us."

He looked at his companions, his eyebrows raised in question.

Cunneglassus said, "I am too old for such cavortings, my friend. And I know Votiporix has his lands to administer. We have been away from our places for too long already. We must get this affair settled and then get back to our proper business."

"But first we must find a successor to Artos," persisted Aurelius. They looked hard at him and he read their dislike of him in that look.

Votiporix said suavely, "You are not the man, Caninus. In any case, you have a job to do when we have finished with Artos. You ride personally to Caer Leon and put your lance through his widow. That is arranged, is it not?"

Aurelius said, "As you say, though it is a task I have little stomach for."

Cunneglassus said, "She is fit only for the whorehouses of Byzantium. We cannot let her live and gain sympathy. She must die when he does. That is decided."

Aurelius, who was the youngest man present, bowed his head, but silently vowed that he would delegate the duty to someone else. He could not bear to think of killing the woman. Though he had to admit that he would be afraid to take her to wife; she was too forceful in her strange way for him.

He said, "What is to happen to Medrawt on the day, then?"

Votiporix answered, "We cannot risk his being at Caerwent to welcome Artos. He might forget our plot and remember his blood-oath at the last moment, then we should be in difficulties. No, he must be kept away from Caerwent. Tell him something to keep him away, Caninus."

Cunneglassus laughed thickly, "Ay, and when you have finished off the wife of Artos, you can sharpen your lance again and put an end to him!"

Aurelius smiled as though he agreed to this rough suggestion. Then he said, "It will be easy to keep Medrawt away from Caerwent. I shall tell him that he must not implicate himself, in case the ambush does not succeed. He must keep the friendship of Artos in such an event."

Votiporix stared him in the eye. "You are plausible, Caninus," he said grimly. "I sometimes wonder whether we should not pay more attention to your own future."

Aurelius, who always had a wine-taster, since he dreamed nightly of being poisoned, showed his teeth again. This time his voice was firmer. He said, "You are too far from your own territory, Votiporix, to threaten me. The men of Dumnonia ask me daily when I shall quarrel with you, for many of them remember the time when you rode into their land, before we came together in this city. They would be glad to avenge their slaughtered families and burnt-out farms."

Such was the expression on his face that Votiporix believed him. He rose from the table and said, "A jest's a jest, Aurelius. Your men would not break the oath of fealty to the three of us, would they?"

Aurelius Caninus said, "Who knows? They are rough men, these from the southwest."

Cunneglassus wheezed and said, "Gentlemen, gentlemen, now is not the time for bickering."

The two men sat at the table again, but from that moment they spoke carefully to each other.

And even as they still talked of the things they should do when Artos returned, a woman entered the city secretly. She wore a heavy dark cloak that hid her face and body, and carried a bundle that seemed to exhaust her. A great hound moved beside her like a shadow.

"Troynt," she whispered, so that the guard should not hear her, "keep to heel, boy, keep to heel." Anir slept deeply from hunger and the weariness of travel; he did not hear his mother's voice. Nor did she speak any more than she needed to, for she was almost at the point of falling onto the roadway. It had been a terrible journey from Lis Pengwern, and at every step she had recalled the old man, Uther Pendragon, lying back in his great chair, his jaws agape, his rigid hand still clutching the cup that had poisoned him.

XXXVII

AS THEY RODE SOUTH OF VIROCONIUM, THE CYMRY SANG, FOR THEY would soon be home again and would have done, at least for a time, with this chafing business of riding on hard saddles from dawn till dusk, eating and drinking on the move and setting a full watch each night.

One of the company, a man originally from Aquae Sulis, and not a cavalryman by upbringing, as most of them were, kept his immediate companions in a high good humour by his songs and stories. He told one story of an old merchant of Aquae Sulis who had married a young wife, a lively young thing with a taste for lads of her own age and not altogether satisfied with the bargain she had made. This lass, he said, driven at last to the extremity of entertaining a Negro slave who worked in a granary three streets away, was surprised one night when her aged husband returned unexpected from a business journey to Londinium. There was no time even for the Negro to escape by the bedroom window, so the resourceful young wife posed him, as a discus thrower, in a dark corner of the room, and when her husband entered, a little dazed from the climb upstairs and the wine he had drunk before coming home, she told him that she had been fortunate enough to purchase this handsome bronze statue at the local market that day.

When the husband saw the Negro he rubbed his eyes and agreed that it was a fine portrayal of primitive manhood, but, he added tipsily, "Whenever I see a statue, I like to give it a kick."

There was no stopping him. He staggered back the length of the room, and launched himself at the posing Negro, who did not wink an eyelid while all this happened.

The old merchant made a better job of it than he had hoped. His foot caught the posing lover with a force and precision that caused a bead of sweat to roll down the Negro's cheeks. Yet his bronze face was as composed as the statue would have been. All he said was, "Clang!"

Artos heard this story and laughed with the others, yet the idea of a wife's betrayal was started once more in his mind. Bedwyr noted his sunken head and his hands gripping the high pommel, the reins hanging loosely over the horse's shoulders.

At length the leader spoke to him quietly, so that the others should not hear. "Though I think I love her, Bedwyr, I would kill her if she was unfaithful to me," he said.

Bedwyr asked, more to pass away the time than to gain information, "How would you kill an unfaithful wife, Bear?"

Artos was silent for a while, then he said, "I do not know, but it would be an original death, something a betrayed husband had never done before, so that all men should remember it!"

Then Artos fell into a long silence once more, almost as though he were thinking of ways a wife might be punished. And it was while he was thinking after this fashion, and when they were cantering down a dark and sunken road, with willow-herb and hawthorn high up to their thighs, and dim boughs leaning over them, shutting out the light, that a man staggered to them, from the gloom, his broken reins still clasped in his hand, his tunic bespattered with blood. Bedwyr spurred forward and levelled his lance at the sudden apparition. Artos dragged out the sword Caliburn and set his teeth for the jolt of the thrust.

But the man in the road raised his mud-caked face and tried to give the royal salute.

"Hail, Artos the Bear," he croaked, "Cei gives you greeting!"

Bedwyr had only sufficient time to swerve his great charger, or the lance would have been in the throat of the warrior. As it was, Bedwyr's stallion brushed against him, tumbling him into the roadway, so that Artos had to rein in his own charger, for fear of trampling his dear friend.

At last they picked Cei up and bore him to the roadside and poured precious water over his face. He opened his eyes and smiled at his master.

"I come to report the news, Bear," he said. "The kings plot your death and are waiting for you at Caerwent. They have massed their warriors in the city and vow that you shall not leave the place alive."

Artos held up the man's head and asked gently, "Who tried to stop you from coming to me, little brother?"

Cei shook his head, "I do not know, Bear," he said. "I rode through a company of horse, men of Votiporix, outside Caerwent and took an arrow in my side. Then, north of our own citadel, three of the second company gave chase and followed me to within ten miles of this place."

Bedwyr rolled him over and examined him. "They did not wound you, Cei?" he said at last.

Cei smiled and said, "I turned on my tracks in a wood and took two of them, slashing from an overhanging bough with my knife. The other turned and went back. But he picked at my horse with his javelin as he went. The beast died under me and I fear has broken my shoulder bone."

His eyes began to close with weariness. Artos shook him gently and said, "What of Medrawt, friend? Is he with the others?"

Cei struggled against sleep, saying, "Medrawt spends all his days hunting and does not seem to know what is toward."

Artos spoke again, more urgently now, for he saw that the man was too exhausted to speak much more. "Tell me, Cei, have they betrayed me, the two of them?"

The tribesman's eyes flickered and his voice was almost inaudible. "They look at each other as merchants do in the market place, when they drive a hard bargain. I have seen no more."

Then Cei fainted away and Artos had him placed in one of the few forage wagons that now remained with them, after the rough and destructive roads of the north. He gave the signal to ride at the gallop. The first company struck spurs into their horses' sides.

"Where are we going, Bear?" asked Bedwyr in amazement.

Artos said, "The gods have cheated us of one battle. We must find another, or our time in Britain is finished, and we may as well sit on the temple steps in Londinium and show our scars for crusts of beggar's bread!"

XXXVIII

AS THEY RODE ON, BEDWYR ASKED ARTOS WHETHER HE WOULD GATHER Medrawt's men from Caer Leon. The Count shook his head. "I am not sure of them now," he said. "Better to attack with a small force that one trusts than a big one that may twist in one's grip, like an ill-balanced sword."

Some miles outside Caerwent, a man waited for them in the roadway, holding up a long strip of white cloth.

Bedwyr said, "I know that man. He stands behind Votiporix in council and carries hidden knives."

Almost immediately the man called out to them, "Hail, Artos! I come as the herald of the Western Kings. Is it peace with me?"

Now they were almost upon him and Artos answered, "Why not, friend? We arc not at war with the west, are we? But why do the kings, my brothers, send a herald to me?"

The man wheeled his horsc about and rode beside Artos. Bedwyr moved in, so as to thrust between them at the first sign of treachery.

The herald said, "My masters send me to bid you welcome back to Caerwent."

Artos replied, "That is thoughtful of them, but why did they think I should not feel welcome there?"

The herald said, "They feared that false reports might keep you from them and from Caerwent."

Artos replied, "I go to Caer Leon, not because of any false reports but because I have matters there which need my attention."

Bedwyr smiled at this crafty reply and edged forward a pace in readiness.

The herald's face showed his concern. "But, Artos," he said, "you must come to Caerwent. The kings await you there with preparations. It would not be seemly to ignore them now."

Artos said, "If they so much want to see me, let the kings come to me in Caer Leon."

"Then die now!" cried the herald, swinging round to plunge his knife in the Bear's side.

The long sword of Bedwyr swept through the air. Its blade took the man at the base of the neck, and shearing the bone of his right shoulder, buried itself deep in his body. The herald gave a high-pitched shriek and leapt from his painted wooden saddle, dead even before his body struck the roadway. Bedwyr found himself holding only the bone hilt of his sword which had snapped when the man had twisted so violently. He flung it at the horse in anger, and the frightened beast started off into the bare moorland at the side of the road, dragging its dead rider with it, his foot still entangled in the stirrup-iron.

Artos said, "I thought I had tempted God too far then, Bedwyr. Thank you, old friend. You shall have the best sword in Caer Leon when we get back there."

Bedwyr said, "Do we not ride to Caer Leon now, Bear?"

The Count of Britain answered, "Not for the moment, my friend. I said otherwise to try this dog's teeth. Now I know that they wish for my death above all other things. I am too dangerous for them still to use me as their battle leader. Now we know the nature of the preparations these kings make to welcome me!"

Then Bedwyr chose for himself a new sword from the armourer's wagon, and they rode on towards Caerwent as fast as their horses would carry them, anxious now to see the end of this affair. After a while, Cei came forward on a pack-horse, his face still drawn with tiredness and pain. "What troubles you, my friend?" asked the Bear.

Cei said, "I have never yet avoided battle, Bear, but today the gods tell me it would not be good for me to go into Caerwent."

Bedwyr heard him and said, "You are still thinking of my words about the raven that caws for you there?"

Cei lowered his eyes. "It would not be good for me today, Artos."

He did not ask to be relieved of his duty; that would have been dishonourable in the code of the times. Artos took him by the wrists and looked into his eyes.

"If your raven should take you in Caerwent after that speech, friend," he said, "I should have a heavy weight on my shoulders all my days. You are too valuable to me to be treated like a worn-out cart-horse. Go, Cei, and find yourself a place among the trees on this road. Wait for us there when we return. If we do not return by nightfall, go to Caer Leon and act as you think I would have commanded."

He took out his hunting-knife and handed it to Cei, who saluted him gravely and kissed the engraved blade before putting it into his belt. Then Cei turned and rode back among the trees. No man spoke to him as he went. He was death's messenger and not to be addressed in ordinary words.

Then the company rode on, and as they came near the squat and brooding citadel, Artos ordered one of his lieutenants to ride beside him, carrying a strip of white cloth as obviously as he could.

"Your horse is of the right colour, comrade," he said. "From a distance they will think the herald has deceived us, and so we shall enter the city untroubled. Otherwise, who knows? There are many spots along this way where we might fall into an ambush."

Bedwyr came close and said, "What is our plan, Bear, when once we are inside this city?"

Artos answered simply, "There can be no plan. We must go into Caerwent and slay or be slain, nothing more."

Bedwyr looked at him in wonder. "Shall we leave no men outside to rescue us if the odds are too great, Bear?"

Artos said, "My friend, we have far too few men as it is to spare a single one of them. Our enemies will lock us in their city, but we must behave in such a way that they will be glad to let us out again! These kings imagine that we shall enter in peace, suspecting nothing. That means they will at first be gentle with us, will await a special signal before attacking. If we carry the war to them without warning, then, they will at least be caught off their balance. I say no more."

Bedwyr saluted him and then halted. "Pass back the word," he said to the next lieutenant, "and say that the order is: 'Sting wasps, and make the hand unclench!' " The man smiled and did as Bedwyr had said. Then the first company set its chargers at the gallop.

So it was that when the great gates of Caerwent clanged behind the last of the Cymry, there was no horseman but had his lance at the ready and his sword loose in the scabbard.

The streets of the citadel were strangely empty, but Artos, staring ahead as they rode up the straight main street, pointed and said, "Look, they have set banners and a great awning in the square. That is to tempt us forward. Their bloodhounds will be waiting, slavering round that trap. There we must not go."

Bedwyr, spurring close to his master, gasped, "What shall we do, Bear?"

Artos answered and said, "Split the company into two halves. I shall lead the one, and you the other. At the crossroads before the square, lead your men to the right. I shall go to the left. So we shall encircle those who would have encircled us. Then must every man of the Cymry vow to kill ten before he falls from his horse. May he who only takes nine with him never reach Avallon!"

Bedwyr saluted, then fell back among the others, and without delay the two troops rode through the waiting city. As they approached the square, the silver trumpets of the Western Kings snarled out in a ghastly parody of welcome. The Cymry who rode in the vanguard even saw the kings sitting upright, expectant, in their gilded chairs, under the gaudy awnings. They saw the many innocent townsfolk who gathered about the colonnades of the square, anxious to greet the Bear, their Count of Britain.

Artos said grimly, "Pray God those good folk go to their homes before it begins, for there can be no delay."

Then they had reached the crossroads, and yelling out their new war cry—"Sting wasps, and make the hand unclench!"—they rode at the charge.

A squad of soldiers sat about in a side street, waiting and throwing dice, their helmets dangling from their arms, laughing and jesting with each other. The troop of Artos was upon them then, and men who had laughed a moment before now spewed blood upon the cobblestones.

Further along the same street, a patrol of picked archers trotted out of a side alley to find out what all the noise was about. They carried their unstrung bows, like festival whips, in their unprepared hands. One man of them only regained the shelter of that lane, for the screaming troop was among them even before they could turn and run back.

Now men lay everywhere, in the ghastly poses of death, while the two berserk troops of Cymry, mad as hunger-driven wolves, scoured street by street, almost lancing each other in their lust to wipe out their betrayers.

Yet this skirmishing, bloody as it was, could not decide the day alone, and Artos knew it. So when his troop passed that of Bedwyr in a broad thoroughfare that led to a group of storehouses, he shouted out, "Now into the square, from opposing sides, and may the gods pour the flagons of death upon our lance ends!"

The news of this swirling massacre had been quick to penetrate to the city's heart, and now men and women ran wherever they thought shelter lay, snatching up their children as they were able, or lying upon them if there was no time to run, to protect them with their own bodies from those merciless hooves and lance-points.

Now the soldiers of the Western Kings poured into the square to form into their ranks. But their movements were impeded by the panic-stricken citizens. Warriors of Dumnonia and Demetia screamed out in frustration and fury, striking at unprotected heads and bodies, as men and women strained to push them aside so as to get back to their homes. The square was now a shambles of excited creatures who tried to fend off death, yet were prevented from doing so by the living. Many an old veteran felt that day as a savage bull must feel on his way to the abattoir, powerful yet baffled by the many weak creatures who hustle about him, pushing him here and there, but never fighting him. . . .

Then that fearful war cry came upon their ears again: "Sting wasps, and make the hand unclench!" Suddenly men looked up to see horses' heads, and, above them, men laughing and levelling their dripping lances. The soldiers of Dumnonia turned and fled towards the other side of the square. But now they met the terror-stricken men of the Demetae, who also fled from the awful stinging wasps on their own side of the square.

Now men flung down their swords and fell howling to their knees, trying to shelter beneath the bodies of those who already lay on the ground. Archers round the square let fly their arrows in a drunken fear that killed their own comrades as they grovelled, helpless. And the horses of the Cymry staggered and rolled as their hooves slithered on the wet cobbles, or on bodies which twisted under their hooves in the last agony. And now the men of the Cymry thrust and slashed, thrust and slashed, until they could have howled from the terror of it all.

And so at last the Cymry were masters of Caerwent; not because of their numbers, which were relatively small, but because of their relentless fury and the savage surprise of their attack. And the news ran like wildfire along the streets of the city that the Western Kings had fled in the haste of their terror, leaving behind them all their treasure. Then many hundreds of men, deserted by their kings, offered themselves to Artos and the Cymry, to follow them to the death.

But the battle was not yet over. Although the hand had unclenched, the city was not yet taken. For here and there men still fought savagely in small bands, in such places, away from the open square, as would allow horsemen no room to turn about or to charge in.

And as dusk came on, the men of Artos and of Bedwyr searched for such dauntless warriors. Horses mounted stairways, or splashed through fountains, or pushed their way through garden walls, tumbling the light stones before them. In gardens that evening, men fought among the flowers, or lay dead with their heads in the carp pools, the lazy fish moving about their starting eyes unperturbed.

Yet even at this moment of victory, the Cymry still suffered their losses. Men of courage crouched beneath walls, thrusting upward with sword or javelin as the questing riders came over, thirsty for still more blood. It was a battle to the end.

Artos, making his last survey, came to a low wall, at which he set his charger. As he approached, with a drumming of hooves, a great hound leapt onto the wall, snarling and preparing to spring at the horses' head. Artos levelled his lance, which passed through the howling animal. Yet this sudden surprise was enough to upset the courser's leap, and it came down heavily on the other side, taking part of the wall with it.

There was a high scream from beneath the wall, and when the horse had regained its balance, Artos turned to see that a woman had been sheltering there in the shadows. Her body had taken the full weight of that disastrous leap. Artos felt a pang of pity that such an incident should mar the final stages of the victory. Then the hairs on the nape of his neck rose, for the hound that still writhed beneath his horse's hooves was Troynt. There was no mistaking that collar now.

Artos leaped from the saddle and ran to the woman. She was dead and the young child in her arms was still.

Artos gave a great cry of anguish then and tore at his hair like a man possessed of devils. And then, when he could no longer express the deep animal grief that ripped his mind apart, he dragged out the great sword Caliburn and with trembling hands set it among the scattered stones, point uppermost.

Bedwyr, seeking the last enemies of the night, looked over the wall to see the Count of Britain fall face downwards with a terrible groan. He leapt towards his lord then and raised him gently from the tumbled heap.

"Thank God, the stones did not hold firm when he fell," whispered Bedwyr. "The wound is not a deadly one."

Artos looked up at him with eyes of agony and said, "I thought the hand had unclenched, yet it still closes me in its grip."

Now others of the Cymry came with lamps to seek their leader. They bent over him in great concern.

"Keep the light steady," said Bedwyr. "He has lost much blood, but with God's help these bandages should hold."

It was only as he rose to wipe the Bear's blood from his hands that he saw the face of the dead Gwenhwyfar. In the lantern's fluttering light, she seemed to smile. Yet as the man turned round and the beam moved away from her face, Bedwyr knew that the expression was the grimace of eternal despair.

"Poor lass," he muttered. "Afraid to go into the darkness alone." He had not seen Troynt, who even in death still stared towards his cold charges.

XXXIX

LYSTRA HAD SPENT THE EARLY EVENING GETTING READY FOR HER lover. Her mute slave-girls, who were safe because she had had them made dumb, had worked on their mistress since the late afternoon so that she might be lovely in the eyes of Medrawt.

They had annointed her olive-skinned body with sweet oils, from Persia and far India, stroking and massaging it into her lean flanks and her rounded thighs. They had smoothed the soles of her feet with pumice, and had trimmed and painted the nails of her feet and hands with gold. While her full breasts were still faintly damp with sweet oil, they had dusted them with fine silver, so that she looked more like a goddess in an Eastern temple than a living woman.

When they had redyed her black hair and painted her eyes blue and her broad lips scarlet-red, they set about dressing her, as she lay supine on the thick skins of bear and wolf and leopard, before the wood-fire. She would wear nothing that Medrawt had ever seen before, she decreed. All must be new, from the precious things she had carried away from the merchant's house in Londinium, things of the East or of the Mediterranean. Her fancy was to appear that night like a princess of Crete, in the lost glory of Knossos, a daughter of Minos himself. . . .

About her hair they fastened a heavy silver coronet, chased with leaping warriors and minotaurs. In her fine ears they stuck great rubies. On her arms, twisted bands of bronze and silver-gilt. About her neck a broad collar of polished leather, set with garnets and cornelians. Her breasts they left bare, in the Cretan manner, for they were ornament enough, Lystra thought sardonically, as she gazed at her reflection in the polished silver mirror that the two girls held out for her. Rubies were too artificial, she said to herself, too cold and contrived when viewed against the real thing.

About her upper body, Lystra wore a little silken waistcoat, thickly encrusted with diamond dust and embroidered with heavy gold and silver wire. Something, she thought, which might easily be slipped off if it were too uncomfortable for anyone. Her skirt was very full, and made of many yards of delicate gauze, pleated accurately and then starched so that it stood out stiffly from her body, yet admitted the light to display the beauty of her limbs.

As the two slave-girls strapped on her light doeskin buskins, Lystra sighed deeply, and one of the girls was so startled, thinking that they had pinched her or in some other way caused her displeasure, that she almost fainted with the fear of the possibilities of such a fault. This girl recalled the surgeon's sharp knife when she had joined the service of the lady Lystra and would have died rather than endure such pain again, for any reason.

But Lystra was only sighing that Medrawt alone would enjoy her preparations. She was a perfectionist and desired that the ideal to which she had attained should be appreciated by as many as possible. If only, she thought, Medrawt could be multiplied, five, ten, twenty times—so that this might not be wasted! One man is not worthy of such a thing. . . . After twenty, one would feel justified in going to such trouble, perhaps, perhaps.

She turned from such speculations with a sigh and in a sharp voice commanded the girls to throw incense upon the wood-fire.

She did not want this done right at the last minute; it would fill the room with smoke. Better get it done now, and then the air would clear and only the faint scent of the stuff would remain, just enough of it to stimulate, without overpowering by its heaviness.

Lystra sent the girls away then and daubed her lips with a delicate gum, compounded of aromatic herbs and honey. This Medrawt must be convinced of her sweetness at every turn. Yet once again, she wondered whether he was worth her trouble. True, he was handsome, almost the most handsome man she had ever seen—except a young Greek officer who had once looked after her in Athens, when she was without a home for a week or two. She had forgotten his name now, for she had known many Greek names from time to time, but she remembered that he was handsome, like a god. He wore the hair long on one side of his face, she recalled nostalgically, because a sword had taken off the lower part of his ear. He was self-conscious about it, though she had laughed at him and had told him that such a thing did not detract at all. There were worse wounds than that a man might have. But Medrawt was quite handsome, in his dark surly way.

Then she thought of her husband, of Artos the Bear. Now there was a man, if only he would forget fighting for a while and recall why the gods had made him a man, and such a fine man, strong and rugged, like his namesake. Not a handsome man, but a strong man. . . . If only Artos could be made to see sense, if only he would give up this stupid quest after a unified Britain with himself as Emperor! The whole thing was ridiculous. Britain had never been that, never, not even in the greatest days of Rome. There had always been a large part of the island which stood outside Roman law. It was a pity that Artos was so uneducated, she thought, or he would have known that. Besides, you could not hold up the course of the peoples. If the Saxon invader was set on coming and living in Britain, then he would keep on coming, whatever Artos did. It was barbaric madness to think that a few thousand horsemen with Roman names and helmets could stifle the land-hungry ambitions of whole races of sea-wanderers. Better to accept the invasions, to meet the Saxon leaders and come to terms with them. Let them have the east, for instance, and build the homes they desired. Then Artos and the Cymry could create a new British nation in the west, living the lives they wished, without disturbance. That would be the civilised thing to do. At that moment, Lystra wished that Artos and not Medrawt were coming to the villa, so that she could explain all this to him while the mood was on her.

She was so deeply engrossed in this thought that she did not hear Medrawt come into the room. He stood for a while, in the fire-light, his torn cloak hanging to the rush mats, his hair upon his shoulders, unkempt, his boar-spear still in his hands. Then she turned and saw him. She gave a little start and then said, "Hail, Medrawt! I had expected you to come dressed for a different sort of hunting."

He said, "I beg your pardon, lady. I was out in the forest beyond Caer Leon surrounded by huntsmen when your messenger found me. I could not leave them straightway, for that would have aroused suspicions. I had to wait until they were sated with killing before I could steal away."

She looked at him through slits of eyes and said, "And now I suppose you are tired out?"

He shrugged his shoulders. "I am as you see, lady," he said. "I am not a Hercules, like another I could mention."

Lystra said, "I have waited so long, a little while longer will make no difference. Perhaps if you went to the baths and cleaned the mud from your body and let the girls comb your hair and put a clean shirt on your back, you would feel better."

She turned away from him and looked at herself in the silver mirror. She felt that she had good reason to feel disappointed.

Medrawt stood, undecided, for a few moments, leaning on his boar-spear. He had no wish to be there that night. This could have waited, until the affair at Caerwent was settled. There would be time to roll this bitch about on the rushes when Artos was safely out of the way. Medrawt almost ran from the room to gallop towards the citadel, to be nearer the place when the news broke, when the kings had set *his* head on the temple-pike.

But it was useless. Weary though he was, Medrawt could not help himself. As he looked across at the woman, he knew that he could not leave her yet. He went quickly to the window and looked out. The young man, Bethlac, was standing, alert, at the garden gate, his sword drawn. No one would enter there without the warning being given. Bethlac had sworn to defend Medrawt with his last drop of blood. He was a true Jute, a faithful one to whomsoever he gave his word. Medrawt smiled towards him and then said to Lystra, "Lady, it is in my heart that we shall have many such evenings together. If this one be short and brutish, pardon me, for I am not yet the master of my own actions. But I swear . . ."

Lystra did not turn. She spoke softly, like a purring cat.

"Swear less, little one, and do more. Go to the bathhouse and then come back and swear to what you will."

Medrawt could not help admiring the steadfast purpose of the woman. He did not love her, of course, for she was not the woman he dreamed of. Yet she had a quality which attracted him in a perverse way. He would see more of her when Artos was killed, but he would have to be rid of her at last. As he followed the slave-girl to the bathhouse, he thought on the problem. He might marry her off to one of the great Cymry; not Bedwyr, of course, because if the day's battle were fully successful, he would have gone down with his master, a javelin in his chest. But one of the others, not so loyal as Bedwyr. . . . Not Cei, to be sure, for he was such a small man, and Lystra would devour him like a female spider!

Medrawt thought long over this situation, and so deeply that he did not even curse the slave-girls for scrubbing his back too hard. A cleanly pair, themselves, having come from the far north where bathing was almost a natural thing to do, they had been disgusted that such a man should come near to their clean mistress.

Back beside the wood-fire, Medrawt said, "Do you approve now, lady? Your girls have dressed me up as though I were going to the great stones, to be sacrificed."

Lystra looked at him with a faint smile, her eyelids heavy over her blued eyes. "Perhaps you are, little one," she said. "Who knows?"

On the low table by the pallet of leopard skins was set a flask and two wine cups. "Drink this," said Lystra, holding out the larger towards him. He noticed that she drank sparingly and commented on her forebearance.

"I eat and drink little," she said. "I even sleep little, so abstemious of the pleasures am I!"

Medrawt drained his cup at a gulp. "The last proves nothing," he said. "Perhaps your time is taken up in other directions."

Lystra looked at him serenely. "Perhaps," she said. "One's private life is one's private life."

Medrawt said, "How private are we now?"

Lystra answered, "I have sent the men-servants away. The two girls could not talk if they wished, and neither can write. So we may consider ourselves as private as if we were locked in a pyramid in ancient Egypt!"

Medrawt drank off another cup of wine, a heavy, resinous vintage of southern Gaul. His shoulders sagged and his legs felt leaden. Lystra beckoned him to share her pallet. He sank down with his head in the crook of her arm and lay still, his eyes closed. He had suddenly had a vision of what must have been happening that day in Caerwent, with the pick of the Cymry tumbling from their horses as the ambush went into action about the square. He saw men he knew and liked, plucking at the arrows in their throats, and he groaned that he would never lead those men, when he became the Count of Britain, the *dux bellorum*, in all truth.

Suddenly he heard Lystra speaking. Her voice was sibilant and sneering. "You do not find the wine stimulating?" she said. "I thought it would ease away your huntsman's fatigue. But perhaps you have been hunting at other villas this night, as well as in the forests?"

Medrawt saw Bedwyr, his mouth wide in a scream, as the arrows stood thick in his back. He shook his head to clear that picture away. He could not speak to the woman. He knew that he should never have come to this place of mockery. No, he should have been with Artos, riding into the square that day. His blood-brother, to whom he had made the vow. Medrawt found the hot tears running down his face. He began to rise from the soft bed. Lystra put her hand inside his shirt and kept him there for a moment.

"Shall I call the girls in to dance for you?" she said. "That might work better than the wine. They are well trained in those things."

Medrawt passed his hand across his eyes, in pain. He shook his head. Lystra smiled and said, "Would you have me dance, Medrawt, then?"

He struck at her caressing hand so that she drew back with something like a sob. Then suddenly he rose and said, "Who passed the window? I thought I saw a shadow pass the window."

Lystra shrugged her shoulders and said, "There is nothing more I can do if that is how you feel. The window is as good an excuse as any, I suppose. I am sorry, Medrawt. I shall not offer you this again."

She began to move as though she would rise from the couch. Medrawt struggled against his tipsiness and fatigue and then rolled sideways to the floor.

As he raised his head and looked up, he was suddenly aware that they were not alone in the room. Artos was standing in the doorway, his great sword in his left hand, his right arm in a woollen sling that was filthy with blood. The Bear's eyes were wide and staring and he seemed to be gazing up through the smoke into the roof itself, as though he could not see. He swayed there for a while, silent, breathing hard.

Medrawt's heart gave a great leap. Artos had not died that day in Caerwent after all. Or if he had, this was his spirit. And Bethlac—why had not Bethlac given the alarm?

Medrawt knew that he could not face this terrible man now. His boar-spear still lay propped against the wall in the bathhouse, and in any case, his arms lacked strength. He was drugged with the wine and the exertions of his hunting. Like a man in a nightmare, not knowing, hardly caring whether he was seen or not, Medrawt moved into the shadows to the far door. He expected at any moment that the Bear would fling a knife into his back, but nothing happened. There was silence. Only the crackling of the wood-fire and the hooting of owls outside. He stumbled on through the garden gate, his head thrown back, staring at the stars. In the narrow roadway he fell his length over the sprawling body of Bethlac, who lay with his hands over his head, as though to protect it from the great blow which had shorn down to his jaw. Medrawt snatched up the sword of the young man from the dust, and then staggered away towards the campfires which burned outside the great city. There at least his own men would be waiting for him, to protect him, if needs be.

In the villa, Artos at length seemed to come back to life again. The sword dropped from his weary hand with a clatter and he shook his head as one who comes out of a deep trance. Lystra, her heart beating so fast that she almost choked with fear, rose from the couch and went towards him.

"Artos the Bear," she said. "Artos the Bear." That was all she could think of saying. He looked down at her and smiled, and for a moment she expected him to put his fingers round her throat and strangle her. Yet he only smiled, and when she dragged him down with her, he let himself sink gently among the skins. And when she placed his hand to a secret part of her body, he let it remain, as though nothing was changed. And so they lay, in the firelight, without speaking.

Then, when she had regained some of her courage, she forced herself on him, hoping to blot out any memory he might have had of that strange night. Artos the Bear smiled and let himself be handled as she willed. Only once did he seem to groan and to roll sideways in a sudden spasm of pain. Lystra looked at him in wonder. Then she drew away from him in disgust, for the gauze of her fine dress was wet with his blood. She stared at it in horror for a while.

"What manner of man are you, Artos?" she gasped at last. "What manner of man who bleeds like this?"

Artos groaned again, and flung himself back on the skins, his teeth bared in a grin of agony. The sudden scuffle with the young fool at the gate had burst apart the bandages that Bedwyr had put into him that day. He would have cursed Bethlac had he been able. Yet he recalled the young man's hands, clasped over his head, as the great sword, Caliburn, came down upon him. He was as helpless as a kitten before such a stroke. Artos was suddenly sorry for that young man, but there was no other way to come to his wife.

He looked at Lystra's horror-stricken face and his lips moved weakly. He tried to ask her to bind up his wound, but no words came from his mouth.

Lystra saw his lips moving, saw the blood upon the white sheepskins, and shrank back towards the door, her hand over her mouth so that she would not scream to wake all the gods.

As she fled into the dark, she looked back over her shoulder, in terror. Artos the Bear still lay on the floor, his hands plucking helplessly at the belt about his stomach, his eyes rolled back in his head. The scent of incense still hung about the room.

PART FOUR

THE VENGEANCE

Lystra, Lustra, Lady of Light,
Come down among us to brighten our night;
Lovely Europa, Bear's heart will be full
To see how your beauty will dazzle the Bull.

XL

IT WAS MANY MONTHS BEFORE ARTOS CAME BACK FROM DEATH. HE lay in his palace at Caer Leon, surrounded by his friends and doctors. They told him that the winter had passed and that spring was almost come again. He smiled calmly and whispered, "I have been for a long journey alone. I have seen strange things that no man has told me of before."

Bedwyr and Cei were there, their wounds long since healed. They wept to hear their master speak so weakly, like a woman after her labour.

"What have you seen, Master?" asked Bedwyr, trying to humour the Bear.

Artos lay still for many minutes, as though he had not heard the question; but at last he answered and said, "It is not as terrible in hell as we were told, Bedwyr. A man can survive it if he has but sufficient courage. That is all a man needs, courage. Not strength, but courage."

He babbled on in this manner for a while and then fell into a deep sleep, for his talking had exhausted him. But later that night he said, fixing his eyes steadily on his two friends, "I have dreamed that Lystra and Medrawt are still in the city. Is that true?"

Bedwyr lowered his head and said gravely, "Yes, Bear. We have them both. They are locked in the prison, in chains. We took them on the outskirts of the city as they tried to escape from you."

Artos was silent for a long while, and then he said, "Is she still beautiful, Bedwyr?"

Bedwyr nodded his head and said, "We have not harmed them,

Master. We have merely locked them up, until such time as you came back to us and told us what to do with them."

Artos smiled up at him and said, "That was a wise course to take, my dear friend. For you know that she is still my wife and he is still my brother?"

Bedwyr said, "We said that to ourselves, when we were almost ready to slay them."

Cei said, "Master, say the word and I will slay them now."

Artos gazed at him as though he had never seen him before. "You are a bloody man, friend," he said. "I do not think you should be allowed to wear a sword. Take it from him, someone."

Bedwyr took Cei's sword. No one else would have dared to ask for it. Bedwyr winked as he took it and later gave it back, when Artos had fallen asleep again. But before he did so, he said, "Are they lodged together, these two, Bedwyr?"

Bedwyr said, "No, Master. They have not seen each other since the night when they fled."

"That was also a wise course," said the Bear. "Tomorrow, dress them as befits their rank and bring them to me. I would like to see them again."

Cei stepped forward, laying his hand on the Count's shoulder. "Master," he said, "you will not forgive them?"

Artos gazed at him strangely and said, "You are the man whose sword was taken from him, are you not?" Cei fell back from the bedside and Artos stared at him and through him, until at last Cei went to the shadows by the wall, unable to meet the eyes of the Count.

And so Lystra and Medrawt were set free, and dressed in their finery once more. They were brought from the dungeon in litters to the palace of Artos. They met in his presence and so could not speak as freely as they would have done.

Artos was propped up in his bed. He smiled at them and touched their hands with his own white fingers. Medrawt could have wept to see the great warrior looking so frail. Lystra smiled with her lips, but hated him with her heart. She was glad that he had suffered in this manner.

Artos said, "At last we are together again, we three."

Then he ordered the doctors and the warriors to leave him. They went reluctantly. Bedwyr and Cei stayed at the other side of the door, in case these two tried to kill the Bear as he lay weak in his sickbed.

When the room was empty of the men, Artos said gently, "I have both loved and hated you while I have lain here, waiting for my body to knit together again. But now that my wound has closed her great mouth, I am my own master again and I say that I have pardoned you both for whatever you may think you have done against me."

Medrawt put on a brazen face. "Artos," he said, "that was something I wanted to speak to you about. I have been locked away from life for many weeks now, and often treated like a slave, not like a nobleman. Men have hinted that I had committed a great sin against you, but would not say what it was. I ask you, brother, to tell me now how I have offended you."

Lystra looked at him sidelong, with contempt, as he spoke, but he disregarded her.

Artos put the ends of his fingers together and said at last, "Medrawt, my brother, I know as little as you do. I have not seen you since the day I set forth for Pictland, have I?"

Medrawt looked hard at the Bear, sensing trickery. But the man's face was innocent of all guile, it seemed. Medrawt thought, Was it possible that he did not see me that night, on Lystra's bed? Was he so weak with his wound that he did not see me then?

He glanced at the woman who kneeled beside him at the bedside. Her mouth was twisted in a wicked little smile.

Medrawt said, "No, brother. We have not seen each other since then."

Artos looked gravely at him. "Then how can you have harmed me, brother?" he said. "Surely they did wrong to imprison you. One day, perhaps, I will punish them. But not now, for I am grateful to God for letting me live again."

Then he turned to Lystra. "Lady," he said gently, "get up from your knees. The floor is cold and it is not yet spring. You must not get a chill, kneeling there. Tell me, lady, are you as glad to see me as I am to see you?"

Lystra said even as gently, "Artorius, the floor of the dungeon was far colder than this is. I have got used to it. There was nothing to do but kneel and pray in the place where they locked me. So do not fear for me."

Artos put out his hand and made the gesture of raising her. Then he indicated that she was to sit on his bed beside him.

"But tell me, my love," he said, "are you as glad to see me as I am to see you?"

Lystra said, "For God's sake, Artos, have done with this foolery. You are almost an old man now, by the looks of you. Do not behave like a boy, torturing a rabbit. Kill me and have done. I am ready."

Artos turned towards Medrawt and said simply, "Why must folk always talk of death? Why not of life? Why should I kill this beautiful woman, think you, Medrawt, my brother?"

Medrawt said slyly, "The only reason I can think of is so that she might always live in your dreams as beautiful as she now is. Age would never come at her throat to wrinkle it then."

Artos said, "Yes, she is beautiful, is she not? Do me a great favour, my lady, and hold this Medrawt in your arms and put your lips to his. I am too sick a man to withstand such heady wine, but he is my brother, and it would be seemly for you to kiss him as I command."

Medrawt started away from the bed with the shock of this order. Now he was sure that Artos was up to some devilry. But Lystra bowed her head in acknowledgement of the Bear's command and took Medrawt by the shoulders. "Like this?" she asked Artos.

The Count of Britain smiled and nodded. "Yes, just like that," he said. "But Medrawt lags behind. Kiss her, my brother. I command it."

Medrawt heard the new tone of menace in the weak voice, and sickened by the situation, obeyed this crazed leader. Yet the lips of Lystra were cold, like that of a dead woman, and the eyes that gazed into his as he bent towards her were the eyes of hatred not love.

Artos said, "That is a picture I shall cherish, whatever happens to me, or to you. I shall always recall it."

Then he called for his doctors to come back to the room. Lystra and Medrawt sat one on either side of his bed, no longer looking at each other. And when Artos said, "We must celebrate my recall to life, dear wife and dear brother, by a great show at the amphitheatre," they merely nodded their heads and did not speak.

Then Artos said, "How is your company of horse, Medrawt? Have they kept in training while I was sick?"

Medrawt's colour rose and he would have spoken in wrath, but Bedwyr, who had come in, answered for him, quickly. "They have trained, Artos," he said. "They are stationed in their own quarters. Cei has commanded them."

Artos said, "Now they will have their own commander back, Bedwyr. Cavalry must know only one master. See that Medrawt's quarters are made comfortable for him."

Then he lay back on his pillows and shut his eyes. Medrawt rose and followed Cei to the door. Lystra stood, indeterminately, wondering where she would be taken now. But at length Artos opened his eyes again and said, "My wife, I am too sick a man yet to risk losing your affection. Give me time, a little time more, and then come to my bed again."

A slave-girl took Lystra's hand and whispered, "Your room is ready, lady. Your two mutes wait to serve you again."

Lystra looked sternly at the girl and said, "By whose orders, girl?"

The girl said, "Artos the Count ordered your room to be made ready, lady. I know no more."

Then a doctor smiled at the lady and opened the door for her, indicating that the Bear of Britain was to be left to his rest.

XLI

AS SPRING CAME AND THE SUN MATURED, THE FOLK OF CAER LEON gazed with wonder at the change which was effected in the ancient amphitheatre. Workmen toiled within the great oval arena, clearing away the rubbish and fallen stones of two centuries. Masons came from far off to replace gateposts and seats, and to render the rough stonework of the barricades with a heavy coating of plaster, just as the legionaries had done when Caer Leon was the home of the Antonine Legion.

A citizen who watched this transformation said, "Getting to be like the good old days again, eh?"

His wife shuddered and turned away. "Good old days!" she said. "It's more as though they were preparing for some horrible sacrifice, if you ask me."

The citizen looked round apprehensively. "Well, no one's asking you, see?" he said. "Come on." And he led the way from the place with steps that marched quicker than usual.

At last, when the amphitheatre had been repainted and gilded, and great silk banners, bearing the sign of Artos, set up above the highest tiers of seats, over thirty feet above the barricades, men began to watch anxiously to see what manner of beasts would be brought to Caer Leon to celebrate the recovery from death of Artos.

One man thought leopards, to fight with wolves: the sleek speed of the one made a pleasant contrast with the rough guile of the other. Another man wagered that those banners gave the clue to what would happen and bet that there would surely be bears, baited by great hounds. That, he argued, would be more economical in the end, for a strong bear, especially one from the German forests, could fight on all afternoon, even when the dogs had torn everything from him but his claws. "In fact," this man said, "I have known them used in three different shows, before . . ."

A third man cut in. "That would be no true celebration of this happy event. Such an affair would be brutal and, er, tedious. Now, if my opinion is anything to go by, I'd say that Artos will provide us with something elevating, man against beast, or man against man—something to illustrate the continuous resurgence of the human spirit. Don't forget, he is officially a Christian."

The other snorted, and then the three moved away, to watch the Jutish company drilling in the great parade ground. Such glorious savages, they thought, as they watched the flaxen plaits bobbing up and down when the men ran in battle order, their short stabbing knives out.

Yet the day came, and no exotic howls were heard from the beast pens below the auditorium. Nor had any foreign-looking gladiators been seen hanging about the taverns of the city. An old man who lived in a shack near the wharf did say that late one dark night he had heard a commotion on one of the barges, a lot of bellowing and snuffling, and then the frightened cries of men. But he knew no more, and his contribution was discounted, since he was in his dotage and a notorious drinker of homemade parsnip wine.

The day of the festival was blessed by the gods. The afternoon sun beamed down upon the arena as though coming to grace the proceedings. Five thousand men and women filled the banks of seats that towered above the empty arena. The company of Artos was given first choice of places, the Dumnonians and Demetae were allowed to seat themselves next, and then the citizens. When Medrawt expressed surprise at this, Cei told him that it was by order of the Count of Britain, who desired the second company and the Jutish troop to stand guard outside, in case of any sort of trouble.

"You never know how civilians will take it," said Cei. "Most of them have lost the taste for these old entertainments and might get overexcited and lose their heads!"

Medrawt pursed his lips. He was not sure he liked the look of things, especially when he saw the entrance gates clang to, and heard the bolts fall into place, from inside the amphitheatre. That meant he would be cut off from his followers.

At last Artos came, in a litter, with Lystra. The gay trumpets brayed and the Count took his place in the seat of honour, Lystra at his side, Bedwyr standing immediately behind him.

When all was ready, Artos turned in his chair for the first time and looked back towards Medrawt. "I see you wear a sword, brother," he said coolly. "Did the ushers not tell you the order of the day? No man is to carry a sword herein."

An officer stepped forward and took Medrawt's sword from him, smiling slightly. Medrawt handed it over automatically, and now he knew that the whole affair was a ghastly nightmare trap. Before him, behind him, on either side of him, the men of the first company sat, wearing their swords and daggers openly.

Then Artos smiled at him and rose, signalling with his staff for the show to begin. All talk faded away and men craned their necks forward to be the first to see whatever wild beasts should run snorting into the sunlit arena. But to everyone's surprise, the pen-gate opened only a little way, and very gently, and three young girls entered, in white and wearing circlets of white flowers about their heads. They bowed to the royal seat and then to the audience, turning towards the four points of the compass and smiling.

Then, standing in the centre of that grim place, they looked up towards Lystra and began to sing, in their sweet and childish voices.

At first there was a titter of amusement at the song, which turned to wonder, and then at last to concern as the significance of the words went home:

"Lystra, Lustra, Lady of Light,
Come down among us to brighten our night;
Lovely Europa, Bear's heart will be full
To see how your beauty will dazzle the Bull!"

Artos sat, expressionless, as the children sang and raised their hands towards Lystra, imploring her. At first she smiled, thinking what sweet voices they had. Then, as they kept their hands raised and began to sing the verse again, she turned to Artos.

"What do they mean, husband?" she said, the nerves of her stomach suddenly rippling with fear.

He did not look at her. His voice was as cold as the northern seas. "They want you to go down there and dance with a bull they have," he said. "That is what they are saying."

Lystra said, "Good God, Artorius, if this is a jest, I do not appreciate it."

Artos answered, "I do not think it is meant to be a jest. But if you conquer their bull as easily as you have conquered Medrawt, you should soon be sitting beside me again, watching the rest of the entertainment."

Lystra looked past her husband, at Medrawt. He was gripping the stone arms of his seat, the knuckles of his thin hands as white as bone. His dark eyes were wide and starting with fear. He had understood what the song meant, as had the vast audience now, by the silence which had descended upon it. Suddenly Bedwyr recalled the words Artos had spoken as they rode down from Pictland: "it would be an original death, something a betrayed husband had never done before, so that all men should remember it." The memory of Artos was a long one. He never forgot an injury or a kindness, Bedwyr knew.

Bedwyr also knew that in the deep places of his heart, Artos had never loved but one woman, that Gwenhwyfar whom he had trampled to death in Caerwent. A woman of his own blood, part of himself, of his own nature. And in killing her he had slain his own finer part. Now Artos had the doom upon him in all truth, and soon the Furies would come gibbering at his door, if they were not there already. Bedwyr looked down at his master's neck. It seemed to have shrunk during his illness, and now from behind he had almost the appearance of an old man, in that shrivelled skin and those great hunched shoulders.

Lystra saw the old age that had come upon him from his pain and grief, from the remorse that daily ate into his spirit, killing him piecemeal. Then her fear was overcome by her great pride and she said, "So you knew, and have never forgiven me, Artos? Now you wish to make an example of me. Is that it, Artos?"

The Bear did not answer. He sat gnawing at the knuckles of his right hand. Bedwyr laid his own hand upon her shoulder. "Come now, lady," he said. "It would be more dignified."

She turned to him, afraid. "More dignified than what?" she asked.

He did not smile as he answered, "More dignified than being thrown, like Jezebel, over the barricade to the beast. That is my own special duty, should your courage fail you, lady."

As she passed by Artos, Lystra said, "You will remember this afternoon all your life, Artos. It will be with you when you would wish it a thousand years away."

In a voice that was not like his own, Artos answered, "No doubt, Lystra. It seems that I can seldom forget anything."

She did not look at Medrawt. But he watched her go out, with terror in his eyes, for now he wondered who would be next, and the answer did not seem hard to find.

For twenty yards or so, she and Bedwyr were out of sight of the audience, in the narrow passageway that led down into the arena. Once in the dusk there, Lystra threw off her dignified walk and, turning, pressed her body close to his, flinging her arms about his neck and putting her warm lips at his throat.

"For God's sake, be merciful," she said to the warrior. "Look, I am terribly afraid. You can feel the fear in my body. I am trembling. Feel it, feel it, Bedwyr."

Bedwyr stood very still, as though all life had suddenly left him. His body was hard and cold, cold as a stone man.

"Bedwyr, oh, Bedwyr," she sobbed again, "cannot you see what I am offering, man? For God's sake, help me, Bedwyr. Let us go away from here. Come with me and have me for your own. Look, I am yours, Bedwyr, to use as you please. Yours, yours, Bedwyr."

Then she drew back from him in horror. He had drawn his short stabbing sword and was walking towards her, his face set for the effort of the thrust.

"Forgive me, lady," he said. "Artos commands it. He knew that your pride would break when we got into the dark here." His voice was passionless and dead. His was only a ritual sorrow, not real, not warm and living. He was placating her ghost in advance, nothing more, as was done with all sacrifices.

"No, no," she said then, running a pace or two from him. "I am myself again. Put up your sword. I am ready."

He followed her closely to the entrance. And here she paused a moment, under the guise of unfastening her girdle. Then suddenly she drew forth a purse of gold, kept for emergencies. She made to press it into the man's hand, letting her breast touch his bare arm with the same movement.

But Bedwyr stared past her. He flung out his arm so that the money rolled in the passageway. Lystra was pinned hard against the wall by his arm. She felt the stone cold against her warm back. Cold, cold death! she thought, and suddenly remembered how hot the sun had been when she had played in the alley-ways of Byzantium as a child.

XLII

WHEN SHE UNDERSTOOD THAT HER LAST BID HAD FAILED, LYSTRA shrugged her shoulders and tried to smile, as though the whole affair was one of little importance in any case. Bedwyr merely stared back at her impassively, waiting for the signal from outside. Lystra could hear the crowds in the amphitheatre talking with wild excitement now. That terrible silence had broken at last. At first she even wondered whether they were going to revolt and rescue her. Then she listened more intently. Her face hardened, for these were the sounds of men who are expectant of blood, not those of men smitten with horror or the desire for mercy.

She began to tear off her fine gown, then stopped as though she had suddenly remembered the presence of Bedwyr. She smiled at him calmly, though her heart was throbbing almost to bursting point.

"Would it not be possible for you to step outside for a moment," she said, "while I make myself ready?"

The lieutenant shook his head, keeping his eyes averted from her exposed body. He gripped the sword tighter, as though he were under some emotional stress, but his hard face showed nothing.

"Very well," she said, as though tired of the whole affair. "Then at least have the decency to turn to the wall."

Bedwyr bowed his head slightly and turned as he was bidden. Then Lystra knew that the man was incorruptible. She tore off the remains of her dress, not caring now whether she spoiled it. She would not wear it again, it seemed. Her long linen outdoor shift she tore into broad bandages, and these she wound tightly about her lower body up to her breasts, to serve as protection, as she had seen the men bullfighters do in Scythia. She wrapped narrower bands about her arms, from wrist to elbow, like the long bracers that Eastern archers wore to guard their arms from the bowstring's lash.

"How do I look, Bedwyr?" she asked, and was suddenly startled to find that her voice had lost its timbre and was now as weak as that of a child, or an old woman. He turned slowly and gazed at her. His eyes were still cold and impersonal, though she sensed that he pitied her plight. She broke down again and said, "My friend, you have known me long enough to do me what favours you can. Is there anything, anything at all?"

Bedwyr did not look at her as he spoke; "Beyond that door is the shrine of vengeance. One might pray there before going into the sunlight. The gladiators used to set great store on it. Perhaps you might find it helpful, in some way."

Lystra went to the door and looked. The grey stones carried no promise, no comfort to her. The little tomb of a shrine smelled of damp earth. It would be the place to find worms and slugs, she thought.

She turned to him with a grimace. "I will pray in the shrine of my own heart, soldier," she said. "It will bring about my vengeance just as effectively, I think, and is cleaner."

Bedwyr sighed with boredom and embarrassment. "As you will," he said. "You know best."

Then he straightened himself and held his sword erect, for outside in the arena the trumpets were sounding and a dreadful hush had settled down once more upon the thick crowds.

"Is it time?" she asked, her insides turning over, her knees suddenly ready to collapse under her weight. He nodded, his mouth pinched hard, his eyes staring away from her. Then he hammered on the thick door with the hilt of his sword, and she heard the two great bolts being withdrawn, on the arena side. The bright sun struck her across the face like a vicious blow. As she stood in the doorway, the air became heavy with silence and all eyes were turned upon her, over the whole circuit of the amphitheatre. Bedwyr spoke out of the corner of his mouth. "Walk forward, lady. They will stone you for cowardice if you stay here longer."

She smiled, though her muscles would hardly obey her. "I would change places with any of them there now," she said. "Even the blind woman selling sour wine."

Bedwyr gave a snort of disgust and stepped back behind her, so that she should not run into the waiting room again and disgrace herself. But she did not turn. She suddenly gained control of her shuddering limbs, and straightening her back, began to walk to the centre of the arena, her face set towards the high seat where Artos sat, with Medrawt so close behind him.

Now from place to place among the audience, shouts were raised, since men saw that she had not been given any weapon, not even a boar-spear, with which to defend herself. Even the Cymry of Artos were dismayed at such treatment. One grizzled veteran, who lacked an eye and four fingers, growled, "Is she meant to fight the damned bull or just offer herself to be sacrificed to it?"

"It would be entertainment either way," giggled a young soldier, tipsily, dribbling the precious liquour from the wine-skin down his chest. The old warrior struck him with the back of his hand, so hard that the young man fell sideways off his seat, rubbing his jaw. Then he rose, and began to shout, "Give her a sword! Give the lass a sword!"

Men looked towards Artos, who made no sign of having heard anything. Medrawt began, "For God's sake, Artos . . ." But Cei suddenly took him by the wrist so strongly that he stopped speaking. The dark man's eyes were narrow. "Look to yourself, first, Medrawt," he said.

Then a young officer in a Roman helmet and cuirass, who sat almost on the barrier, dragged out his sword and kissed it before he flung it over the balustrade towards her. "May it serve you well, lady," he said, "for you are very beautiful." Few heard his words. They only saw his gesture, and all men agreed that it should be done.

Lystra ran to the sword and took it up, clumsily, as a woman might, and then bowed her head towards the officer. Those who sat near him saw the tears gather in his eyes. He did not look again into the arena that day, but knelt and prayed, his head in his hands.

Now Lystra took up her position again in the centre, and this time so much of her courage came back to her that she smiled up at Artos and held the sword towards him, as she had seen gladiators do, as though dedicating the bull to him. The crowd loved her gallantry and good-humour and began to cheer her, lightly. Artos stared down at her, his chin on his hand, never smiling at all.

Then there was a shout from the stables beneath the great circle, and suddenly the broad oak door burst open. The two stable hands who were in the ring ran to the barrier and leaped over the low stone balustrade to safety. Lystra stared with fascination and horror to see the creature she was condemned to face. For an instant she thought she had gone blind, for a grey mist passed across her eyes. She wiped her hand over them. It was the sun. She had stared upwards too long in mocking Artos. She realised now that she must not look up again if she wished to see what was happening about her.

Then the bull was out of the stables and into the arena, snorting and bewildered in the sunlight. For a few moments it stood still, as though carved from shining black rock. Then it turned towards the balustrade over which Artos sat, and made a vicious pass at the shadows there, for it, too, was blinded momentarily by the sun.

Here and there voices rose from the crowd. "You are going the wrong way, bull!" "Hey, bull, don't you know it's bad manners to keep a lady waiting!" "Wait till you see her, bull, you won't go the wrong way then—or perhaps you will!"

Lystra did not hear any individual cries, but only a vague and uninteresting rustle. Nor did she see anyone now. The clustered faces seemed to her but a grey wall about her, and only the bull and the sword in her hand mattered. The hilt was wet with the sweat of terror.

Now the black bull turned, pawing the earth and snuffling, sensing her presence. He sighted her at last and, almost without any apparent preparation, launched his bulk towards her. Lystra felt the weight of his body through the soles of her feet. Then suddenly her body felt very light, as though it did not belong to her. She had known this sensation before, when she had swirled out before a great company of noblemen at some feast in Byzantium. It was a form of physical elation just before she went into action. Even the sword in her hand now seemed as fragile and as light as a willow wand. It seemed impossible that it could kill anything.

Lystra knew nothing of bullfighting, but she was an exquisitely trained dancer. As the black shape came towards her, she remembered the bull dance of Crete, a delicate thing of great intricacy, meant to represent the gyrations of a maiden who eluded the Minotaur before at last she poised herself and surrendered. Lystra smiled wryly; this time there must be no surrender.

As the beast swirled in upon her, the dust shooting behind his hooves with the force of his rushing, the lithe girl's body swung before his horns, like a strip of gossamer, only inches away from him, to left and then to right, leaving him blinking and bemused in the sunlight, the foam already collecting at his muzzle.

So great was her artistry that the crowds shouted with joy to see this inexperienced woman facing such a creature so expertly.

Once again the bull charged, and once again Lystra swirled about him maddeningly, elusive, safe. Now the bull stood still and regarded her as though he was the one who should be afraid.

Someone near the barrier suddenly shouted out, "They have an understanding, these two! I heard tell she was descended from Europa! She'll caress him next!"

Lystra heard this crude jest and turned to smile towards the barrier. As she did so, the bull charged once more. A great gasp went up about the amphitheatre. The girl, sensitive as a tuft of thistledown, swayed aside, and the heavy body lumbered past her. Yet she was too close and his rough flank brushed her out of her stride as easily as a man's hand may brush away a cobweb. She stumbled a pace or two and then went down upon one knee. And then the bull had turned and was on her again.

Among the crowd a group of voices began to chant, "Mithras, Mithras, Mithras!"

Then somehow, miraculously, the girl rolled free, a lithe bundle of arms and legs, leaving the furious beast goring the dust, sending up great spurts as he sank his horns to his forehead.

Now Lystra was on her feet again, smiling despite herself. She was amazed that it could be so easy, this terrible fighting with bulls. Now she stood erect, poised on her toes, tensing her muscles in this new confidence. And now she remembered the sword in her hand.

Somewhere voices began to call, rhythmically, "Kill! Kill! Kill!" as they did when they thought the bullfighter should put an end to his beast.

Lystra looked at the bull. He stood now with his head held low, his eyes staring with the great exertions he had made, his flanks rising and falling terribly, in great gasps of exhaustion.

Lystra swept towards him like a light breeze across a summer meadow, the bright blade of the sword glittering in a long streak of silver light. Yet even as her arm fell, a great wave of compassion surged through her, as though it would be cruel to cause suffering to the great red-eyed beast who slavered onto the ground. Yet the impetus of her movement carried her forward, the point of the keen blade wavering across the bull's shoulder blade, scoring the tense hide, and sinking into the thick muscle on his shoulder.

He raised his head with the sudden pain and grunted savagely. Lystra saw the long horn slide through the linen bandages about her body, and as she leaned against him, she felt the heavy thudding blow of his forehead against her groin. That dull pain that swept through her broke up into a number of knife-points that seemed to rip through every nerve of her body.

Then she was on the ground, and the sweat from the beast's head fell into her eyes again and again, and the wool of his forehead thrust hard against her breast time after time.

Now there was nothing more she could do. She was no longer conscious that she had a body at all. She was only an awareness, lying in the dust, laughing at herself for thinking it all so easy, laughing at the world for taking itself so seriously, and then just laughing, into the sun that was blotted out again and again as the crazed brute came at her, tossing the strip of bloody flesh from side to side, a scarlet ribbon now, in his blind fury.

XLIII

A GREAT CRY OF HORROR SWEPT ACROSS THE AMPHITHEATRE, FOLlowed by a heavy, vibrant shocked silence. Five thousand pairs of eyes turned from the mutilated body of the girl, and fixed themselves in reproach upon Artos, who still sat smiling dully.

Then suddenly Medrawt found himself standing on his stone seat, his eyes up to the sun, screaming.

"Artos is a butcher! We shall all come to this, Cymry, unless we kill this man of blood! I prophesy, friends! Mark my words . . ."

Cei dragged him down, and the two fell, scuffling, among the lower rows. A heavily built man, not a soldier but a camp contractor, took Cei by the scruff of the neck and lifted him up, then punched him with all his might in the mouth. Cei's head lolled on his shoulders and he fell from the man's fist. Now on all sides men began to fight, some siding for Medrawt, some for Artos, though with misgivings now, it appeared. A hundred young Jutes, who had been kept outside the arena, now pushed down the doors and surged up into the auditorium. They struck at every man who did not shout "Medrawt" as a war cry. Now many of Medrawt's own company had regained their bewildered senses and began to cry for their leader.

Artos found himself thrown sideways and downwards by the great rush of men's bodies. Bedwyr, by his side, held his arm about the weak king, and tried to keep others from crushing him. Above them an immense and hostile press of folk came along the seats at them. The selected few of Artos, the comitatus, encircled him, their swords already dripping with blood.

"Down, down, Master," said Bedwyr. "Into the arena, there we are safer." He grasped Artos about the body and leapt down onto the sand. The comitatus followed them. The bull who had torn Lystra had now lost all his fury and his courage. He stood amazed to see this great mob of men suddenly leap towards him. Now he was as frightened as a young calf. He hung his head and bellowed piteously, his red-rimmed eyes staring about him in terror. One of the Cymry ran lightly to him and passed his long sword through the beast's throat. He sank to his knees, slavering and then spewing blood. No one looked at him again, for the battle of Caer Leon had begun.

Now to the sick eyes of Artos, the sky was overclouded with the flying bodies of men. Stones hailed down upon the warriors in the arena. Men about the Bear fell senseless as these missiles struck their unprotected heads. But soon the arena was crowded with friend and foe alike and no more stones could be thrown. Now men fought silently, like animals in the dark, unable to spare breath to speak.

And then Bedwyr said to the fainting Artos, "Over there, a man is shouting your name. He is coming towards you, Bear. Here, take my sword, it is a shorter one than Caliburn and better for use in a press."

Then as the man came nearer, still shouting the name of Artos, Bedwyr and the Count saw that it was Medrawt, yet so altered by a cut that had opened his forehead that it was little wonder they had not recognised him before. Medrawt had snatched a sword from the first man who fell near him, and now pressed towards the Bear with a horrible surge of vengeance.

Once, twice, a man of the Cymry barred his road, and each time Medrawt struck with the long cavalry sword, and his man fell. Now he was within a yard of Artos, and for a second he halted, his chest rising and falling as he breathed painfully, his dark eyes starting with tiredness and bloodlust.

"Bear, Bear!" he yelled, his throat working like that of a maniac. "Oh, how long have I waited, how long, how long!"

Then, like some dark bird of prey, he launched himself at Artos, who stared at him, like a man in a trance, unable to move. Medrawt struck once and his blade fell upon the brooch that Artos wore on his left shoulder, a massive thing of bronze and cornelian. The stone shattered and pieces spattered the faces of men around. The sword-blade sheared into the heavy piece of bronze, but did not cut through it to wound Artos. Medrawt dragged at the blade, and then, to his horror, he found that his hand held only the wooden hilt, for his blow had splintered the tempered steel.

He flung the heavy hilt into the face of Artos. It struck him on the temple, and the Bear seemed to shake himself back to life with the shock of the blow. His lips smiled faintly and he sucked in his breath, like a man who steps into icy water. Then he passed his sword into Medrawt, who shrieked and fell among the other men, on the sand.

Bedwyr dragged him away, for he thought that Medrawt was dead. Then men closed round the king again and he was pushed towards the temple of vengeance. Medrawt lay still, though he feared being crushed to death by the many feet that passed over him. The sword of Artos had shorn through the muscle of his left breast and had opened up his arm in its passing. But it had not pierced his heart, as Artos had intended. Medrawt shut his eyes, pressing his arm as tightly as he could to his side, to save what blood he could.

Now the battle moved away from him, and the Cymry were defending their leader in the very doors of the temple of vengeance. Now the major force of the Cymry had organised itself and was attacking the Jutes and the second company that was for Medrawt, ruthlessly. The battle was already lost to Medrawt. His men were falling where they stood, here and there, asking no quarter and giving none. The Jutes alone tried to form into a shield-ring, but the Cymry of Artos broke them up again and again, and now only a handful of the men who had come with Bethlac were left. Yet still they fought, even on their knees.

Medrawt lay as still as his pain would let him. But at last he looked from behind the dead man who sheltered him and then made to rise. At that moment, Cei, his leather jerkin almost slashed from his body, a sword cut reaching the length of his thigh, so that he dripped blood wherever he walked, staggered blindly towards him. Medrawt would have lain down again, but the man at his side, wounded terribly, shifted in his death throes and flung Medrawt sideways. Cei's fearful eyes lighted on him. He gave a grim smile of recognition and shambled forward with his javelin upraised. Medrawt shut his eyes and sobbed with the anguish of waiting. But Cei had lost too much blood and could not make his stroke. He thrust at Medrawt's stomach, but the spear turned in his grasp and the thin point passed through the thick muscle in the man's side, to do him no fatal injury. Medrawt gave a high scream and fell backwards. Cei laughed and tried to strike again, but fell from weakness, and was trampled on by the next rush of the Cymry.

Then Medrawt himself fainted with pain and loss of blood. A great silence settled on the amphitheatre. At length, only the birds made a sound, for the Cymry of Artos had withdrawn, victorious, to tend their wounds and to pursue what fugitives they could.

It was twilight when Medrawt regained his senses. He moved

with a groan and sat up. His arm had stopped bleeding, by some miracle, but the whole of his left side throbbed with a frightful heat and pain. He turned his head and saw the faint glimmer of a torch. Some men and women were turning the bodies over, at the far side of the arena. He heard an old woman's voice say, "Artos will give us bread for a year if we find him."

"Aye," the rough voice of a man answered, "and a hundred lashes if we don't. Come on, we shall burn our torch out before we have found the traitor."

Medrawt knew for whom they were searching. As silently as he could, he moved from the heap of bodies among which he had lain and staggered towards the barrier, where the shadows were thickest. They did not see him go. They did not hear the sobbing gasps he made, for by now the night breeze had risen and filled the air above with its sad sighing.

Medrawt tottered along the wall, towards the entrance gates. The pain in his side was almost unbearable and his arm began to ooze blood again. He felt its wet warmth down his tortured side. He bit his lips to keep himself from screaming, until at length he had finally gained the high gates. At first he thought they were closed and he began to weep with disappointment. But they were ajar and he was able to creep between them and so out into the fields that fell down to the river. He did not dare cross by the bridge, so made a detour to a place where he had sometimes bathed before. There he found a raft left by some boys and pushed it with painful effort into the stream. Then he lay on it and drifted for a while. The moon came up and he was afraid that he might be seen. As he passed under the citadel, he saw bright lights and heard the sound of hoarse voices singing. The Cymry of Artos were celebrating their victory, he thought. Artos could not be dead, then, or they would not be singing.

Then Medrawt fainted away, lying on the rough boat, his useless left arm dangling in the cold water. Before his senses left him, he heard his voice whisper, "Aurelius, my friend. I am coming to you as you said, at last. Aurelius, King of Dumnonia! Ah, my friend!"

A late bird flying back to its nest passed over the raft and swooped down to see what manner of creature this was. He skimmed over the prostrate body and then rose with a harsh shriek of fear. To Medrawt's fading senses, this was the cry of doom. He rolled over as though dead.

PART FIVE

TOWARDS BADON

Thought shall be the harder, heart the keener,
Courage the greater, as our strength faileth.
Though here lies our leader in the dust of his greatness,
Who leaves him now, be damned for ever.
We who are old shall not leave this battle,
But lie at his feet, in the dust with our leader.

(THE BATTLE OF MALDON—adapted)

XLIV

A GREAT SADNESS HAD FALLEN ON ARTOS. HE WALKED NOW LIKE AN old and suffering man. The gods had placed a heavy load upon his shoulders. Whoever came near him seemed to suffer, and those whom he loved, most of all. Artos thought of his dead father, Uther Pendragon, poisoned in Lis Pengwern; of his dear woman and her son, Anir, crushed to death in Caerwent; of Lystra, who had brought some joy to his body though little to his heart, gored by the bull in Caer Leon; of Medrawt, his blood-brother, bleeding in the sand of the amphitheatre. All who called him friend were doomed for that friendship, he thought.

He spoke to his comrades, Bedwyr and Cei. "What ritual cleansing is there, my friends, to wash the doom from me?"

Bedwyr was not knowledgeable in such matters. He said, "All I know is that a man is what he is. He must put up with his own destiny!"

Cei, who had been a little fey since his wounds, took the matter very seriously and said, "There is a wise woman, a witch, some say, beyond Caerwent. She would know, Bear. Shall I ask her for you?"

Artos turned away from them, forgetful now, thinking of other things and sighing deeply like a worn old man. He did not trouble to answer Cei. He had forgotten what he had asked them.

Cei smiled at Bedwyr and went from the room. He rode to Caerwent alone, feeling himself to bc thc cmissary of the Count of Britain. It was a warm day and he stopped in the city of Caerwent, looking for a tavern. His thirst was great.

Many of the streets were still deserted, for some families no longer cared to live on in the city where their sons or menfolk had been slain. Yet at length Cei found a low-roofed hovel with the bunch of leaves, signifying an inn, above the door.

Cei sat in the warm shadows of the long room and called for a flask of grape wine, a dry vintage that would slake his thirst. The girl who carried the wine to him went back into an inner room and spoke to a thick-lipped man who wore a catskin cap, its flaps long enough to hide the furrowed scar that laid open his head.

"Are you certain?" this man asked the girl. She nodded.

Then the man went into the long room, swinging his right leg awkwardly as though it would not obey him adequately. He sat down beside Cei at the long table, wiping his mouth as though he had just drunk.

Cei regarded him amiably. "The wine is good here, friend," he said. The other man nodded, then leaned over the table confidentially. "But they haven't brought you the best, friend," he said. "I know this tavern well. They have cheated you."

Cei drank from his flagon and said, "I shall not call out the magistrates to them for that! I was thirsty and what they brought me was good enough for the occasion."

The man looked round as though he did not wish to be observed. Then he leaned over and took Cei's flagon, smiling secretly. "Wait a moment, man," he said. "I'll get you a drop of the real wine. I know the tricks of their kitchen!"

Cei smiled and let him go. The man came back a few moments later. "Here, man," he said, "try this and tell me if I speak the truth or not!"

Cei felt in his pouch and found a silver coin. "Take this, friend," he said, "for your trouble."

The fellow shook his head. "Nay, man," he said, "taste it first and then give me a penny or two for my trouble. Don't pay before your drink, that is not good business!"

Cei smiled at the fellow's strange honesty and drank deeply from the flagon. The man watched him carefully. Then Cei said,

"You are right, friend, it is a good wine. You have earned your penny!"

He tried to put his hand into his pouch, but the strength had left his arm, and now the side of his mouth was pulled down by a great pain that tore across his stomach.

The man watched him quietly until he fell into the straw beneath the table, his eyes starting and a bloody froth gathering on his lips.

The man went back to the kitchen. "I did not think it could have been so easy," he said to the girl. "So perish all the Cymry!"

So did Cei's raven find him at Caerwent, as Bedwyr had said long before. His body was taken at night and flung among the gorse-bushes on the road out of the city.

When Artos heard the news at last he was greatly angry. Then, when his fury had worked itself out, he said to Bedwyr, "I have sinned, old friend, and the gods will never let me forget it. Leave me now, Bedwyr, before they take you from me too."

But Bedwyr said, "Artos, you talk like a green girl. I have always been with you, since we were little lads together. If the gods cannot stomach that, then they must kill me and have done with it, for I shall never leave you in life."

The Count of Britain turned away to hide his tears. He said, "I always knew that you were a fool, Bedwyr. Very well, choose your own fate and die for following me."

"So be it," said Bedwyr, smiling. Then he went out, and taking the fiercest stallion in the citadel, put him at all the fences and walls in Caer Leon, until the strange emotion had gone out of him. Men who saw him lead back the half-dead charger said, "Bedwyr is either very happy, or suffering a great sickness of the heart!"

But no one jested with him that night, for he was now the second-in-command of the Legion and one who might well become the *dux bellorum* himself before many months were passed, unless Artos found some medicine to cure his grief of mind and of body.

Another day Artos said to Bedwyr, "My friend, I have sinned so greatly in the first part of my life that I must spend the second part in placating the gods for my evil deeds."

Bedwyr was cutting his fingernails with a keen hunting-knife and did not bother even to look up, for Artos was saying things like this every day now.

"Yes," answered Bedwyr, "that is why we are allowed to live so long. Obviously those who die young have no sins to pay for."

This answer angered Artos, who suddenly thought of little Anir, and felt that Bedwyr was taking his death lightly. But he recalled Bedwyr's long service to him, and controlled his anger. Instead, he said, "I have many debts to pay to the gods. I shall start to pay them soon, while I have life still in me."

The next day, Artos sent envoys to find the Western Kings, and to take offerings of gold to them as a token of his good intentions, for now he thought that he had robbed them and was anxious to make amends. Two of the messengers returned, one from Cunneglassus and one from Aurelius. The one sent to Votiporix was tortured and then killed in an adder-pit by the suspicious King of the Demetae. The others brought no consoling news. Cunneglassus had sent word back that he would never trust the Bear again, and that he would live in his own way from then on, even siding with the Saxon should Artos try to force his rule upon him.

Aurelius was less bold. He sent word that his country was too poor and his people too disaffected to allow him to accept the renewed friendship of Artos. One day, he said, when times were better, they might meet again.

Artos heard these messages and bit his lip in self-hatred.

"Now I know that I am alone, Bedwyr," he said. "I no longer lead the armies of other men, no longer act as *dux bellorum*."

"You are your own master, Bear," said Bedwyr. "You lead your own army, and it is a greater one than Britain has known since the greatest days of Rome."

This reply seemed to please Artos, who gave orders that his armour was to be cleaned and his sword burnished. He slept well that night, and did not call his physician to give him a sleeping-draught, as he usually did.

Then Artos called a great parade of the Cymry, and told them that they had rested long enough and that the time was come for them to show themselves in peace through the land, so that men should know that Britain was well protected.

The Cymry roared out agreement to these words. They had feared that their Bear had lost his claws. All the same, some of them shook their heads as they looked at him astride his great horse, for his body seemed to have shrunk. His armour was too big for him now, and the great sword Caliburn seemed to have been forged for a stronger man.

The last thing that Artos did before the Legion left Caer Leon was to have the amphitheatre filled in with soil and gravel, and the supporting pillars round its sides dragged down and cast to the ground.

"He wants to forget Lystra," said a woman tearfully.

"He wants to forget Medrawt," said her husband, "for he loved him more than he ever did that Eastern bitch."

"Artos has such a strange way of showing his love, then," said the woman. "I'd as soon be hated by such a man."

"Take care you never are," said the man. "There'd be no more of you left than would feed a small cat."

XLV

A BLACK THING LAY ON THE SHORE OF THE BROAD ESTUARY, HALF IN, half out of the water. The white gulls wheeled and screamed over it, curious that only one of its arms should move up and down as the lilting waves caught it. This black thing had been lying there for two days now, moving higher up the shore when the tide came in, and sliding down again when the waves withdrew. It was alone, the gulls decided. They had seen the raft on which it came slither from under it and then go bobbing away into the deep Irish Sea. As night came on, they lost interest in it and moved away to the island where they rested. Perhaps they would come back again tomorrow and see if it was still there.

In the night a woman came with a lantern, looking for anything the sea might have brought. She came at night because then there was more chance of finding something, when the lazy men were fast asleep. They only searched in the daytime, when the sun was hot.

This woman was past her youth and had never been very handsome. Yet she was well made and strong. Her black hair was bound back from her brown face by a length of cord. Her thick body was clothed in a woollen shift which had once been blue, but which was now much faded from sun and sea water. She bore a long wicker basket on her back and trod barefoot in and out of the sea-pools without any fear, for her feet were as hard and calloused as leather.

She was a brave woman, having had to fend for herself since her second husband had been killed in a rock-fall five years before. But even so, she shrank back with a little scream when her lantern's faint light showed her the black form, lolling among the pebbles. She knew well enough what it was. She had seen them before.

Then, regaining courage, she moved forward to see what had happened to the man, perhaps what he carried about him still, if anything. The beam of her lantern shone on the heavy gold armlets that Medrawt was once so proud of. She took him by the feet and dragged him a little further up the shore, away from the lapping water. Her eyes glistened with anxiety as she stripped away the ring that clasped his right arm, just above the wrist. But when she came to twist the other one off, she saw the gaping wound in his arm, that seemed to gasp at her, its mouth washed clean by the salt waters of the estuary. In the light of the lantern, it was almost as though that terrible sword thrust in the amphitheatre had come near to severing the arm completely.

The woman did not dare to touch the arm-ring then. It would bring bad luck to take it from such a limb. She would stand in danger of losing her own left arm one day, she feared. Yet it was a shame, to have to leave such a treasure. She turned away regretfully, when the man spoke. His voice was low, so low that it seemed like the whispering of the waves at first. Yet it was a voice, a human voice, though cracked and harsh with suffering and exposure to the waters of the sea.

Medrawt said, "Forgive me, Ambrosius, I was mad."

The woman turned but his lips were still again. Yet she was sure he had spoken. She could not have mistaken the name of Ambrosius, for he had been one of the great heroes of her old father, many years ago, though the woman had never thought about him in her life. She turned her lantern-light onto the man's white face. It was immobile, but he was breathing, lightly, unevenly, as though each breath was the last he would breathe.

She stood over him, wondering. If she cared for him, for the little time he had to live, then she would have a right to that rich arm-ring; the gods could not deny her that. But it was too cold here, on the bare shores of the wide estuary with the cold night wind blowing across from Siluria's mountains.

The woman hoisted the limp body of Medrawt onto her broad shoulders and set off inland, among the gorse-grown moors, her lantern now bobbing at her leather girdle. After a while, she unslung her wicker basket, for it was too much to carry. She pushed it under a bush that she knew well, and left it there. The other burden was more precious at that moment. With those two bracelets, she would be the richest woman of her small tribe. This man, useless as he was, was a thing to be guarded now. He was the richest harvest the sea had ever brought her, or any one she knew. Surely the gods had sent her down to the shore with her lantern that night, she thought.

Her home, such as it was, lay about a mile from the broad Sabrina. It was a small cave, the entrance hidden by hawthorn and high rushes. It lay in a round hollow, grown high with coarse grasses. In the hollow ten families had their tents or wattle hovels, set round the stone-enclosed fireplace, at which they did their communal cooking and about which they sat at night, when the beasts of the woodland howled and snuffled above them in the darkness.

This small settlement was one of many in the west; some of the folk who composed it had once been proud to call themselves people of the agricultural Durotriges. But their Roman overlords had taken away what land they had, and had almost made them slaves. And now their blood was mingled with that of the malcontent Bacaudae who had murdered their Roman masters and had wandered, lawless men, over the countryside, finding their homes and their women where they could. For such villages, the clock had stood still for four hundred years. They had forgotten what little the Roman had ever tried to teach them; they had forgotten whatever laws their once great tribe had laid down. They were displaced persons, even in their own land, men who owed loyalty to no one, hopeless men. Provided they had a horsehide to cover them and a platter of soaked herbs or grain to hold away the gnawing of hunger, they thought they had done as well as a man unblessed by the gods could do. They asked for little, took as much as they could lay hands on, and spoke a primitive prayer into the fire-smoke on those nights when they went to their bracken beds with a full stomach, which was very rarely, and so the occasion for a special thanksgiving to the malevolent powers that watched over such folk in those hard days.

The woman bent low as she carried Medrawt into the little cave; even so she knocked his head and shoulders on the door-top. He was unconscious again and did not know. Even had he known, such a blow would not have troubled him. His body had gone beyond pain now; he had bled for two days before the salt sea had staunched his wounds and the chill of the water had numbed his nerves. Only the faintest spark of life still lingered in him. The intermittent beam of his consciousness was so small that it might almost be said that he was a corpse in all but final death.

The woman laid him on her fern-bed at one side of the cave.

She shone her lamp on his face again and saw that his black hair had turned white in a broad streak, starting at the left temple.

"I'll call thee Brock, if life stays in thee, lad," she said. Then she flung a length of sackcloth over him and went to a younger woman who groaned deeply from a pallet at the other side of the cave.

This young woman was her sister. Her labour pains had come on two days before, yet the child had not yet been born. There was no one among the tribe skilled in bringing on labour, and few children were born live among them. Those that were, lived but a few days, unless they were males. The females were laid at the fringe of the upland woods to die of exposure or the visitations of bear or wolf. In a way, the folk of the hollow thought of this as an offering to whatever deities resided among the dark avenues of trees on the hillside.

The woman in the bed called out weakly, "Come, sister! Come, Mamag! I think it is the last pain. Come!"

Mamag took the lamp and looked down at her. The woman's emaciated face was thick with sweat and her white lips were drawn back over broken teeth. Mamag knew that she was dying, that this last pain was not the coming of life. She sat by her sister, holding her hand and crooning softly, and before dawn came the woman died, twisting suddenly in her bed as though her child had come at last.

Mamag placed the cold hand back onto her thin breast. She looked at Medrawt and said, "You will live now. The gods have the life they wanted from me. Now you will live. Yet I had rather you lay as she does."

She wept a few tears for her dead sister and then lay down beside her and went to sleep, like a tired animal, almost as soon as her head sank into the bracken.

XLVI

THE LEGION OF ARTOS RODE THROUGH SOUTHERN BRITAIN, AND wherever they billeted themselves, men came to join them. They grew in strength each day, until at last Artos decreed that he could use no more of them. He formed a force of militia now, men who would act as permanent garrisons in such cities as Verulam, Camulodunum, Vricon, Deva and even Eburacum. The ironworkers of the Forest of Dean kept their forges glowing into the night, making helmets and armour and swords for the great army that had grown throughout the land. All men were anxious to share in the new glory.

And indeed a glory seemed now to have settled on Artos, not the fiery warrior glory that once he had dreamed of, but a more sober and more responsible glory. Now when men saw him, they saw not a headstrong young colt of a fighting man, but a grave general, his hair already greying and coming out, his shoulders stooped with the weight of his armour, his hands shaking a little. While they were stationed in Verulam, Artos found himself a Greek scholar who sat with him and told him tales of the old heroes, and translated the ancient Roman laws to him. The Bear paid attention to his lessons, though when the teacher offered to instruct him in Latin, he shook his head and said that he was now too old to learn it. He did, however, take a Roman name from this time on. He became Artorius, and had all documents made out under the style of "Artorius, Count of Britain, Dux Bellorum of the Emperor in Rome, whoever he may be."

A long letter, written in Latin, came to Artorius from Auxerre in Gaul. It begged him to attend to the matters of the Church in Britain. Artorius consulted with his Greek teacher, who told him that it would be fitting for the Count to patronise the Christian

Church in Britain. Artorius said that he was ill trained in these matters and gave the Greek full licence to set up a commission which should elect new bishops in Britain and put into repair as many churches as they could. For this he gained a new title, that of Protector of Christ in Britain, though it was a description which he seldom dared to employ, not fully understanding its implications.

Bedwyr was of little use to him in such matters, for he had always been a heathen and had no desire to change his ways now. Artos used to tease him about his taboos, such as never killing a hare or eating the flesh of a hen. But Bedwyr merely smiled and said, "You may know what Caesar wrote in his book, but I know what I do know, and that is enough for me."

"But you are my successor, now, friend," said Artorius gently. "You must begin to learn these things."

Bedwyr shook his head. "No, Artos," he said, making a face as though he had taken a draught of vinegar instead of the wine he had expected. "No, if the gods should take you, I should go back to the west. I should build me a house above Lis Pengwern and die quietly. I am no Roman, in spite of this helmet!"

Artorius mused at this, and wondered what had become of Medrawt, if he still lived. They had not found his body in the arena, despite long searches, but that did not mean he was still alive. His followers might have carried the body away, to bury it secretly. Medrawt would not have spoken as Bedwyr had done.

Artorius said, "Why do you ride with me, Bedwyr, if you do not mean to follow me when I am gone?"

Bedwyr said, "I do not love Rome, or even Britain. I love you, Artos, that is all."

He would say no more, but glared at Artorius angrily when he tried to take the matter further. Artorius left him alone and went into his council room to go through the accounts with the Greek, though almost anyone could have cheated him because he was so little used to counting the revenues.

Yet there was much to be attended to, even though he did not understand the words very often. In many of the towns he had given permission for theatres to be reconstructed, for dwelling houses to be demolished and rebuilt, for municipal offices to be erected—and the staffs needed to run them, appointed. Now Britain began to have a new system of tax officials, for these improvements had to be paid for.

Yet before men could pay taxes, they must have work to do. So Artorius sent out many large detachments of the Legion to protect all men willing to work in the fields, growing corn, or on the moors, rearing cattle, or along the coasts, gathering in the harvests of the sea. Crops, cattle and fishing improved then, for men were anxious to share in the profits of the new times.

Elsewhere, regiments of the Legion worked on the roads, or at rebuilding fortresses, or harbours and their wharves. A vast tract of the eastern marshes was redrained and irrigation channels cut through them to let the sea run out again. So that this might be done, the fortress of Lindum was reclaimed and garrisoned with soldiers.

Now there was activity everywhere in the east; in quarries, in woods, in cities. The administration was primarily a military one, the commander of each garrison being held responsible for the entire state of the area in which his fortress was situated. And as each of these men was personally known to Artorius, the administration was not a corrupt one; it was such as had not been known before for two hundred years. Not because the commanders were necessarily virtuous men, but because they knew that they would be called to council with Artorius himself, and not one of them wished to appear in a bad light before those eyes which had the trick of spying out any defects in a man, as in a horse.

Artorius himself was no longer the western tribesman he had been. There had always been some basic greatness in him, inherited from old Uther Pendragon. Among tribesmen he had been as savage as any; among statesmen, he had learned to show a grave dignity until his quick brain had accommodated itself to the new situation before him.

And what had first been a young savage's escapade, a desire for power which his father had held from him, now became a mission. There was nothing else Artorius wished to do in life but be the ruler of this new kingdom. He had lost his wife and her son; he had lost his blood-brother. He was alone with old Bedwyr, and the Greek tutor, who had now become more than a mere teacher, but something like a chancellor. There was nothing left to do but rule the country he had, by some strange chance, founded.

And since those first battles in the south, and the reputation that had grown about him as a fighter after Caerwent, no enemy seemed to wish to test the Bear's claws. Britain was at peace for the time being. Trading ships began to arrive from Europe and the East, only a few, but enough to bring hope for the future.

XLVII

A LONGSHIP PULLED INTO THE SHORE A LITTLE BEYOND THE HARBOUR of Tribuit. Men began to leap from her, splashing in the sea up to their waists, laughing at the shock of the water and dragging at the ship, to get her well aground before they left her.

They were led by a tall strongly built young man, whose reddish hair was chopped short to keep the lice out of it. He wore a thick blue tunic over which clanked a breastplate of iron. His face was thin and foolish-looking in repose; yet there was a sharpness about his nose and a quick movement of head and eyes that warned men not to be taken in by his expression. No warrior who really knew him would call Cissa a fool, and certainly not in his hearing. Cissa spoke little, and was more used to striking than to arguing. Only those of his oldest followers stayed close to him. The new ones gave him a wide berth, unless he called them to him, to give his brusque orders, a stupid smile curling his lips. No man paid any attention to that smile, for it meant nothing.

Cissa called a big warrior to him, an oldish man who wore a

heavy black bearskin about his body and a little round woollen skullcap on his bald head. His flaxen beard reached low over his chest and gave him a patriarchal look. This was Aesc, a Nithing, one beyond the law for killing a child in a shore-side foray in Jutland. Cissa did not hold that against him. He was drunk at the time and said he struck at something which moved, he did not know what.

Aesc shambled through the water to Cissa and grinned at him, tugging on his beard as another might have tugged on his forelock.

"What is it, shipmaster?" he said.

Cissa pointed up towards the thick woodland that grew above them. "Camp there tonight," he said. "I see smoke above the trees."

Aesc scratched his chin. "They may not want us," he said.

Cissa looked through him with pale blue eyes and said, "We shall burn their houses if they do not welcome us. We camp there tonight. Leave six men to guard the ship. Old men with sons. Bring their sons with you, then the fathers will not sail away when we have gone. Tell them about it."

Aesc tugged at his beard again and went back to the men who were still dragging the longship up the beach. Cissa did not wait for them. He turned and began to walk up the hill towards the village. Forty men followed him rapidly, fearful lest he should turn on them and punish them for cowardice. They were all South Saxons, with light fair hair, and faces as brown as old leather, from voyaging up and down the German Sea. They carried small shields and short swords; otherwise they went unarmed, wearing only light hide tunics and shoes. This was the first of five ships belonging to Cissa to beach again on British shores. After Bassas he had been back to Germany, gathering the right men for this new attempt. This time he was determined to carve out a kingdom for himself.

When the party reached the village, it was deserted, though smoke still came from the chimneys. Cissa laughed. "They saw us coming," he said. "They seem to be afraid of us, Aesc."

Aesc grinned. This happened everywhere now. If the men did

not find an enemy soon, they would get out of practice in fighting. Aesc hoped they would meet an enemy before long.

A man came back from one of the houses, holding a head-ring and a sheepskin coat. "Jutes, Master," he said to Cissa. "They were not British who lived here."

Cissa said, "What does it matter? Jutes have lived here so long they are like British. They are all enemies."

The men set about making themselves comfortable, until such time as the other shiploads arrived.

"What is the plan then, Cissa?" asked Aesc.

Cissa fixed his eyes on the point of Aesc's thick nose, making him feel uncomfortable. "Then, when we are all met," he said, "we push northwards towards Londinium, and kill every man we see. The scribes shall set down that Aelle went through the land like fire and slew all the British."

Aesc looked at him, bewildered. "Aelle is dead, Master," he said. "He died at Dubglas. The same lance nearly killed me."

Cissa blew into his face, contemptuously. "Aelle still fights," he said. "He fights in me, sailor. It shall be his victory; then I shall find victories of my own when his ghost lies quiet again."

He walked to the door of the hut and pointed towards the old Roman harbour of Tribuit. "I shall have my place there," he said, "and I shall call it Cissaceaster. Mark that, Aesc. Poke out my eyes if I do not do as I say."

Aesc tugged at his beard and said, "I will do that, shipmaster."

Their other vessels beached later that night and the men joined them in the village. As they all sat about the fires, jesting, a horseman rode among them, proud and fearless, his sword ready at his hip. He wore chain armour and carried a long square shield. But he was not a Roman. He carried a high conical helmet on his pommel and men saw that his hair was as fair as their own.

He rode straight up to Cissa, who sat shaking dice with Aesc by the fire. His voice was firm and carried authority.

"Greetings, Cissa," he said. "I come from Cerdic the West Saxon."

Cissa had heard of this Cerdic, half Briton, half Saxon, but had no idea where he might be found. Cerdic was getting old now, men said, and it was best to keep out of his way until he was weak. Then things would be different.

Cissa said, "What message does my brother Cerdic send?"

The warrior looked down at him with a sneer on his face. "Cerdic sends no message to men such as you," he said. "All Cerdic says is that he will have no midden-cock crowing on this heap. Cerdic is the bull of the farmyard here."

The man looked down at Cissa and then turned to ride away. Aesc had reached for his knife and was about to run after him but Cissa laid his hand on the old man's thigh.

"Tell Cerdic I go about my business," called Cissa. "Tell him I look forward to meeting him when that business is done."

The man did not reply, but rode back into the darkness that hung about the woods. Cissa's rage was great then, and his men drew away from him and went to their huts.

The next morning, the great slaughter of Pevensey began. Cissa vented his wrath against Cerdic on every man he found.

XLVIII

MEDRAWT CAME SLOWLY BACK TO LIFE AMONG THE RUDE FOLK IN THE hollow. But he was not the same man as had followed Ambrosius to the west. And now his name was Brock, the Badger, because of the streak of white that ran across his head. Brock was simple-minded. His weak voice and slobbering words made communication with him difficult. His thin head shook from side to side as he sat. Brock looked like a very old man. He was not yet thirty-five.

Brock's left arm was dead and had withered away to the size of a stick through the summer. Mamag had feared that he might catch it on a bough and tear it off. Then he would bleed to death again. So she had made him a little hide cradle for it and this kept it close to his body. He wore his arm under a tight short-coat, and those who saw him for the first time thought he had only one arm. Mamag was his wife now. She had declared this in a tribal gathering, so that no one could contest her right to the gold rings. But to Brock, she was his mother again, for she made him do things, and fed him, and spoke to him as though he were a little one. She did not know that he was brother to Artos, Count of Britain. Nor did Brock. He had forgotten that he was anybody at all. The men of the village thought of him as the half-wit that Mamag had been given by the gods when her sister died. He was like a pet dog, a poor thing with a useless leg, that did no harm, and was incapable of doing any good. Brock wandered about the hollow, shaking his head, bothering no one. When he was in the way, they pushed him aside. If they found meat, they gave him the pieces they could not eat. He did not mind whatever they did. He had died in the Sabrina estuary.

As the summer wore on and the autumn came, Brock made a discovery. One bright morning he sat at the door of the cave, trying to draw with a stick in the dust. Then suddenly he felt a pain in his head and after a while looked round to see if a boy had thrown a stone at him. But there was no one in sight, except a very old woman who sat in the ashes of the fire, her shawl over her head, mourning her husband who had been dead for forty years. She would not throw a stone, Brock's mind told him. He began to cry, for the pain was getting worse. Then it suddenly stopped and Brock said some words to himself. They came to him naturally and he had never heard them before. They came to him like another voice speaking inside his head. He said them clearly, in a way that he did not usually speak. Suddenly his mouth felt empty; his tongue could move about in it again; he did not have to fight with the words and weep inside his heart when they would not come onto his tongue. Now the words came onto his tongue and were his friends. Brock said:

"Oak and Ash, Fire, Water and Rock,
I praise Thee.
Sun fling gold upon the earth;
Moon fling silver.
Oak give me a bow;
Ash give me an arrow;
Fire give me a long life;
Water give me a fish;
Rock give me an altar for sacrifice."

Mamag heard him and ran out of the cave, bumping her head on the low doorway. She was angry because it hurt her and at first cuffed Brock and knocked him over. Then she remembered his words again and stared at him in fear. He began to whimper now, for he had hurt his arm when he fell.

"Say those words, again," said Mamag sternly, her fear overcome by her wonder. Brock tried to say them and could not for a time. Then his tongue became smaller once more and the voice began to speak in his head and he said them.

Mamag ran away from him, to the top of the hollow, and there she took up the cow's horn and blew on it and all the folk came from wherever they were.

"What's the matter, woman?" they called. "Are you mad, like your new husband?"

She told them to come down into the hollow and listen to him. Brock shut his eyes, and when she told him, he said the words again, in a thin, clear, reedy voice, like the one in his head. Now the words came easily to him.

The headman of the village groaned in astonishment.

"Fall on your knees before him," he shouted at the men and women. "This is the voice of the Old One. We have given shelter to the Old One and did not know it."

The villagers fell on their knees and did not dare get up till the headman told them to. Brock began to cry, for he was afraid they were angry with him. But the headman knelt before him and put a bowl of fermented grain into his lap as an offering.

"When you pray tonight, Brock," he said, "tell Merddin that we love him. Tell your master that we have used his servant well."

The words meant nothing to Brock, who forgot them as soon as he heard them. Mamag took him into the cave, very respectfully now, and dried his eyes. Her fear of him was tempered by her new realisation that now she was the guardian of Merddin's servant. It was an honour no woman had known for many generations, since the old faith died.

XLIX

WHEN ARTORIUS HEARD OF THE MASSACRE AT PEVENSEY, HE WAS angry and sent down three regiments of Cymry to clear out the Saxons from Anderida Silva.

They were ambushed in the forest, and though far superior in strength to the men of Cissa, were cut to pieces, since they were trained to fight in the open and were greatly hampered by being forced to go into action in a wooded country.

Artorius received the news with a strange calm. It was Bedwyr who was angry this time. But Artorius said, "This is the answer we need. We have been getting slack and easy in our new cities. This reverse will teach us to watch closely. Now we know that the enemy is coming at us again, but more strongly this time."

"Let us attack them and sweep them into the sea," said Bedwyr, his eyes aflame for war.

Artorius said, "Winter is coming on. They will not come any further inland, but will try to consolidate their position. Let them wait, let them feel secure. Others will join them. They will have many mouths to feed soon. By spring they will have to make a move, but before they are ready we will fall on them with a great force. We have men enough to surround them now, to attack them in front and in the rear, to cut them off from their ships! They will be wiped out as though they had never been, Bedwyr, my friend."

Bedwyr saw the old glint in the eyes of Artorius, and he smiled, too, glad that the Count had not lost all his wits, studying those books that the Greek kept bringing to the city. Bedwyr did not like that Greek. He wore his black hair oiled and in tight curls. At a feast one night he had gilded his fingernails and put silver on his eyelashes. Bedwyr did not like that sort of behaviour. He felt that there must be something contaminating in those books the Greek kept showing to Artorius. He half feared that one day his old friend might put silver on his eyelashes too, and then the world would be at an end for Bedwyr.

However, he did not disapprove of Camulodunum, which the Cymry shortened to Camulod, and even Camlod, being unaccustomed to the long Roman termination of the word. It was the Greek, Thykristion, who had suggested this as the new capital of Artorius. Bedwyr had come to like the place. There were taverns enough and a cockpit, and some long tracts of flat land outside the city where he could exercise his cavalry. Bedwyr asked little from life—but insisted on getting all he asked for. Since the death of Cei, he had no close friend, for the confidant of a king usually finds himself friendless. Bedwyr did not worry on that score. He was not a man who liked many friends, though he was a hail-fellow-well-met with the larger number of his great company. He knew every man of them, paid them and punished them regularly. They would have died for him, without knowing why. Yet he had no close friends. It was as though he had dedicated himself to Artorius, and to no other. Artorius had himself spoken of it all, one day. "A great captain must have no friends," said Bedwyr simply. "At any moment he might be called on to send them to death. That would break his spirit. It is better not to have friends."

"Yet you and I are friends," said Artorius seriously. "What if I am forced to send you to your death?"

"That is different," said Bedwyr. "I took the blood-oath to you when I was yet a little lad. I am your thing, like your knife or your horse. If you wish to break your knife, or kill your horse, no one has a right to stop you. It is the same with me. I am more than a friend, I am your knife, and your knife is a part of you, like your hand."

Artorius patted him on the back. Thykristion, who was present in the room, smiled in a superior manner and said some words about the simple savage being a more honourable man than the well-educated patrician. Bedwyr heard what he said and turned slowly towards him, his hand upon his broad-bladed hunting-dirk. The Greek bowed in a genteel manner and left the room without delay, saying there were some scrolls in the library which had to be catalogued.

When he had gone, Artorius said sternly, "If you hurt him, I shall be angry with you, my knife!"

Bedwyr said, "Hurt who? I was only going to show you this knife. I've had it for ten years and it carries as good an edge now as when I got it from the forge above Glevum. I wish I had another like it."

Artorius said, "Why don't you make a trip out there before the snows come and get another, then? You have my permission to go, with your troop."

Bedwyr looked up at him in alarm. "What, and leave you alone?" he said. Artorius was so moved that he kissed him on the cheek and then left him, for he could not trust himself to speak after such a show of loyalty.

Above Tribuit, Cissa began to build his settlement, Cissa's fortress, Cissaceaster. Fresh ships came in every week, bringing new followers to his standard. They were all set to work, to build a fortification which might stand against a sudden assault, from Artos or from Cerdic. Cerdic was wise, it seemed, and did not wish to risk an encounter now. He had moved further along the coast, past Vectis. Aesc had counselled Cissa not to trust Cerdic, and not to take it for granted that he had given up any idea of attacking. Cerdic was a master of the surprise assault, he said, and Cissa must beware.

Cissa, who had been drinking when Aesc spoke to him thus,

struck the old man between the eyes and laid him flat. Aesc forgot himself then and, rising, took the younger man by the throat and would have dashed out his brains against the lintel, but two men who were near by dragged him away from Cissa.

Cissa dashed the blood from his nose and put his arms about Aesc. "You are a brave man, Aesc," he said. "Thank you for your advice about Cerdic."

Neither of them spoke of the incident again. The two who had saved Cissa were not even thanked. They vowed to let him die next time.

So through the winter, Cissaceaster grew and grew. Cerdic knew all about it, for he had a dozen spies inside the fortress. Men who built busily through the day and brought him messages at night. Artorius knew about it, for he had sent a whole shipload of Saxons to join Cissa, at his own expense. They were friendly men, to whom he had promised citizenship in Verulam after their task was over. They swore a blood-oath to him and set sail from Camulodunum to Cissaceaster, just round the coast.

Of them all, Brock perhaps suffered most through that winter. His voice came to him more often now, telling him to say different things, some of them prayers to the old gods, some of them songs, which the voice sang in a high nasal tone. This always left Brock exhausted and gasping as though he would die. And now, what was worse, his mind had begun to clear a little and to let him know what he was saying when these fits came on him. He began to dread the voice inside his head and to pray that it should not come to him again.

Brock did not understand why Mamag touched her forehead on the ground before she spoke to him now. Nor why the folk would not play with him as they had done. The boy-children ran away when he walked about the hollow now. They used to bring birds' nests for him to look at and hold, and once they had taken him on a rough barrow to see the great estuary from which he had risen, like a messenger of the gods. Now they did not dare speak to him and crossed their fingers before their faces when he looked at them.

Mamag did not sleep in his bed any more. He missed the warm comfort of her body. It was like a big warm mother's body to him. Now it was cold in his fern bed at night, even though he had been given blankets and wolfskins by the tribesmen.

He remembered that there was a time when the year was not cold and when the sun shone and the birds sang in the trees. He cried and asked the gods to send this time of the year back to him, because he was cold.

The headman heard him and went to the others and said, "Have courage, my friends, the winter will pass soon. I have heard Brock commanding them to send spring to us again."

They brought Brock an offering of sheep meat then.

L

SPRING CAME AT LAST, IN SPITE OF BROCK, AND CISSA AND ARTORIUS, Count of Britain. It broke early, after a hard winter, and all men were so glad that they turned their minds to war.

Even Brock felt a strange disquietude. The hollow suddenly seemed to him a place of loathing. It was not that it stank when the snow went away, he did not mind that, or the midden-heaps and the piles of human rubbish that lay about, for now his own personal manners were not as they had once been. But it was because the hollow was the place where the voice first came to him. He felt that it must live there, in the cave, and that if he could get away from the hollow, he might lose the voice.

One day he said to Mamag, "Brock must leave you, go away." At first she wept, thinking the gods were angry with her. Then she asked whether she might come too. Brock cried when he understood what she meant. He wanted her to come. He would have been afraid to leave the hollow without her.

Then Mamag knew that the gods still favoured her. She went to the headman and told him what Brock had said. The headman wondered whether the gods looked with favour on him and his people too. He asked Mamag to ask Brock if they were to come.

When she asked him, he shook his head as though he meant "Yes," though in fact he could not hear her words, and only shook his head because he could think of nothing else to do.

Although the headman had lived in the hollow for most of his adult life, he was glad when Brock said that they were to come. For it meant that the gods smiled on them and that they would have good fortune in the coming year.

"Brock says that the gods will visit the hollow with their vengeance," he told the tribesmen. "They will cast thunderbolts into the place and burn it up. We must leave and go where Brock takes us."

The villagers were so excited by these words that many of them began to get their belongings together immediately, so as to avoid the terrible death that would fall on all who remained.

This headman was a knowledgeable man. "We cannot let the voice of the gods walk, as we must do ourselves," he said. "A journey would kill him. Then we should never know what the gods wanted us to do. We must find a horse for him."

Some of the young men went out that night and found a broken-down old horse that wandered in the forest. It had been there for years, to their knowledge, and had once belonged to a warrior of the Dumnonians who had been killed when he struck an overhanging branch. The horse had stayed more or less in the same spot and had grazed his life away. Now he was as thin as a rake, after the hard winter. They decked him with coloured ribbons and one day, when the new sun was shining, they set forth, acting on Brock's whim, and taking the way towards the east. Brock rode at their head, with Mamag by his side to keep him from falling off the sheepskin that acted as a saddle. He had forgotten how to ride, and needed someone to look after him now.

They took the ancient high roads, for as long as they could, letting Brock lead them. He in turn trusted to the horse.

Artorius was on spring manoeuvres that took him almost as far as Calleva Atrebatum when news reached him that Cissa was about to move northwards. His informant, one of the shipload of Saxons in his pay, said that Cissaceaster was overcrowded. That there was nothing to eat with so many mouths to feed, and that unless Cissa brought them a victory soon, they would all rebel and kill him. He must march inland now, or give up all hope of a kingdom.

Artorius smiled grimly at this news and nodded to Bedwyr, who nodded back. The first Company of the Legion halted and made immediate plans. Artorius would ride to make a frontal attack on Cissa, and Bedwyr would take a smaller number to line the shore, so that if Cissa retreated he would fall into their hands. Then they sent fast riders to Camulodunum and Verulam, calling for an immediate marching of all troops there. Further messengers went northwards to Lindum, calling on the garrison there to send half its strength south, to hold the cities which would be emptied by this sudden call.

Artorius waited two days, then began a slow ride towards Anderida Silva. He took the high road, so as to be outside the reach of Cissa's spies, who would watch the metalled roads. It was on one of these high roads that Artorius and his vanguard passed a ragged procession of tribesfolk, led by a shrivelled creature on a starved horse.

Though the man was heavily shrouded with a tattered cloak, Artorius sensed a curious power in him. As they drew alongside, Artorius saw that the man had but one arm, and that the locks of hair which escaped from his hood were white. A heavily built woman crooned to him and held his bridle as they went along.

The tribesmen got off the road and walked in the lush grass to let the great cavalcade pass, but the lone rider held his course and did not seem to notice them.

Artorius called to him, "Hail, great captain! Are you bound for war, my friend?"

Those about Artorius laughed at this jest, but the man on the horse did not seem to hear the words.

When Artorius and his comitatus had passed, Mamag said to Brock, "Do you know that man who greeted you, Brock? He called out to you?"

Brock struggled with speech for a while and then said, "Yes, I know him. That is Ambrosius who is dead."

The woman passed this news back to the headman, who told his children in later years that once on the hilltop he had been passed by the ghost army of Ambrosius. Since they did not believe him, the mistake did not matter at all.

As for Cissa, such was his fear of rebellion and his confidence in the might of his berserker army, that he did not take even the commonest precautions, and was met without warning by a force of cavalry in an open valley. The Cymry rode down on him, from either side, and killed until they were too weak to strike another blow. Some of them, quite unwounded, fell senseless from their horses with exhaustion.

Cissa took the few that remained into the woods, and tried to get back to his city. When he reached the hillside above Cissaceaster, he saw a thick cloud of black smoke. His fortress had disappeared and was now only a great heap of charred wood and blackened stone. He was met by his spies, who told him that all his ships in the harbour were either burned or scuttled. He was indeed a prisoner in the land he had come to conquer. So Cissa turned back into the deep woods and with a handful of men lived like an animal among the trees. When he heard that Cerdic had come eastwards, too, his heart sank, for he knew that he might expect less mercy from the West Saxon than from the Bear of Britain himself.

When Artorius knew that Cissa was crushed, he withdrew Bedwyr's army from the coast; he had no great wish to kill the man, remembering how well he had fought beside his father at Dubglas. Instead, Artorius stayed at the edges of the forest for a few days, hunting, to pass the time pleasantly before he returned to Camulod.

One afternoon, as he rested in a glade, with Bedwyr at his side, a squat black-haired horseman cantered past them, and seeing them suddenly, reined in his horse and sat looking down at them for a while. They noticed the richness of his dress, and the pride of his bearing. He wore a heavy silver-gilt coat of mail, over which was slung a red baldric that carried a massive curved sword, rather of the Eastern type, in a studded scabbard of sharkskin. He wore a long sky-blue cloak that set Bedwyr's eyes wide with envy.

This man smiled at them pleasantly, twisting his dark moustaches. Then he said, "My thanks, Artos of Lis Pengwern. You have taught the young hound a lesson. Take care he does not bite you next time, though!"

Then he set spurs to his horse and galloped away into the woods, by the path he had come. Bedwyr sent scouts to find him, but he had gone too fast for them.

"Who could it have been?" he asked.

Artorius said, "There is only one it could have been. That was Cerdic of the West Saxons. He, too, is a great captain."

Bedwyr smiled sourly. "That would not have kept my knife out of his belly if I could have got to him," he said. "He will give us trouble."

Artorius said, "What does that matter? That is what we are here for, to fight all of Britain's enemies."

It was while Artorius was in this mood that a messenger rode into the glade with the news that the sons of Gomer had broken their treaty, and were leading the Picts south. They were at Mount Agned, said the messenger, and had vowed to take Eburacum before they stopped.

Artorius swore a great oath. The men who were about him shrank back from him, afraid. When his passion had left him, he turned to Bedwyr and said, "I dare not go, friend, for I would not know when to stop, such is my anger now at this treachery. You shall go, and shall punish the sons of Gomer. Take as many men as you need, for we shall not be troubled by Cissa for many a year now."

Bedwyr said, "I shall go, Bear. I shall kill the sons of Gomer and decimate their followers. Then I shall ride on to their villages and shall burn every house in Pictland."

"Do that," Artorius said, "but no more than that. They will remember us then, and will not break the Roman peace again."

Bedwyr rode out towards the north that very day, and Artorius set off back to Camulod, for the country about Anderida Silva could not feed his great company of horse.

That night, Brock and his strange procession arrived in the wood, having followed the Cymry. They set up their flimsy encampment in a glade and ate bark and green shoots from the trees.

When the moon was high, Brock stirred from his damp bed of grass and fern fronds and crept out of the tent. Mamag, exhausted by her long walk, was sound asleep. Brock walked out into the glade. He was hungry and thirsty and the voice was beginning to whisper in his head again, for the first time since they had left the hollow. He wanted to escape from it and began to run as fast as his weak legs would take him. The moon looked down at him madly and the questing night-owls shrieked at him as he passed. He became terrified and tried to turn back, but the thick undergrowth shielded the little encampment from his eyes and he could not find his way. Brock began to run wildly, calling out for Mamag, like a little child.

At length he saw a light burning and ran towards it. There were tents in a glade, and men talking together. He thought it was his own encampment, and that Mamag would be where the light was. He ran to the tent and pushed open the door with his one hand.

Cissa was sitting at a rough table with Aesc and three others. They were drinking from a wine-skin, and were red-eyed and tired. Aesc had a great red gash down his face and was trembling with fever. Cissa looked up at Brock, like a wolf at a hare that strays into his den.

Brock came forward, conscious that there was something different, but not sure what it was. Cissa stared at him for a while and then said, "By Woden, but do you see who this is? By the gods, but he has travelled far since he blinded us at Bassas!" Then he began to shout in a drunken frenzy, "Medrawt! Medrawt! Medrawt!"

Medrawt said weakly, "Where is Mamag? Where is she?" They all began to laugh at him, sitting and staring and drinking.

Then they hung him up by his one sound wrist to a bough outside the tent and, laughing, cut away his manhood from him. And all the while Medrawt screamed and screamed for Mamag until no sound came from his raw throat. And at last they left him alone and the light in the tent burned down and only the moon shone and the owls hooted and Brock heard the slow and regular dripping of his blood among the ferns.

And when Cissa awoke in the morning he saw that the man was white-haired. He called to Aesc and said, "He still lives. Get rid of him. He will bring us misfortune. There is that about him which bodes no good."

Aesc shivered with fever. He said, "It is not his manly parts, then, Cissa, for they are no longer about him." Then he went away to tell his fellows what he had said, for he wanted them to laugh too. Cissa cut Brock down with his own hands. He even spoke to him. But Brock only stared now, for he could no longer understand any language, even that of his voice.

Cissa said, "Poor devil."

"What shall we do with him?" asked Aesc, taking out his knife again.

Cissa said, "We shall send him to Cerdic. It might be a warning to him, in a way. Though we have no teeth to bite him with yet awhile."

Back in the wood, Mamag and the headman searched for Brock, and then gave up the search, convinced that the gods had called him back to them. The procession began its journey home to the hollow.

LI

THAT YEAR'S HARVEST WAS A GOOD ONE. MEN BLESSED ARTORIUS FOR their prosperity. In some temples he was hailed as a God Emperor. When he was told this, he was amused at first; but Thykristion pointed out to him ironically that it was the custom of such gods to die for their people. That was the other part of the contract, so to speak. Artorius said that after all he would prefer to be the plain Count of Britain!

Bedwyr had been highly successful in Caledonia, and now the Picts had withdrawn back across the Bodotria estuary, shattered, to build themselves new homes before the northern winter set in. As a sign of good faith for the future they had sent three of their princes to be educated at Eburacum, as hostages, more or less. Artorius was satisfied so far as the Picts were concerned.

Nor was he dissatisfied with the general state of Britain. Iron foundries were set up again in the old kingdom of the Cantii, many of them now worked by Jutish immigrants. Lead and tin mines were turning out their metal and the marshes about the Abus were gradually being drained. All told, he felt that his schemes had proved themselves.

And now the citizens of Londinium had sent a deputation to Camulodunum, asking that Artorius accept their fealty and include them in his commonwealth. Artorius listened to their plea, seated in his high chair, beneath an immense Christian cross carved from Midlands alabaster. When they had finished and waited for his answer, he merely shook his head slowly, but did not speak a word. The burghers waited, bewildered, until Thykristion told them it was time to go and that their audience was at an end.

One of them said, "But, Artorius, what if the Saxon capture the city, and take its treasures from the land?"

This man was of Saxon blood himself, his grandfather having come with Hengist. But he spoke with sincerity for he was a wealthy merchant now.

Artorius deigned to speak. "I would not lift a finger if the devil himself took Londinium. As for its treasures, they mean nothing to me, though they may mean much to you. Britain has never profited by them in the past, and does not hope to profit in the future."

Then he turned his back on them and they were forced to go from the audience chamber. The man who had spoken up stopped at the door and called back, "You will live to regret this day, Artos the Bear."

Then a guard bundled him out of the palace and the deputation went back angrily to their city.

Artorius said to Thykristion, "Did I do right, friend?"

The Greek smiled, and said, "One can never tell, Artorius. Men are not like mathematical symbols, static factors; they change with the years. And one never knows how they will change."

Artorius said, "Do you mean they may join with the Saxon?"

Thykristion answered, "They hate you as much as you hate them. We can be assured of that. I know no more."

But that did not trouble Artorius, for he was confident of the loyalty of the Province. And his Legion was in good heart, the finest army in Europe, he was told, by military attachés who now came to Camulod.

Yet there were other worries. The Western Kings did not live in amity now. Votiporix of the Demetae had recently picked a quarrel with one Maelgwn of Gwynnedd, Lord of Anglesey, and it looked as though this feud might spread into more northerly and southerly areas. If that happened, the west might well be closed to Artorius, should he need men or supplies while on a campaign in that territory.

Bedwyr pointed out to him that Cerdic had lain quiet a suspiciously long time. It was well known that he had landed many ships' companies west of Vectis and was living on the south coast more or less as a permanent settler. The danger would arise, thought Bedwyr, if he were joined by Saxons or Angles coming inland along the valley of the Tamesa. If they took that route in sufficiently large numbers, and Cerdic pushed northwards to meet them, it would produce a pincers movement which would cut off the whole of southeast Britain—and that could be very dangerous.

Artorius replied that the Saxon would have to pass Londinium to get up the Tamesa, and so would be seen.

Thykristion, who was with them, said, "Have no doubts, Artorius, the men of Londinium would welcome such a move. It would not change their outlawed position and it would give them revenge against you. Do not forget that you have hurt them deeply and they will not forgive you in a lifetime."

Artorius scratched his head and then said, "Send to Votiporix and the chieftain Maelgwn. Tell them to stop fighting before the month is out or I shall march to punish them."

A scribe took down the message and a horseman was called from the outer court to deliver it straightway. As he rode away, Bedwyr said, "I had better sharpen my sword. They will never heed you now, Artos. You are no longer their man, one of them. They think of you as a Roman now."

It turned out exactly as Bedwyr had said. And Artorius was forced to march west to make good his threat. Yet, when he was only halfway there, news followed him that Cerdic was indeed pushing northwards to meet Saxons who had come along the Tamesa, and were now forging hard through the woodland that shrouded the upper reaches of the river. Their combined armies would be formidable, the messenger said. There would be no time for Artorius to quieten down the quarrelling kinglets. He must turn and meet the Saxons without delay if he was to save the southeast.

Artorius sat in his tent and eyed his charts with a worried look on his thin face. Bedwyr was no help to him in a matter like this, and Thykristion was left back at Camulod, rearranging the new Law Library there. There was no time to send for him. Artorius had never met a situation of this complexity and he did not know quite what he should do. He wished Medrawt were there. They would have come to a conclusion, have made a plan of some sort. But now he stood on his own, alone.

"Whatever we do, we must do it fast," said Bedwyr, who had no head for strategy and only wanted to smell the dust of battle again.

They were riding through undulating country now, to the north of the Midlands, taking the old Roman road that led to Calleva Atrebatum, when suddenly a forward scout rode back to them, pointing and crying excitedly. They followed his finger and saw above them, on the old ridgeway that had served men long before Rome had risen, a dark mass of men, many hundreds of them, it seemed. They were cutting across the path of the Cymry, to meet others. Bedwyr would have spurred forward, but Artorius restrained him.

"God alone knows how many of them there must be up there," he said, "they are coming from many directions. It is as though they planned to meet here."

A horseman rode back to the vanguard then, to say that he had encountered an immense body of Saxons, with some companies of Angles among them. Cerdic was riding at their head, with a huge banner on which was embroidered a dragon. His son Cynric was thought to be riding with him, in command of a section of Jutes. All told, there must be ten thousand of them, all laughing and in high spirits. It seemed that they had heard the sound of the Legion on the hard Roman road and had withdrawn a little higher up the hill and now overlooked them, for the Saxon host was largely on foot, and could move over any type of terrain, whereas the Cymry were forced to take the hardest and smoothest tracks and avoid the rocky stretches of countryside.

By midday, the Saxon army had climbed higher up the slope, and now occupied the hilltop of Mons Badonicus, an ancient earthworks at least nine hundred feet high. They stretched for a distance of a thousand yards along this hill, supported in the rear by many ranks more.

Artorius gave the order for the Legion to mount towards them, until they were halfway up the slope. Then, with his array laid out in the order of battle-charge, he and Bedwyr rode hither and thither to take stock of the position.

The western flank of the hill was far too steep for any cavalry attack, and so was the rear, which could only be reached by a long detour. That had the consolation that it would be equally difficult as a way of retreat, Bedwyr thought grimly, for he never considered the possibility of the enemy gaining the victory.

"We must attack up the eastern slope," said Artorius, "for that is the slighter. We cannot call this battle ours until we have routed them from the hill-top and destroyed them."

Then he gave the charge on a long bull's horn that he carried, and the first ranks of cavalry set their chargers at the slope, crying out "Mary and Britain," for recently they had listened to the churchmen, who told them they were fighting for Christ as well as for Britain and Rome.

When they were two hundred yards from the hill-top, a thick hail of arrows fell amongst them. The Cymry toppled from their horses. No arrow struck Artorius that day, by some miracle. Yet all about him, men were pierced by the deadly rain of missiles. The Cymry were brave men and would have kept on up the hill until the last one had fallen, but Artorius did not wish to lose more men than he had to. He sounded the withdrawal and the horsemen turned and cantered back down the slope. As they went, the Saxons on the hill-top cheered them ironically and began to sing songs about the Bear having his fangs drawn. Bedwyr was so furious that he almost went berserk and tackled them alone. His friend restrained him, with a grim little smile.

"Wait, friend," he said. "They will be singing a different song before the day is out."

Artorius had observed that the heaviest flights of arrows came from the eastern side, and so he called together the captains of the swiftest cavalry, men mounted on the little ponies of Exmoor. He selected a hundred of these and ordered them to ride like demons to the top of the hill, and once there to cause as much confusion as they could. He told them that he would follow on their heels with the heavier chargers and consolidate the victory. These men saluted him, and laughing up the hill into the wintry sun, they galloped like madmen. Some were taken by the arrow flights, others by sling-shot when they got closer. The last of them almost reached the first line of Saxons, and then struck the many obstacles, the stakes and caltrops, which were waiting for them. Horses reared with agony as the sharp points drove into their hooves. Men were thrown. The first ranks of Saxons rushed down the hill and butchered them where they lay, among the threshing hooves.

Artorius halted his heavy cavalry in the middle of their charge.

"Back, back," he cried. "We run into a trap. We shall suffer worse than they."

The Cymry did as he said, and in many hearts that afternoon there ran the thought that this was the beginning of defeat. This was the final throw, men thought, which beggared the gambler. Artorius must look to it, or his Britain would crumble after all.

Artorius took counsel with Bedwyr and a dozen old captains who had followed him for many years. They were in the Count's round pavilion, which was set at the foot of the hill, below the ridgeway, at a place where two Roman roads crossed.

Artorius said, "Is there a man among you who knows this hill-camp?"

One old warrior stepped forward and said that he had been up to the top when he was a boy. Artorius asked him if there was a stream at the top.

"No, Bear," said the man. "It is as dry as a bone. I remember we searched for a stream, for we were thirsty from running."

"That is well, brother," said Artorius. "That shall be their doom. We must see to it that they work hard this day and tomorrow. Ten thousand men should get very thirsty on that exposed hill."

They laughed at his words now, seeing the drift of his meaning. Then Artorius called for a wine-skin and all the captains drank deep.

Artorius said, "That's the way, my boys, drink, and think of the host of Cerdic as you drink! It will be long before some of them set a wine-skin to their lips as you are doing."

The men laughed again at this grim jest. Of that twelve, only three survived the battle, however. It was their last drink, too, though they did not know that then. So they relished the wine.

Then Artorius sent a strong company behind the hill, so as to cut off any possible escape of the Saxons, and having done that he gave orders that wave after wave of horsemen were to pretend to mount the hill until darkness fell. This would keep the Saxons on their feet and cause many of them to run down the hill in pursuit when the horsemen turned, as seemed to be their undisciplined habit.

So, as an ancient writer put it, stationing his companies, he made hardy assault upon the Saxons, who were ranked wedgewise in battalions. But all day long did they stand their ground manfully, although Artorius made assault upon assault. And at sundown the Saxons still occupied the hill, which seemed all the camp they needed.

That night Artorius called Bedwyr to him and said, "All goes well. Though we have lost many from arrows, we are in a good position. They cannot go on shooting at us, for they will run short of arrows and sling-shot and cannot replace their losses. Let us pray for a hot day tomorrow, brother. The sun would be our strongest ally."

They talked like this for a while, and then Artorius said, "Sleep now, Bedwyr, for we must be up betimes. Our first attacks must start at dawn and then continue while there is light in the sky, and after if needs be."

The Cymry slept well that night, for the Bear's plan had been passed along the ranks. They set strong watches, however, who were able to cut down many Saxons, trying to escape in the darkness. The troop behind the hill was also fortunate in that respect. The Saxons on the hill, however, put on a good face and lit fires there. Many of them sang all night, as though to show the Britons that they were confident of victory still.

The great attack began when the first birds called in the dawn sky. Many times the Cymry assaulted the hill, and many times the Saxons dashed down after them. But these foolhardy berserkers always died, for though they struck their blow, they could not get back to their vantage point before the next assault cut them down. In this way, both sides lost heavily during the morning.

The sun came out early and stayed, despite the lateness of the season. No rain fell that day to slake the thirst of the thousands on the hill-top.

Then in the afternoon, Artorius became angry at their stubborn resistance. He sent word to the troops of horse that all men must eat and drink now, for they would get no other chance to do so that day. Then, when all was in readiness, he sounded the charge and himself rode in the vanguard of the attack.

This thrust was timed by chance at the most opportune moment, for on the hill-top the three separate contingents of Saxons, Angles and Jutes, under their own sub-chieftains, were in a state of disagreement. Many were for a wholesale retreat towards the back of the hill; others were for charging the Cymry down the forward face; the others voted for continuing to hold the hill summit, despite the great thirst that now tormented every man.

The first wave of Cymry hit them at this moment, and the company of Artorius actually gained the summit and rode here and there striking down at the unprepared footmen.

Artorius pointed. Bedwyr saw a group of men in fine armour standing beneath the dragon standard. One of them, a dark squat man in a sky-blue cloak, was smiling and talking resignedly to those about him. Beside him stood a youth, his son, judging by the similarity of his appearance and dress.

"Cerdic and Cynric," said Artorius. "If only we could take them, the battle would be over and our men could eat and drink their fill."

Bedwyr saw the triple rank of axe-men that surrounded this

party under the dragon banner. He said, "It would cost a company to take them, Artos. Yet I will go, if you wish it."

Artorius said, "No, Bedwyr. I wouldn't lose you in exchange for all the Saxons in Valhalla. Come, we will wait. Cerdic will come to us before the day is spent."

Then he gave the order to withdraw, since his troop was hard pressed.

So the bloody day wore on. And each wave of Cymry as they returned brought back news that the Saxons were weakening. Now many of their foremost ranks of archers had to withdraw because of thirst, and others, hardly less thirsty, took their places for a short while. The Cymry attacked and attacked, losing men and horses with each foray. Yet they lost them gladly, for the smell of victory was in the air, mingling with the heavy scent of blood.

On the hill as light faded, the Saxons tried again and again to thrust back these vicious horsemen, but the Cymry were fired now with their success and only death could make them loose their hold. Everywhere there was chaos, man against man, horse against kneeling man, his hand held over his head pathetically to ward his brain from the descending sword blade. The skull was split and the brain spilled out over the grass and the man, no longer a man, sank to the earth without a prayer. Perhaps in some dim and flickering brain cell that shivered in the harsh wind on the turf, there still remained a memory of home and flaxen-haired children, of the baby that was to come next spring. But the horses trampled on over the turf and the man was trodden into the clay, together with his memory of the son who should carve himself a kingdom in this dark island.

On the hill slope, men hacked at any moving shadow now, friend and foe alike. No one spoke; the battle cries were ended; men fought like animals, silently, only grunting as iron sheared through nerve and flesh. Artorius, still in the front, watched a Saxon spear-point slide into his thigh, unmoved. He saw the bright blade dull itself with the warmth of his flesh. He saw his enemy's teeth as he grinned with the exertion of the thrust. Artorius saw all this and felt no pain. Indeed, he would have praised the man's aptness with his weapon if he had had the breath to spare. But his own breath was all expended in bringing down the great sword Caliburn upon the man's exposed shoulder. It was an automatic action, born of long practice in combat, with no hatred in it. Just as silently as Artorius had taken his wound, the Saxon took the death blow, his shoulder and half of his ribs shattered by that reply from so high above him. He swung round and seemed to dissolve into the twilight beneath the horse's hooves. And the Bear rode on, shaking something from his blade that had seemed to alter its balance for the moment, feeling his leg warm and his feet sticky, but unaware that his riding boot was half full of blood.

"Sting wasps, and make the hand unclench!" he found himself shouting. And all those who had been with him at Caerwent took up that ghastly cry until the ancient hill echoed again in the dusk.

And that night lesser men knew what it was to kill, or to be killed. There was one of the Saxons, Gurth by name, a man from one of the smallest of the Friesian Islands. He had had quite a thriving farmstead back there and had only been persuaded to sail with Cerdic, at the last minute, by a second cousin who had promised him acres of good cornland and a ready-built wooden hall.

This Gurth had had the luck to find himself a good position on the hill before the light failed. At his right was a thick clump of hawthorn, and at his left a great heap of tumbled stones. Behind him his comrades stretched back to the ridge. Before him, only one of the enemy could approach at a time. And Gurth had a good spear which he could trust, because he had made it himself, out of a stake from his own ash fence at home, and a rim of a discarded wagon wheel from the next farm. So he waited, confident in the outcome of the battle. This Gurth had the good fortune to tear open the bellies of four horses in the first charges, for he had waited discreetly behind the hawthorn as the Cymry edged through the narrow gap. Once the screaming mounts were down, their riders were helpless for a few moments. And it was in these moments that Gurth remembered the cornland he was promised and went to work with the little skinning-knife, easily, happily, regarding it all as a business proposition.

Only when the light finally faded did Gurth meet death and lose his fields. He was tired then and not quite so careful. He was waiting for another horse to come, but instead a footman came, another Saxon, a man from a farmstead not five miles as the crow flies from Gurth's own steading; but a Saxon, like many more that night, who suddenly saw more profit in following Artos the Bear than in scrimping along under this Cerdic, who was a hard man anyway, and whose promises like piecrusts were too often broken.

This man came round the hawthorn, turning his head from side to side, like anybody else who didn't know where the next blow was coming from. He looked at Gurth, and Gurth looked back at him. They even smiled, for they knew many of the same folk back home. Then, as Gurth sat down again on a flat stone that he had used all day, the other just leaned forward as though he were going to join him, but instead slipped his little knife under Gurth's ribs, gently and without hurry, just under the shoulder bone.

Gurth sighed and looked up at him, suddenly powerless, yet thinking what a rogue this man was, thinking how glad he was that he had not offered him a job at the farm he was going to get when this battle was over.

LII

ARTORIUS LAY BACK IN HIS CHAIR WHILE THE DOCTORS PUT HEALING ointments on his wound and bound it up. His captains, such as were left of them, sat about him, for they were so tired that he could not bear to have them standing, tottering with fatigue.

He was grave, for this battle of Mons Badonicus had cost the Cymry two thousand men and horses. Bedwyr tried to console him by reporting that the Saxon losses were more than twice that number. And that was only on the battlefield, said Bedwyr. God only knew what their further losses had been in the rounding-up when the fighting was over, for the Cymry were relentless, and each one had a comrade to avenge when all was over.

"Cerdic will be lucky if he has four thousand left, out of the host that climbed the hill yesterday," said a captain.

"We cannot hold them," said Artorius wearily. "They must be sent back to the coast, without a guard. They are weaponless men and broken in spirit. They will go away from Britain now. They are a beaten people."

He groaned a little as he tried to move his heavily bandaged leg. "This wound will keep me quiet for a while, eh, Bedwyr?" he said.

Bedwyr's right arm was in a sling and he had lost much blood from a slash across the back. He stood up stiffly, though he was almost dead with fatigue, for the pain would not let him sit down.

"I hope that we were struck with clean swords," he said. "It helps the healing then. We shall be right again by spring."

He turned rigidly to tell a young lieutenant that it was a point of honour among veterans to thrust the sword into the clean earth between each death or wounding, for that lessened the risk of one man's poison being passed to another. The young warrior listened gravely and said that he would remember that.

Just then the Celtic war-horns howled again and the tread of many feet could be heard approaching the tent of Artorius.

"They are bringing him, bringing Cerdic," said a captain. Artorius sat upright at his table and put on his look of gravity. The soldiers about him stood and folded their arms, looking, as nearly as they could, like the Romans they had heard so much about.

Cerdic came into the Count's pavilion, still dressed in his finery, but looking white with weariness now. He leaned on the shoulder of his son, Cynric, who had his hand and forearm bound up after a deep lance-thrust at the very end of the battle.

For a while the two captains looked at each other. The face of Artorius was set and stern; Cerdic smiled tiredly, but with an easy courage.

Artorius spoke and said, "Sit down, Cerdic of the West Saxons." He made no show of noticing Cynric, who swayed on his feet for tiredness.

There was a silence in the pavilion and the veterans kept their eyes lowered. Only Bedwyr snorted from time to time, but he was the right hand of Artos and was privileged.

At last Artorius spoke and said, "You have invaded a peaceful land, Cerdic of the West Saxons, and have brought much suffering to it. Your host has been fairly defeated in battle. You are their hostage now and must suffer for the harm you have done."

Cerdic still smiled. He spoke thickly and said, "Artos the Bear, let us have done with this mummery. I am no play-actor, I am a man seeking a kingdom. It matters little what you do to me, my friend, for I carry a disease within me which will not let me ride much further. I am unconcerned with your threats to me, so say what you will. But I ask you this, that my son Cynric be set free to go his way and find his own kingdom somewhere where one may be found."

Artorius looked hard at the young man, who returned his stare in silence.

"He has fought well today, the young man," said Artorius. "He shall not suffer for the sins of his father. He is a free man."

The young princeling gave a dry sob and kneeled before his father. Cerdic slapped him on the back and said, "Have no fear, son, I am well enough served if I know that you may one day gain your kingdom. As for me, I should have left you soon, in any case."

Some of the officers in the tent were moved by this. Bedwyr alone seemed impervious to such words. He snorted again and Cerdic looked across at him with a smile.

"You came badly out of it today, Bedwyr," he said. "I was waiting for you myself, but you never came close enough."

Bedwyr smiled grimly back at him. "That was your good fortune," he said, "for I should have left neither of you with any hands to get a kingdom with."

Cerdic shrugged his wide shoulders and, turning, said, "Well,

Artos, let us have it over with. I am ready to go outside when you wish."

Artorius passed his hand wearily over his forehead, and then said quietly, "I have killed enough for one day, Saxon. I shall not end the day by spilling blood uselessly. I make you an offer, warrior."

Cerdic smiled and said, "Speak on, Bear. I do not care either way."

The Count of Britain said, "You may either join my Legion, in a position of great honour, being next after Bedwyr here, or you may go with your son to the coast and sail whither you will, having vowed never to trouble us again."

Cerdic smiled up at his son and then said, firmly and without any hesitation, "I am not the man to play second fiddle to any, Bear. I am too much like you. I cannot join you, though I thank you for the offer. I will take the other way and go, let us say, to Brittany with my son. There may be a few acres of unwanted land there for us to set up our house on."

Artorius said, "Consider again, Cerdic. Will you come with me and be among my great captains?"

Cerdic rose and went to the table and placed his hand on that of Artorius.

"Bear," he said, smiling, "you and I are too much alike ever to get on well together. We should kill each other when the spring got into our blood, and that you know. No, I refuse your offer. But I tell you this, upon my word, I shall never fight you again. I shall never trouble Britain again—in your lifetime."

"What of that disease which will kill you," said Bedwyr slyly.

Cerdic said, "Why, have we not all got a disease within us, the disease of humanity? We must all die sometime, soldier."

Bedwyr ground his teeth then, for he felt that Artorius had been tricked. Cerdic was well known for his lies, and being of mixed blood, was distrusted by both sides.

"Do not let him go, Bear," he said, stepping forward urgently.

Artorius looked at him gravely and said, "Would you have me break my word, Bedwyr?"

Bedwyr said, "It might be best if you did, Artos, for this snake will sting the moment he is set free."

Cerdic looked at him tolerantly. "You are grown too mighty, Bedwyr Kiss-the-Cow!"

This remark referred to an incident which took place when Bedwyr was a lad of fifteen. In a blindfold kissing game during the spring festivals, someone had wrapped a shawl round a cow and had led her before Bedwyr and he had been taken in by the jest. He had taken long to live the silly incident down, and no one now dared to mention it. Only Cerdic had been crafty enough to use such a childish means of embarrassing the warrior. He struck the table with his free hand, but could not speak for rage. Cerdic stood and laughed at him, and soon the other captains dared to join in, but gently.

Cerdic said at last, "While I live, Britain shall not forget Bedwyr Kiss-the-Cow." Then, turning to the stern Artorius, he said more seriously, "A gift for a gift, Bear. You give us our lives; I shall give you one who shall put Bedwyr's nose out of joint again!"

"What do you mean?" asked Artorius, suddenly pale.

"Your blood-brother," said Cerdic, "the Count-elect of Britain, though I fear he will be useless in council. He seems to have lost his tongue, or at least to have found one that no man can understand. Perhaps he would fit well among your councillors, though, I know such men usually talk gibberish."

Artorius got to his feet painfully and clutched the arm of Cerdic. "Do you mean Medrawt?" he said.

Cerdic nodded. "Yes, friend, I mean Medrawt," he said. "But not the man you once knew. This one is sadly chastened by the gods and will never do any more damage, I fear."

Artorius made a movement of anger towards him, but Cerdic held up his hand confidently. "No, Artos," he said, "the blame is not mine. I have tended him with care, against this day, when he might be a bargaining point. He has had good treatment from us, I can assure you. What damage he has suffered came to him before we got him. Indeed, he is more of a man now than when the brute Cissa flung him in at my window."

Cerdic went to the door and called. Two men came forward, carrying Medrawt. He sat in a chair, his head lolling on one side. In the light of the lamp, he looked up and saw Cerdic. His eyes brightened a little with recognition and he smiled.

"You see, Bear," said Cerdic, "I am his friend."

As he spoke, Medrawt looked towards Artorius. And now a great yearning seemed to come into his face. He held out his right hand towards Artorius and tried to get down from the chair.

"See," said Cerdic, "he is quite overcome. He is weeping. Why, you are both weeping!"

PART SIX

CAMLANN

Lavender's blue, dilly, dilly!
Lavender's green;
When I am King, dilly, dilly!
You shall be queen.

Call up your men, dilly, dilly!
Set them to work;
Some to the plough, dilly, dilly!
Some to the cart.

Some to make hay, dilly, dilly!
Some to cut corn;
While you and I, dilly, dilly!
Keep ourselves warm.

EPILOGUE

IT WAS LATE SUMMER AND SOME OF THE LEAVES ON THE TREES about the palace at Camulod, or Camlann as it was now called, had already changed colour and seemed almost ready to fall. Yet it was still warm, and the air was filled with the humming of midges and the mellow purring of pigeons from the red-tiled rooftop.

There was an atmosphere of somnolence in the garden. It was part of the somnolence that pervaded the whole of Britain now. A summer that never seemed to end, that had lasted so long now that even grown men with families could not recall its beginning. Now men, and women, too, walked unarmed about the lanes by night, and slept with their windows open when they went to bed. The ironworkers of the Forest of Dean and the Weald had so little to do, making weapons and armour, that they swore to rebel unless there was another war soon.

For twenty years there had not been a poor harvest, and the seas as far as Jutland teemed with good fat fish. Men were rich enough now to wear wool next the skin and silk over that. A man who dared walk the streets in a sheepskin jacket was pointed out as one of those barbarians who had overrun the Province before the battle of Mount Badon. Now each week the wine ships of Cyprus and Crete put into the port of Camlann, and no man drank water any more. It was a lovely late summer.

Yet, as in all summers, there were occasional rumblings on the horizon, as though the thunder might come at last. But men only laughed and put on a heavier coat so as not to be caught in the spots of rain. It could be nothing serious, they thought. True, it was becoming more difficult to gather in the taxes since their administration had been taken out of the hands of the army, for few Britons had a talent for that sort of thing, and now the officials were mostly of Levantine origin, men who had been introduced during the viceregality of Thykristion, before he was disgraced and beheaded for corruption. Sometimes, it seemed, some citizens paid twice while others paid not at all. Yet they seemed to have so much to pay with, that no one ever bothered overmuch about it, save those who paid, of course.

True, also, since the Cymry were disbanded and a regular army of foot soldiers, in the style of the old Legions, introduced, many young men who had heard the tale of the Legion of the Bear, had taken their swords elsewhere in Europe, to sell them to the highest bidder.

True, the Picts had forgotten their oath, once more—a habit of theirs, it seemed—and had come south over the great Wall of Hadrian. But that was of little importance. They were allowed settlements in the cold and inhospitable north, and apart from an occasional drunken outburst, did little harm.

As for the other migrants, they were allowed their own territories, without let or hindrance, along the coasts, and in the most marshy areas, provided they paid their taxes when called on to do so, and provided they did not carry arms. Angle, Jute and Saxon seemed amenable, and after Badon had never found themselves a leader who might be considered too dangerous.

Only the dyed-in-the-wool old pessimists, such men as had fought at Glein, a lifetime ago, saw anything but peace and pleasure ahead for Britain. In the taverns they sometimes said, "We have no real army now. Not one of them ever fought in a battle. The government is corrupt. It is full of easterners. The farmers are rogues and do not pay their taxes. It is all left for the townsman to pay. We are surrounded on all sides by the Saxon. He is ready, when the moment arises, to strike us down. We are prevented by law from carrying swords in the streets any longer. We cannot even protect ourselves."

The young men, who had never known anything else, would sneer and say, "Well, grandad, it hasn't happened yet, has it? And you still have Artorius, the Count, to look after you, haven't you?"

The men who had fought at Dubglas would say then, "Artorius! He is an old man now. He is not the man who led the charges at Badon. He lost his manhood when he took mad Medrawt back to his bosom. And there is no one to follow him, for old Bedwyr is as stupid as his master."

The young men would laugh then and say, "To hear you old ones talk, one would think that everything was wonderful in the years gone by! Nothing is ever so good after a man has turned thirty, you know!"

And on the horizon the thunder went on rumbling through the late summer, and the midges kept on whirring their tiny wings, and the pigeons lulling themselves to sleep on the red roofs with their never-ending purring.

And Artorius sat in the garden in his gilded chair, his back now bent and his thin hair quite white. Medrawt lolled beside him, dressed in a long black habit, his one hand shaking, his head continually shuddering. Occasionally, old Bedwyr, who now leaned on a thick staff, would lean forward and wipe the spittle from the breast of Medrawt's black habit, like a nurse, and Medrawt would stare before him, unnoticing, his head still shuddering.

Before them, on the cropped green grass, at the edge of the marble-rimmed carp-pool, a little girl played. She was flaxen-haired and merry, and had her long brocade dress tucked up into her gilded girdle so that she could run about freely. Artorius watched her intently, his pale eyes never leaving her. From time to time she would look back at him and smile mischievously, as though she loved him.

This little girl was an Angle, seven years old, whom Artorius had found in the ruins of a burnt-out steading in Essex, when the Cymry had been forced to put down a small village rebellion. She had been left behind when her parents had fled or been killed. Bedwyr had flung her across his saddle out of pity, and then Artorius had claimed her. She reminded him of someone, he had said, but he could not remember who it was. Bedwyr could remember, though, and he gave the child to the Bear without any argument.

Now in the garden the little girl looked back at Artorius. "Uncle Arthur," she said, "I am tired of playing alone. Play with me, Uncle Arthur."

The Count of Britain left his chair and got onto his hands and knees. She climbed astride his back and he pretended to be a war-horse, though the pain in his stomach and his stiff leg prevented him from being a very agile one. The little Anglian did not seem to mind but jogged up and down violently on his back. The old man's face showed that this exertion was too much for him. He said, "Let us play something else, I am getting to be too old for such things."

The little girl pouted and then dragged him back to his chair. She climbed onto his knee and tied his beard in knots. He let her do what he would have killed another for, in the years gone by.

Medrawt looked at her vacantly, trying to remember who she was. He thought he had seen her before. She had been there since the age of two, so he was right. He thought he had seen Artorius somewhere before, but when he tried to think of this, a great pain came into his head and he fell down.

The little girl said, "Uncle Arthur, I know. Let us play kings and queens!"

Artorius looked stern for a moment. This was against his principles. But he loved the little girl more than anyone save perhaps his dream of Anir, that now came to him nightly. He turned and said to Bedwyr, "Make crowns, Bedwyr. Her ladyship commands it."

The old warrior shuffled into the house and brought back two strips of parchment. They were tax accounts, but he could not read the things, and Artorius never bothered to look at them any more, now that the Greek had gone. Artorius and Bedwyr twisted the parchment and made two crowns. Artorius set one on the head of the little girl, and Bedwyr set one on the head of the Bear of Britain.

"You should have a throne of your own, lady," said Bedwyr, trying to enter into the spirit of the thing, although he was not very good at playing. The little girl looked at Medrawt, half expecting him to let her sit in his chair. But Medrawt only stared back at her. He wondered why she was wearing that strange hat. He thought he would like one like that and wondered how to ask for one.

Bedwyr came forward hurriedly and with difficulty got down onto one knee. It made him perspire to do this and his joints creaked with rheumatism. He made a throne for the little girl. "Sit here, lady," he said.

The little girl gave him a kiss on the forehead. He made a grimace of disgust, but did not wipe away the dampness that she left.

She sat quite still, trying to look as she thought queens must look. Artorius gazed at her, and then stretched out his hand and touched her flaxen hair. His eyes were filled with moisture. He said brokenly, "Gwenhwyfar, oh, Gwenhwyfar!"

The little girl said, "That is a pretty name. That shall be my name when I am playing at kings and queens."

Artorius still gazed at her, passing his hand over his brow to wipe away the tears. "One day," he said, "men will say that I had three queens, no doubt. They will perhaps call them all Gwenhwyfar. But they will never know how beautiful my third queen was, my dear."

The little girl said, "Don't cry, Uncle Arthur. I will be your wife, and will look after you and we will play every day in the garden at kings and queens."

The old man suddenly rose and gave a great sob. Medrawt wondered what he was doing with that strange hat on, and weeping. Then Artorius did something very peculiar. He took Bedwyr's staff and held it up before him, as he stood by the pool. He was making the sign of the cross, but the flash of fire that came into Medrawt's head made it look like a sword, like Caliburn.

Artorius was saying, "May God protect this little one when I am gone. May she always be as happy as she is this day in the garden."

Then Medrawt heard his voice come again, the one that had first spoken to him in the hollow. And over his opaque mind passed a picture of a deserted forum and the grim skulls gleaming up at him beneath the paving-stones. He smelt the altars of Lis Pengwern again and felt the keen knife that cut him as he hung outside Cissa's hovel.

Then suddenly he slithered from his gilded chair while Artorius was still praying and Bedwyr was holding the little Anglian girl. The spittle dripped onto his breast as he ran across the grass, three paces, towards the carp-pool. Then all at once his tongue was loosed again and he spoke so that men could understand him.

"Ambrosius, you devil!" he shrieked, and buried his little fruit knife to the hilt in the neck of Artorius.

The Bear of Britain turned with the shock, a smile still on his face. He tottered and tried to prevent Medrawt from falling, not knowing that his own death had come upon him.

Bedwyr flung the little girl from him, so that she rolled over the grass in her paper crown. And then dragging his own dagger from its sheath he struck Medrawt through the head, the tears streaming down his withered face.

Medrawt gave a thin cry and plunged head foremost into the pool, his blood already tinging the water. Artorius the Bear was sitting down, trying to take the knife out of his neck, his eyes already glazing.

The little girl threw herself onto him and cried, "Uncle Arthur, don't cry! Don't cry! I will be your queen!"

Artorius spoke once again before he died, and said, "Take my sword, Bedwyr, and fling it far from you so that no man will ever find it."

He had to say this again before the old man could understand the faint words. And then with a great cry Bedwyr took back his own staff that Artorius held out to him, and flung it over the wall of the garden.

As he did so, the gate burst open and Bedwyr saw a group of faces, faces he did not know, angry faces.

The men of Londinium stood in the gateway for a while, watching the Bear of Britain dying. Behind them a serried mass, of Briton and Saxon, swarmed, cudgels in their hands.

"We have come too late," said the leader of the rebels. "He is beyond our reach!"

They ran forward now. "But his dog isn't," said one, bringing down his oaken staff on the head of Bedwyr, who now stood helpless, watching them as they trampled over the king's garden.

The little Anglian lay across the body of the Bear, crying, and asking him not to pretend any longer. She was still wearing the paper crown when they dragged her away, forgetting that they had children of their own in their mad fury.

Sources

In the preparation of this story, I have consulted the following works: *Everyday Life in Roman Britain,* by the Quennells (Batsford); *Roman Britain,* by Ian Richmond (Collins); *Early Britain,* by Jacquetta Hawkes (Collins); *Anglo-Saxon England,* by F. M. Stenton (O.U.P.); *Roman Britain and the English Settlements,* by Collingwood and Myres (O.U.P.); *An Historical Geography of England Before 1800,* edited by H. C. Darby (C.U.P.); *Arthur of Britain,* by Sir E. K. Chambers; The Preface to *Le Morte d'Arthur* by John Rhys (Dent); *The Battlefields of England,* by Lt-Col. Alfred H. Burne D.S.O. (Methuen); *The Amphitheatre at Caerleon on Usk,* by Sir Mortimer Wheeler; *The Legionary Fortress of Caerleon on Usk,* by Dr. Nash-Williams, Keeper of the National Museum of Wales; also the following correspondence: *Arthur's Battles,* W. G. Collingwood, in "Antiquity," September, 1929; *Arthur and His Battles,* O. G. S. Crawford, in "Antiquity," September, 1935; *The Battle of Badon,* Lt-Col. Burne, in "History," September, 1947.

I am indebted to the following old texts: *The Anglo-Saxon Chronicle* (Dent); *Histories of the Kings of Britain,* by Geoffrey of Monmouth, (Dent); *Historia Britonnum,* by Nennius; *The Mabinogion,* by Gwyn Jones and Thomas Jones (Dent).

I have visited the excavations of Romain remains at Caerleon on Usk and at Caerwent.

I am conscious of a debt to *The Golden Bough,* by Sir James Frazer (Macmillan), and *The White Goddess,* by Robert Graves (Faber), but cannot name specific instances.

The sequence of Arthur's battles is taken from Nennius and runs as follows:

> "*Primum bellum fuit in ostium fluminis quod dicitur Glein; secundum et tertium et quartum et quintum, super aliud flumen, quod dicitur Dubglas. . . . Sextum bellum super flumen quod vocatur Bassas. Septimum fuit bellum in Silva Celidonis, id est, Cat Coit Celidon. Octavum fuit bellum in castello Guinnion. . . . Nonum bellum gestum est in Urbe*

> *Legionis. Decimum gessit bellum in littore fluminis, quod vocatur Tribuit. Undecimum factum est bellum in monte, quod dicitur Agned. Duo decimum fuit bellum in monte Badonis.*"

My authority for Camlann is the *Annales Cambriae*, under the date 537 A.D.

H.T.

ABOUT THE AUTHOR

HENRY TREECE is a man of many parts: ex-boxing captain of Birmingham University, Flight Lieutenant in the R.A.F. during the last war, performing villain for his local drama club, lecturer in England and America, reviewer of Broadway plays for the *Manchester Guardian* during a recent visit to New York, and currently head of the English Department of the Barton-on-Humber Grammar School.

Mr. Treece studied at the universities of Santander and Birmingham. He and J. F. Hendry founded the Apocalyptic Movement in England, whose membership included Robert Melville, Alex Comfort, Dylan Thomas (briefly) and others. He has served on the editorial staffs of three literary magazines, *Seven, Kingdom Come* and *Transformation.* Several years ago he lectured at the Poetry Center of New York, at which time he became acquainted with W. H. Auden, Conrad Aiken, George Freedley of the American National Theatre Association and other poets and dramatists.

He is a distinguished poet himself and has written several volumes of verse, as well as criticism, short stories and radio plays and features. It is hardly strange, therefore, that both poetic and dramatic concepts should find their way into *The Great Captains.* He says, "The novelist is someone who keeps the reader's heart beating."

Though he was born in the English Midlands and enjoys life with his wife and two children in Lincolnshire, his cultural heritage stems mostly from Wales, toward whose landscape and history he is constantly drawn in his studies of the Celtic tragedy, subject of this book and his other novel, *The Dark Island.*